By
ROYAL
APPOINTMENT

A. O'CONNOR

POOLBEG

Published 2018
by Poolbeg Press Ltd
123 Grange Hill, Baldoyle
Dublin 13, Ireland
E-mail: poolbeg@poolbeg.com
www.poolbeg.com

1

A catalogue record for this book is available from the British Library.

ISBN 978-1-78199-828-1

Typeset in Sabon by Poolbeg Press Ltd
Printed by CPI Group, UK

www.poolbeg.com

About the author

A graduate of the National University of Ireland Maynooth and Trinity College Dublin, A. O'Connor is the bestselling author of twelve novels, including *The House, The Secrets of Armstrong House, The Legacy of Armstrong House, The Footman, The Left-Handed Marriage* and *On Sackville Street*.

He has also written one children's book on Irish patriot Michael Davitt, and one on the history of Kilmainham Gaol. (Also published by Poolbeg.)

Acknowledgements

A big thank-you to Paula, Kieran, David, Caroline and all at Poolbeg and to my editor Gaye Shortland.

To Sue, Justin & family

Historical note

In 1861 nineteen-year-old Albert Edward, Prince of Wales, began an affair with the Irish actress Nellie Cliffden. The following is a fictionalised account of their story, based on true events.

PROLOGUE

1871

Queen Victoria sat on her couch in the audience room at Windsor Castle as the Prime Minister William Gladstone was shown in. As she watched him respectfully approach her, she was not looking forward to the meeting. She had never liked Gladstone. He was austere, a perfectionist who never tired of pointing out perceived imperfections in others. Even Victoria was not exempt from his disapproval.

"Your Majesty," said Gladstone as he bowed to her.

"Prime Minister." She nodded to him.

"I understand the Prince of Wales has been ill? How is his condition?" enquired Gladstone.

"He is poorly, Prime Minister. He has taken to his bed in Sandringham but is getting the best of care and I have no doubt will recover soon."

"Typhoid is a terrible illness. But I do not need to tell you that, ma'am, when it caused the premature death of your dear husband."

"That, amongst other things," muttered Victoria under her breath.

"With the Prince falling ill and the approach of the tenth anniversary of your husband's death, I thought it might be an apt time to discuss concerns surrounding the royal family, ma'am," said Gladstone.

"I should think these events make it anything but an apt time, Prime Minister," said Victoria.

1

"Perhaps so, but the issues need to be discussed in any case."

"What exactly needs to be discussed?" Victoria said curtly.

"Ma'am, I do not think I can remember a time when the royal family have been so out of favour with the country as they are now."

"Out of favour?" Victoria sounded more irate than concerned.

"Ma'am, the press is openly critical of you and the public is equally dissatisfied."

"The press is always critical and the public never satisfied. To try and make them otherwise is a fruitless exercise."

"You have not been seen in public for many years, ma'am. The country is beyond puzzled at this stage at your continued absence from public life and, quite frankly, angered by the perceived neglect of royal duty."

"Prime Minister, may I remind you that I am in deep mourning for my beloved husband." Victoria's tone was at its most icy.

Husband *and* first cousin, thought Gladstone, wondering whether the close blood relationship had made the attachment excessively intense. "I understand that, ma'am, but the country does not. They think that two years, maybe three or four, may be sufficient to be in deep mourning. But ten years, ma'am? The country is perplexed and your popularity is at its very lowest."

"My aim never was to be popular, Prime Minister. I have done everything out of a sense of duty."

"Indeed." Gladstone bowed slightly. "But the situation has now become so unsatisfactory that the press is openly questioning the need for a monarchy at all and calls for a republic are getting stronger every day. May I remind you that Napoleon the Third has just been ousted in France and that country has become a republic again?"

"There is no need to remind me, Prime Minister. I assure

you that I am fully informed of international affairs, despite what you may think. Your fears of Britain becoming a republic are unfounded – that will never happen here. One thing you can always be sure of in Britain is monarchy and rain!"

"Ma'am, I have urged you before that if you feel you are not up to performing your duties in public then you should allow the Prince of Wales a role in government and let him represent you. At least then the country would have a royal presence, rather than this gaping void we have had for ten years."

"That is quite out of the question. My son is simply not ready to assume an official royal role and I will not jeopardise this monarchy by giving him a role that he is not prepared for."

"But, ma'am, the Prince desperately wants the active role that you are denying him."

"What he *desperately* wants and what he is capable of are two entirely different things."

"I think him more than capable," objected Gladstone.

"And I think I know my own son better than you do."

"The reality is – because the Prince has been denied an official role by you – he too has become deeply unpopular. As he has no official function, he and the Princess of Wales are seen as frivolous and uncommitted. He has acquired the image of a playboy more interested in parties and alcohol, amongst other things, with his decadent set – the Marlborough set, I believe the press calls them – than showing any interest in his royal duty."

"If the Prince has that reputation, then perhaps he deserves it and it is through no fault of mine that he acquired it," said Victoria.

Gladstone looked at the small dour-looking woman dressed as always in mourning black and realised he was wasting his time. He and previous prime ministers had tried to make her see that her all-consuming grief, along with her distaste and distrust for her son, was destroying the institution that her husband had worked so hard to build up during his lifetime. The situation was now so critical that her family's future was in real jeopardy, but she refused to see it.

There was knock on the door and a footman came in.

"Excuse the interruption, ma'am, but an urgent telegram has arrived for you from Sandringham," he said.

Victoria nodded to the footman and beckoned him to come to her. She took the telegram and as she read it she paled.

"What has happened, ma'am?" asked Gladstone.

Victoria stood up. "The Prince of Wales' condition has deteriorated rapidly. They have asked me to go to Sandringham without delay."

"But – I thought he was recovering?"

"That was what we were previously informed. I must go, Prime Minister."

"Of course, ma'am, and I hope the news is better when you arrive at Sandringham."

Victoria nodded and quickly left the room.

As Victoria's carriage drove through the grounds of Sandringham to the main house, she was overwhelmed with a terrible sense of foreboding. It was December and it would soon be the tenth anniversary of her dear Albert's death. It was true what Gladstone had said, that typhoid was the official cause of his death. But everyone in the family knew Victoria had other ideas about that. And, now here she was, nearing the tenth anniversary of her husband's passing and being told that her eldest son and heir was suffering from the same illness and that he was in grave danger. Victoria knew that she would not have been sent for if the doctors did not think the situation was extremely serious. She could not help thinking that history was repeating itself. That she would lose her son in the same terrible fashion as her husband at the same time of year. As she thought of her son – Bertie as he had always been known to the family and close friends – she could not even imagine him being sick or physically impaired. He was a young man of thirty, a father to five children. He was always so strong-looking and cheerful. Victoria could not imagine a person so full of vitality being struck down so young. But life could be cruel – had the same thing not happened to her husband at a young age? And she had never recovered from the shock of that. And now she was being blamed by her prime minister for not appearing in public when she felt every day was a case of mere survival without her darling husband.

She thought of her relationship with Bertie. How they had become so distant from each other in recent years. As the years passed by, they had grown ever more estranged from each other. She had lived in her court of mourning, Bertie had lived in his court of decadence. There had been nothing in common between the two courts. But, through it all, she had never imagined that anything could happen to him, that he would ever fall ill or that his life could be in danger. She knew how sometimes doctors could get things wrong and how her own family were prone to exaggeration – she could only hope and pray that this was the case.

The carriage came to a halt and she was assisted out. Inside, she was escorted through the vast rooms and corridors of Sandringham.

Her daughter Alice and her husband had been visiting from Germany when Bertie had taken ill. Alice, who prided herself on her nursing skills, had remained to nurse her brother. As she was escorted down the corridor to the room Bertie was in, she saw Alice deep in conversation with Bertie's wife Alexandra outside the door. Victoria knew she had to be strong for them all. Not only was she the head of the family and Bertie's mother, but she was also the queen. She knew in this time of crisis she had to show strength.

As she reached the two women she could see they had been crying.

"Mama!" Alice came and kissed her cheek.

"Your Majesty," Alexandra managed to say as she tried to pull herself together in front of Victoria, but her tall elegant figure was trembling.

"How is he?" asked Victoria. "How is our dear Bertie?"

"We must prepare ourselves for the worst," said Alice.

"I fear there is no hope," said Alexandra as she raised her handkerchief to her beautiful face to stop herself from sobbing out loud.

Victoria suddenly felt weak and held on to a nearby chair for support.

"But – this cannot be – it just cannot be," she whispered. "Not Bertie . . . I had been informed he was improving."

"He had been, Mama, but then he had a relapse," said Alice.

"I must go to him at once," said Victoria.

Suddenly she could hear the sound of groaning coming from the other side of the door.

"You must prepare yourself, Mama, he is quite delirious. Sometimes he is not making much sense. He will not recognise you."

Victoria nodded. "Take me to my son."

Alice nodded and, offering her mother her arm, led her to the door and opened it. As Victoria entered the room she could see a group of people gathered around the four-poster bed – doctors, nurses and some of the household staff at Sandringham. With Alice's support she walked across the room.

The medical staff stepped away from the bed and bowed to her.

Then Bertie came into full view. She saw his deathly white face, his brow covered in sweat, his eyes closed as he tossed and turned alarmingly on the bed.

She let go of Alice's arm and went to the side of the bed.

"Bertie, my darling Bertie, it's your mama," she said.

But he seemed not to hear her as he continued to toss and turn.

"Bertie!" Victoria reached out, took his hand and held it firmly.

He gripped his mother's hand and looked towards her. "I need to go – I need to go now and see her," he gasped.

"He's not making much sense, Your Majesty," said the doctor beside her. "He hasn't for some time – it's the fever."

On the other side of the bed, Alice took a cloth and wiped Bertie's forehead as Alexandra tried to suppress her tears.

"Bertie – can you hear me?" Victoria said, squeezing his hand tightly to try and get a response.

"You don't understand!" he said, his voice rising. "I have to go and meet her now – she's waiting for me – she's been waiting for me all this time."

"Who – my dear? Who is waiting for you?" asked Victoria.

"Nellie – Nellie is waiting for me. Can't you see? I can't keep her waiting any longer. I must go to Nellie – I must go to my Nellie now!"

Victoria's eyes widened in shock. She looked across at Alexandra and Alice who looked utterly horrified.

"I must go to Nellie now," repeated Bertie. "I must see her – I must see her now."

CHAPTER 1

"What shall we do about that boy?" Victoria asked as she gazed out the window from the upstairs sitting room in Buckingham Palace.

"Bertie needs ... careful handling. He's not a leader, he needs to be led," said her husband Albert who was sitting beside the fire in an ornate armchair, his legs crossed.

Victoria swung around from the window, her face a mask of concern. "If *ever* a man needed to be a leader and not to be *led*, it is our son. How can you have a king who is not a leader?"

"Modern-day monarchs often need to be counselled, to rely on and be led by their prime minister's advice and judgement," Albert pointed out, his accent still displaying his German origins. "You have done it enough times yourself."

Victoria raised her eyes to heaven and moved across the room to her writing desk as she spoke. "If I were to leave my decisions to the sole judgement of my prime ministers, I and indeed the country would have been doomed long ago. A prime minister is like a gown and can be discarded by the end of a season when it falls out of fashion. Some of the cleverest prime ministers who have served me have been thrown out of office by the whim of the people and replaced by dimwits."

"Yes, I do see your point. Bertie in the hands of an incompetent prime minister would lead to a sorry state of affairs," sighed Albert.

"The blind leading the blind!" scoffed Victoria.

Albert sat forward. "That is why it is paramount that a good marriage is made for him. He needs the right woman beside him as queen."

"An intelligent, clever, *dedicated* and diligent woman who will serve this institution to the best of her abilities –"

"And will keep Bertie on the straight and narrow, curb the idleness and pleasure-seeking he is prone to, and turn him into the monarch that this country deserves."

"And I am of the opinion that Princess Alexandra fits just such a role," said Victoria confidently.

"The woman Vicky speaks highly of."

"Yes, the Danish girl."

"I am still concerned that Bertie marrying a Dane will cause problems with our German relatives. Are you quite sure, Victoria, that there isn't any German princess as suitable as she?"

"Vicky has searched high and low to no avail. Ah – you haven't yet seen the photograph of Alexandra that Vicky sent me." She reached out to a drawer in the desk and, taking out a photograph, brought it over to Albert.

Albert studied the photograph intently.

"She is beautiful, is she not?" Victoria asked as she sat in an armchair opposite him.

"She is pleasing on the eye, I agree. But she is a Dane, Victoria, hardly a good choice politically."

"In any case, I fear Alexandra is the last resort, Albert. She is the only suitable princess left in Europe."

"Have you discussed it any further with Bertie?"

"I have constantly tried to raise it with him, but he seems bored by the whole subject," she said with an air of despair. "Vicky has said that when she met Alexandra she got on very well with her. She thinks she is quite perfect as Bertie's future wife."

"Well, if Vicky thinks so then it must be true!" Albert's tone was slightly mocking, amused at how his wife had always had such a high regard for their eldest daughter's opinion, even more so since she had married Frederick, heir to the Prussian throne, three years previously.

"Well, I do trust Vicky's opinion, in the same way that she relies on mine. Vicky has been vigilant in her search and her choice is Alexandra – so that is the end of it."

"Alexandra may be Vicky's choice, and may well be our choice – but it is still ultimately Bertie's choice that matters."

"Which is what depresses me!" said Victoria. "If only children would do what they are told!"

"He's hardly a child any more – he is nearly twenty, may I remind you!"

"He acts like a child to me."

"But we must remind ourselves of his good points," Albert insisted.

"Yes, do remind us!" she said sarcastically.

"He has done very well since going to Cambridge –"

"Which surprises me greatly. He was just short of being a dunce when his tutors schooled him before university – unlike Vicky," said Victoria.

"Regardless of that, he has surpassed himself at university – so much better than we thought he could. And then his tour of America and Canada last year was by all accounts a staggering success. He strengthened the links between us and those countries and was admired and loved by all who met him."

"Perhaps they see something in him that we do not?" mused Victoria.

"I have heard back from many a source that they find Bertie charming with a natural flair for diplomacy – the makings of a great monarch, one could say."

Victoria looked sceptical. "One could say many a thing about Bertie . . . we could debate him for weeks and still not reach a conclusion on him. On a more urgent note – are we to allow him this journey to Ireland?"

There was a knock on the door and a footman entered.

"Your Royal Majesty, the Prince of Wales has arrived and is waiting to see you."

Victoria and Albert exchanged a glance before Victoria said, "Show him in."

The footman backed out of the room, and a minute later a young man, smiling broadly, walked confidently in.

He bowed to his mother before leaning down and kissing her cheek. He then turned to his father and bowed to him.

Victoria looked at her son and thought he looked very well. He was a handsome young man with brown hair and sallow skin – though Victoria had always thought it unfortunate that he did not look like his father who in her mind was the most handsome man she had ever met.

"You are looking well, my boy, Cambridge must suit you," said Albert.

"Very much, Papa, I am enjoying myself immensely there," agreed Bertie.

"Not too much, one hopes?" said Victoria. "Do sit down, Bertie, and stop hovering there like a seagull about to take flight."

Bertie sat in an armchair between his two parents.

"We were just discussing you," said Albert.

"All good, I hope?" smiled Bertie.

"Quite," said Victoria, arching an eyebrow at her husband, "but we are not convinced this holiday to Ireland is what is called for at present."

Bertie's smile faded. "Hardly a holiday, Mama! I will be stationed with the army in Kildare. An excellent opportunity to acquaint myself with the military and learn how it operates while I train to be an officer. After all, I will be Commander in Chief of the army one day and I feel I should have the men's respect and they should feel that I am one of them."

"You will never be 'one of them'. And may I remind you that I am Commander in Chief of the army at present, and I should hope that I hold the men's respect without ever having felt the need to take up residence in a barracks in Kildare!"

"Yes, Mama," said Bertie, looking down at the floor.

"We are not completely against the idea," Albert said quickly, seeing his son looking crestfallen. "In fact, I have pointed out to your mother that this would be an excellent opportunity for you to learn some badly needed discipline. A spell in the army, no matter how short, could be the making of you."

"Thank you, Papa," Bertie smiled through gritted teeth. "I should have thought my tour of America and Canada would have proved how capable I am already."

"We have heard positive reports of your tour, we will not deny it," said Victoria.

"Well, then!" said Bertie. "Being stationed in Kildare for a while could improve relations with our subjects in Ireland. After all the damage that was done to our family's reputation during the Famine and the strengthening republicanism that is taking root there, surely a visit from me could only improve matters?"

Victoria looked at Albert and he nodded. "Oh, very well!" she said with a sigh. "You may go to Ireland. One never knows, perhaps you are even right – goodness knows our popularity is its lowest ever in Ireland and anything that helps to bring us closer to the people there can only be good."

"If I may make a suggestion?" said Albert. "That we arrange for Bertie to be in Ireland at the same time as our official tour there in August. That way we can meet with him and he can even accompany us to Killarney for that part of the tour."

Victoria's face lit up at the suggestion as she clasped her hands together. "Marvellous idea, Albert!"

Bertie knew this plan served only as a means to keep him under surveillance by his parents. "Indeed – a marvellous idea," he said, managing to smile.

"And now to other matters," said Victoria as she pointed at the photograph of Alexandra which Albert had placed on an occasional table by his chair.

Albert picked it up and handed it to his son.

Bertie studied the photograph and then looked up. "Who is she?"

"Well, it is Princess Alexandra of Denmark of course!" said Victoria. "The young woman I have been discussing with you!"

"Oh – I see," said Bertie, looking down at the photograph again.

"Well?" asked an impatient Victoria. "Is she not beautiful? Is she not delightful?"

"Yes, I suppose. It is so hard to judge from a photograph," he said, handing it back to his mother.

"It is not that hard to judge! We think she is exquisite," said Victoria, her face souring. "Your sister Vicky is presenting you with a bright, intelligent and beautiful princess with excellent pedigree – surely you must have an opinion on the matter?"

"I – I just think of myself as too young to be contemplating marriage."

Victoria's face soured further. "Your sister Vicky was three years married by the time she had reached your present age, Bertie, and your younger sister is already engaged to be married next year!"

"Ah yes – but they are women, Mama! Of course they should marry earlier."

Albert sat forward, irritated. "Nonsense! I was engaged to your mother when I was nineteen and married to her at twenty-one. And here you are at the same age without any indication of settling down or inclination to do so!"

"I believe I am too young to settle down," said Bertie.

"One is never too young to settle down, Bertie," Victoria snapped. "But we fear you may turn out to be the type of bachelor who thinks he is *always* too young to settle down!

As your father and I have discussed, you need the right wife to help you carry the burden of this institution, in the same way I have been blessed with your father's support through all these years."

"And for many a year to come, one hopes, Mama. You are still young and in such fine health that hopefully the time for the burden to handed to me will not be for many a year!" Bertie allowed a faint mockery to seep into his voice.

"I have every intention of reigning for many a year and decade yet before you become king, Bertie – do not concern yourself about that!" said Victoria.

"But you are being selfish as always, Bertie," said Albert. "You have been born into this life but the woman you marry will not have been. Surely you want to give your wife time to prepare for her role as queen by marrying her as young as possible?"

"I hadn't given it much thought!" said Bertie.

Victoria raised her eyes to heaven and looked despairingly at Albert.

"Perhaps we should continue this subject over dinner tonight before you leave for Cambridge in the morning?" said Albert.

Bertie realised he was being dismissed and stood up quickly. "Oh, yes, of course. Actually, I hadn't planned on being here for dinner tonight."

"*What*?" shrilled Victoria.

"I have made alternative plans. I do apologise!"

"Alternative plans with *whom*?" demanded Victoria.

"With some friends who are down from Cambridge in London," said Bertie.

"Out of the question, Bertie. If you want to meet your friends here in London then you can invite them to have dinner with us here," said Victoria.

"Your mother is right, Bertie. You cannot just – head out – for a night in London without the proper protocol and plans put in place."

Bertie hid his anger. "As you wish."

He turned and left the room.

"We must fear for the future of this monarchy, Albert, when *he* is supposed to be the future!"

"I share your concerns, but let us hope that this stay in Ireland will bring him to the level of maturity that he will need to prepare to be king one day."

"We live in hope," sighed Victoria.

CHAPTER 2

Nellie Cliffden walked confidently towards the footlights in the Palace Theatre in Dublin before a packed audience as she finished singing –

"Where are you going, my lovely?
Wouldn't you like if I went there with you?
I'm not asking to go there forever . . .
I'd be happy with one night or maybe with two!"

The theatre erupted in laughter and applause as Nellie took an exaggerated bow in front of the audience.

"More, Nellie!" shouted one man.

"Sing it again!" shouted another.

"I'm afraid that's all I can do tonight, my friends!" Nellie projected her voice to the audience before winking. *"I've got a special appointment I can't break!"*

"No, Nellie! Don't leave us! Stay for another song!"

"I'll be back tomorrow at the same time, on the same stage – *when I'll be once more all yours!"* said Nellie as she gave a courtesy. Then, smiling broadly at the audience who were giving a thunderous applause, she walked off the stage.

Backstage, her smile dropped as she walked quickly past the stagehands there and the members of the next act who were preparing to go on.

"That was wonderful performance tonight," said her assistant Sadie as she put a shawl over Nellie's bare shoulders and arms.

"I thought I was off-key on the second song," said Nellie as she walked down a corridor to her dressing room.

"No – you were in perfect key all night, Nellie," Sadie assured her as she tried to keep up with Nellie's quick pace.

Once they reached her dressing room, Nellie swung the door open and entered.

"Unbutton me, will you?" she said as Sadie closed the door behind them.

As Sadie rushed to unbutton her gown, Nellie glanced over at her dressing table which had several bunches of flowers on it.

"I have to go to a special party tonight, Sadie," she said as she stepped out of the gown. "What can I wear to make me stand out?"

"What about the emerald-green gown with the crystals, Nellie?" said Sadie, helping her into a golden satin dressing gown. "You always look so beautiful in that one."

Nellie nodded as she inspected the flowers and quickly read the cards attached. They were from members of the audience complimenting her and asking if they could call on her. She regularly received flowers during her performances from admirers.

Nellie sat at her dressing table and began to clean off the theatrical make-up she was wearing.

Sadie busied herself taking the emerald gown from the wardrobe, where Nellie always kept a choice of attire, and finding matching shoes.

When Nellie had removed her stage make-up, she stepped into the gown which had a low neckline and generous crinoline. Sadie fastened up the gown over her tightly laced corset. Nellie slipped into the shoes and sat again to apply some more subtle make-up.

Then Sadie arranged her hair.

Nellie regarded herself critically in the mirror. "I've been thinking, Sadie," she mused. "My hair won't be that colour forever . . . and, as a girl gets older, it's the colour of real gold she needs."

Sadie laughed as she stood back and admired Nellie – her golden hair, her tall full figure and her face which had a refined beauty. She caught sight of herself in the mirror. She was now in her mid-fifties, and she knew she had not aged well. She had a face that showed a life of hardship and struggle, her hair now greying with only a faint trace of the chestnut-brown it had once been.

"Who is holding this party tonight, Nellie?"

"It's a soirée being organised by Captain James. He's collecting me as usual."

"Will there be lots of important people there?"

"I'd say so. Captain James seems only to know important people, Sadie."

There was a knock on the door.

"That'll be him," said Nellie, taking a final look in the mirror before standing up and asking, "How do I look?"

"Magnificent!" declared Sadie.

Nellie nodded. "Open the door."

Sadie rushed to the door and, opening it, ushered a man in.

"Miss Cliffden, Captain Marton is waiting for you outside," he announced with a bow.

"My cloak, Sadie," said Nellie.

Sadie hurried to fetch the hooded cloak and helped Nellie into it.

Then, with a wink and a smile for Sadie, Nellie swept out the door.

She walked to the back door of the theatre, followed by the man. Outside, a carriage waited. The man opened the door and assisted Nellie in.

As the carriage drove off, Captain James Marton scrutinised Nellie who was sitting opposite him.

"Will I do?" she asked eventually.

"You'll do," he said. "Though in future, not so heavy on the rouge. It makes you look common."

"I thought they liked the rouge," said Nellie.

"Oh, they like it all right. Just not as much as you are wearing tonight."

As Nellie looked at James she could see why she had once so easily fallen in love with him. With his slicked-back black hair and dark-brown eyes which contrasted so starkly with his pale skin, he was strikingly handsome.

"Where is this soirée?" asked Nellie.

"It's in the home of Gilbert Frampton, the wine merchant."

Nellie immediately recognised the name. Framptons was one of the biggest wine merchants in Dublin.

"He lives in a manor house in Rathgar, quite private on its own grounds. His wife is away and the house is not overlooked by neighbours, so it's quite safe."

"Will there be many there?"

"I believe he has invited about ten of his acquaintances. And there will be a number of ladies as well, of course."

"And who am I to charm?" she asked.

"Frampton himself, of course. I selected you for him."

"He knows about me?"

"I've informed him all about you . . . he's quite looking forward to the pleasure."

"Frampton must be a very rich man. How much does this job pay?"

"Ten pounds, as usual divided equally between us."

Nellie bit her lower lip. She had wanted to have a certain conversation with James for a long time but never had the courage to broach it. Frampton was a step up from their usual clients and so she decided it was the perfect time to say what she had to say.

She sat forward, smiling. "James – do you think it's fair that I get only half. After all, I do all the work."

James's face soured. "Of course it's fair! It's more than fair! How would you meet these men if it weren't for my contacts?"

"It's just –"

He reached over and took her chin roughly in his hand. "Don't you ever forget where you were before you met me! And if it wasn't for me you'd be still back there!"

"I know, James, and I will always be grateful for what you have done for me," she said, trying to pull away from his grasp.

"Remember where I found you? Would you like to go back there?"

"Don't, James, please!" she begged, the horror of her past coming back in a flood of memories.

He let go of her chin and riffled a hand across her expensive dress. "Never forget who you are, Nellie. It doesn't matter what dress you wear or how much applause you get on the stage, you are what you are. And you belong to me. Do you understand?"

Nellie nodded and looked out the window as a tear fell down her cheek.

CHAPTER 3

The carriage drove down a leafy street in Dublin's Rathgar and slowed on reaching a large imposing gateway. Turning into it, it continued up the driveway and stopped in front of a four-storey manor. Nellie could see through the windows that the party had already commenced. Gentlemen in tailcoats were laughing as they smoked cigars while women in elaborate crinolines swept around the spacious room.

The driver dismounted, opened the door and offered his hand to Nellie who allowed him to help her down the step onto the gravel driveway. James stepped out after her.

"Madam?" James said with a note of sarcasm as he held his hooked arm out to her.

She took it and he escorted her up the steps to the front door and knocked loudly.

"Try to smile, Nellie! Look as if you're enjoying yourself!" he hissed at her as they waited.

"As soon as I go into the house I'll smile – don't I always? It's called being an actress."

The door opened and a butler stood there.

"Captain James Marton and Miss Nellie Cliffden," announced James.

"We've been expecting you, sir," said the butler as he bowed and ushered them in.

There was the sound of laughter and merriment in the house as the butler took their cloaks.

"This way, sir," said the butler and they followed him down the hallway.

Nellie glanced around at the marble floor and the high ceiling dominated by a chandelier. The butler led them through a double doorway into the drawing room. Nellie felt her stomach flutter with nerves. You'll be fine, Nellie, once you get into character, she thought. Remember, you're an actress!

There were at least a couple of dozen people in the drawing room. They were mostly men, with a handful of women. She recognised some of them. They were actresses like her. She knew their names and had met them at similar parties in the past. She had even worked in the same theatres and music halls as them on occasion, though they never acknowledged they knew each other. There were a couple of very young women there who she did not recognise. Unlike the actresses, they looked out of place, despite being well dressed. They were overawed by the surroundings they found themselves in and were acting loudly and drunkenly. Although some of the gentlemen appeared enamoured with them as they joked and flirted, Nellie realised they would not be invited to such parties or events in the future. For women like them to gain entry into this world, they were expected to act a certain way and the girls' lack of training would mean their foray into high society would be brief and they would be discarded after the night. Nellie hoped the girls would make the most of it.

There was also an older woman present, in her forties, dressed expensively and bejewelled. The woman gave Nellie a filthy look when she saw her. Nellie knew who she was. Connie Reagan. Rumoured to be from gentry stock, she had fallen from her position in life when she had a child out of wedlock in her youth. She was rumoured to be involved in many things but she was known to such men as were here as an organiser of parties and a fixer. A fixer for liaisons.

"*Marton!*" came a booming voice across the room and Nellie saw a well-dressed man in his fifties cut across the floor to them.

"Good evening, Gilbert," said James.

"I was beginning to doubt you were going to come at all!"

"We were slightly delayed – Miss Cliffden's performance at the theatre ran over schedule."

Gilbert turned his attention to Nellie, took her hand and kissed it. "Ah, Miss Cliffden! Do you mind if I call you Nellie?"

"I'd be insulted if you called me anything else, Mr. Frampton!" said Nellie as she smiled broadly at him.

He patted her hand as he still held it. "And you must call me Gilbert, I insist."

"Gilbert," she acknowledged, lowering her eyes modestly.

Gilbert had a ruddy complexion that Nellie was sure was born out of too much rich food and fine wine. His frame was large and also showed the signs of an appetite that had been too rich and greedy.

"Well, I've heard so much about you, my dear, that I feel I know you already!" said Gilbert. "Your reputation travels before you."

"As long as it doesn't trail behind me as well, Gilbert!" she quipped.

"Enchanting!" His laughter boomed as he looked her up and down. "Marton has told me all about you and I'm glad to see he was not lying or exaggerating. You are as pretty as a picture."

"You are too kind, Gilbert."

"Come, let me introduce you to the others and find you a drink," he said.

He winked and nodded his approval at James as he led her away.

"Gentlemen, we have in our midst a famous actress tonight," Gilbert announced loudly, causing all eyes to turn to Nellie. "May I introduce to you to Miss Nellie Cliffden!"

James took out his pocket watch, looked at the time and saw it was nearly one in the morning. The party was still in full swing. The drink had flowed all night and now many looked

24

to be very drunk. The younger women, who he hadn't seen before, had passed out on a sofa. One was hiccoughing loudly as she slumbered. He shook his head in despair at the sight of them. Amateurs who should not have been allowed at a gathering like that. He wondered how they had got there. He couldn't imagine they were Connie Reagan's girls. Connie wouldn't have risked her reputation as a fixer by bringing amateurs like that. No, he figured one of the other guests had found them and thought it would be a laugh to bring them along. That guest had got it wrong. The purpose of these parties might be considered sordid to some, but they should always have a veneer of class. As he looked at Nellie, he admired her. She was a true professional. She never let herself down. He watched her work the room, entrancing all the men. She laughed at their jokes, listened intently to their opinions. Nellie knew her part and, as much as these men vied for her attention, she knew the deal had been done and she would be with Gilbert that night. Nor would she let the compliments or flattery she was receiving go to her head. She graciously accepted them out of politeness, but they were like water off a duck's back. Nellie knew who she was and what she was and would never let herself fall for any of this sweet talk men like these would treat her to. She knew her purpose at the soirée and she was, like James, only interested in the business of making money.

"You have a beautiful home, Gilbert," she said as he handed her a glass of red wine.

"Yes, it's been in my family for a hundred and fifty years," he said.

"Where are your family?" she asked, looking up at a portrait of Gilbert with a rather severe, matronly-looking woman who was clearly his wife.

"They are taking the waters in Switzerland. I was too busy with work to join them," he said. "So –"

"So – when the cat's away!" she said with a smile.

"Exactly, my dear . . . But you've only seen this part of the house. Would you like me to give you the grand tour?"

"I would be honoured." She smiled as she took his arm.

As they left the room she glanced over at James who nodded approvingly at her.

"This staircase is hand-carved," said Gilbert as he led her upstairs.

"Most impressive."

"And the ceiling hand-painted," said Gilbert.

"So many hands!" said Nellie, causing him to laugh out loud.

"The house has ten bedrooms," he said proudly as he led her along the landing on the first floor.

"How can you ever choose which one to sleep in each night?" Nellie mocked lightly.

"Well, I'm a creature of habit, Nellie. So I always sleep in the same bedroom." He stopped at a door and put his hand on the handle. "This one actually – would you like to see it?"

"That's the best offer I've had all night," she said as he opened it for her and she walked in.

She looked around the luxurious bedroom where a four-poster bed stood in pride of place.

"I don't think I've ever seen such a beautiful bedroom," she said as she wandered around.

"And I'd say you've seen the inside of many bedrooms," he said as the smile disappeared from his face and he stared at her.

There was another portrait of his wife hanging on the wall.

"I think I shall just turn this around," he said, taking the painting and turning it to face the wall. "Violet was always such a prude!"

He walked towards Nellie and stood hovering in front of her.

"Well," he said as he finally pushed her down on the bed. "We know what we are here for, so let's get on with it. I think I've waited long enough."

Nellie saw the light coming through the bedroom windows.

She turned to see Gilbert's snoring frame beside her. She got out of the bed and began to dress in the clothes that had been hurriedly discarded on the floor.

Once dressed she said, "Gilbert? I think I'll be off now, unless there's anything further?"

Gilbert grunted and turned away from her.

She went to the mirror on a dressing table and fixed her hair before turning to leave the room. Before she left she spotted the portrait of Gilbert's wife Violet, facing the wall. She walked over to it and turned it back around the right way – Violet once again firmly stared out onto the room and the four-poster bed. Nellie giggled to herself, thinking of Gilbert waking to the sight of his wife's cold judgemental eyes staring down at him.

She walked along the landing and down the stairs. The house was now in silence, all guests either having left or found their way to one of the other nine bedrooms in the house. She knew James would be long gone home.

As she passed the open door of the drawing room she peeked in and saw the room was a mess from the soirée the night before. Empty glasses and bottles of champagne and wine were strewn everywhere. On the table were trays still half filled with uneaten food. She walked in and looked down at the sandwiches, salmon and cakes just left there to be thrown out once the staff returned. She had a flashback to the Famine years before. The starving desperate people she had seen scavenging for food. The parents who watched their children die as they were unable to find food for them. She shuddered at the memory. She quickly grabbed a few napkins and began to fill them with leftover food and tied each one with a knot once full.

"Good morning, madam," said the butler, appearing from nowhere beside her.

"Oh, eh, good morning," said Nellie, going red with embarrassment.

"Will you not be staying for breakfast?" asked the butler.

"No, thank you. I need to go. I have a play on tonight and I need to rehearse before my next –"

"Performance?" The butler looked her up and down disdainfully as he finished her sentence for her.

She nodded and smiled and, grabbing the food, made for the front door.

She walked down the long avenue until she reached the street. She felt unnerved by the butler. His haughty disdain for her was hurtful – his attitude implying that he knew what she was and there was no point in her pretending to be anything else. She looked up and down the street in the hope of spotting a hansom cab. But there were none. The area was residential and so she imagined it would be unusual to see a cab there at that time of the morning. Tired and emotional, she set off towards her home.

CHAPTER 4

Nellie pushed the door of the building where she lived open and walked into the main hallway. It was a smart building in Leeson Street which had been divided up into flats. She climbed to the top floor, unlocked the door to her flat and let herself in, closing it behind her.

The flat was small but cosy and decorated, if not luxuriously, then very comfortably. Nellie reminded herself every day of how lucky she was to be able to live there. Beside the fireplace, the fire in the hearth was now just smouldering. Sadie was asleep in an armchair. Nellie tiptoed over to the table and put the napkins of food on it before taking a rug off the couch and going to put it over Sadie.

Sadie stirred and her eyes flickered open.

"I was trying not wake you," said Nellie.

"Oh, I didn't mean to fall asleep," said Sadie, sitting up quickly. "I was waiting for you to get home."

"I've told you before, Sadie, there's no need for you to sit up and wait for me. You should have gone to bed and got a good night's sleep."

"I like to sit up and wait for you, Nellie. I worry until I see you come safely back through the door."

"You worry too much," said Nellie as she went to the mirror over the fireplace and removed her jewellery. "I brought you some food. Some lovely cakes and sandwiches."

Sadie went to the table and untied one of the napkins.

"Look at this feast! I'll put it in the larder and we can have it for lunch. Were they just going to throw this food out?"

"It looked like it."

"How anyone can waste a morsel of food after the Famine, I'll never understand," said Sadie.

"People like that didn't see or experience what we did in the Famine, Sadie. They'll never understand," said Nellie, turning and facing her.

"How was the evening?" asked Sadie.

"Fine. It was very glamorous, the house was beautiful and, as you can see from the leftovers, the food was scrumptious."

"And the gentleman?" asked Sadie cautiously.

Nellie smiled, rolled her eyes and laughed. "He was that drunk he passed out after five minutes."

"I wish you didn't have to do that. It breaks my heart to think of you!" said Sadie, becoming upset.

"Oh, stop that, Sadie! I've no time for your nonsense! Aren't I lucky that I am where I am? There are a lot worse places to be. Never thought I'd have a place of my own, let alone a place like this."

"But I was thinking, if you asked the theatre owner for a pay rise, then you wouldn't have to go to those parties any more. You deserve a pay rise, Nellie, the amount of business you bring to the theatre!"

"Even if my salary was doubled at the theatre, I still wouldn't be able to live here or pay my way. Let alone put some money aside for the future, for when my golden hair turns grey and I won't be invited to soirées any more and they won't want to see me on a stage either."

Sadie went to Nellie and began to unbutton her gown. "Did you speak to Captain Marton about increasing your earnings, like you said you were going to?"

"I did, and he said no. Told me straight away he wasn't going to do that."

"But that's not fair, Nellie. Why should be keep such a large portion of your earnings?"

"He said if it weren't for him I wouldn't be invited to the soirées or introduced to the gentlemen who hire me. He's right, Sadie. He's the fixer. I'd be nobody without him." Nellie stepped out of her gown.

"That's not true, Nellie! You're an actress!"

"Of a sort . . ." Nellie's eyes had a distant look in them. "I owe everything to James. He found me. He turned my life around. Trained me how to walk and talk proper. Introduced me to the right sort of clients. I had never met people like that before. And, with his training, I had enough airs and graces to get on the stage."

"Well, he's been well rewarded for his work!" spat Sadie. "He's earned a lot of money on your –"

"Back?" Nellie finished the sentence for her and the two women burst out laughing.

"Aye, one way of saying it!" said Sadie. "You get yourself off to bed now, and I'll bring you in a nice cup of tea when the kettle is boiled."

"Thank you, Sadie. I don't know what I'd do without you," said Nellie as she walked down a corridor to her bedroom.

"It's me who doesn't know what I'd be doing without you!" Sadie called down the corridor after her.

CHAPTER 5

Queen Victoria looked her son up and down as they stood in the upstairs drawing room in Buckingham Palace.

"You look presentable," she announced.

"Thank you, Mama."

"What time is the royal train leaving for Liverpool?" asked Albert.

"Two o'clock, Papa. It will arrive in Liverpool in time for me to get the night boat to Dublin."

"I have written to Major Hazeldon," Albert said.

"Who is Major Hazeldon?" asked Victoria.

"He is in charge of the camp in Kildare where Bertie will be stationed."

"Carry on!" said Victoria.

Albert coughed and continued. "I have informed Major Hazeldon that you are not to be given any special treatment or favours just because you are the Prince of Wales, Bertie. I have asked him to treat you in the same manner as he treats all the other military personnel."

"Yes, Papa."

"Strict discipline," said Albert. "Rigid training, curfews, early rising in the mornings, plain fare when it comes to diet, cold-water baths – absolutely no alcohol. No gambling, no socialising and no female company."

"It makes a stretch in Pentonville prison sound more appealing," muttered Bertie.

"Bertie! What did you say?" demanded Victoria.

"I said – it sounds most appealing!" said Bertie.

"This is an opportunity for you to prove yourself, Bertie. And for once in your life to make your parents proud!" said Albert.

"I will try my level best," said Bertie.

"Your best often falls short of what is required, Bertie," said Victoria.

"Remember you are representing not just your mother, but this whole institution while you are in Ireland," said Albert.

"I will remember," said Bertie.

"These are such turbulent times in Ireland," said his mother. "And your stay there, coupled with our own visit to the country later in the summer will, one hopes, appease one's subjects there and put an end to all this talk of Irish independence and republicanism."

"We will kill this talk of independence with kindness," said Albert.

"Better to kill them with kindness than with starvation and another famine," said Bertie.

Victoria raised her hand to her forehead in despair. "How you can be flippant about such a subject is beyond me!"

"Bertie!" snapped Albert angrily. "I strongly suggest you leave your boyish jokes in Liverpool before you get the night boat. You will find your sense of humour will be lost on the Irish people who do not view the loss of one million of their fellow subjects during the Famine in the same glib manner!"

"Yes, Papa. I profoundly apologise. If that is all, then I shall take my leave. The royal train awaits!" He bowed to both his parents before hovering beside his mother.

"You may kiss me," said Victoria, raising her cheek to him.

Bertie planted a light kiss before leaving the room.

"Must we despair? To think an empire's hopes rest on those shoulders!" said Victoria as she sat down abruptly on an armchair.

Albert sighed. "These weeks in Ireland will change him. It will teach him responsibility and discipline. You wait and see. He will be a different man by summer's end."

CHAPTER 6

Major Hazeldon sat at his desk in his office in the military camp of the Curragh in Kildare, reading a letter. His eyes widened as he continued to read. Then he folded the letter and placed it on the desk in front of him. He took off his spectacles, laid them beside the letter and massaged his temples.

There was a knock on the door.

"Enter!" called Hazeldon.

Captain Charles Carrington walked in and towards the desk.

"You wished to see me, Major?"

"Yes, Carrington," said Hazeldon. "How are the preparations progressing for the Prince of Wales' arrival?"

"Everything is in order, Major. His quarters are prepared and the men are prepared for his presence. Most of them are very excited about His Royal Highness's stay here."

"I have received a letter from His Royal Highness's father. Prince Albert is insisting his son is treated to a regime so harsh during his stay with us that I fear it will leave a bad impression of us with the future king."

"I am sorry to hear that, sir."

"Be seated, Carrington," ordered Hazeldon.

Charles sat in the empty chair on the other side of the desk. Hazeldon studied him for a few moments. Charles had a very honest and trustworthy face, he thought. Pale-blue eyes set in a heart-shaped face with neat straight fair hair.

Yes, Charles's looks reflected his personality. A man who could be trusted with the role he was about to give him.

"I believe you are acquainted with the Prince."

"Yes, sir. My family are acquainted with the Royal family and I have met His Royal Highness socially."

"That is why I have put you in charge of him during his stay here. What kind of a fellow is he?"

"Well, Bertie – ahem, the Prince of Wales – is an affable sort of chap. Friendly and outgoing, surprisingly modest for the position he holds."

"That is my understanding of his character. The facts are that His Royal Highness is not going to have a military career, he will never see battle or go to war. His destiny is to be king which will exclude him from any military duty in his lifetime. Although I wish for the Prince to learn about the military, I do not want to bestow on him a bad impression of it. I do not see it as my role to harshly prepare him for a career in the military that he will never have."

"Yes, sir."

Hazeldon's forehead creased. "Nor do I see it as my role to provide parental guidance and supervision to a young Prince in lieu of his own father's guidance and supervision."

"Yes, sir."

"If I implement the strict regime his father is recommending, then I fear all I shall achieve will be to make the Prince's stay here unpleasant – and leave a lasting bad impression with our future monarch of not just our camp here but of my own good self as well."

"Yes, sir."

"I have no desire or intention to make an enemy of our future king, Carrington."

"Very wise, sir."

"So, I shall not be implementing the more stringent of his father's suggestions, but of course want the young prince to receive all the military training that we can give him. In short, I want the Prince to enjoy his time with us and to hold fond memories of his time here that he may carry forward into the future."

"Yes, sir."

"His father has asked for his son to be treated the same as all the other men here – but he is not the same as all the other men here – he is not nor ever will be or can be." Hazeldon put the letter in a drawer in his desk and closed it with a firm thud.

"Of course, sir."

"And, Carrington – I caution you to remind all the men, and particularly your fellow officers, of the importance of the Prince of Wales' visit is to us. Everyone must be on his best behaviour at all times."

"Of course, sir."

"We cannot let our guard down for a moment. No crude talk or behaviour from anybody will be tolerated. Every single man must act as a gentleman at all times," Hazeldon raised his eyes to heaven, "whether he be one or not. I know some of the officers like to occasionally gamble and have one drink too many – that will not be tolerated for one minute during the Prince's stay."

"I fully understand, sir."

"I insist that the Officers' Mess is elevated to the standard of the finest gentlemen's club in London for the Prince's visit. This is our opportunity to shine before the Prince and before Her Majesty the Queen when she comes to inspect his progress here."

"Yes, sir."

Hazeldon sighed. "Although I do not know how we are to turn a young man with no military experience into a shining example of officer material within a few weeks – to display to his parents by the time they arrive here."

"Well, I'm sure we can do it, sir, if we all pull together."

"I admire your optimism – I, for one, will be glad when he is dispatched back to England and is no longer our responsibility. That is all, Carrington."

"Yes, sir – thank you, sir." Carrington stood and saluted before marching out of the room.

Charles walked through the door of the Officers' Mess and looked around. It was late afternoon and the mess was quiet with only a few tables occupied. The room was huge with a bar at the end of it and a series of tall windows which looked out over the rolling Kildare countryside. The walls were panelled wood and a series of portraits of military heroes decorated them. In pride of place amongst the portraits was a painting of a stern-looking Queen Victoria, gazing into the distance with a disinterested look. Charles spotted some of his friends sitting at a round table by one of the windows. There were four officers there, all young men in their early twenties.

"The usual, sir?" asked Dickie, the chief barman in the mess. Dickie was a small man in his forties with a ginger moustache and a quick eye that could spot an Officers' empty glass before he did himself. He was very popular with all the officers.

"Make it a double," said Charles.

"Coming right up, sir."

Charles made his way over to his friends' table. "I need a stiff drink!" he said as he pulled up a chair and joined them.

"Well – what did he want?" asked Captain Donald Kilroy, a sandy-haired young man of twenty-two with a permanent smile of his face and twinkling blue eyes.

"He wanted to discuss the Prince's visit, as expected."

"And?"

Dickie arrived with a glass of whiskey on a tray which Charles quickly took. He waited for Dickie to retreat before he continued.

"And – we are to treat the Prince with kid gloves, we must make his stay as pleasant as possible, create dear memories for him which he can hold on to in the future – oh, and we must turn him into a first-class officer by the time Her

Majesty the Queen arrives to visit." Charles raised his glass to Victoria's portrait. "God bless you, ma'am!"

"Oh, it all sounded quite civil until you mentioned the last part!" smirked Donald.

"Hazeldon is going quite against Prince Albert's wishes. He not only doesn't want his son to be treated any differently to others but is looking for a harsh regime to be inflicted on him."

"Hazeldon is probably concerned his hopes for a knighthood would be dashed if he made an enemy of the Prince," suggested Donald.

"Most probably," said Charles, swigging back his drink.

"Well, I think it's all a bit of a cheek, I really do," said Edgar Forrest, a young man with soot-black hair, dark eyes, and lips set in a thin straight line. "Whose idea was it to foist the Prince on us? The whole camp has been turned upside down for his visit and we have the ludicrous sight of grown men – soldiers, mind you – acting like a group of giggling girls!"

Charles laughed out loud. "I can't ever remember as much excitement in a camp before, I admit!"

"Ridiculous, I tell you," confirmed Edgar. "I, for one, will not be treating the Prince any different from anyone else. I don't care whose womb he came out of!"

"Forrest! Best you get that attitude in check before his Royal Highness arrives!" Charles smile faded as his face turned cold. "These are Hazeldon's orders and my job is to ensure they are complied with."

"*Pah!*" snorted Edgar. "This must be the first time in the army's history that we are under orders to be *nice* to somebody! The empire is lost surely!"

"I don't know about that," said James Marton as he sat back in his chair and looked out of one of the tall windows at the countryside, "but I am quite looking forward to royal company."

"*You* would, Marton! You were always a social climber," scoffed Edgar.

"I shall be delighted to make the acquaintance of the Prince," continued James. "And the whole experience will be much more pleasant for everyone now that we must be nice to him, rather than ghastly."

"It must be hard being the Prince of Wales," mused Donald. "Everyone having an opinion on you before you've ever even met them. I think I should hate it."

"I think I should love it!" said James as he reached for his drink and tossed it back. "And Hazeldon has the right idea, in my opinion. Why make an enemy of our future monarch when we can so easily make a friend of him?"

"As I said – social climber," Edgar muttered under his breath to Charles as James rose from the table.

"And now, gentlemen, if you will excuse me. I have a date with a young lady," said James.

"Another one?" asked Charles.

"Of course! I must hurry – I have to get to Dublin to meet her." James smiled as he turned and left them.

"I never quite know what Marton is up to," mused Donald as he watched him go. "I know he is not from a moneyed background like the rest of us, and yet he seems to have more cash than the rest of us put together. And it's not coming from an officers' salary, let us face that fact."

"Perhaps one of his lady friends is a rich widow funding his lifestyle," laughed Charles.

"It wouldn't surprise me in the least!" said Edgar, his dark eyes following Marton out of the mess.

CHAPTER 7

Nellie walked up the steps of the Shelbourne Hotel and the doorman opened the door for her.

"Good evening, madam," he said and she nodded to him as she walked past him into the foyer.

It was a busy evening in the hotel and the foyer was populated with well-dressed patrons. A gentleman raised his hat to her as she walked past him towards the restaurant. As she passed two women, she saw one of them quickly lean towards the other and whisper into her ear.

"Hello, Miss Cliffden, how are you this evening?" said the maître d' as she entered the restaurant.

"Very well, Pierre, and you?"

"Very well, Miss Cliffden. Captain Marton is already at your table. If you would like to follow me?"

She followed him across the packed restaurant. As she walked, she felt the eyes of the other diners on her. The admiring glances of some of the men, the shocked faces of some of the women, the judgemental looks of others.

James was at a corner table, waiting, smoking a cigar.

Pierre pulled out a chair for her and she thanked him as she sat down.

James studied her for a few moments and then put out his cigar in an ashtray on the table.

"You look beautiful tonight, Nellie. New gown?"

She shrugged and smiled at him. "Yes."

"It suits you. Red was always your colour."

"You may take our order, Pierre," said James. "We are both having the smoked salmon to start, followed by the venison."

"A very good choice, Captain Marton," said Pierre. He filled Nellie's glass from the bottle of white wine standing beside a red on the table. Then, with a bow, he left.

Nellie glanced around the restaurant, where diners were stealing glances at her.

"You love it, don't you?" he said. "The attention?"

"Well, if I'm going to get it, I might as well enjoy, don't you think?" she retorted.

"I wonder what they are thinking? What they are whispering about? Are they commenting on your looks, or the fact you are a well-known actress? Or the fact you are rumoured to be a women of no virtue?"

She raised her glass and took a sip. "They might be commenting on all of those things – or they might be wondering why a respectable officer like you is keeping the company of a woman like me."

His smile dropped for a second before he responded. "You always have the witty retort, Nellie."

"You have to in my profession as a –"

"Whore?" he cut in.

"Actress," she corrected, smiling at him sweetly.

He laughed. "I do love you, Nellie, I really do!"

"I might have fallen for that line when I first met you, James, but I'm a little long in the tooth to fall for it now. You love what you can get out of me . . . even the looks we are getting tonight. You don't care what the rumours might be about me or that you are being seen with me, because all you care about is that they are looking at us. It's you that enjoys the attention, not me. I get as much attention as I need when I'm on stage."

He sighed. "You're right, I do enjoy the attention. I deserve it. I never had it when I was growing up. The poor relation to a rich and powerful family who took pity on me by making sure I got a good education and then sent straight into the army to make sure they didn't have to worry about me again."

She stifled a yawn theatrically. "We've heard it all before! Poor James, life has been so hard for you!"

"It has, actually – relatively speaking, in any case."

"I suppose everything is relative in life, James."

"Anyway, Frampton was most pleased with you at the soirée last week," said James.

"I'm glad to hear it. He was the most boring man I ever met in my life, and he has had some stiff competition!"

"Not so boring, one hopes, that you won't meet him again? His wife is away next month and he has requested for you to attend another soirée at his house. A private party this time, with only you and he present."

"The same payment?" she checked.

"The same," James confirmed.

"In that case, I will listen to his boasting and his silly jokes with glee. Although I don't think I could put up with his snoring again. Even for that money it was too much to bear. Tell him I want my own room."

James's eyebrows rose. "Well, he won't allow you to have your own room, Nellie! Defeats the purpose!"

"For after, when he conks out which will be pretty soon judging by his last performance. Just somewhere I can have a restful night's sleep, is that too much for a girl to ask for?"

"Well, it very well might be. I tell you what, you ask him yourself when you get there. But, whatever you do, don't fuck up this arrangement. He's a very good contact and customer."

"And I'm providing a very good service," she said.

"The salmon," said Pierre, placing the plates in front of James and Nellie. He then refilled their wineglasses before leaving them alone.

"This looks scrumptious!" said Nellie, lifting her knife and fork and taking a mouthful.

When she glanced at James again, he was looking at her curiously.

"What?" she asked.

"Don't you ever get sick of it?"

"Sick of what?" she asked as she chewed.

"The life you lead?" There was a slight look of disgust on his face.

"Well, you're the one that led me into it, so why ask such a question?"

"Because – because, surely you could leave it any time?"

"And live off the wages I get paid at the music hall? It wouldn't even keep me in petticoats."

"You could find a cheaper place to live, cut down on your expenses," he suggested.

"It's not as if I live an expensive life, James."

"You could get rid of that leech Sadie for a start. Surely you could do without a maid?"

"I'll never get rid of Sadie. What would she do, where would she go?"

"Who cares?"

"I care! Sadie is much more than a maid to me. She's the only person who has ever really loved me for me and not for what she can get out of me. I suppose she's the only person I've ever truly loved as well."

"I thought you loved me?" he asked, smiling.

She laughed dismissively. "I don't love you, James. I did once, when I first met you. You'll never know how much I fell in love with you. But I was a fool, and that will never happen to me again – ever!"

"I haven't been such a bad friend to you, have I?"

"We use each other, James. Let's not have any other ideas about it. We use each other to make money that we both badly need. A business transaction, pure and simple. And it works very well."

A waiter removed their plates. Then Pierre arrived at the table, accompanied by a waiter carrying two plates of venison and another who served them vegetables.

Pierre then filled their glasses with red wine.

"Will there be anything else, sir?" he asked.

"No, thank you," said James, and Pierre and his waiters retreated.

"Anyway, Sadie doesn't cost me that much," said Nellie.

"So, if Sadie doesn't cost you that much and you claim you don't have an expensive lifestyle, what do you do with all this money you earn?"

"I put it aside. One day I will have earned enough to leave this life behind. I will be wealthy enough to say what I want and when I want it. I won't be at the beck and call of the Framptons of this world, or you. I'll be independent. I'd like to own a hotel one day, maybe a small boarding house by the sea. Then I'll do well and move up." She looked around the Shelbourne. "Maybe even own a hotel like this one day."

James choked on his venison and stifled his laughter. "Oh, come on, Nellie! What world are you living in? *You* owning a place like this?"

"I don't know why you are laughing, James. If you had told me some years ago that I would even be allowed into a place like this, let alone sit here eating with the crème de le crème staring at me, I wouldn't have believed it. And yet here I am. Anything is possible, they say. Ten years ago, I felt lucky to have survived the Famine. Lucky that I had something to eat. And yet here I am eating venison in the restaurant of the Shelbourne with a dashing and handsome captain!" She raised her glass and took a sip before winking at him.

"You are so full of shit, darling," James said, shaking his head.

"And that, my dear James, is why you love me!"

CHAPTER 8

The carriage swept into the huge forecourt of the military camp in Kildare. There, several hundred soldiers were standing to rigid attention, every button, every boot, every buckle polished and shining in the afternoon sun. Major Hazeldon, with a group of officers, stood to attention on the steps of the vast Victorian building that was the epicentre of the camp.

The carriage door was opened by a soldier and Bertie, dressed in officer uniform, stepped out and squinted in the sun.

Hazeldon peered at the young man with the handsome face and pleasing smile. For a moment he was shocked. He hadn't known what to expect on meeting the future monarch but couldn't help experiencing a feeling of disappointment. Perhaps he had expected somebody with the presence of a Julius Caesar, a Napoleon, a Henry the Eighth. Instead, he was viewing a pleasant-looking young man who seemed quite ordinary.

Hazeldon quickly stepped forward, gave a smart salute and said loudly, "Your Royal Highness, Major Hazeldon reporting. Welcome to Ireland."

The army band assembled on the forecourt began to play 'God Save the Queen'.

Bertie saluted and stood to attention with the rest until the music ceased.

He then looked around, seeming a little baffled.

"If you would care to follow me to my office, sir?" said Hazeldon.

"Oh, yes, of course, thank you," said Bertie and then followed Hazeldon up the steps into the building.

Inside, soldiers who were administrative staff stood along the corridors, saluting as they walked by.

Hazeldon indicated that Bertie should follow him up the stairs and they walked in silence until they reached his office.

They entered and Hazeldon closed the door.

"If Your Royal Highness would care to take a seat?" he suggested as he pointed to the empty chair in front of the desk.

"Oh, yes, of course," said Bertie, sitting down.

Hazeldon sat down behind his desk.

"I trust His Royal Highness had an enjoyable voyage?"

"Yes, thank you. The sea was a little choppy, but I got here in one piece, which is the main thing, don't you think?"

"Eh, yes . . . em, tea?" said Hazeldon as he reached for the bell on his desk and rang it loudly.

A few seconds later the door swung open and three soldiers entered carrying trays of sandwiches, cakes and tea. They placed them on the desk between the two men.

"Oh, this does look tasty, and I'm famished," said Bertie as he inspected the food.

The soldiers stared at Bertie in amazement as one of them poured the tea. Hazeldon then waved his hand at them and they hastily retreated.

"You'll have to forgive the men, sir – they haven't met a member of the royal family before, and so their curiosity is piqued."

"Understandable, of course, though I hope their curiosity will wane quickly. It's such a chore being a figure of curiosity." Bertie smiled broadly. "When I started at Cambridge, it took the other fellows a full two months to come to the realisation that I breathe, eat and sleep like everyone else."

Hazeldon nodded. "Eh, quite! Em . . . I received a letter from your father –"

"Yes, so I believe, and I understand he said I was to be treated just like everyone else." Bertie lifted a sandwich and took a large bite from it. "That is my dearest wish also. Just to be treated as everyone else is here."

"Yes, well, em – the training you will undergo will be quite intensive."

"Good! Jolly good! I've always been fascinated with the military. In fact, I was determined to have a full-time career in the army but I was overruled. That's the problem with being the Prince of Wales, Major – one is always overruled!"

"Yes, I see."

"There are perks to the job, as you can imagine. But the disadvantages far outweigh the perks as far as I can see. One is told what to wear, and where to go, and what to say, and which lady one should marry even!"

Hazeldon's eyes were wide open in surprise at these confidences. "Yes, I suppose that could be difficult."

"Damned difficult, Major! And yet, here I am in the beautiful countryside of Ireland, at last free of all that, if only for a short while. This could be the only chance of freedom I ever get in my life, Major!"

"Well, one man's idea of freedom is another man's prison, sir. The army isn't known for providing freedom to its soldiers."

"It feels like freedom to me, Major! Beautiful freedom!" Bertie inhaled deeply and smiled. "So where am I to sleep?"

"Your quarters have been prepared. Captain Charles Carrington will show you there once we have finished lunch. You are familiar with Captain Carrington, I understand?"

"Charlie Carrington? Oh, yes, I've met him. I didn't realise he was here. Excellent! He was always good for a laugh!"

"Indeed . . . And then your training starts in the morning, first thing – if that's all right?"

"Absolutely."

"Seven o'clock in the morning – is that too early?"

"Not at all!"

"Good. Jolly good. More tea, sir?" asked Hazeldon, picking up the teapot and managing to smile.

"Yes, please," said Bertie, smiling back.

Tea poured, Hazeldon reached for the bell on his desk and rang it again. "I will call for Carrington now, as he has been charged with your training here, and we can discuss your, eh, stay – if that is acceptable, sir?"

"Yes, fetch Charlie and we can have a good chat about what one is expected to do," smiled Bertie as he took a bite from another sandwich.

"Well, well, Charlie! Fancy meeting you here!" said Bertie as Charles walked him across the forecourt in front of Hazeldon's building after lunch.

"Yes, I've been stationed here for a while to complete my officer training, sir. Then I return to Cambridge in the autumn to round off my education there."

"Excellent! Well, it's good to see a friendly face."

"Well, most faces are friendly here, sir, I think you'll find."

Bertie looked around at all the soldiers busy with their duties and trying not to stare at him. "How many men are based here, Charlie?"

"Twelve thousand, sir."

"Twelve thousand! But that's larger than many towns!"

"Indeed it is, sir. It's one of the biggest garrisons in the empire, and certainly the hub of the military here in Ireland."

They turned into one of the streets off the main forecourt.

Bertie looked at the buildings which seemed to stretch on forever. "Quite a place!"

"Yes, sir – and the garrison runs like any town – every soldier has his own duties and jobs to ensure the camp is run efficiently. And, like in any town, there is a hierarchy. We officers are naturally at the top and there is strict non-fraternisation with the lower ranks."

"I understand."

"Discipline among the ranks is very important and so I urge you not to be too pleasant to the lower ranks – they won't respect you for it," Charlie advised him. "I know you will probably want to fit in here, but there is a strict code of behaviour and being friendly to your inferiors is out of the question."

"Thank you for the advice, Charlie – so much to learn, so little time."

Charlie pointed out different buildings and points of interest as they continued walking through the camp.

Eventually they reached a large manor on the edge of the camp which looked out over the beautiful rolling fields.

"And this is the house your quarters are in, sir," said Charlie.

Bertie wandered over to a fence and looked out over the countryside. He breathed in deeply. "What a beautiful smell! Do you know what it is, Charlie?"

"Eh, cow dung?" said Charlie, sniffing the air.

"No! Freedom! That is the smell of freedom, Charlie!"

Charlie stifled a laugh. "Indeed, sir!"

Bertie turned and followed Charlie into the house and up the stairs to the top floor. Charlie opened the door and showed Bertie in.

It was a large well-furnished flat with tall windows looking out over the countryside. The furniture was much more luxurious than Bertie had expected.

"This is your sitting room, and over here," Charlie went to a door and opened it, "is your bedroom."

Bertie went over and took a look. Again it was a large room with a comfortable bed and tapestries on the wall.

"The bathroom is to the right," explained Charlie. "I'm afraid it's not what you are used to, but I hope it's adequate."

"On the contrary, Charlie, it's more than adequate. I never expected it to be quite so nice. You officers certainly know how to live in style here in the Curragh!"

Bertie went over and inspected the bed. Then, with surprise written on his face, he inspected the armchairs before looking at one of the tapestries.

He swung around, dismayed, "But – all this furniture is brand new!" He pointed to the tapestry. "The price-tag is still on it!"

"Eh, yes, sir. The quarters were refurnished for your stay."

Bertie's face dropped in disappointment and upset. "But I never asked for new furniture! I didn't want it!"

Charlie shrugged. "It was thought, sir, that the original furniture was not good enough for your visit."

Bertie slumped down on the bed and dropped his head. "But – that defeats the whole purpose of me being here. I wanted to live the life of an ordinary officer and not be treated any differently."

"I apologise, sir, if you have been offended in any way," said Charlie in dismay.

"Not offended, Charlie, just disappointed," Bertie said, looking around the large room. "This isn't the typical quarters for an officer, is it?"

Charlie shook his head and smiled. "No, sir, our quarters are considerably smaller than the one that has been assigned to you."

"Blast it!" Bertie stood up, his face suddenly red with anger. "Are my father's and my own wishes to be ignored? Was it not my express wish to be treated just like any other man here? What is Hazeldon doing, ignoring our wishes?"

Charlie approached him, looking embarrassed, and spoke kindly. "It's really not Hazeldon's fault, sir. He – we all – just want to make sure that your stay here is as comfortable and enjoyable as possible. We just want to please you."

Bertie sighed and calmed down. "Perhaps I expected too much – to be treated as any other when the distance between everyone else and me is so great. The gap can never be breached, even here in a garrison in Kildare."

A soldier in his twenties appeared at the door. "Oh, pardon me, Captain Carrington, I didn't realise you were here."

Charlie turned to view the man. "That's quite all right. Do come in. Sir, this is Tommy Spillane. He is to be your batman during your stay here."

Tommy stepped forward and saluted. "Your Royal Highness!"

"Tommy will run your bath, prepare your uniform, clean the quarters, run messages for you," Charlie explained.

Bertie viewed Tommy coolly, not impressed by his impish face and ready smile. "And do all officers get a manservant, or is this too a privilege reserved for the Prince of Wales?"

Charlie smiled. "No, all of us officers have a batman – this is nothing special for you. I have a most irritating batman from Cork – he seems incapable of doing anything he is told!"

Bertie looked relieved as he took off his coat and threw it on the bed. "In that case, run a bath for me, there's a good chap, Tommy."

CHAPTER 9

Sadie was fixing Nellie's hair as she sat at her dressing table in her bedroom.

"There! You look as pretty as a picture!" declared Sadie.

Nellie inspected herself in the mirror. "Can you make the bun a little higher, Sadie?"

"I certainly can," said Sadie as she set to work again. "Where is the soirée you are going to tonight?"

"It's in Dalkey. Though it's not a soirée."

"Not a soirée? Who is going to be there then?" asked Sadie.

"Just the gentleman himself, a man called Anthony – he's an art dealer, according to James."

Sadie stepped back from Nellie and looked at her. "But Captain Marton will be there?"

"No, he won't. He cannot get leave from the Curragh tonight as the Prince of Wales has come to stay there, no less," said Nellie, giving a fake look of being impressed.

"But – have you met this man before?"

"No."

Sadie frowned. "I don't like the sound of this, Nellie. I don't like it when you are going to be alone with a man."

"But I always end up alone with them in the end, Sadie!"

"Yes, but that's different. There are usually other people there first and Captain Marton brings you and introduces you. It's not safe to meet a stranger on your own."

"I'm sure if Captain Marton says it's all right, then it's all right, Sadie. He only knows the best of people."

"I think you should not go."

"I can't do that, Sadie. I can't let James down and, if I get a reputation for being untrustworthy, then who will want to meet me again?"

Sadie sat down beside her. "Say you have a cold and can't go – nothing can be said then."

"No, Sadie," said Nellie, standing up and inspecting the cream gown she was wearing. "I'll be fine, stop worrying. I can look after myself, I always could." Seeing her words hadn't comforted Sadie, she reached down and took her hand. "I'll be fine, Sadie! I'll just get a hansom cab to the house and I'll only be a few hours. I'll be back before it's light."

In the Officers' Mess, James was drinking whiskey with Donald Kilroy and Edgar Forrest.

"So, has he settled in?" said Edgar, looking displeased.

They had all been present for Bertie's arrival earlier that day.

"He looks like a pleasant sort, not what I had expected," said Donald.

"He's looks like a spoilt brat!" said Edgar. "And a fish out of water! What a waste of time having him here. What purpose does it serve?"

"Well, I think we should all give him a chance," urged James.

"We will hardly ever see him, I'd say," said Edgar. "He'll be tucked up in those beautiful quarters Hazeldon had refurnished for him, far too good to condescend to interact with any of us."

"Watch up! Here he is!" said Donald.

James swivelled his head around to see Bertie and Charles walk into the mess.

Donald grabbed his whiskey glass and threw the contents

in the plant pot behind him, Edgar quickly put his glass on a neighbouring table and James knocked his drink back before putting the glass on the tray of a passing waiter.

The men all then sat up straight and buttoned up the top buttons of their red tunics.

Charles was pointing to different portraits on the walls, then spotting his friends he led Bertie over to the table. The men all stood up and saluted.

"Your Royal Highness, if I can introduce Captains James Marton, Donald Kilroy and Edgar Forrest."

"Your Royal Highness," the men said, bowing their heads.

"Good to meet you all," smiled Bertie. "And you really can dispense with the formalities – you may call me Bertie or sir, whatever you are more comfortable with."

"Thank you, sir," said the three men in unison.

Bertie grabbed a chair and sat down. "Please, be seated."

The other men sat down and an awkward silence ensued.

"I hope His Royal Highness has settled into his quarters all right?" asked Donald at length.

"Oh yes, very much so, thank you."

"And everything is to your liking?" asked Edgar.

"Very much to my liking."

More silence reigned for a while.

"If His Royal Highness needs anything, then please just ask," urged James.

"Oh, I have everything I need, thank you. And I have been given an excellent batman who ran me a perfect bath – temperature was just right."

"Eh, Dickie, tea for everyone!" Charles called across the mess to the barman.

"Coming right up, sir!" said Dickie as he went behind the bar. He was amused. The men never ordered tea after six, only alcohol.

"So – where are you all from?" asked Bertie.

"I'm from Buckinghamshire – my family are landowners there," said Edgar.

"And I'm from Yorkshire – my family are mill-owners," said Donald.

"And I'm from Meath – my family are –" James thought quickly, "farmers."

Bertie smiled at them. "And I'm from London, and my family are monarchs!"

The men looked at him, surprised, and Charles laughed.

"So what do you do for fun around here?" asked Bertie.

"Well, there isn't much time for fun, sir. Early to rise, early to bed, training continuously," said Donald.

Dickie arrived with a tea tray, unloaded it and poured for them.

And the men lapsed into silence again.

The officers around the table had endured an hour of Bertie's company. The conversation had been polite and cordial, but everyone was on tenterhooks. They now listened, feigning interest as Bertie told them stories of his tour of America and Canada the previous year.

"Have any of you ever been to the Americas?" he asked.

They all shook their heads.

"Though I had an uncle who emigrated there," said Donald. "He's caught up in the civil war there now."

"How ghastly!" said Bertie.

Edgar looked at Charles and discreetly raised his eyebrows before flicking his eyes towards the clock on the wall.

Charles took his cue and looked up at the clock. "Gosh, is that the time? It's time for bed, chaps."

There was a quick agreement from the other men.

"So soon? But it's not yet nine o'clock!" objected Bertie.

"We always go to bed at this time. We have to in order to be up bright-eyed and bushy-tailed in the morning," said Donald.

"Oh, eh, yes of course," said Bertie.

Charles stood up. "I shall walk you back to your quarters, sir, to make sure you get back safely."

"I think I'll be able to find my way back on my own," said Bertie.

"The streets in the garrison are like a maze – best I see you home – it's easy to get lost when you are new here," said Charles.

"Oh, yes, all right in that case," said Bertie, standing up. "Well, it's been a pleasure meeting you fellows."

The officers quickly stood up and saluted him.

"We shall just finish our tea and we'll be off to bed as well," said James.

"Goodnight," said Bertie.

Charles discreetly winked at the others and led Bertie out of the mess.

They walked through the streets and lanes of the garrison until they reached Bertie's quarters.

"Tommy will be waiting inside so, anything you need, just let him know," said Charles.

Bertie nodded. "Thank you, Charlie, for everything."

"You are welcome, sir."

Charles hurried back until he reached the mess building. He raced upstairs.

"*The coast is clear!*" he announced loudly as he stepped into the mess.

There was a cheer from all the officers. The waiters quickly went around and gathered up all the pots of tea they had been drinking and replaced them with beer. The games of scrabble the officers had pretended to be playing were cast asway, decks of cards quickly appeared and games of poker commenced.

"*Dickie! A bottle of your best Irish whiskey to our table!*" Charlie shouted.

"*Coming right over, sir!*" Dickie called back.

"What a thumping bore!" said Edgar as Charles retook his seat.

"He's not that bad!" said Charles.

56

"I thought he was quite pleasant," said James, "in a dull way."

"How long do we have to suffer him being here?" Edgar asked as Dickie arrived at the table with a bottle of whiskey and began to fill glasses.

"Ten weeks!" said Charles.

"I don't think I can continue drinking pots of tea for two hours every night waiting for him to go back to his quarters," said Edgar.

"Well, we shall have to put up with quite a lot – but it is for only ten weeks," said Charles.

CHAPTER 10

The hansom cab swept through large gates, up a driveway and came to a halt in front of a large house.

The driver dismounted from his sprung seat at the back of the vehicle and helped Nellie out. She paid him and turned to the house as he drove away.

The lights were on downstairs. She walked up the steps to the front door and banged the knocker.

She waited a minute and was just going to knock again when the door opened. A handsome man in his forties stood there, well dressed and with a warm face.

"Nellie?" he asked as he looked her up and down.

"Yes."

"I'm Anthony. I've been expecting you, please come in." He stood out of the way and gestured to her to enter.

She smiled at him and walked in. He closed the door after her.

She looked around the grand hall.

"May I take your cloak?" he asked.

"Yes, thank you," she said, taking it off and handing it to him.

He hung it on a hook near the door.

"James wasn't lying to me when he said you were beautiful," said Anthony as he admired her.

"Thank you," she said.

She followed him into the front parlour. There was a

grand piano in the corner, and a bay window that looked out to the sea, now darkening under the lowering sun.

"Drink?" he asked.

"Yes, please – red wine," she answered as she sat down on one of the ornate couches.

He went to the drinks cabinets, took up a decanter and poured two glasses before going to the couch, handing her a glass and sitting down beside her.

"Cheers!" he said as he held up his glass to her and she clinked her glass against his.

As she looked around, she sensed that he must be alone in the house, without servants. She was accustomed to this. If she did house calls, her clients often got rid of their servants for the night, not being able to rely on their discretion. She quickly eyed him up and down. He had a kind and gentle face and a nervous awkward manner about him. She imagined he would have been very good-looking in his youth but now seemed to have the weight of the world on his shoulders, with too many lines on a face that had not yet reached fifty.

"So, James tells me you are an actress?"

"Yes, I am at the Palace Theatre," she said.

"I don't think I've ever been to that theatre – what play are you in?"

She smiled at him. "Well, I'm not actually in any play – at the moment. I sing."

"Oh, like opera?"

As she thought of her repertoire, she laughed. "No, not opera either. I sing more – popular music."

"Oh, that does sound exciting!" he said. "My wife likes opera."

"Does she?" Nellie began to feel slightly uncomfortable.

"She, in fact, loves opera. The amount of times I have been forced to accompany her to the opera you would not believe – and I hate it!"

"I've never been to the opera, so I wouldn't know."

"Oh, you're lucky in that case – it's such a bore! But my wife loves it. In fact, that's where she is tonight." He looked away and then took a drink from his glass. "Or, at least where she says she is."

Nellie took a sip of her wine and looked around. "You have a beautiful house."

"Yes, the art business pays well. Did James mention I was an art dealer?"

"Yes." Nellie nodded.

"Interesting man, James. He knows so many interesting people. Where did you meet him?"

She smirked at him. "Well, it wasn't at the opera! As I said, I've never been!"

He looked at her and laughed. "No, I imagine it wasn't . . . I imagine you've had a very interesting life, Nellie."

"I can't complain."

"I'd say you've never had it easy. Unlike my wife. She's had everything easy. She has never had to work for anything. Expects to be given everything on a plate."

"Well, if she can get that – why not?" giggled Nellie.

He laughed again. "Indeed – why not? She's a beautiful woman – in fact, she looks a lot like you."

Nellie nodded. "Perhaps that's not a good thing?"

"Oh, yes, it's a good thing. Very good indeed. Her name is Maud."

"That's a pretty name," said Nellie.

"She won't be home tonight," he assured her.

"I didn't expect she would be!"

"She's at the opera."

"You already did mention that."

"But she's not."

Nellie was confused. "She's not at the opera?"

"No, she's in bed with my best friend," said Anthony.

"Oh!" Nellie frowned. "I'm sorry, Anthony."

"Oh, don't be sorry. I'm well used to it. He's not the first lover she's had and I don't think he'll be the last."

"Why – why do you put up with it?"

"I don't know, Nellie – you tell me. Perhaps because I love her. I've never cheated on her before. Not once. I don't make a habit of bringing a woman to my house."

"Then – then why have you tonight?" Nellie was struggling to understand him.

"I don't know. To get some kind of revenge on her perhaps. Not that she would give a damn even if I ever had the courage to tell her."

Nellie sipped from her drink and placed it on the table beside the couch. "Do you know what I think, Anthony?"

"Tell me, Nellie."

"I don't think you really want me here tonight. I think the only reason I'm here is because you felt it would make you feel better about your wife's affairs. But it won't. It will probably make you only feel worse."

"Do you think so?"

She sighed and nodded. "Yes, I do. It's hard being in love with somebody who's not in love with you. I know, I've been there too. It's hard to be in love with somebody, knowing they are only being with you for what they can get out of you. But this – me being here – isn't the answer to your problems."

"You're a very wise woman, Nellie. Where did you learn such wisdom?"

She laughed. "From life."

He took his glass and drank it back.

She reached forward and placed her hand on his. "I think I should go. Do you want me to go?"

He took her hand and held it softly. "No, I want you to stay, Nellie. I never wanted anything so much in my life."

Bertie sat in the sitting room of his quarters and looked at the clock. It was eleven o'clock.

His batman Tommy knocked on the door and came in. "Excuse me, sir, I wanted to ask is there anything else you need tonight?"

"No, that's all, thank you, Tommy," said Bertie.

"Right, sir," said Tommy and left him alone.

Bertie sighed. His first day at the garrison had not been what he had hoped for or expected. The feeling of freedom he had initially felt had quickly evaporated. Everybody from Hazeldon to Tommy his batman had treated him in a cool detached manner. He had spent a couple of hours with Charles and the other officers in the mess, but the conversation had been muted and strained as they drank endless cups of tea. He had not experienced the camaraderie he had expected to experience there. He had not felt the warmth and sense of belonging he had desperately craved amongst his fellow officers. Alone in his quarters, he felt more lonely than he ever had in his life as he began to realise that coming to Ireland and spending these weeks in Kildare was a mistake. He should have listened to his parents. They were right – he was not like other men but he was unfit for the role he had been born into. He was uncomfortable with being the Prince of Wales and yet he did not have the common touch needed to allow him to fit in with the people. He would forever be isolated from the real world in a role he was not suited to.

He sighed as he looked up at the clock on the wall again. Standing up, he went to one of the windows and looked out at the countryside now lit up in the moonlight. It was hard for him to comprehend that he would be king of this land one day, a land he didn't know at all and was desperate to get to know this summer. He walked into his bedroom and, going to the wardrobe, he took out a greatcoat and put it on over his tunic. Even if he was alone, he would go for a walk and familiarise himself with his new home. Donning his new officer's hat, he left his quarters, walked down the stairs and out of the manor house.

Outside, he went to the nearby fence that marked the perimeter of the garrison and gazed out at the fields. Then he turned and began to walk back into the garrison. It was very quiet compared to the hustle and bustle during the day. The troops had retired for the night but he passed the occasional soldier on his way to or back from some duty. No one took any notice of him, still less recognised him.

At last he found himself in the courtyard in front of the building that contained the Officers' Mess. He heard music coming from somewhere together with laughter and loud talk. He looked up at the windows of the mess on the second floor. The loud music and laughter were coming from there. He backed away from the building until he had a better view through the windows. To his astonishment he saw the mess was full of men who looked to be enjoying themselves immensely.

Pulling up the collar of his greatcoat and pulling down his hat, he hurried into the building and up the stairs. Luckily, he didn't encounter anyone. At the door of the mess, he stopped and cautiously looked in.

His eyes swept over the crowd inside and he saw Charles Carrington standing in a circle with Donald Kilroy, James Marton and Edgar Forrest. They were drinking beer and seemed to be swapping jokes and funny anecdotes, judging by their hilarity.

Horrified, Bertie realised they had been lying when they had said they were going to bed earlier in the evening and did so every night at that time. They had been lying to get rid of him. As Bertie gazed at them, he was overcome by a feeling of fury at their lies, hurt over their deceit but mostly loneliness for being so cruelly excluded from their company.

Turning, he hurried down the stairs and left the building.

CHAPTER 11

Anthony was kissing Nellie as they sat on the couch in his drawing room in Dalkey.

He drew back from her and said, "Let's continue this upstairs."

She smiled at him and nodded. Standing up, he offered her his hand. She took it and let him lead her out of the parlour and up the grand staircase to the first floor.

He led her into a bedroom and closed the door behind them.

He embraced her from behind and kissed her neck before turning her around and continuing to kiss her.

Then he pulled away from her and stared at her for a while.

"Is anything the matter?" she asked.

"Why do you do it?" he said.

"Do what?"

"Have these affairs with men?"

Her forehead creased in confusion. "Why do you care?"

"Why do I care?" he asked incredulously and the kindly look on his face disappeared. "Because I'm your husband, for fuck's sake!"

Nellie's mouth dropped in shock. "You're not my husband, Anthony."

His face twisted in anger. "Well, you certainly don't act like a wife! Sleeping with my best friend! How many have there been, Maud? *How many?*"

Her heart began to pound but she said quietly, "I think I should go."

As she went to walk to the door he blocked her way and said angrily, "Oh, no, you aren't going anywhere, Maud! Where do you want to go to all in a hurry? To *his* bed?"

"Please, Anthony, I don't know what game you are playing, but you are frightening me," Nellie said.

"You are right to be frightened," he said threateningly, "because I've put up with your whoring for all our marriage and I'm not putting up with it any more! That's what you are – *a whore!*"

"Please, Anthony –"

She backed away from him. He looked like a different person to the gentle kind man he had been downstairs. He now looked like an angry monster.

He reached out and grabbed her and held her by the arms, his fingers digging into her flesh.

"*Please, Anthony, you're hurting me!*" she cried as she struggled free.

"By the time I'm finished with you . . ." He forced his mouth on hers and began to kiss her roughly.

"I want to go now!" she cried, fighting him off. "If you don't let me go, I'll scream!"

He pulled back from her and, raising his hand, he slapped her across the face and threw her on the bed.

"Scream all you want, Maud! There's nobody here to hear you."

Nellie held her hand against her face where he'd struck her. Her eyes were burning with tears. She was terrified, terrified of this stranger who was now looming over her. She raised her knee and thrust it between his legs.

He screamed in pain as he pulled back, grabbing at his groin.

"*You little bitch!*" he yelled.

She jumped out of the bed and shoved him with all her strength. He fell backwards to the floor.

She started for the door but he grabbed her ankle, pulling her back and felling her to the floor beside him.

"*Let go of me!*" she shouted as she tried to kick him.

But he was crawling on top of her and pulled her around to face him. He pinned her arms down on the ground.

"*You shouldn't have done that,*" he snarled, his face a mask of fury. "*I've paid for you, you belong to me, you whore!*"

He released one of her wrists, pulled back his arm and went to hit her across the face again, but with her free hand she reached up, dug her nails into his face and dragged them down, causing blood to spring up.

"*Ahhh!*" he shouted as he clapped his hand to his face, freeing her other wrist.

She pushed desperately with both hands and managed to push him off her. Scrambling to her feet, she raced to the door and swung it open.

"*Come back, you bitch!*" he yelled as she ran down the corridor.

Her heart was pounding wildly as she reached the corner of the stairs and began to race down. She could see him staggering after her, blood pouring from the wounds on his face. As she reached the bottom step, she tripped and went sprawling on the tiled floor. She could hear his footsteps come heavily down the stairs as she struggled to her feet. But there was a shooting pain from her ankle and she realised she had twisted it badly. She lurched forward.

"*I'm going to fucking kill you!*" he snarled as he reached the bottom step.

There was a large marble fireplace beside her in the hallway and she grabbed a long poker that was resting there and swung it with both hands above her head.

"*Take one step nearer and I'll knock your fucking head off!*" she screamed at him.

He put his hands in the air and laughed. "A feisty one, aren't you?"

"You'll see how feisty I am when you get your head cut

off as if this poker was a guillotine!" she threatened, her eyes blazing with fear and anger.

"Put the poker down, Nellie. You know you don't have the strength. Even if you hit me, you won't get out of the house without me catching you."

She glanced down the hallway lined with side-tables laden with expensive ornaments.

She swung the poker in the air and smashed it into the huge mirror over the fireplace, causing it to shatter and fall to the floor.

"*What the fuck do you think you're doing?*" he roared as he looked at his priceless mirror destroyed.

She followed that up by sweeping the poker across all the ornaments on the mantelpiece and smashing them to the floor.

"*Stop! Please stop – they are seventeenth-century French!*" he squealed at the top of his voice.

"*They're not any more!*" roared Nellie. "*They're broken bits of shit now!*"

She quickly swung her poker in the air and held it over a sideboard laden with vases and ornaments.

"Get on your knees or I'll smash these in a second!"

Anthony fell to his knees. "Please, Nellie! Please! Don't do any more!"

"Oh, you remember my name now, do you? I thought you thought that I was your cheating slut of a wife, Maud!"

"*No – please!*" he begged as she brought down the poker and smashed all the vases and ornaments on the sideboard.

She looked up at a painting on the wall of Anthony with a beautiful woman. "I take it this is her? The cheating wife?"

Nellie dragged the poker down the painting and ripped it apart.

"Explain that to Maud when she gets back tomorrow from your best friend's bed!"

Horrified, Anthony went to stand up from where he was kneeling.

Nellie quickly grabbed a golden jewel-encrusted ornament in the shape of an egg from another sideboard.

"*Please – don't – it's Fabergé!*" shouted Anthony.

"Well, it's going to be faber-smashed in two seconds if you don't get back down on your knees!" she said, holding the egg high in the air as she moved towards the door while keeping her eyes fixed on him.

Anthony quickly resumed his kneeling position.

"Now, I'm going to leave this house," said Nellie, "and if you try and stop me I'm going to smash this egg on the ground. Do you understand me? *Do you understand me?*"

"Yes! Yes! Please just go! Leave me and my ornaments alone and go!" he pleaded.

She backed carefully to the door, not taking her eyes off him. As she got to the front door she dropped the poker and opened it, all the while holding the egg in the air.

"You are to stay there for ten minutes," she said. "If I hear you move, I'll smash this fucking ornament on the ground outside. If you're a good boy and don't move from there, then I'll leave it unharmed at the bottom of your driveway behind your gate. Do you understand me?"

He nodded enthusiastically. "Yes, yes, I won't move until you are gone. Just please don't harm my Fabergé!"

She took the key out of the door, stepped outside and locked the door behind her. She then ran down the long driveway, throwing the key into a bush as she went. As she reached the gate at end of the long drive, she looked frantically up and down the road. The few houses on the road were behind large gateways like Anthony's house. She realised it would be a long walk to get a hansom cab. She lifted the Fabergé egg into the air and was going to smash it on the ground but stopped short. It would take a long walk to find a cab and if Anthony found it smashed he would likely go into a rage and pursue her. If, on the other hand, he found it safe behind the gates he would be so relieved to have it back and for her to be gone, that he would never want to see her again. She had become a good judge of people's likely actions over the years with the life that she had led. As much as she wanted to destroy his precious Fabergé, it wasn't worth the risk of further provoking his anger.

She quickly placed the ornament behind the gate and then began to run down the road. Continuously looking over her shoulder to make sure Anthony wasn't following her, she pushed herself onward as quickly as she could until she reached Dalkey Village.

There, she managed to find a hansom cab. The driver looked at her askance and insisted she pay before he let her into the cab. It was little wonder, she thought. She had left her cloak at Anthony's house and, unkempt and sweating profusely, her face injured, her nails bloodied, she realised she must look like a madwoman to him.

With some difficulty and a little privacy, she managed to extract some coins from the secret purse she wore hanging from the waistband of her petticoats – a necessity for one in her profession.

She paid, and gratefully sat into the cab, still shaking.

Sadie heard the key turn and sat up from her seat by the fireplace.

"Nellie, is that you?"

Nellie stumbled into the room and Sadie got a shock when she saw her, looking so upset and shaken, a red mark blazing across her face.

"Nellie, what happened?" Sadie asked as she rushed to her.

"Oh, Sadie!" cried Nellie as she slumped into her arms and allowed herself to burst into tears.

Some time later Nellie was sitting on an armchair staring into the fire, a warm shawl about her shoulders, as she nursed the hot tea Sadie had made for her.

A shocked Sadie sat across from her, having heard the whole story.

"It was terrible, Sadie," Nellie said. "He suddenly became a different person . . . such anger . . . so frightening . . . he kept calling me his wife's name and I thought – I thought I wasn't going to get out of there alive."

"He sounds like a monster!"

"He's just somebody who is not well and very angry and he wanted to vent that anger on someone – that's why he hired me – to say and do all the things he wants to do to his wife but can't do."

"You had a lucky escape," said Sadie.

"I'd have laughed towards the end if I hadn't been so terrified! He was so frightened I was going to destroy any more of his priceless ornaments."

"He didn't know what he was taking on when he took on Nellie Cliffden!" said Sadie proudly.

"But it could have gone so easily the other way. If I hadn't managed to escape his clutches in the bedroom, if I hadn't managed to grab that poker – if I hadn't been inspired to attack his ornaments – it doesn't bear thinking about." Nellie shuddered.

"So what now? Captain Marton has a lot to answer for, Nellie. He should have never let you go to a new client on your own. He should have checked the man first and made sure he was safe."

"Captain Marton doesn't care about anyone but himself, Sadie. He doesn't care that I was in danger tonight. All he cares about is that he gets paid."

"So are you going to the police?" asked Sadie.

"I can't go to the police, Sadie. They will know what I am when they investigate. I'll be the one who ends up in jail for destroying his property. He'll deny it all and say I broke into the house."

"He can't just get away with it!"

"He hasn't got away with it. I've cost him dearly with his precious antiques and he has to explain to his wife what happened to everything when she gets back . . . he can't blame burglars – smashing everything would be the last thing they'd do! To say nothing of ripping her portrait! But I don't care about him. He means nothing to me. Let him get back to his miserable life with his miserable marriage. But it's made me realise I can't go on with this life, Sadie."

"What do you mean?"

"I can't meet any more clients for James or anybody else. It's too dangerous and – and I just can't do it any more," said Nellie.

"Oh, Nellie, I'm so happy!" said Sadie, going to her and hugging her.

"We'll miss the money, having to get by on my wages as an actress and I'll have to give up my dream of opening a small hotel one day."

"But we'll get by – that's the main thing," said Sadie. "You're doing the right thing."

CHAPTER 12

"*Stand to the right!*" called Bertie. "*Stand to the left . . . Face forward . . . At ease!*"

The soldiers who stood in front of him in the forecourt shifted uncomfortably as they tried to follow his orders which were not in the normal sequence.

Charles and James stood apart from Bertie, looking on.

"He's a disaster!" whispered James.

"It is only his first day!" Charles defended him.

"I know – but he's not getting anything right! The soldiers are all over the place!"

"*Hmmm*," mused Charles.

"And he has no authority in his voice – he sounds apologetic giving the orders!"

"*Hmmm.*"

"He doesn't even know his left from his right!"

"All right, Marton! You've made your point!" snapped Charles irritably.

He approached Bertie.

"Sir?" he said quietly. "I think we need to do some more homework before we let you loose on the troops!"

"I'm not very good, am I?" asked Bertie, his face red with shame.

"I wouldn't say that, sir, but you are a novice being thrown in at the deep end. Perhaps if we dismiss the troops and practise on our own, there wouldn't be so much pressure?"

"Whatever you think," said Bertie, dejected.

Charles turned to the troops and with a loud voice of authority dismissed them.

James sauntered over to the two men.

"It's really not fair on you, sir, to learn on the job as it were," said Charles. "Let's try and get you up to scratch before we have an audience."

"I think I shall never learn this, I never had a good memory for manoeuvres," confided Bertie.

"Let's not be defeatist, sir," said James. "I shall be the soldier – let's start the drill again."

James stepped in front of Bertie and Charles and stood to attention.

"Now, the first thing is to get our lefts and rights correct, sir," said Charles. "You are facing the soldiers and so when you say turn to the right, it is their right they are turning to which is your left. Similarly, when you are commanding them to turn to the left, it is their left which they are turning to which is your right – understood?"

Bertie's face went even redder as his mouth dropped open in confusion. James discreetly rolled his eyes at Charles.

Bertie was exhausted after three hours of practice in the hot sun with Charles and James.

"I think we shall call it a day, sir. Too much information at once can be hard to take in," said Charles.

"I'm not sure if any of it went in," said Bertie.

"We'll reconvene tomorrow," said Charles. "Would you like to accompany us to the Officers' Mess for a spot of tea and evening dinner?"

Bertie remembered the shame of finding out the previous night that they had not wanted him there and pretended to be going to bed just to get rid of him.

"No, I think I shall retire to my quarters for the evening," said Bertie.

"Very good, sir, as you wish," said Charles.

As James and he walked away across the forecourt in the direction of the Officers' Mess, James whispered, "Thank goodness for that!"

Bertie looked after them, feeling deeply disheartened.

In the Officers' Mess Charles and his group were gathered around their usual table having had dinner. They were now enjoying whiskies as they recounted the day's training with Bertie.

"You should have heard Carrington!" laughed James. "*Project your voice, sir – project your voice!*"

"Is he an imbecile?" asked Edgar.

"We finally managed to get him to understand that the right hand of the person he is facing is on the opposite side to his!" informed James, causing the group to burst out laughing.

"All right, Marton, that's enough!" snapped Charles.

"I'm only telling the truth," said James.

"His Royal Highness is not here to be laughed at but to be trained – it's more of a reflection on us if he can't pick up the training correctly," said Charles.

"Or the reflection of a dimwit!" said Edgar, causing them to burst out laughing again.

"At least we are spared his presence tonight. I don't think I could take any more tea!" said Donald.

In the room behind the bar, Bertie stood with Dickie.

"Are you sure about this, sir?" asked Dickie who had been in shock since Bertie arrived in through the servants' door at the back of the mess ten minutes before.

"Quite sure, Dickie," said Bertie as he watched Dickie put the bottles of beer and large bottle of whiskey onto a tray.

Bertie lifted it up.

"Can you manage, sir? Would it not be easier if I carried the tray?" asked Dickie.

"That would defeat the purpose, Dickie," said Bertie as he precariously balanced the tray.

He walked out of the back room into the bar and began to

cross the mess. As he walked various officers spotted him and whispered to their companions, until most of the room was staring at him in amazement.

Bertie made his way to the table in the far corner where Charles and his friends, not having spotted him, were still laughing and joking.

"*Sir!*" said Donald loudly, jumping to his feet when he saw him.

The others followed his gaze and jumped up too.

Bertie silently and carefully placed the tray of drinks down on the table and then stood and looked at them one by one.

"Well – get me a chair, somebody!"

"Yes, sir!" Edgar rushed to a neighbouring table, grabbed a chair and placed it by Bertie.

Bertie sat down and began to fill the glasses on the table with whiskey as they all looked on, confused and amazed.

"Well, what are you all waiting for? Sit down and have a bloody drink!"

Shamefaced, they sat down.

"Unless you would prefer tea?" said Bertie mockingly.

"No, sir, whiskey will do just fine!" said Charles, smiling warmly at Bertie who smiled back at him and winked.

It was after midnight by the time the officers left the mess.

As Bertie walked out of the building he fell flat on his face on the cobblestones outside.

"*Sir!*" cried Charles as he and James bent down quickly and picked him up.

"I'm fine! Absolutely fine!" slurred Bertie.

"With the greatest respect, sir, you don't seem very fine!" laughed Charles.

"He's pissed! Pissed out of his head!" said Edgar, not sure whether to be disgusted or impressed.

"Happens to the best of us!" laughed James as he and Charles each put one of Bertie's arms around their shoulders and tried to hold him steady.

"Let's get you back to your quarters, sir," said Charles.

The group made their way through the narrow laneways.

"I think somebody must have put something into my glass!" slurred Bertie.

"Yes, you would be the person guilty of that charge yourself, sir!" laughed James.

"S-s-such an enjoyable night," stuttered Bertie.

"We are glad you enjoyed yourself, sir," said Charles.

"He didn't drink any more than the rest of us," said Edgar. "There's no reason he should be in that condition."

"He's obviously not used to alcohol, or certainly not to the extent he consumed tonight," said James.

"Well, you would think he'd know his limits!" said Edgar.

"Oh, stop being such a judgemental prude!" snapped Charles.

They managed to get Bertie back to the manor house and up the staircase to the top floor where they opened the door and manoeuvred him inside.

In the bedroom they laid him on the bed, then all gathered around staring down at him as he fell quickly into a drunken slumber.

"There lies the Prince of Wales!" mocked Edgar. "If Her Majesty could see him now!"

"Well, I for one am delighted he enjoyed the night," said James. "Isn't that what Hazeldon wanted – for him to have good memories of the time he spent here?"

"I doubt he'll have any memories of tonight he's so intoxicated," said Charles.

"Are you going to report back to Hazeldon about the condition he is in?" asked Edgar.

"Of course not!" snapped Charles. "Why would I do such a ridiculous thing? I'm not his nanny! Bertie is a fellow officer of ours, and he has proven tonight he wants to be treated just like the rest of us and be one of us."

"Bertie! We are on first name terms with his Royal Highness now, are we?" asked Edgar.

"Well, it was he who insisted we call him by his first

name," said James. "Charles is quite right – Bertie is one of us and we should now close ranks around him and treat him as such. I, for one, am delighted – it will make his stay here much more pleasant for us all."

"You are just trying to curry favour with royalty, Marton!" said Edgar.

"You take that back!" demanded James.

"Will not!" Edgar replied.

"Gentlemen – *please*!" interjected Charles. "Remember you are officers and not squabbling children! From now on, I say, Bertie is one of us and there will be no more excluding him from our social diary or making him feel like an outsider. We are to welcome him with open arms. Agreed?"

"Agreed!" they said in unison with the exception of Edgar.

"Forrest – agreed?" Charles demanded.

"Agreed," Edgar said reluctantly.

"Good," said Charles, taking a blanket and putting it over Bertie.

"I thought you said you weren't his nanny?" mocked Edgar.

"Oh, shut up, Forrest!"

They left the room and closed the door.

"I say, look at the quarters he's been given! Fit for a prince, if you pardon the pun," said Donald as he walked around the sitting room.

"All the better for us," said James. "I'm sure Bertie won't mind us using his quarters for our social events."

"Always looking for the benefit in it for you, Marton," said Edgar.

"Let's go," said Charles. "We'll be rising early, may I remind you?"

"As should the Prince, though I can't see much chance of that!" said Edgar as they filed out.

Ten minutes later James was back outside the manor house. He checked there was nobody around before slipping inside, using the key he had pocketed earlier.

He headed to the bedroom and, cautiously opening the door, peered inside. Confident that Bertie was still unconscious, he crept in and looked down at him. Then he went to the wardrobes, opened them and started examining the clothes inside, more than impressed by the Saville Row suits and shirts there. He closed the wardrobes over and started looking through the drawers in the dressing tables. With starry eyes, he touched all the jewellery there – watches, cufflinks, pins, clips. He had never seen so many precious items in one place. He opened more drawers and to his shock saw a large amount of money there.

Bertie grumbled in his sleep and turned over, causing James to quickly close the drawers.

With a final look at Bertie, he left the building.

His mind was working overtime as he made his way back to his own quarters, different ideas flying through his head. When he got back to his own quarters he poured himself a whiskey and sat down on his couch.

"Life has just handed you a golden opportunity, old boy," he said to himself.

Bertie stirred from his sleep.

"Sir – sir!" came a voice from somewhere in the distance.

He opened his eyes to see his batman standing over the bed.

"What – what time is it?" said Bertie, struggling to sit up.

"It's eleven o'clock, sir," said Tommy.

"*Eleven o'clock!*" shouted Bertie. "Why didn't you call me before, man?"

"I – I didn't want to disturb you!" said Tommy.

"*Disturb me!* But I'm horribly late – oh, for goodness' sake!" He swung his legs onto the floor, but the sudden action caused him to feel sick. "Oh, my head!" He sank his face into his hands.

"May I suggest tea, sir?" said Tommy.

"Yes, tea! And run me a bath – and lay out my uniform for the day – and do it all quickly!"

Bertie made his way onto the main forecourt where he spotted Charles and James going through drill practice with soldiers.

"Good afternoon, sir, how are you today?" asked Charles.

"That stupid boy Tommy didn't wake me!" complained Bertie.

"He might have found it impossible to do so, sir?" suggested James.

"I can't remember getting home last night," said Bertie.

"No need to worry, we took care of you," James assured him.

"And we covered for you with Hazeldon this morning – we said you were up and ready on time and gave a drill," said Charles.

Bertie smiled appreciatively. "Thank you. I don't know what to say."

"No need to say anything – that's what we officers do – look after each other," said Charles. "Now, let's get to work and start practising."

"Yes, let's," said Bertie.

"Oh, and we are all going to the mess tonight for seven o'clock if Your Highness would like to join us?" said James.

"Yes – yes, I'd like that very much!" beamed Bertie.

CHAPTER 13

Nellie waited anxiously in Bewleys restaurant on Grafton Street. She was twisting a napkin in her hand with worry. She spotted James as he approached her table.

He looked very angry as he sat down opposite her.

"You are very late," she said.

"Yes, I told you it's hard to get away, what with the Prince of Wales' visit," said James. "But that is the least of your troubles. What the fuck went on between you and Anthony? He has told me you smashed up his house! He said you took a poker and smashed priceless ornaments, ripped apart a portrait of him and his wife, and some story that you held a Fabergé egg as hostage!"

"I had no choice, James!" she said.

"No choice!" He was erupting in anger. "Do you know how much damage you have done? He said those ornaments cost a fortune!"

"I had to do it, James. He was going to kill me!"

"What are you talking about?"

"When we got to the bedroom he changed. He had been kind and nice until then. But then he became angry –"

"Well, you must have done something to displease him!"

"I did nothing! It's his wife, Maud, who has displeased him! She is having affairs behind his back. He became this monster and started confusing me with his wife and calling me by her name. Then he attacked me!" Nellie's eyes filled with tears.

"Attacked you?"

"Yes, he hit me – look, you can still see the mark on my face." She pointed to her cheek. "He shoved me on the bed and grabbed me. And I had to kick him to escape. But he followed me and I had to break his precious ornaments and threaten to break the Fabergé to get out of there alive."

"It sounds to me like you are exaggerating."

"I'm not exaggerating, James," she said as the tears slid down her face. "He was going to kill me, I'm sure of it. I'm lucky to be here today."

He reached out and patted her hand. "There, there! I had no idea he was such a brute."

"He's more than a brute, he's a madman."

"I'm sorry. He came recommended to me. I should have done more checking on him. If the Prince of Wales hadn't been staying, I would have brought you to the house myself and collected you. You do realise that, don't you?"

She nodded, then took a napkin and wiped away her tears.

"The problem is that this may affect business," said James. "If he puts out the word of what you did, clients might not want to see you again."

She became angry. "What I did? It's what he did that matters!"

"I know, but your reputation could be affected."

"My reputation!" she scoffed. "What reputation do I have?"

"You're an actress, Nellie, an actress of the stage," he said.

"Well, that is all I will be in the future. Because I'm giving up the other life I've led."

James looked horrified as he reached over and took her hand. "That's a bit of an overreaction, Nellie!"

"It's not. What happened the other night has made me realise I don't want that life any more," she said, looking away. "I never wanted it in the first place."

"But you've done very well from that life, haven't you? A nice flat on Leeson Street, nice dresses, jewellery and a maid! Not bad for girl where you came from."

"The price is too high for those things," she said. "I won't be visiting any more of your friends, James."

"But – you've had a shock, I understand that. But that's no reason to walk away from something so lucrative. We've worked hard to get you where you are."

"Nothing you can say will change my mind, James."

He smiled warmly at her. "Look, I've set up a meeting with you and a very nice chap for next Tuesday night. I'll bring you there myself and wait the whole time you are there and drive you home afterwards. I can't do fairer than that, can I?"

"You can tell your friend I won't be there, James. Find another girl to take my place. It won't be that hard to find another me."

"There's only one you, Nellie. You're irreplaceable." He leaned towards her, smiling.

"Your sweet talk won't work this time, James. It's your sweet talk that got me into this life in the first place. I, the misguided fool, thinking that if I did what you wanted I might stand a chance with you, that we could have a future together!"

He spoke earnestly as he held her hand tightly. "We can still have a future together, Nellie. I adore you, you know that."

"You adore yourself, James, there's no room for anyone else. As for you and me having a future . . ." She shook her head slowly. "A man like you would never marry a woman like me. Not with your ambition, your greed, your social-climbing. I know you too well – because there's actually no difference between us – except our gender."

"Exactly! There is no difference between us – we're the same – you and I. We belong together," he said.

She pulled her hand back from him. "Why don't you

introduce me to your new friend, the Prince of Wales, in that case? Introduce me to him as your fiancée."

He looked at her with a mixture of horror and amusement. "You are being silly, Nellie."

"Yes, I've been very silly for far too long. But no longer – from now on I do what is best for me."

His lips thinned in a tight smile. "And how long do you think you can live without the money you earn from my clients? How long do you think you will be able to stay in that flat and have the nice things you have become accustomed to, on the wages of a music-hall actress?"

"I'll manage just fine – I'll have to."

"And what about your dreams for the future? About being rich one day and having your own hotel? Didn't you want to own a hotel like the Shelbourne one day?"

"It won't be the first dream I've had that's been broken." She looked at him sadly. "I've had to get used to living with broken dreams."

She stood up and picked up her beaded handbag.

"I'd better go. I have a show on tonight at the theatre."

"At the music hall, you mean?" he said nastily.

"An actress or a prostitute, a theatre or a music hall – what does the difference of a word matter?"

"So – is that it then? The end of us? We shall not see each other again?"

"Goodbye, James," she said as she turned and walked out of the restaurant, leaving him glaring after her.

CHAPTER 14

Bertie marched along in the blistering heat. He was walking alongside a company of soldiers as they trekked through the countryside. Charles was on horseback beside him, leading a second horse along with him by the reins.

"How much further?" asked Bertie.

"Another four miles, sir."

Bertie tried not to let his exhaustion show as he marched ahead.

"Sir – why don't you travel the rest of the journey on horseback?" suggested Charles.

"No, I'm quite all right," said Bertie.

"But sir, you are going beyond the call of duty! It was never expected that you, as an officer, should trek the twenty miles on foot! You are meant to supervise the march on horseback not on foot!" Charles was exasperated. He had said the same thing several times earlier to the Prince and had been ignored.

Bertie stopped marching and turned to face Charles who pulled his horse to a halt.

"I want to march alongside the men. If it's good enough for them to trek through the countryside in the midday sun, then it's good enough for me."

"But, sir, they are used to this exercise, you are not! It's their job to march twenty miles, it's not yours!"

"Regardless, I want them to respect me as one of them.

How can they ever respect me as one of them if I am not prepared to do what I command them to do?"

"As you wish, sir!" said Charles as Bertie began to march forward again.

Although Charles thought the Prince insane, he could not help having a grudging respect for him as he marched on. News had spread that Bertie was doing a military exercise that day and many locals had gathered along the route in the hope of getting a glimpse of him.

"Your Royal Highness! Your Royal Highness!" shouted a group of peasants gathered ahead who had excitedly spotted Bertie.

On reaching them, Bertie broke away from the marching soldiers and walked towards them. Delighted, the crowd curtsied and bowed.

Charles rode over to Bertie. To Charles's disapproval Bertie had stopped several times along the way to chat to locals.

"You're welcome to Kildare, Your Royal Highness!" shouted a man at the front of the crowd.

"And I'm very pleased to be here. What a fine sunny day it is to meet all you fine people!" Bertie walked along the row of people, smiling at them.

Charles kept a watchful eye on the crowd with a hand on his revolver inside his tunic, looking for any troublemakers or possible Fenians amongst them. But like the others they had encountered that day, they seemed to be just well-meaning locals anxious to get a look at the future monarch.

Charles also marvelled at Bertie's interaction with the people. He seemed to genuinely want to meet them and please them.

"Anyway, I must catch up with my regiment. So good to meet you all!" said Bertie as he waved to them and marched quickly ahead to the onwards-marching soldiers.

"I think you've made their day, sir," said Charles as he rode along.

"These poor people have suffered so much during the

Famine – I want them to know that I care for them. I don't want to rule them from a distant palace in London like my mother does."

Charles went to say something but stopped short, surprised that Bertie for the first time seemed critical of his mother.

That evening, Bertie got into a carriage outside his quarters. Charles, Donald and James were already inside.

"Where are we actually going to?" asked Bertie.

"We are going to a tavern in the local town!" said Donald excitedly.

"A tavern! But do we not need permission from Major Hazeldon to leave the garrison?" asked Bertie as the carriage took off.

"Officially, I suppose, yes! But we are officers, Bertie, so we come and go as we please," said James.

"But a tavern! What kind of a place is that for officers to be in?" asked Bertie, who looked scared at the prospect.

"Wait and see!" said Donald.

The carriage drove through the streets of the town and pulled up outside a tavern from which loud laughter, shouting and Irish music could he heard. Charles jumped out of the carriage, followed by James and Donald.

"Well, come along, sir!" urged James as Bertie still sat in the carriage looking out at the tavern in trepidation.

Bertie hesitantly stepped out of the carriage.

"You cannot be serious about entering there?" he said.

"Yes – why not? We've been lots of times," said James.

"It's rather good fun, once you get used to it," said Donald.

"Unless you'd rather not, sir?" Charles asked.

"Eh, no, I'm game, I think," said Bertie.

He followed them through the front door. The sight inside assaulted his eyes. The tavern was packed with what looked to him like a rough-looking crowd of men and women who were obviously drunk. In a corner a group of musicians were beating out the loudest traditional music from their instruments that they could.

"Best not let anybody know who you are, if they should ask," Charles said into Bertie's ear. "They will think you are just a new officer."

Bertie nodded as he followed the others through the crowd to the back of the bar. A woman fell down in front of him, drunk out of her mind.

He quickly bent down and helped her up. "Are you all right, madam?"

"Ah, sure, aren't I as right as cold beer on a hot day!" she said as she got to her feet and to Bertie's surprise threw her arms around him.

Charles intervened, removed the woman's arms from around Bertie's neck and pulled him on to the back of the bar. An empty table there was up on a platform which looked down on the rest of the pub and the officers sat down around it.

"Welcome, gentlemen, and is it your usual you'll be having?" asked a man in his sixties who seemed to appear from nowhere.

"Yes, landlord! And send over Florrie with the beer!" shouted Charles.

"I will surely, sir!" said the landlord as he disappeared back behind the bar.

Bertie stared at the antics being played out in front of him in the tavern.

"But, surely – surely these are all peasants?" said Bertie.

"Well, if they are not, they are doing a good job of impersonating them!" laughed James.

"But – I've never been to such a place – I never thought . . ." said Bertie.

"It's such good fun to come slumming, sir! Just enjoy!" urged Donald.

An attractive woman with green eyes and pale skin came

up the steps to the platform with two large pewter tankards
of beer in her hands, another attractive young woman
following her with two more tankards.

"Well, aren't ye a fine sight for sore eyes!" said the
woman as she plonked the tankards down on the table in
front of them.

"Not as fine a sight as you are, Florrie!" said James.

"Charmer!" winked Florrie before looking over at Bertie.
"And who have we got here? Who's this fine young
handsome fella?"

"He's our friend, Bertie, new to the regiment!" called
Charles, fighting to be heard over the noise.

Suddenly, to Bertie's astonishment, Florrie plonked herself
down on his lap and threw her arms around his neck.

"Where are you from, my lovely?" she asked.

"E-e-e-ngland," stuttered Bertie.

"Ah, sure the English lads are always the most
handsome," she said and suddenly she put her mouth on
Bertie's and kissed him.

"Steady, sir!" laughed James as the officers clapped loudly.

Florrie stood up and winked at him. "More of that later, if
you like!"

As she and the other barmaid walked away, Bertie wiped
his mouth with the sleeve of his tunic and stared at the others
in shock.

"What – what kind of a woman is that?" he demanded.

"The best kind – alive!" laughed Donald and they all
burst out laughing.

"Cheers, everybody!" James raised his tankard and the
others clinked their tankards against his.

"Sir?" asked Charles, seeing Bertie hadn't lifted his
tankard.

"Oh, yes, cheers," said Bertie meekly as he raised his
tankard and feebly clinked it against the others and took a
sip.

As he sat there he looked around and saw Florrie behind

the bar smiling up at him and winking, her cleavage in full view. On the other side of the bar a couple were groping and kissing each other so intently that Bertie felt nauseous.

"Maybe I should go," said Bertie to Charles and James.

"But why, sir? We've only just arrived!" said James.

"I'm not sure if I'm comfortable here – I feel like a fish out of water." He pulled a stressed face. "If it ever emerged that I was here . . ."

"But, sir, why would it ever emerge? The only ones who know you are here are us, and we'll certainly never say anything," said Charles.

"I just – it's all a bit shocking – I keep feeling my parents' disapproving eyes on me."

"Sir, your parents are across the water in England, gloriously unaware that you are here. So I suggest you drink up, shut up and relax!" said James.

Bertie nodded and nervously raised his tankard of beer and took another sip.

Florrie came back and forth from the table all night, delivering more and more beer. All the time, she focused on Bertie.

"She likes you!" said Charles.

"Does she?" said Bertie as he watched her behind the bar. "How can you tell?"

"Well, it's obvious, from the way she looks at you, and flirts with you!"

"I – I'd say she's just being kind," said Bertie.

"Nonsense! She's totally smitten with you," said James, who was rather drunk at this stage. "If you asked her to take a walk with you, I'm sure she'd be delighted."

"Take a walk!" Bertie was horrified. "But she's a barmaid!"

"I think that might be a bridge too far, Marton," cautioned Charles. "The Prince of Wales cannot be seen with a peasant woman in public."

"I'm not suggesting being seen with her public, but who

would know about a quick knee-trembler?" said James.

"A fumble in the dark!" laughed Donald.

"Pretty much out of the question!" insisted Charles. "The Prince of Wales does not keep company with barmaids – regardless of how attractive they are."

Bertie was shocked as he listened to them discuss him as if he wasn't there, and using such vulgar language.

"Besides, I'm sure Bertie has a sweetheart back in England he is loyal to – am I not right, Bertie?" said Charles.

Bertie shook his head. "No, I haven't."

"But there must be somebody in Cambridge?" asked Charles, surprised.

"No." Bertie shook his head.

"But why ever not?" demanded James.

"Where am I to meet this sweetheart?" asked Bertie.

"But you are the Prince of Wales – I have no doubt the women are throwing themselves at you," said James.

"I have certainly met many young ladies, but there is a lot of supervision," said Bertie.

"At *all* times?" repeated James, eyes wide with horror.

"Yes," said Bertie. "I always have courtiers and diplomats around me making sure that I am not alone."

"But how is one ever to find the space to fall in love if one isn't permitted to court first?" asked Donald.

"Falling in love for the Prince of Wales is a complicated matter, usually involving the foreign office to ensure it is of good diplomatic advantage," sighed Bertie as he downed his beer.

"So you can't – just call on a woman that you find attractive?" said James.

"Not out of the blue, no – there are diplomatic channels that I should go through."

"That doesn't sound in the least romantic!" said James.

"No, no – I don't suppose it does," said Bertie. "Any female I am introduced to has first been vetted and checked as a possible bride. I have very little say in it."

"I see. And have you then been introduced to any possible brides?" asked James.

"Oh, yes, quite a number. My parents are very alarmed that I have not yet announced that I intend to marry one of them," said Bertie cynically. "They think I am being slow and dilly-dallying when there is the future of the monarchy to secure and heirs to be produced."

"I don't think I envy your life, Bertie," said Charles truthfully.

"At the moment they are actively soliciting that I agree to marry a certain Princess Alexandra, a firm favourite of my sister Vicky. She fits all the criteria for a future queen, according to my parents."

"And do you like this Princess Alexandra?" asked Charles.

"Well, I haven't met her, have I? I've only seen a photograph. She's Danish."

"Oh dear, the Danes are always so dull!" said Donald.

"I can see how this time spent here in Ireland is so important to you, to be free of all that even for a short while," said Charles.

"So important!" confirmed Bertie. He downed the rest of his beer then shouted across the bar. "Florrie – another round of beers!"

James took out his cigarette case and lit a cigarette.

"A smoke, sir?" said James, offering his case.

"Oh, no, I don't smoke," said Bertie.

James raised a cynical eyebrow as he continued to hold the box out. Bertie reached out and took a cigarette. He placed it in his mouth while James lit it.

"Now – just inhale!" urged James.

Bertie sucked on the cigarette and started coughing and spluttering.

"That's vile!" said Bertie.

"Keep trying, sir, and like everything in life you will come to enjoy it!" said James.

CHAPTER 15

Nellie was consumed with sadness after her last meeting with James. He had been an important part of her life for a long time. She had loved him once. He had told her he loved her. There hadn't been much love in her life. But she had become painfully aware over the past couple of years that James had never loved her. She had been a meal ticket for him. She didn't want to play the victim in the relationship because she had gained a lot financially from it as well. But she knew herself that part of the reason she had continued to see clients over the last while was to keep James happy, as she couldn't bear the thought of losing him forever. But now she knew that she had to lose him. She knew he would have no more interest in being part of her life once she stopped earning him money. Regardless of everything, it hurt that she would not be seeing him again.

"Will we manage?" Sadie asked her after Nellie had gone through her finances one afternoon in the flat.

"Of course we will, Sadie. I've a bit put by, and I can sell some jewellery if needs be. But we'll manage just fine on my wages as an actress."

The truth was Nellie wasn't sure how they were going to manage with her sudden loss of income. She had got so used to receiving that money. She would have to be very careful in the future.

That evening she headed to the theatre. It was a packed

night, and she saw a lot of the regulars in the audience. She loved going on stage and becoming a different person during the performances. She loved hearing the laughter and applause. That night was no different and she brought the house down. Smiling and curtsying to the crowd, she walked confidently off the stage. As she caught sight of herself in one of the backstage mirrors, she examined the beautiful cream gown she was wearing. She realised that the first thing she would have to cut back on was her wardrobe. She would have to cut down the amount and quality of gowns she bought. And there would be no more fashion bought from the fine stores on Sackville Street that ordered in Parisian fashion. She bit her lower lip in worry as she knew these dresses added so much to her stage performances. The audiences expected to see Nellie looking glamorous and dressed in high fashion. She would have to look around for dressmakers who could make similar dresses at a cheaper price than the stores.

"O'Brien wants to see you, Nellie," said a stagehand as he hurried past her.

"Thanks, John," she said and turned away from the mirror.

She began to walk down a corridor to O'Brien's office. O'Brien was the theatre manager. Nellie had always got on well with him. He knew how popular Nellie was and how the audience always came back to see her. She was always on time, never missed a show and didn't cause any arguments with the staff. Nellie also knew O'Brien could be a complete bastard. She had seen him reduce some of the other actresses to tears. She wondered what he wanted to see her about and thought this might be a good opportunity to ask for a raise in her wages. She knocked on his door.

"Come in!" came the response.

She opened the door and entered, closing the door behind her.

"You wanted to see me, Mr. O'Brien?"

"Ah, yes, Nellie, take a seat."

She walked across his office and sat down in the free chair on the other side of his desk.

He was writing away at his desk and eventually looked up at her and put down his pen.

"Is everything all right, Mr. O'Brien?"

"Em, it was a good night tonight?" he asked.

"Yes, very good. The crowd seemed to enjoy the new songs I've entered into my act," she said, smiling.

"Good," he said, studying her. "Nellie, how many nights a week are you working here now?"

She wondered at the question. As manager he should know. "I'm working five nights a week, Mr. O'Brien. But, actually, I can increase my workload to more than that now, as I have some more free time on my hands," she said, delighted at the prospect of earning more money.

"I'm afraid I have to cut your hours here. I'm cutting you down to two nights a week."

Nellie's mouth dropped open. "But, that makes no sense! Why would you do such a thing? My act has never been more popular – and I'm the most popular actress you have. I'm the star of your show!"

"Stars come and go, Nellie. And I'm afraid your star is going."

"But I didn't hear you have employed any new actresses to take my place! Have you employed a new actress?"

"No." He shook his head. "Not yet, but I soon will."

Nellie was bewildered. "But – what will I do? I rely on the money I earn here."

"That's not what I've heard," he said, raising his eyebrows.

"What have you heard?" she demanded.

He sat forward. "Look, Nellie, what you do in your free time is not my business but when it affects my business then it does become my business. Understand?"

"No, I don't understand at all!"

"Do I have to spell it out, Nellie? Your nocturnal activities are reflecting badly on my theatre."

"My nocturnal activities?" she asked as realisation dawned. "I don't know what you're talking about."

"Sure you don't!" he said cynically. "Look, I don't care what any of the girls do – you're not the only one, let's face it. I don't judge anyone morally – I'm certainly in no position to do so. But that nasty business in Dalkey. I can't have that going on with one of my actresses. The police could come and God knows what they could find if they came sniffing around my door."

"That wasn't my fault, Mr. O'Brien. Whatever you heard, I was defending myself!" Who had told him? How did he know?

"Maybe you weren't and maybe you were, I don't really care. But I can't take the chance."

"How did you find out about it?" Nellie asked.

"I got a visit from a young officer from the army who told me all about it. That you smashed up a house of a client of yours and caused a huge amount of costly damage."

"An officer?" Nellie was shocked.

"He said he was a friend of the client's and that if I didn't get rid of you he would make sure that none of the officers or army ever came here again. I can't alienate the British army, Nellie – they make up half my audience any given night!"

"Tall, black hair, dark eyes, good-looking man – the officer?" said Nellie as everything suddenly made sense to her.

"That sounds about right."

"But he's not a friend of the man in Dalkey!" she said, slamming her hand on the desk. "That's James Marton! He's my . . ."

"I don't care what he is, Nellie. He's very angry and he threatened he'd close me down if I had anything more to do with you!"

"What a bastard!" she said, slamming the desk again.

"He wanted me to fire you on the spot, but I wouldn't do that to you, Nellie. So I'm reducing your nights to two until you can find something else. Though best that I warn you – this Marton man has done quite a job of blackening your name around town. I'd say it would be hard for you to get a job in another theatre."

She nodded, her eyes blazing with anger.

"Is there anything else?" she said, standing up.

"No. And I'm sorry, Nellie."

"Not half as sorry as I am – or Marton will be when I get my hands on him!" she said, turning and stomping out.

Nellie flung the door of her dressing room open and slammed it shut.

"Nellie! Are you all right?" asked Sadie, turning and jumping up from her seat where she had been knitting.

"No! I am bloody well not all right! James has come to the theatre and spoken with O'Brien, told him about the incident in Dalkey and threatened O'Brien with closure unless he gets rid of me!"

Nellie began to furiously pace up and down.

"But – he can't do that!" said Sadie.

"He has, and he did! O'Brien has reduced me to two nights a week here. I'm lucky he didn't get rid of me altogether and only didn't because he's frightened he'll lose the other half of his customers if I suddenly disappear from the stage here!"

"Well, you can leave, Nellie! You're an actress in high demand. You'll get another position without any problem."

Nellie slumped into a chair. "O'Brien says James has badmouthed me across town with all the theatre owners. He says I won't get another job and I believe him."

"But why would Captain Marton do such a thing?"

"Isn't it obvious, Sadie? He's angry that I have left him. He's trying to force me back into his clutches. Force me back into making money for him. He thinks if he squeezes me this way, I'll have no choice but to go back to that life." Nellie sank her face into her hands.

"Oh, love!" said Sadie, rushing to her and putting her arms around her.

Nellie looked up. "I'm going to kill him when I see him!"

"Calm down, Nellie!"

"I will not calm down! He's such a bastard! I've a good mind to go down to the camp in the Curragh right now and make a show of him in front of all his fine friends!"

"Calm down, Nellie. It would be a wasted journey as you wouldn't be allowed into the camp and none of his fine friends would believe it anyway if you told them the truth."

"Oh, what am I to do, Sadie? You're right, he knows I won't be allowed within an ass's roar of him. Having said that, I could visit every restaurant and theatre in Dublin until I find the bastard and make a show of him when I do find him!"

"What good will that achieve, Nellie? All you'll be doing is making a show of yourself and whatever you say publicly to him will only destroy your own reputation for good in this town."

"Always the voice of reason, Sadie. And he knows it. He knows he's untouchable."

"So, what do we do now?"

"I don't know. I know what he expects me to do. He expects me to write to him, arrange to meet him and go back to servicing his clients and making him money."

"And – and is that what you're going to do?"

"No, I am not. I don't know *what* I'm going to do, but I'm not going to do that," said Nellie with determination.

CHAPTER 16

Queen Victoria sat in the upstairs drawing room at Buckingham Palace as Prince Albert opened a letter from Bertie. Placing the letter-opener back on the mantelpiece, he stood beside the fireplace as he began to read aloud.

"'*Dear Mama and Papa . . . I bid you fond greetings from Ireland. I hope you and my brothers and sisters are keeping well. I am keeping very well in Kildare. I have settled in and have taken great joy in my training exercises. Major Hazeldon has said I have made good progress and I work hard so as not to be a disappointment to him and to you. I have made friends with the other officers here who, as Papa wished, treat me the exact same as if I were a regular officer. They are good fellows and very welcoming. The work is very hard and there is no time for relaxation or any pleasure pursuits. I go to bed at nine o'clock each evening and rise at six to begin training at seven. Last week I marched a twenty-mile trek cross-country with my battalion. I am greatly enjoying the whole experience. Ireland is a wonderful country, the people friendly. The weather is very hot and I suggest packing appropriately for hot weather for your forthcoming visit. I look forward to seeing you here. There is much excitement about your forthcoming visit. I remain . . . your dutiful son . . . Bertie.'*"

"Well, that wasn't very informative. Short and to the point," said Victoria. "He was never a detailed letter writer

98

like Vicky, who brings the court in Prussia alive with her prose. All Bertie says is – the weather is hot and people are nice!"

"Sometimes the shorter the better with Bertie! At least he has no complaints, which is what I had feared he might," said Albert.

"Yes, I am surprised he has settled in so well. Twenty-mile treks across the country, early rises, early nights – I would have thought he would despise such a regime."

"On the contrary, he's flourishing in it. You see, I told you all Bertie needed was discipline and he would become responsible. I think we shall always be grateful to Ireland for turning Bertie into the son we always wanted."

"We live in hope. And we shall judge for ourselves when we visit Ireland in August. Although, I must admit, I regret we ever agreed to the visit in the first place. It is so soon after Mama's demise and I cannot seem to shake the feeling of grief that has overcome me." Victoria took out a handkerchief and dabbed her eyes.

Albert came and sat beside her. "There, there, my dear, try not to fret," he said, putting an arm around her. "I think this holiday to Ireland will be just what you need to try and distract you from your grief."

"I don't think anything could distract me. And I so miss Vicky at this time. I could always confide and speak with her and now I must rely on letters."

"Vicky is getting on with her own life and family," said Albert, "which is how it should be. Little Wilhelm needs all the care she can give him."

"Children always demand so much of their mother's attention! At least now Vicky can experience herself what I have endured for years!" said Victoria. "Of course, Bertie makes no mention of the Princess Alexandra! I daresay he doesn't give her a thought while he plays soldiers in Ireland!"

"I am sure he is giving her plenty of thought," said Albert.

"Well, she won't wait for him forever!"

"We can broach the subject again with him when we visit him in Ireland. Surely he will have reached a decision on Alexandra by then."

"Can Bertie ever reach a decision?" said Victoria. "In any case, we must continue to prepare for our Irish visit. Our ministers inform me that our visit to Killarney is designed to promote the tourist industry there. They believe that our presence there can promote visits to Ireland in the same way our presence at Balmoral promotes visits to Scotland."

"Yes, this is true, and after the Famine anything that helps bring industry and an influx of capital into Ireland is a wonderful thing. You see, Victoria, the service that you are providing to your Irish subjects. Does that not lighten your mood?"

"Not considerably! It makes me feel more like a tourist guide than a monarch!"

Charles sat down at their usual table in the mess where the others were waiting.

"Where's Bertie?" asked Donald.

"He'll be along in a short while. He had to do something in his quarters."

"How was today?"

Charles raised his eyes to heaven. "He's trying his level best, but let's just say it is as well he will be king one day as he really isn't officer material and never will be."

"If you can just get him past his parents' inspection when they come, you should consider that a job well done," said Donald.

"Other than that, I think we have achieved our goal in having provided him with a wonderful time here," said James.

"Oh, yes, he loves it!" agreed Charles.

"I cannot believe that he has never had an affair!" said James. "How can he expect to make a good marriage if he has no experience of such things?"

Donald smiled brightly. "Ah, I have been thinking about our friend in this regard. And it is really high time that we introduce him to some women who can 'educate' him in how to deal with the opposite sex."

"Anyone in mind?" asked Charles.

"Well, as it happens, my own paramour is hosting a soirée this Friday at her residence in Dublin," said Donald. "I suggest we take Bertie along to meet a few of her friends."

"Is your paramour not a married woman?" asked James.

"Yes, Henrietta Fitzgibbons. She will have many friends there – mostly married."

"But Bertie can't be with a married woman, if that is what you're suggesting," said Charles.

"Why not?" said Donald. "Married women are perfect for such a purpose. They do not expect anything in return and their discretion is guaranteed as they have a lot to lose should the affair ever become known."

CHAPTER 17

Nellie stood at the window in the sitting room of her flat, looking down at the street below. It was a Saturday afternoon and the street was, as ever, busy. Queen Victoria and her family had arrived in the city that day for a royal tour of the country and there was much excitement in evidence. Carriages going back and forth. Ladies and gentlemen in their fine clothes walking up and down the pavements.

Nellie was in no mood to join the people in the streets to try and get a glimpse of the Queen as she passed by. She turned from the window and looked around her. She liked living there. She loved the area and the flat.

Sadie was working at the theatre. She had taken on extra shifts to try and help with their finances. Nellie had pretended to Sadie that everything would be all right. She knew how Sadie fretted and worried and wanted to protect her as much as she could. But the reality was Nellie didn't know that everything would be all right. She had to fight the feeling of panic that was continually overwhelming her. How would she manage? How would she be able to afford to continue living there? How could she afford to pay the rent, buy the food? Before O'Brien had cut her nights working, all she had to worry about was a change in lifestyle and not being able to afford the clothes that she was expected to wear on stage. But now she was consumed with worry about how she would afford anything. Damn James! How could he do this to her? She was so angry with him and so hurt. And yet she knew James so well – she knew she should have expected nothing more or less from him. He would do anything to get what he wanted and to keep her in his control. He had changed her life so much and yet she wished she had never met him.

And, as she stared out the window again, she was consumed by a feeling and a fear she thought she had left behind long ago and would never have to face again. Fear of poverty, fear of hunger. She had known that feeling so well and now it had returned to her.

Nellie's earliest memories were such happy ones. She had been born and grew up on a tiny farm in the west of Ireland. Her home was a small thatched cottage perched on a hill that overlooked the wild Atlantic. Her parents were loving if dirt poor. She was the youngest of the family, with two older brothers. What she remembered most was the love they all had for each other. And she remembered the sense of community. How all the neighbours pulled together and helped each other out. It wasn't surprising, she thought, as most of them were somehow related to the others – if only by the marriage of a cousin or a relative. Like everyone, the small farm they rented was part of a huge estate owned by a landlord. She remembered seeing the landlord once drive by in his fine carriage with his wife and daughters. She had been overawed by the glamour of them. It was hard for her to imagine the world they lived in, which was so different from her own. The landlord never spoke or had anything to do with the tenants. He employed land agents who dealt with the tenants directly. She remembered these land agents being harsh and unpleasant and all the tenant farmers were frightened of them.

Then she remembered that summer in 1845. She had been just five years old at the time. Her father had come in and said that the crop of potatoes had failed – they were destroyed by potato blight. She remembered the disbelief the whole community felt as the crops failed on all the farms on the estate. And then word had come that the potato crops had failed throughout the entire country. There was panic and fear as the potato was the staple diet of the people – indeed, practically their only food as other crops grown had to be sold to pay their rents. They had struggled through that harsh winter as best they could. It had been a hungry winter with her parents struggling to feed the family with what they had. They waited and hoped for the harvest the following year, hoping that the crop would be a good one and they could get back to normal. But when the crop failed again the following year, catastrophe struck. Hunger turned to famine as food ran out.

And then came the evictions. Nellie shuddered as she remembered the awful day the land agent arrived and threw them out of their cottage. It was a day of mass evictions as so many farmers on the estate had been unable to pay their rent. In scenes of violence that Nellie would never forget, her family and their neighbours were thrown out of their homes and escorted from the estate. They filed in a long line, making their way through the country roads to the nearest town. The scenes they saw on the road frightened Nellie as the devastation the Famine was causing outside the estate unfolded before their eyes. Swarms of starving people begging on the side of the road, their emaciated bodies causing such weakness that many were lying in ditches, waiting for death. "Don't look! Don't look!" ordered her mother as they hurried on until they reached the town.

There they had made their way to the nearest workhouse and joined the queue waiting for admittance. They waited all night and the next day until they were finally seen by a doctor. The Cliffden family were lucky. The doctor passed them as none of them had infectious diseases. The workhouse, teeming with people, was terrified that the typhus that was breaking out around the country would be brought into it. Once inside the huge grey-stone building, Nellie didn't know whether they had been lucky to get admittance or had been better taking their chances on the outside. She and her mother were immediately separated from her father and brothers and shown into a giant room where they were to live with another hundred women. Nellie could still remember the dank smell in the room, the little light, the despair of being thrown into such close quarters with so many strangers. The food was scare, provided by government subsistence and charity.

"We're the lucky ones," he mother kept telling her. "At least we have something to eat and a place to stay."

But as Nellie looked at her mother's face that had seemed to age ten years in a few weeks, she wondered was she trying to convince herself of this rather than convince her daughter. Nellie barely saw her father or brothers after that. They were kept apart all the time. The work they were given to do was backbreaking and the conditions atrocious. The government wanted to dissuade people from flocking to the overcrowded workhouses and so kept conditions as bad as possible. The reputation of the workplaces was so bad that people on the outside feared them more than the certain death they faced from starvation on the outside.

Nellie's father finally got approval from one of the charities involved in the workhouse to pay for a passage to America for him and her brothers. But Nellie and her mother did not get approval.

"They want strong men to build the new world, they don't want us," Nellie's mother explained.

The family were reunited for an hour the week before her father and brothers were to set sail.

"I have no choice, I have to go – otherwise we'll all die here," said her father to her mother as the two of them wept.

"I know," said her mother.

"As soon as I find work in New York, I'll save the money for your passage to come and join us," said her father.

"But how long will that take?" asked Nellie.

"It won't take that long. I'll work like a slave until I can send for you and then we can all be together again," promised her father.

Nellie's heart was breaking as she watched her father and brothers leave.

"You'll see," promised her mother. "We'll be in New York soon and we'll all be working and together. And we'll never be hungry again."

But within a few short months there was an outbreak of the dreaded typhus in the workhouse and her mother died. Nellie was all alone and heartbroken. All she wanted was to be with her father and brothers. She waited anxiously every day for news from her father and the passage fare to bring her to New York to join them. But it never came. She wondered had they even made it to New York as stories of the so-called 'coffin ships' that were taking the Irish emigrants to New York came back to Ireland. The ships were overpacked and riddled with diseases with little food and water. Nellie heard that nearly a third of the passengers making their way across the Atlantic on those ships died en route, so bad were the conditions. Nellie liked to think of her father and brothers alive and well in New York, having made new lives for themselves. But sometimes, when they never sent for her, this upset her more than the thought of them dying on the ships going to their final destination. As the months went by, Nellie kept her head down in the workhouse, worked hard and tried not to think too much. It was a case of survival.

Nellie knew that what she and her family had gone through was no different from what millions of others had suffered in Ireland. As the Famine wore on into its third and fourth year, news came that over a million people had perished. Nellie could understand why it had happened: the potato was diseased. But she couldn't understand how it was allowed to happen. She knew nothing of politics or power, but surely there must be a government somewhere that would stop this suffering?

"Nellie Cliffden!" came the shout one morning while she was busy at work.

Nellie left her needlework and followed the supervisor through the dark corridors to the manager's office.

"You wanted to see me, sir?" she asked as she hovered before his desk.

"Yes, Nellie. You turned sixteen last week, according to our records."

"Yes, sir."

"In that case, Nellie, it's time you left us and made your own way in the world."

"What?" Nellie was shocked.

"The Famine is now over, Nellie, and government funding is cut. We can't afford to keep you here any more."

"But what will I do? Where will I go?"

"A bright girl like you should be all right. Get yourself up to Dublin where I am sure you'll be able to find work."

"Can't I stay a little longer, sir? I don't want to go out there," she pleaded as tears came to her eyes.

"I can't allow that, Nellie. There's no funding left. We have to use that for the young and the old and the sick. You'll be all right, you wait and see." He counted out some money and gave it to her. "Here is some money for the work you have done here."

Nellie took the money and wandered back to the workroom in a trance.

"He's kicking me out," she said to an older woman she had befriended.

"Good for you, Nellie!"

"What's good about it?"

"You don't want to waste any more of your life in here. I tell you, if I was young and able I'd be gone. Get out into the world and try to make something of yourself."

"But I don't know anything of the world out there. All I remember is the people dying on the sides of the roads when we made our way here," said Nellie with a shudder.

"The Famine is over now, Nellie, those that were dying are all dead. It's a different world out there now. You're a pretty girl. If you are stuck, get yourself up to the army garrison in Kildare. There's thousands of soldiers there and they'd pay a pretty penny to go with a girl like you!"

Nellie looked at her, horrified. "I'd never . . . I'd starve first."

Nellie left the workhouse that afternoon, carrying her few belongings. It was true the world had changed in the years since she had gone into the workhouse. Gone were the teeming masses of starving people. Nellie was struck by how there seemed to be so few people around compared to before. But she realised that, with a million dead and more than another million emigrated, of course the country would look more empty.

She made her way to the train station and bought a ticket to Dublin. Everything felt so unreal and different and frightening as she sat on the train and it transported her through the countryside to Dublin. The journey took hours and when she arrived she got off the train and walked in awe through the station, looking at the high glass roof and the hundreds of people teeming around.

She walked out onto the street and didn't know which way to go. She followed the crowds. She felt so lost and alone and everything was so big.

By evening she had walked for hours and headed back to the train station. She sat on a bench there and fought the overwhelming need to burst into tears.

Then a man came up to her and smiled.

"Are you all right?" he asked.

She looked up at him. "No. I don't know where I am or where I'm going. I just got off the train today and I know nobody in Dublin."

"Follow me," he said.

She hesitated for a moment and then, when she realised he was the only person who had spoken to or smiled at her, she stood up and followed him. He didn't speak much as he led her through the streets until they came to a small tea room. He opened the door and ushered her in. There were a couple of waitresses cleaning up and it looked like it was about to close. A stern-looking woman was behind the counter.

"Who's this, son?" she asked.

"I found her at the train station. She knows nobody and has nowhere to stay," he said.

The woman shook her head. "I don't know, son. You're always the same – bringing back waifs and strays!"

"You said you were looking for a girl to work in the kitchen," said the man.

"Yes, but somebody with a bit of experience. This girl is straight out of a workhouse from the look of her." The woman looked her up and down. "Where's your family?"

"I don't know," Nellie said.

The woman tutted. "A famine orphan. As if we didn't see enough of them during the Famine when they started teeming into the city with nowhere to go, with their diseases and their woes!"

"That's in the past. Do you want to hire this girl or not?" asked the man.

"I'll give her a try." She looked at Nellie. "You can start tomorrow. But you'd better work hard."

"I will," Nellie promised.

"*Hmm* . . . Come on – I'll make a bed up for you tonight and we'll find someplace tomorrow for you. I'm Mrs. Yardley, and I better not get any cheek from you or you'll feel the back of my hand."

Mrs. Yardley was kind once Nellie got past her abrupt manner. She lent her some money to get lodgings in a nearby lodging house. It was bleak and uncomfortable, but Nellie was delighted to have it. She worked extremely hard in the kitchen and after a while Mrs. Yardley trained her to serve tables. Nellie could hardly believe her good fortune, dressed in a prim uniform taking orders from the customers and serving them tea.

One day she spotted a man in a corner table, dressed in an officer's uniform. He was very smart-looking and handsome, and very polite when she took his order. He came back the next day and the next and always smiled at her and was very polite. He became a regular at the tea room and she would notice his eyes on her as she served tea.

One evening when she finished work, she left the tea room and had turned to walk back to her lodgings when she saw he was waiting for her outside.

"Hello," he said.

"Hello," she answered as she walked past him.

"I am Captain James Marton," he said, putting out his hand for her to shake. "And who might you be?"

"I'm Nellie Cliffden," she said, shaking his hand before going to walk past him.

"Why are you in such a hurry?"

"I just need to get home," she said.

"That is a pity – I was rather hoping you would come to dinner with me."

She blushed and hurried past him and ran all the way back to the lodging house. But he was at the tea room the next day again, trying to engage her in conversation. And he regularly appeared after work, asking her to go to dinner with him.

"I don't know why you keep waiting for me after work – I will not go to dinner with you!" she snapped angrily at him one evening.

"But why?"

"Because why would an officer like you want to go out with the likes of me?"

"Because you are the prettiest thing I have ever seen," he said, smiling at her.

She blushed profusely.

"Really, Nellie – what harm would it do for you to come to dinner with me?" he asked.

She looked at him and was mesmerised by him.

110

"All right," she said. "But just this once!"

He brought her to a lovely restaurant and told her she could order anything she wanted. She listened to him talk about himself. He was from outside Dublin, from a farming background, but had wealthy relatives who had paid for his education. After school he had joined the army as an officer. She fell in love with him that evening, listening to him speak. She had never met anybody from his world before.

She continued to see him over the following weeks and they soon became lovers. It wasn't long before he rented a small flat for her where he would come to stay when he wasn't at his garrison. She lived for those hours when she was alone with him. Soon he was teaching her things she never knew before – how to sit properly, talk properly and walk properly and eat "like a lady", as he would describe it. He soon put pressure on her to leave her job in the tea room.

"You are too good for that place, Nellie," he said.

So she left.

He paid for singing lessons for her and to her amazement she found she was an excellent singer. She never knew such happiness could exist.

"I think you would be excellent on the stage," he said to her.

"Me on the stage! Never!"

But he introduced her to a theatre manager and suddenly she had a small part in a show. And it wasn't long before she was giving performances on her own. Looking back, Nellie now knew, James had the whole thing planned. He had plucked a pretty naïve girl desperate for love and polished her and made her into what he wanted her to be. But she realised after a time that he didn't do that because he loved her. He didn't want her to become the perfect woman for himself. He wanted her to be the perfect woman for others. James didn't have much money and had expensive taste. And she blindly followed his instructions when he started suggesting she go to parties he arranged and all she had to do was smile at the men there. That's what he told her: smile at a certain man and make him feel important. Soon she realised James expected her to do more than that. And she loved him so much she went along with his instructions. After another year he stopped coming to the flat and their personal relationship was over. He never gave an explanation as to why he ended it with her.

But their business relationship continued. Nellie nursed her broken heart as she realised James had only been using her for financial gain. But she was now a star of the stage and had made such important friends and had as much money as she wanted. She had come a long way and she tried to convince herself that that was something to be proud of.

The door of the flat opened and Sadie came in, bringing Nellie back from the past and her memories and into the present.

"You look exhausted, Sadie," said Nellie.

"Oh no, I'm fine. Just been working hard at the theatre," said Sadie.

"I hate how you have to do these extra hours."

"I'm lucky O'Brien gives them to me, so I'm not complaining. Anything that helps us with a few pennies," said Sadie, taking off her cloak.

"It won't be for long," said Nellie.

Sadie's face lit up. "Have you managed to find another position?"

"No, not yet. But I will." Nellie was forcing herself to look positive. She knew part of the reason Sadie looked so exhausted was because she was so worried about their future.

"You look lovely," said Sadie.

"Oh, Sadie, I could be wearing a coal sack and you'd pay me a compliment!"

"Are you going anywhere nice?"

"I'm going to a sitting for a drawing at Oliver's and then he's having a soirée afterwards."

"I wonder – Mr. Oliver knows many people in the theatrical world – maybe he could get you a new job if he asked around?"

"There's a thought! I'll ask him when I'm there," Nellie said with a smile.

Nellie sat in an upright position in front of a tall window in Oliver's studio, in his fine house in Fitzwilliam Square, as he sketched her.

"Is everything all right, Nellie? You seem distracted today?" asked Oliver as he continued to draw.

"Everything's fine. I'm just trying to concentrate on not moving and disturbing your drawing."

"Oh, no fear of you moving, Nellie. I've never had a model sit as still as you do . . . I would very much like to paint your portrait one day."

"Oh, that would be a fine thing, Oliver!" She smiled with enthusiasm.

She studied him as he worked. His dark hair was wavy and worn that little bit too long, as bohemians tended to wear it, curling down to his shoulders. "Tell me, Oliver, do you earn money from your art?"

"I make enough, but I am still very much in the struggling-artist class. I need a rich patron to fund me!"

"Don't we all!" she said, laughing. "I don't mean to be personal, Oliver, but if you don't earn that much from your art, how do you fund your lifestyle?"

"This –" he gestured around the room, "owes everything to an inheritance I received from my grandmother and nothing to my art."

"Ah – I see!" she said, nodding. "It all makes sense now!"

"But one day my ship will come in," he said.

"As will all of ours?" she laughed. "So, who will be at the soirée this evening?"

"Oh, the usual crew, with a few newcomers as well. We have a German poet coming who is here in Ireland for the month of

August to research Celtic folklore." Oliver sounded scornful.

"He sounds like a bore!" she said, pulling a face.

"Doesn't he?" agreed Oliver. "How is the theatre?"

"Oh fine. I think I'm getting a little bored there – might be time to move on."

"Really?"

"Do you know of any theatres looking for actresses?" she asked.

"Well, maybe, Nellie. But they are probably looking for Shakespearean actors not music-hall dollies!" he teased her.

Her face clouded in anger. "If I am merely a music-hall dolly, then why do you insist on sketching me all the time? Why not sketch one of your Shakespearean actresses?"

"Because the Shakespearean actresses all look like walruses and I should never sell a drawing for the rest of my life if I painted them!"

"I never know with you if a compliment is an insult or if an insult is a compliment!"

They lapsed into silence again and he continued to draw.

"How does one become a Shakespearean actress anyway?" asked Nellie. "I'm sure it can't be that different from what I do?"

"I think you might be disappointed by the wages a Shakespearean actress gets, Nellie. They won't be getting anything higher than you, maybe less. What's all this talk of change anyway? I thought you were happy where you are?"

"A girl needs a change sometimes."

"What does Captain Marton say about it?" He looked at her curiously.

"Myself and Captain Marton have parted ways."

"Really?" He put down his drawing board. "Why?"

She shrugged. "No reason."

"But you and Marton have been an item for years. We all thought you were his girl."

"I have never been anything more to James than a passing entertainment."

"Come now, Nellie, you do yourself an injustice. James was enthralled with you, everyone could see that."

"James was not enthralled with me, Oliver. James used me like he uses everyone else. If you only knew the truth about me and James –" She stopped talking abruptly.

"Has this something to do with that business in Dalkey?" he asked.

Nellie swung around and stared at him. "How did you – what do you know?"

"Not much, Nellie – only that there was some nasty business at a party that ended up in a fracas."

"Do you know what I was doing at the party?" she asked, afraid of the answer.

"No, but I can guess. That's the great thing about our bohemian world, nobody ever knows, but everyone can guess."

"Is it common knowledge what I am – what I was?" She was terrified by the answer he would give.

"Not common knowledge, but people speculate. They wonder where your money has come from, and I am guessing that you, unlike me, do not have rich grandmother."

She smiled and shook her head. "I don't know what I'm going to do, Oliver. I've got myself into a right pickle."

"You'll do what everyone does – survive. But be careful of James – he could be a bad enemy and from the whispers I've heard he was somehow involved in that fracas in Dalkey."

CHAPTER 18

As Nellie looked around the drawing room in Oliver's house she found she knew most of the crowd there. They were, as Oliver described them, mostly bohemians. Artists, writers, actors, journalists who all saw themselves as far too interesting to be part of the bourgeoisie. As most of them were from upper or middle-class backgrounds they attracted other more conventional friends who wished to be acquainted and associated with their fashionable reputation. Nellie never felt as if she was one of them. Although not all of them boasted wealthy connections, she doubted any of them had a background as bad as hers. She knew she was there only by the license of having beauty and wit. Also, as she always appeared to have money, this gained her entry into this world. For no matter how this bohemian crowd liked to pretend to have a disdain for money, its importance to them was without question. Now that Nellie had lost her income, she wondered how long she could continue to impress them.

Carl Jennings was at the fireplace with a circle of people around him, including Nellie, as he pontificated while drinking champagne. Carl was a journalist, a large loud man in his forties who Nellie had often enjoyed bantering with.

"So – my good people, how many of you turned out to see the arrival of Her Majesty the Queen in our fair city of Dublin today?" he asked, his voice full of humour.

"Do not tell me that you, Carl, joined the crowds in the

116

street to wave as she passed by?" asked Nellie derisively.

"I did of course, my dear Nellie! I stood amongst the masses as she rode by!"

"Do explain yourself, Carl – has the Queen's visit changed you from being a lifelong republican into a monarchist? Were you standing in the rain waving a Union Jack flag and singing 'Rule, Britannia' as Her Majesty passed?"

"Not in the least, Nellie. I merely went as a spectator. My curiosity got the better of me and, as she has only visited this country she claims to rule twice before, I thought I might never again get a chance to see her in person in my lifetime."

"And were you impressed by the sight of the Queen?" asked Nellie.

"Not in the least. I don't know quite what I was expecting, but I wasn't expecting somebody quite so dull and dumpy-looking," he said.

"Careful what you say, Carl, or you might end up in the Tower!" said Nellie with a laugh.

"Detained at Her Majesty's pleasure!" he laughed back. "On a more serious note, I was far more interested in seeing the reaction of the crowds than the good lady herself. I could scarcely believe it. Irishmen and women cheering as she went by – how short our memories are! Where was she during the Famine? Did she care or come to the rescue of her subjects as they lay dying of hunger while she sat in her ivory tower?"

"I scarcely think the Queen herself was responsible for the potato failing," said Nellie.

"That I won't accuse her of." Carl's face became angry, all signs of joviality gone. "But I will accuse her and her government of standing idly by while a million people perished. And I'll admit she gave two thousand pounds from her own purse to aid the starving masses but, when the Ottoman Emperor wished to give ten thousand pounds to aid our fellow countrymen, she asked him not to give so large a donation as it would make her donation seem ungenerous – what kind of behaviour is that?"

"Perhaps if she saw the starving people and the suffering for herself, she would never have done such a thing," said Nellie, a faraway look in her eyes.

"My point exactly, Nellie! She didn't come and see for herself, did she? And she arrives over now, safe that she will not be confronted by any of the horrors we all saw at the height of the Famine, and expects us to wave and cheer for her."

"Well, many who were on the streets of Dublin cheering her today probably did not see the horrors of the Famine for themselves either. They were probably as removed from what was happening around the country as the Queen was herself in her ivory tower," Nellie said, looking around the circle of people listening to her and Carl. She was confident that none of those present had seen the horrors of the Famine. She was sure they all stayed in their large houses, to keep away from the suffering and disease that was sweeping the country, and were every bit as guilty as the Queen for turning a blind eye. "If you'll excuse me, please," she said with a smile and turned and walked away.

The conversation with Carl had turned morose. She had come to the soirée to try and forget all her troubles, not be brought back to the horrors of her childhood. And yet how far she had come. To be mixing and mingling with these people. Even if she wasn't really one of them, and even if they whispered about her behind her back, she was there amongst them. How far she had come! And she didn't want to go back to where she came from. She couldn't bear the thought of it.

"Nellie, come here please," said Oliver. "I'd like to introduce you to somebody."

Nellie turned and smiled at the couple with him.

"George and Teresa Langton, may I introduce Nellie Cliffden, the famous actress."

Nellie smiled at the couple who looked uptight and snobby. George with his round spectacles and pinched face looked like a typical banker. Teresa with her tight bun, high collar and turned-up nose looked like a typical banker's wife.

"How do you do?" said Nellie formally.

Teresa was looking her and down. "Famous actress? I can't recall ever hearing of you before. What plays are you in?"

"I perform at the Palace Theatre," said Nellie.

"Oh!" Teresa's uptight face became more disapproving. "I see! Well, I've never been there and I don't imagine I never shall!"

"Such a pity, Mrs. Langton, as I'm sure you would fit in a treat!" said Nellie.

"How so?" said Teresa. "From what I understand, the majority of the audience is male."

"You never know until you try!" said Nellie and, as she looked at George Langton again, her face dropped. The man was looking distinctly uncomfortable as he shifted from one foot to another. She remembered him well. She had been introduced to him at a special party James had arranged a couple of years ago. George Langton had been one of Nellie's clients.

"What exactly are the talents ones needs to perform in such a theatre?" asked Teresa condescendingly.

"Talents? Well, I couldn't say for sure . . . some have said that Mother Nature has been kind to me." Nellie put her finger under her chin and raised her face.

"Hardly a talent!" said Teresa.

"What do you think, Mr. Langton – what talents do you think I possess?" Nellie said, staring at him.

"Well, yes, I really wouldn't know about such things – wouldn't know anything about the world of theatre or whatever it is," said George as he grabbed Teresa's arm and led her away. "Come along, dear, we must mingle."

"Really!" whispered Teresa to her husband as they walked off. "Whatever is Oliver thinking of, inviting that woman? I mean she is nothing but a music-hall singer!"

"*Hmmm*, quite!" said George as sweat broke out on his brow.

Nellie stood in a corner, sipping her champagne. She had watched George Langton and his wife circulate, steadfastly avoiding her. Occasionally George would give her a glance and then quickly look away. As Nellie watched his snobby wife, she wondered what she would think if she knew Nellie had been in her house and had bedded her husband. She knocked back her drink. She felt a headache coming on and needed to leave.

"I'd like to leave," she said to Oliver as he walked by.

"I'll fetch you a cab," he said.

He walked her to the door and helped her on with her cloak.

In the cab, she looked back at the soirée and wondered how long she could keep the masquerade up. Now that her money was going, how long would she be invited to these gatherings? And part of her wondered whether would care if she left that world. She would never have what she yearned for most. A husband that she loved and who loved her, a proper home and family. Women like her were excluded from having that. Men like George Langton might play with women like her, but they married women like Teresa Langton.

CHAPTER 19

Bertie looked nervously out the window as the carriage drove into Mountjoy Square with its fine townhouses looking onto the park in its centre. In the carriage were Donald, James and Charles. They had arranged to take him to a party being hosted by a friend of Donald's. Bertie now regretted having agreed to come. His mother and family had arrived in Dublin that day for their tour and were staying at the Vice-regal Lodge in Phoenix Park. Bertie felt uncomfortable that his parents were only a few miles away while he was attending a party they would be outraged to know he was going to.

"I don't think this is wise," fretted Bertie.

"Why ever not?" asked Donald.

"Well, what if Major Hazeldon discovers we have left the camp?"

"Bertie, we are officers," said James. "We are allowed to leave camp as long as we are not on duty."

"Yes, but I am supposed to be in Ireland to receive military training, not to attend soirées in Dublin," said Bertie.

"But who will ever know?" asked James.

"Word may filter back to my family. One of the guests at the soirée may gossip," said Bertie. "Especially as my parents are in Dublin now."

"Bertie!" said Donald, leaning towards him. "There will only be a select few at this soiree. They are old friends, and old friends cover for each other."

"They may be old friends of yours, Donald, but they are not old friends of mine," said Bertie.

The carriage pulled up in front of one of the townhouses and the driver came to the side of the carriage and opened the door.

James, Donald and Charles filed out while Bertie remained seated.

"For goodness' sake, sir, we're already late!" said Charles, becoming exasperated.

Bertie climbed out of the carriage and followed them up the steps to the front door.

Donald knocked and, a few moments later, the door was opened by the butler.

"Good evening, Captain Kilroy," said the butler.

"Good evening, Vernon," said Donald, removing his cloak and top hat and handing them to him.

The others removed their cloaks and hats as well and Vernon took them all. As Bertie handed him his, he noticed the butler was trying not to stare at him but his expression showed a mixture of excitement and nervousness. Bertie realised the tall, distinguished-looking butler clearly had been told who was coming to the house that night but was under strict instructions not to show any sign of recognition.

"This way, gentlemen," said Vernon. He led them down the corridor and into the drawing room where about a dozen people were drinking and chatting.

"*Donald!*" came a cry across the room and a tall glamorous woman in her late twenties approached and kissed his cheek.

"Hello, Henrietta, you look beautiful tonight," said Donald.

"Thank you, Donald," she said with a smile and she quickly eyed his companions.

Indeed, thought Bertie, Donald was right. Henrietta was a raving beauty with her auburn hair, hazel eyes and a figure she was proudly displaying in the latest fashion.

"You know Charlie and James," said Donald.

122

"Good evening, gentlemen," she said, nodding at them.

"Hello, Henrietta," they said in unison.

"And this is – Bertie," said Donald.

Her eyes sparkling with delight, Henrietta made a curtsy and said, "I am honoured to have you visit my house, Your Royal Highness."

"Come, come, Henrietta," said Donald. "I told you Bertie insists on being called by his first name tonight."

"If His Royal Highness permits?" asked Henrietta.

"I insist," said Bertie.

"In that case, let me introduce you to my guests," she said, taking his arm and leading him into the drawing room.

As Henrietta smiled flirtatiously at Bertie, James and Charles exchanged satisfied looks.

Bertie took a nervous gulp from the glass of wine he was holding as he stood surrounded by Henrietta and three other women.

"You look so handsome, Bertie, in your tunic!" said Henrietta, placing a hand on his arm.

"T-t-thank you," he said.

"Donald has told us all about you," gushed a woman called Clarissa who was again a glamorous blonde woman.

"R-r-really, what has he been saying?" asked Bertie.

"Oh, just that you are brilliant at commanding the company of men!" she said with a giggle.

"A – a – little exaggerated in his praise, I must say," said Bertie.

"So modest!" said Henrietta. "I saw your parents today as they toured through Dublin! I was so excited to see the Queen. She waved at us as she passed by."

"Really?" said Bertie.

"And to think I now have her son here in my house!" said Henrietta excitedly.

Clarissa fanned her face with her hand. "Is it me or is it very warm in here?"

"Yes, it is very warm," said Henrietta. "Bertie! Why not take Clarissa out for some fresh air in the garden?"

"Oh, yes, do!" said Clarissa, seizing Bertie's arm.

Henrietta took his glass and Clarissa led him across the drawing room and through the French windows which were open, into the garden.

They walked down some steps into the garden and past a fountain.

"What a lovely garden!" Bertie remarked.

"Isn't it? Henrietta is known for her gardening skills," said Clarissa, staring into his face with a broad smile.

"Has she lived here long?" he asked.

"Oh, a number of years. Ever since she married Jack," said Clarissa.

"I see!" he said, becoming uncomfortable at the mention of Henrietta's husband. "Where is – Jack – tonight?"

"Why, he's in South Africa on tour."

"South Africa? You mean he's in the army?"

"Of course – he's a Colonel."

"I see," said Bertie, shocked that Donald was seeing a fellow officer's wife behind his back.

"Is something the matter?" asked Clarissa.

"No – yes – are *you* married?" he asked cautiously.

"Naturally! I'm thirty years old, Bertie. If I wasn't married by now then I never would be!"

"And where is your husband tonight?"

"He's a diplomat – he's away on foreign affairs," she answered, moving closer to him. "I, however, am much more suited to affairs closer to home."

"Eh, yes, I think I've had enough air now, so I shall head back in," said Bertie, turning and leaving her there as he made for the French windows.

Bertie stood in the corner of the Henrietta's drawing room, nursing his drink as he looked around him. The guests had become drunker as the night went on. Donald and Henrietta had disappeared some time ago and Bettie had seen them sneak up the stairs.

Charles was engrossed in a conversation with Clarissa in another corner of the room.

"Are you all right, sir?" came a voice beside him and he turned to see that the speaker was James.

"Yes, quite all right," sighed Bertie.

"Are you not enjoying yourself, sir?"

"Oh, yes, very much so. Everyone has been very kind." Bertie paused, looked about and then back at James. "May I ask you a question?"

"Of course."

"Are Donald and Henrietta having an affair?"

James nodded. "Is it not obvious?"

"Yes, very obvious," said Bertie. "But she's married to a fellow officer!"

"I am aware of that," said James.

"But that is disgraceful behaviour!"

"Is it? Her husband knows what Henrietta is like, Bertie. He's not exactly shy himself when it comes to affairs."

"And Charles and that woman Clarissa – they will no doubt be acquainted with each other in a similar way by the time the night is over by the look of them," said Bertie.

"I do not know. But the lady did try to seduce you first, or so you said, and when you gave her the cold shoulder she moved on to pastures new. You can't blame her, can you?"

"No, but her husband may blame her when he finds out," said Bertie.

"Sir, her husband won't find out. Everyone here is very discreet – there is no chance the truth will come out."

"Somebody in my position cannot take chances with other people's discretion. They all know who I am, do they not?"

James nodded. "Yes."

"That no doubt explains my popularity with the ladies present."

"You underestimate your charm, sir!"

Bertie flushed, wondering if James was mocking him. "I shouldn't be here. If my father found out!"

"Sir! We thought it would be good for you to come here tonight. It's good for you to meet some ladies in a calm and relaxed atmosphere!"

"For what reason? I am to be married to a suitable princess and the only person I need to get on with and have experience with is her!"

"But, Bertie, life isn't all about duty. Surely you are entitled to enjoy yourself as well?"

"Not when one is born the Prince of Wales. Duty comes first. You can't be expected to understand, James. My father is incredibly strict on these matters. He has never looked at another woman all his life, despite being surrounded by court beauties who outrageously flirt with him, if for no other reason than to irritate Her Majesty the Queen. He has never faltered once and he expects the same from me. To make a perfect marriage and live in contented bliss for the rest of my life. He would be horrified that I am here."

James sighed. "It is not my place to advise you, sir, but I do believe you are making a mistake in living your life by another's terms."

"I have no choice," said Bertie.

"In that case, would you prefer if we leave and return to camp?" asked James.

"I think I should, though there is no reason for you to leave as well."

"It's quite all right, sir, I shall leave too," said James as he turned and headed towards the hallway.

As Bertie put down his glass and turned to follow him, he saw Charles and Clarissa walk out the French windows. He watched as they walked through the moonlit garden to the fountain and stop there to speak intimately. He was overwhelmed by a feeling of jealousy and envy.

"Sir? The carriage is waiting outside," said James.

Bertie nodded. With a final glance at Charles and Clarissa

126

in the garden, he left the room and made his way out to the awaiting carriage.

Bertie sat in silence as the carriage drove through the city streets.

"Is everything all right, sir?" asked James, snapping Bertie out of his thoughts.

"Oh yes . . . I just feel a little deflated. I wish I could be like Donald and Charles and be able to throw caution to the wind. Alas, I will never be able to do so!"

"The purpose of tonight was not to make you depressed, sir, but to entertain you."

"I understand you all had the best intentions. However, I'm afraid all that you have done is show me a cornucopia and then it has been snatched away from me. Shown me an Aladdin's cave that I am forbidden to enter."

James studied him for a while and then leaned out the carriage window. "Change of course, driver! Take us to the Palace Theatre!"

"Yes, sir," said the driver as he changed course.

"What is happening? Where are we going?" asked Bertie.

"The night is still young, sir. Perhaps Henrietta's party was not the best idea and I understand how you might have felt exposed there. Sometimes Donald forgets the restraints that you have to live by. But I think it is far too early to travel back to Kildare where you'll just sit in your quarters feeling morose!"

"So . . . what kind of theatre is the Palace?" asked Bertie.

"May I suggest that you trust me, sir. Sit back and enjoy the night. I shan't put you in any difficult or compromising position but I can promise you entertainment the likes of which you have never witnessed before!"

Bertie sat back, puzzled and yet relieved that the night was not going to end just yet, and might be redeemed.

The carriage pulled up outside the Palace which was at the top of St. Stephen's Green.

Bertie stepped out of the carriage and looked up at the building which was ornately decorated at the front. There were a number of carriages parked outside the theatre and people, mostly men, were walking in and out of it. Many of them were soldiers.

"Come along, sir," said James walking confidently to the entrance.

"James, what if somebody should recognise me?" said Bertie.

"For goodness' sake, sir, it's only a theatre – it's not a house of ill repute!"

"I know, but –" said Bertie.

"Nobody will recognise you, Bertie – just keep your head down and follow me."

Bertie did as he was told and followed James, keeping his head bowed and the collar of his cloak up.

"Good evening, Captain Marton. A pleasure to see you again," said the girl at the ticket desk inside the door in the foyer.

"Good evening, Sally. Do you have you a box free tonight?"

"Always have a box free for you, Captain Marton. Up the stairs on the right and sixth box down," said Sally, smiling.

"Thank you, Sally," said James as he beckoned to Bertie to follow him up the stairs.

Upstairs they walked along a corridor which had curtained boxes to one side.

"Ah, here we are!" said James as he pulled back the curtain and gestured to Bertie to enter.

Bertie hesitated and then walked into the box. It was a small box, one in a row of a balcony of boxes that ran along the back and sides of the theatre. The box looked down on rows of seats, all occupied. It was close to the stage with an excellent view of it. Although the layout of the theatre did not seem that different from the opera, the atmosphere was completely different. The packed audience was loud, laughing and talking even though there was a performance going on.

"Is this a music hall?" questioned Bertie as he sat in one of the seats and James sat beside him.

"Some might call it that, but it calls itself a theatre."

"In the same way a man might call himself a gentleman but is in actual fact far from it!" said Bertie, looking slightly shocked at the raucousness of the crowd in the seats beneath them.

The curtain of the box was pulled back and a waitress walked in.

"Good evening, Captain Marton – I brought in your regular," she said as she placed a full bottle of rum and two glasses on the table at the front of the box.

"Good girl," said James, giving her a big tip.

"Thank you, Captain Marton!" said the delighted girl before she retreated.

James poured them two glasses of rum as Bertie stared at the stage. There was some kind of comedy sketch being performed on the stage. There was a group of people, some dressed as clowns, running around the stage pretending to hit and fight each other which was causing much laughter in the audience.

"How extraordinary!" said Bertie as he took a gulp of his rum and followed the comedic play that was being enacted on the stage.

James pretended to be looking at the sketch but he was seated a little behind Bertie, watching him and his reactions.

As the play on the stage became ever more chaotic, Bertie suddenly burst out laughing.

"Did you see that? Did you see what the little fellow did to the woman?" he said.

"Yes, sir!" said James who laughed along too as he topped up Bertie's glass with rum.

As the night wore on, Bertie was captivated by the antics on the stage. He laughed during the comedies, loved the musical acts and was mesmerised when the troop of dancing girls came out.

"What fun!" declared Bertie. "I never thought a theatre could be so much fun or provide such wide-ranging entertainment!"

"Much more fun than going back to the camp for an early night!" said James, raising his voice to be heard over the loud music as the dancing girls kicked their legs in the air.

After the dancing girls had skipped offstage to loud applause, the master of ceremonies walked out on the stage and addressed the audience.

"*And now – what you have all been waiting for – without further ado – may I present – Miss Nellie Cliffden!*" he shouted and the audience exploded in applause and cheering.

Bertie watched intently as a woman walked onstage, her golden hair piled high, dressed in a golden gown that twinkled under the stage lights. She was carrying an open parasol over her head. She waited patiently for the audience to calm down and the cheering and clapping to stop.

"*Are you expecting rain, Nellie?*" shouted a man once the audience had become quiet, seeing Nellie twirl her parasol.

"*A girl always has to come prepared to expect anything! Isn't that right, boys?*" she called out, winking at the audience and they all began to clap and cheer.

The band started up and Nellie began to sing her signature tune. As she strolled up and down the stage, twirling the parasol over her head, she sang –

"*Where are you going, my lovely?*
Wouldn't you like if I went there with you?
I'm not asking to go there forever –
I'd be happy with one night or maybe with two!"

As she finished singing, the audience again exploded in applause with loud whistles and shouts of praise.

Nellie closed her parasol and flung it to the side as she walked towards the footlights.

"*Good evening, gentlemen – and ladies of course!*"

"*There's no ladies here, Nellie!*" shouted a man from the audience.

"*None that would look at you twice in any case!*" Nellie shouted back, causing the audience to laugh loudly.

She strolled up and down the stage, looking at the audience. "*What a wonderful crowd we have in tonight! Half of you look like you're here hiding from your wives and the other half look as if you're hiding from your mothers!*"

Bertie, with the rest of the audience, burst out laughing.

She spotted a young man in the front row and bent towards him. "*My, you are a handsome lad! What's your name, my lovely?*"

"*Jack!*"

"*Hmmm – Jack of all trades and master of none, I bet, by the look of you!*"

She moved along the footlights and stopped again.

"*What a beautiful suit you're wearing, sir!*" she said.

"*Thank you!*" said the man, embarrassed by the attention.

"*Did it cost much?*"

"*Quite a bit,*" answered the man.

"*Hold on to that suit and keep it good, sir – it will be a lovely suit for you to be buried in. I can see you laid out in your coffin, wearing that suit, after your wife kills you when she finds out you were at the Palace tonight!*"

The audience cheered.

"What an unusual girl!" said Bertie as he stared, mesmerised by her.

"Nellie Cliffden is one of the most famous actresses on the Dublin stage, sir," said James.

"Amazing!" said Bertie.

"*Now, gentlemen, I am hearing a rumour that good old Queen Vicky has arrived in our fair city,*" said Nellie, causing some in the audience to start booing.

James looked quickly at Bertie who was staring fixedly at the stage.

"*I wish somebody told her we have no need for another queen in the city – because we have our very own palace – right here – and I am the Queen!*"

The audience laughed and clapped.

"But if good old Queen Vicky would care to pay us a visit here at the Palace Theatre – we'll show her a good time, eh, boys?"

At that, most of the audience stood and clapped, while they laughed and cheered.

James abruptly stood up. Blast, he thought, just when things were going so well! "I cannot apologise enough, sir! I had no idea that such lack of respect would be shown to Her Majesty. We shall leave at once."

"Sit down, Marton! I am trying to watch the show!" said Bertie.

James subsided, amazed.

As Nellie continued with her repertoire she held the audience's attention in her hand. She finished with a performance of 'She Moves Through the Fair'. It was unlike the other songs she had sung and her voice sounded haunting as she echoed the sad verses that carried to the back of the theatre.

Bertie sat transfixed as she sang, her voice now so sweet and soft.

"I think she is the most beautiful woman I've ever seen," said Bertie quietly as she finished the song.

As she curtsied, the cheering audience rose to their feet and James was stunned when Bertie jumped to his feet like the rest and clapped enthusiastically.

"Bravo! Bravo!" he cheered loudly.

"Did you enjoy yourself tonight, sir?" asked James as the carriage made its way back to the garrison through the countryside of Kildare.

"Yes, very much!" said Bertie who was smiling from ear to ear. "I'd never dreamed, never thought . . . I mean I'd obviously heard of those kind of music halls but I never imagined they could be so much fun!"

"They are a welcome release from the daily grind!" said James. "A place where a gentleman can go, have a few drinks and enjoy the show undisturbed."

"Oh, yes! So true. One isn't expected to chat or be diplomatic or impress anybody," said Bertie. "That girl, the actress –"

"Nellie Cliffden?"

"Yes, what a voice! Such a beautiful voice! And the way she spoke to the audience – I never heard the like of it from a woman!"

"Yes, Nellie is quite a character. The audiences love her."

"Yes, I could clearly see that . . . I never thought a woman could act in such a way. And yet she is so dainty and beautiful."

"She is even more beautiful close up," said James.

"Have you met her – in person?" asked Bertie, becoming excited at the idea.

"Oh yes, I've had occasion to meet Nellie socially."

"Really! And what is she like?"

"A very witty woman, beautiful, independent."

"Is she married?"

"No, she isn't."

"But she must have a fiancé or a beau . . ."

"Not that I am aware of. Nellie always struck me as being too independent to allow herself to enter into a relationship and risk being controlled by a man."

"Such independence – hard to fathom a woman being so independent," said Bertie.

James chuckled.

"What's so amusing?" asked Bertie.

"It's ironic to hear you say that, sir, when your mother is an empress!"

Bertie raised his eyebrows and nodded. "I suppose it is. But I don't view Her Majesty primarily as a woman, due to her being a monarch. And besides, she is not as independent as one might think, being controlled by governments and politicians and doing and saying what is expected of her . . . I should know more than anyone else in the world, for I alone was born to fill the same role."

Suddenly Bertie's good mood evaporated. His face creased in frowns and he looked as if he had the weight of the world on his shoulders again.

"Is anything the matter, sir?" asked James.

"It's just – your mention of my mother brought me crashing back to earth. My family are already in Dublin and will be visiting the garrison to watch what I have achieved here in a couple of days."

"But that is good, is it not? To see your family again and let them be proud of you in the field, commanding the garrison?"

"Let's be honest, James, I have not done well in my training. I can see the disappointment in Major Hazeldon's face when he has come to observe me. I greatly fear I will disgrace myself on the field in front of my parents."

"Nonsense, you will be excellent!"

"There is no need for you to flatter me like the other officers do, James. I am all too aware of my shortcomings."

As the carriage turned into the garrison, James said, "May I suggest, sir, that we rise considerably earlier than usual tomorrow and head out to the plains to do extra practice and training before the others are up? I will endeavour to tell you exactly where you are going wrong and where you need to improve – I will be brutally honest and refrain from any flattery."

"Would you, James? Would you do that? I sometimes think my training is being hampered by people fearing to tell me the truth."

The carriage pulled up outside the manor house.

"I shall collect you at five thirty in the morning and we shall head straight to the plains," said James.

"Oh, thank you, James. I cannot tell you how I appreciate this!"

Bertie stepped from the carriage and, smiling, headed into his quarters.

James's smiling face became thoughtful as the carriage took him back to his own quarters.

CHAPTER 20

The next day, after James had finished training with Bertie, he headed back to Dublin. He walked through the back door of the Palace Theatre and made his way through the corridors until he found what he was looking for. He had been backstage at the Palace many times visiting or collecting Nellie and so was familiar with the layout of the building. Not bothering to knock, he opened a door and walked into O'Brien's office. The manager was seated behind a desk and, looking up, was surprised to see James standing there.

"Captain Marton! I wasn't expecting you!"

"I can't imagine you were," said James, closing the door behind him and walking towards O'Brien's desk.

"Is anything the matter?"

"You could say that, O'Brien. I had occasion to be here at the Palace last night and I was surprised, nay, shocked to see Nellie Cliffden on the stage!"

O'Brien went red in the face. "Yes, well, I can explain –"

"Please do, because I thought we had come to an understanding?"

"I have cut Nellie's nights after our last conversation. She is working only two nights a week here now."

"But that is not the arrangement we came to. Why have you not severed all links with her as I requested?"

"Well, it's not that easy, Captain O'Brien. Nellie has been here at the Palace a long time. She's our most popular actress

135

here. To suddenly cut ties with her – well, the audience would be in uproar!"

"Actresses like Nellie are two a penny – she is easily replaceable," said James.

"That's not true – Nellie's –"

James suddenly raised the cane he was holding, swung it into the air above his head and brought it down on the desk in front of him hard, causing O'Brien to jump.

"We had an agreement, O'Brien," said James, his voice low and menacing. "You assured me Nellie Cliffden would be booted out of the Palace. I do not like when people go back on their word to me."

"I – I apologise, Captain Marton."

James walked closer and half-sat on the desk. "I told you what would happen if you did not get rid of Nellie. I said I would spread word to all the army personnel not to patronise this theatre again – that I would threaten any soldier found here with court martial. Let us see then how big your audiences are."

O'Brien nodded. "Rest assured, Captain Marton, Nellie Cliffden will not be appearing at the Palace again – not even for one night a week."

"Good. I am glad to hear that, O'Brien. And I think it is the safest thing for you and your theatre – I would hate for anything to happen here. Sometimes my soldiers can become rowdy when they drink too much. It wouldn't take much for a fight to break out and your theatre to get smashed up. That would be a shame, wouldn't it?"

"Sounds like a threat, Captain Marton," said O'Brien.

"More of a prediction than a threat, I would say. Do we understand each other?"

O'Brien nodded, "Perfectly."

"Good," James stood up and walked to the door. "And may I compliment you on the new waitress you have employed – a pleasure to deal with."

O'Brien stood up as James left the room. He quickly

walked to the door, closed it over and locked it. He then mopped the sweat that had broken out on his brow and tried to stop himself from trembling. He had been very stupid not to get rid of Nellie altogether when Marton paid him a visit before. He would give Nellie her marching orders when she came in for her next performance the next day. O'Brien didn't know what the nature of the relationship between Nellie and Marton was, but the officer was not going to let her go under any circumstances. O'Brien hoped for Nellie's sake she would manage to get away from him.

Nellie was in her dressing room, being prepared for that's night's performance.

"We don't have time for you to do my hair this evening, Sadie. Just fix me with one of my wigs," said Nellie.

"Are you sure?" asked Sadie.

"Yes, we still have to do my make-up," said Nellie.

Sadie combed Nellie's hair back into a tight bun and then fixed the wig with the exact same colour of Nellie's real hair on. Nellie often used a wig during her performances. It saved time and looked wonderful under the stage lights.

"O'Brien wants to see you, Nellie," called a stagehand as he hurried past her dressing-room door.

"What does he want now?" sighed Nellie as Sadie finished putting on her stage make-up.

"Better go and see," said Sadie, standing back and letting Nellie stand.

"Wish me luck!" said Nellie as she left.

She made her way to O'Brien's office. She knocked and entered.

"You wanted to see me, Mr. O'Brien?" she asked.

O'Brien looked up from his paperwork and gestured for her to shut the door.

He shook his head. "It's no use, Nellie, I have to let you go."

"Let me go!" She was shocked.

"I can't even have you do two nights here any more."

Nellie's eyes flashed in fury. "But why?"

"You know why, Nellie. Your friend has been back paying me a visit."

"James?" She whispered his name.

"Yes, Captain Marton. He was very unhappy to see you still on the stage. He gave me a stern warning that he'd see that my audiences would be halved if you were not dismissed altogether."

"*The bastard!*" Nellie's eyes filled with angry tears.

"He also made threats that he would have my theatre smashed up," said O'Brien solemnly.

"He *said* that?"

"It might be an empty threat but I'm not willing to take the chance. I have enough trouble, Nellie – I don't need an enemy like that. And neither do you, whatever you have done to upset him so."

"I haven't done anything to upset him, Mr. O'Brien, except try to get away from him," said Nellie.

O'Brien nodded. "I'm sorry, Nellie, but there's nothing I can do. I certainly don't want to lose you – I don't know how I'm going to replace you."

"I understand, Mr. O'Brien. Thank you for being honest." She turned to go.

"Nellie?"

"Yes?"

"Look after yourself. Be careful of that Marton man – he seems dangerous to me."

"Don't worry, Mr. O'Brien," said Nellie. "I can look after myself – I've been doing it all my life."

CHAPTER 21

The day before the royal family's arrival at the garrison in Kildare, there was a frenzied atmosphere as every button, boot, doorknob was polished. Every road, path and step was swept. Every horse groomed, very bayonet shone. Union Jack flags hung at full mast everywhere in the garrison. Victoria, Albert and their children Prince Alfred and the Princesses Alice and Helena were the most important visitors the camp had ever had and there was nothing that was left to chance for their visit.

Bertie invited his friends to his quarters that night and they sat playing poker. Bertie had never played poker in his life before arriving in Kildare and was amazed at how quickly he had picked it up. He now loved the game. He wished he had managed to pick up commanding a battalion half as well.

"If ever there was reason to have a dry night it's tonight," said Donald as he placed his cards down on the table.

"I would have thought if ever there was a need to have a whiskey it's tonight!" said Bertie.

"It would be very unwise for you to indulge," advised Charles. "You need a clear head tomorrow for Her Majesty's arrival."

"I know!" said Bertie.

"And I think we all should all get an early night so we are fully rested," said Charles.

"You make it sound like Christmas!" said Donald.

"Well, in a way it is a little like it, isn't it?" said Charles.

"I'll be under inspection and on best behaviour," said Bertie. "Hardly fun!"

"Speaking of fun –" Donald turned to Bertie, "the ladies were most disappointed you left the party early at Henrietta's, sir."

"Really?"

"Yes, they were quite taken with you and wished you had stayed longer," said Charles.

"Well, you two looked as if you had your hands full," said Bertie them.

"Well, no harm done," said Donald. "Just a little diversion."

"I think Bertie felt the situation was a little too exposed for somebody in his position," said James.

"Oh, we didn't mean to put you in any compromising position, sir," said Charles, feeling awkward.

"You didn't, Charlie. I appreciated the invitation. I just felt I shouldn't overstay my welcome – as tempting as it was to do so. Besides, as I said to you before, I imagine when my parents arrive tomorrow they will want to discuss my thoughts on my engagement to the Danish Princess – it wouldn't be right for me to stay talking to those women, when I am to be married to another."

The men nodded their understanding.

"Now, if you gentlemen will excuse me, I will retire to bed," said Bertie, standing.

"Yes, we shall all go," said Charles and they stood up.

"No, please, gentlemen – continue your game. You haven't nearly finished it by the looks of it. You won't be disturbing me. I'm a sound sleeper."

They sat again as he walked across the sitting room and into his bedroom, closing the door.

Bertie took off his tunic, sat on the side of his bed and rubbed his temples. He wished the following day was over.

140

He felt overwhelmed at the thought of being on the open Kildare plains, commanding a battalion in front of his parents. He turned off his light and stretched out on the bed. He could hear his friends in the sitting room talking in low voices, trying to keep quiet so as not to disturb him. After a while curiosity got the better of him and he got up from the bed and went to his door where he strained to hear. He could just about make out what they were saying next door.

"Poor Bertie – what a life! To be married to some foreign woman he hardly knows," said Donald.

"She might snore!" giggled Charles.

"She may have many more unpleasant habits than that!" said Donald.

"Well, we have tried our best, chaps, but if Bertie is intent on the life of a monk until he marries a bride chosen for him who he might not even like, then it is his choice," said Charles.

"It's not that he doesn't want to live his own life, but he feels he is restricted from doing so," said James.

"He is going to be king one day," said Donald. "If he can't even stand up to his own mother, how can he be the head of an empire?"

"Let's not be harsh – Bertie is merely putting duty before pleasure," said James.

"And Bertie can compliment himself on that when he is trapped in a loveless marriage for the rest of his life without ever knowing what a real woman or real love is like," said Donald.

With a heavy heart Bertie returned to his bed.

CHAPTER 22

Victoria stepped off the train in Kildare, followed by Albert and three of her children, Alfred, Alice and Helena, aged respectively seventeen, eighteen and fifteen. There was a company of soldiers awaiting them and an army band that started to play 'God Save the Queen'. The royal family stood in line on the platform until the band finished playing. It started raining as they made their way through the station to the waiting carriages.

"I thought Bertie had written to say that the weather was good and dry!" tutted Victoria to Albert as she reached the carriage.

"As in the case of all things with Bertie, weather reports should be taken with a pinch of salt!" said Albert.

As the carriages made their way through the countryside they saw that people had gathered at the sides of the road.

"Oh, look, Mama, they are so pleased to see us!" said Alice in delight, her big eyes wide in her oval face which was set off with a perfect pointed nose.

"They appear to be. They do look rather ragged. Not as well dressed as the peasantry in England," observed Victoria.

"Who cares how they are dressed as long as they are being welcoming to us," said Albert. "There were reports that a republican newspaper had urged the people to throw potatoes at the royal party as we pass!"

Victoria recoiled in horror. "Such brutish writings! To even imagine such a thing!"

She smiled at a group of cheering children, raised a hand and waved at them. "As you said, Albert, it is of little interest to us how they are dressed – as long as they do not fling potatoes at us!"

At the garrison the carriages came to a halt in the main forecourt and Victoria and her family were helped down.

A company of men was waiting and Victoria was greeted with another rendition of 'God Save the Queen'. Bertie stood beside Major Hazeldon and his fellow officers on the steps in front of the forecourt. He felt extremely nervous as he viewed his parents and family standing to attention as the band played. In the few weeks he had been stationed there, he felt he had changed. He hoped he had changed and he hoped his parents would see that change. That they might appreciate his abilities and consider him more deserving of respect and responsibility. Though even being in their company again seemed to make him regress. He felt intimidated. Particularly about the drill he was to perform in front of them.

"Your Majesty is most welcome!" said Hazeldon, stepping forward and saluting once the band had stopped playing.

"Major," nodded Victoria.

Bertie stepped forward and saluted. "Your Majesty."

Victoria nodded. "You are looking well, sir. Your time in Ireland has suited your complexion."

Bertie nodded. "Thank you."

"And if there is no objection from Her Majesty," said Major Hazeldon, "the company awaits its drill, to be commanded by the Prince of Wales."

"We are looking forward to viewing it, Major," said Victoria.

Bertie began to tremble as the moment of truth neared and preparations started for the company to travel to the plains outside the garrison.

The royal carriages were parked on the plains outside the camp as a battalion of soldiers stretched out before them.

Victoria and the royal family remained seated in the carriage as they looked on.

Bertie stood in front of the battalion to begin the drill.

"Bertie looks so handsome in his uniform!" said Helena, her usually serious face lit up with a smile.

"Yes, a uniform is guaranteed to make the most mundane-looking man look appealing," said Victoria.

"I'm so proud of him," said Alice.

"*Shhh!*" said Albert. "Let us pay attention to the drill."

"Sorry, Papa," said the princesses in unison.

"*Attention! Stand at ease! To the right! Advance! Halt! Left incline!*" Bertie's voice carried feebly across the plain.

Albert strained to hear his son's commands. More troubling was the fact the soldiers seemed to be straining to hear Bertie's voice too as they tried to follow orders, not always successfully. Suddenly the light rain that had been falling turned into a torrential downpour.

"Goodness!" cried Victoria as she struggled to open her umbrella.

The drivers of the carriage quickly raised the roof of the carriage to protect the royal family from the rain.

"Oh, now we can hardly see anything!" complained Victoria as they strained to look out at the drill.

"And I can't hear a word Bertie is saying now!" complained Alice, upset.

As Albert watched Bertie try to lead the battalion in the torrential rain, his voice barely audible over the downpour, he didn't know whether to feel sorry for or angry with his son.

"Rotten luck with the damned rain!" said Charles.

"Rotten luck!" agreed Donald.

"Indeed!" sighed Bertie, furious that the weather had not held out for the drill.

He was in his quarters with his friends. His parents and family were due to arrive soon to have tea there and meet his fellow officers. Tommy and three other batmen were hastily rushing around laying out food and checking that everything was in place.

"But you performed magnificently!" enthused Charles.

"Splendid job!" agreed James.

"Hardly, boys!" snapped Bertie. "I lost command of the battalion halfway through."

"Hardly lost command!" Donald objected.

"Well, what would you call it?" demanded Bertie.

"You're being too hard on yourself, sir – you performed well," said James.

"Just 'well' doesn't cut it with my family," Bertie said with a grimace.

"The rain would have thrown the best of us!" said Charles.

"And considering the limited amount of time you have been here and the intensive training you have received and been expected to master in such a short space of time, I'd say you have performed magnificently!" said Donald.

"*Here! Here!*" they all agreed loudly

The door of the quarters opened and they all quickly stood to attention as Major Hazeldon walked in with Victoria, Albert and the rest of the royal family.

Bertie stood and saluted like the rest of the officers.

"At ease," said Hazeldon and they all relaxed.

"Good day to you all," said Victoria as she approached them.

"Your Majesty!" they all greeted her in unison.

James stared at Victoria and felt he needed to pinch himself. The last few weeks had felt surreal for him. To be in the Prince of Wales' company so much and for him to befriend him had felt unreal to him. The other officers, though impressed, took it more in their stride. But James had at times felt overawed. The other officers did not come from the same background as he did, he knew. As the others had enjoyed Bertie's company, James had made it his business to get to know him. To know him as a person. That's what James did. He got to know people, got to know their strengths and their weaknesses. It had been his gift in life to be able to do so. He had used that gift through his life to manipulate and control people. With this stroke of luck of having the Prince stationed at the garrison at the same time he was, James had been given a golden opportunity that he had never dreamed of. An opportunity to get to know and befriend the Prince of Wales. He had carefully and shrewdly befriended him. He hadn't stood out from the other officers. He had not tried to be a special friend to the Prince. James was sure that such action would quickly be seen through by the Prince and the others. But he had always been the one there at the end of an evening to listen to Bertie's problems and offer subtle advice. Slowly gaining his confidence and trust. It was a relationship now secured that he would not surrender easily.

But now here he was in front of the Queen. As Hazeldon introduced her and the royal family to the officers, James maintained a serious conscientious look on his face. As the other officers smiled and grinned, James made sure to come across as sincere and trustworthy.

"We are famished!" said Victoria as she sat down on the couch.

"You must excuse our rough arrangements and simple fare," said Charles.

"It will be rather like a picnic, I'm afraid," said Bertie.

"One must expect manly arrangements and fare in a garrison!" said Albert with a smile.

Cups and saucers, plates, cutlery and napkins were already set out on occasional tables positioned next to each guest. Charles signalled to the batmen and they began to circulate, first with pots of tea, jugs of milk and bowls of sugar, then with trays of sandwiches. The officers eyed the batmen anxiously, afraid of blunders brought on by nervousness. However, all went reasonably well.

146

"I trust Her Majesty has enjoyed her time in Ireland so far?" asked Charles politely when everyone had been served tea and food.

"Quite so! It is good to be back in this part of our Kingdom. But the changes are immense."

"How so, Your Majesty?" asked Donald.

"There are far fewer people than there were on my previous visits. We remember travelling through the countryside before and being struck by the large population. Now, great swathes of the countryside are empty. One can travel for miles without seeing a house or a person. Alas, the Famine seems to have changed the landscape!"

"It has all been very difficult," agreed Hazeldon.

"But the last occasion we visited Ireland was in 1853, a good three years after the Famine finally ended, and we do not recall the countryside being quite so empty on that occasion."

"There have since then been hundreds of thousands of people who have emigrated to escape the poverty left in the wake of the Famine," said James.

"You seem to know a lot about the situation, young man," said Albert.

"Yes, Your Royal Highness. My family are from County Meath and so I am a countryman, so to speak," smiled James.

"I see," said Albert.

"That is why the royal visit is so important right now. To help bring industry and investment to the country," said James.

"Indeed," said Albert, moving closer to him. "What is your opinion of the state of industry in Ireland at present?"

"It's in a sorry state, sir. Although I do know Ireland does not have the raw materials that England has, I do think so much more can be done. For example – I am a great admirer of the Great Exhibition that you organised in London, Your Royal Highness."

"Were you a visitor at the exhibition?" asked Albert.

"I certainly was," lied James. "I was very young at the time but I was enthralled by it. I do believe that if a similar exhibition could be arranged in Dublin, the benefits would be tremendous for Ireland."

"A Great Exhibition in Dublin," pondered Albert aloud. "Indeed – yes."

Albert sat down across the desk from Major Hazeldon in his office.

"I would like to express again how privileged we are that you and Her Majesty have visited us today in the Curragh. It is a great honour," said Hazeldon.

"Yes, we have much enjoyed our visit. It is unfortunate the rain was so torrential," said Albert.

"Yes, well, rain is never too far away in Ireland."

"So I believe. It was difficult for us to fully judge the Prince of Wales' performance due to the rain. How would you judge it?"

"Oh, very good, Your Royal Highness," said Hazeldon.

"Not exemplary?" asked Albert.

"The Prince has been a very diligent student and has given his all to his training. It has been a pleasure to have him here."

"Would you say he has a glowing career ahead of him in the military?"

"I – I – it is hard to make such judgements when the Prince has been with us so little time. But he has shown himself to be more than capable in carrying out his duties."

"*Hmmm* – there seemed to be some confusion during the drill today. Some soldiers seemed unable to carry out Bertie's orders?"

Hazeldon looked affronted. "Any failing to carry out orders is not the fault of my soldiers here who are the very best in the world, Your Royal Highness."

"In that case the confusion must have originated from my son's instructions?" said Albert.

Hazeldon opened his mouth to speak and then closed it again. As he looked at Albert's stern face, he realised he was hanged if he did tell the truth and hanged if he didn't. Clearly, the mistakes that were made during the drill had been noted by Albert and he was determined to discover whose fault it was. Hazeldon decided it was better to tell the truth. He did not want the Royal family to leave Kildare with the impression that his troops were disorderly, untrained or undisciplined.

"Your Royal Highness, as I said, the troops here are the best in the world. The Prince of Wales has been a pleasure to have here and is greatly admired and respected by all. However, in my opinion, he lacks the natural ability to be a first-class officer. His voice lacks authority and does not carry well, especially in the rain as we experienced today. He also would not have a first-class memory for the run of things, often stumbles over orders, and can be easily distracted." Hazeldon finished speaking and set his mouth in a thin tight line before adding, "In short, I would not like to see the Prince ever being entrusted to lead a company of men into battle."

"I see," said Albert, standing up. "Well, I thank you for your honesty."

"It is meant with the kindest of intentions," said Hazeldon who stood and saluted.

"I thank you again for all the kindness you have shown to our son," said Albert as he turned and walked out of the office.

Later that evening, alone with his parents in the sitting room of his quarters, Bertie noticed Victoria look at Albert and nod at him.

Albert cleared his throat before speaking, "Bertie, your mother and I wonder whether you have given any more thought to the Princess Alexandra?"

"I must admit that I haven't, Papa," said Bertie.

A look of despair came over Victoria face as she raised her

149

eyes to heaven and demanded, "Why in heaven's name haven't you?"

"Well, I haven't been given much time to think about any such matters, so intense was the training I have received here," said Bertie.

"And a welcome distraction to exclude thinking of more important matters, no doubt," said Victoria.

"Really, Bertie!" said Albert. "We would have expected much more of you. Why else do you think that we permitted you to come here and receive your military training – was it not that it would give you some time away to think and make up your mind about whom you wish to marry!"

"Vicky says you will do no better than Princess Alexandra," said Victoria.

"Oh, well, if Vicky says it's fine then it must be!" said Bertie sarcastically. "But I'm afraid Vicky is not the one who will be married to the Princess Alexandra and have to live with her for the rest of her days!"

"I don't know what is to become of you!" said Victoria, "When you are presented with an ideal woman as a wife, you dither and dather like a fool!"

"Well, if a man cannot take time to decide whom he wants to marry, then what hope is there for us all?" demanded Bertie.

"Indeed – what hope! What exactly is the problem with Alexandra that you have apparently noticed but none of the rest of us have?" demanded Victoria.

"I am not saying there is any problem with her," said Bertie. "But I do not know her! And she does not know me."

"Thank heavens for that!" said Victoria under her breath.

"How can I be expected to commit to somebody I have not yet met?" said Bertie.

"But we are asking for your consent to arrange a meeting!" said Albert. "That should decide the matter – your mother and I knew we were right for each other the moment we met."

150

"Well, you and Mama were very lucky," said Bertie.

"And not only did we know we were right for each other," said Victoria, "but our love developed and grew over the years. This too is what can happen for you and Alexandra."

"Will you consent to meet her?" asked Albert.

"I – I need more time," said Bertie, becoming stressed.

"Time waits for no man, Bertie, even the Prince of Wales," said Victoria. "We had very much hoped that you would have reached your decision by now and are very disappointed in you that you haven't."

Bertie became angry. "Have you not seen how hard I have worked here? Are you not proud of what I have achieved?"

"But what have you achieved?" Victoria's anger bubbled. "Your performance today commanding the company was lacklustre, to say the least."

Bertie's face fell.

"And Major Hazeldon commended your efforts but left no doubt in my mind that you lacked the real ability of a first-class officer," said Albert.

"Major Hazeldon said that?" Bertie's mouth opened in shock as his eyes became misty with hurt. "But I've worked so hard and the men – I've worked so hard to be one of them."

"Do not misunderstand me, Bertie. Major Hazeldon said you were perfectly adequate," said Albert quickly.

"But the Prince of Wales is meant to be so much more than merely adequate," said Victoria. "The Prince of Wales is meant to be a leader – a shining example of leadership!"

"Major Hazeldon did, in fairness, commend your ability to fit in and said you were very popular here with the troops and officers," conceded Albert. "But left me in no doubt that you lack leadership qualities."

"I – I don't know what to say," said Bertie, disheartened.

"The reality is, Bertie, that it is all very nice to be well liked but being a king is not a popularity contest – we leave that to our prime ministers in their elections," said Victoria. "Being a monarch is all about leadership and strength. To be a constant in everchanging times for one's subjects. A rock of stability to changing governments. A figure of unwavering stability in an otherwise shifting uncertain world."

"I realise that, but –" began Bertie.

"That is why you should be married to a strong woman who can give you that strength and why we are so in favour of Alexandra," said Albert. "Your time here has proven to us to again that your character is . . ." Albert searched for the right word.

"*Weak?*" suggested Victoria.

"Indecisive," corrected Albert.

Bertie rose to his feet, his face red with anger. "I will never be good enough for you, will I?"

"*Bertie – remember yourself!*" ordered Albert.

"I do remember myself! I remember everything. The constant disapproval, the constant remarks, the constant – *can do b-b-better!*" spluttered Bertie.

"And now we resort to temper tantrums!" sighed Victoria.

"Bertie, if we push you it is only so that you can realise your full potential," said Albert.

"But, do you not see, Papa, this *is* my full potential and my full potential is not good enough for you!" Bertie ran his hands through his hair. "I do not know what you expect of me, but I do know your expectations are too high. And I am tired of living in your shadow, your constant disapproval!"

"We fear that this spell in Ireland has only added insolence to your failings, Bertie," said Victoria.

"My failings! My failings are my own business and I will not be judged by you any more!" said Bertie and he stormed out of the room.

Victoria and Albert looked at each other.

"Words fail me!" said Victoria.

"I hope we didn't push him too far?" said Albert.

152

"In my opinion we have not pushed him far enough. That is the trouble with Bertie – he has been allowed too much of his own way," said Victoria as she slapped her hands down on her lap in frustration. "And what are we now to write to Vicky on the subject of Alexandra? The poor girl has been left hanging yet again on a thread, unsure if she is to be the future Queen of England or not!"

CHAPTER 23

After returning from Kildare to Dublin, the royal party was due to travel to Killarney for the next stage of their tour of Ireland.

Bertie was unenthusiastic about joining his family for the trip. He realised how attached he had become to the garrison in Kildare as he left it to get the train to Dublin. If he felt this lonely when he was leaving the garrison for a few short days, he wondered how dreadful it would be in three weeks when the time came to leave the garrison for good and return to his life in England. The idea of being trapped over the next few days with his parents was distressing. Especially after the last conversation he had with them. He knew himself that he had not performed his duties on the drill with excellence, but he felt shame at it being pointed out so candidly by his parents. Not that he expected anything less – they had made it a mission in life to point out his shortcomings. And in their minds, his shortcomings gave them licence to command him to do what they wanted with the rest of his life.

He met with his family in Dublin and, as they made the journey to Killarney on the royal train, the atmosphere was stilted between him and his parents. He occupied himself on the journey by reading and writing in his diary as the others chatted. The train slowed as it passed through villages and towns where crowds had gathered to wave and get a glimpse of the royal family. Dutifully the family waved to the crowds as they passed by.

"The women are handsome if rather dishevelled-looking," commented Victoria as she gave the royal wave to the onlookers as they passed through Tipperary.

"How they must have suffered during the Famine," sighed Alice. "I think if I had been of age at the time I would have come to Ireland to assist with the hospitals and charitable works."

Victoria raised her eyes to heaven. "You are a goodhearted girl, Alice, but it is hardly the place of a royal princess to be assisting in hospitals."

"Why ever not, Mama? When I am married to Prince Louis, I plan to spend much time improving the hospitals in the Grand Duchy of Hesse and doing charitable works. My friend Florence Nightingale has kindly offered to advise me on the works I intend to carry out there."

"Alice, never forget the public expect royalty to maintain a distance from them. There should always be an air of mystery – what mystery can there be about a princess seen emptying bedpans?"

"I think Alice is quite right," said Bertie.

"Do you indeed, Bertie?" said Victoria, sarcastically.

"Times are changing, Mama, and people expect more from us than just being remote figures living in ivory towers," said Bertie. "I experienced it on my tour of Canada and America."

"Did you indeed?"

"Yes, people expect to have access to the royals and for us to be seen as one of them – somebody they can admire but can talk to," said Bertie.

"The common touch, I expect is what you are referring to," said Victoria as she turned from her children and gave the crowd another wave.

Suddenly she took out a handkerchief and began to dab her eyes as tears sprang up and began to trickle down her cheeks.

"Are you all right, Mama?" asked Alice, rushing to her side.

"I am just thinking of your poor grandmother – how she would have loved to be here with us," said Victoria as she quickly wiped away her tears.

"Oh, Mama!"

"I think I shall go for a lie-down before we arrive in Killarney. I am tired." She rose from her seat.

Bertie put down his book and stood up.

"I will assist you," he said, taking her arm.

She smiled at him. "Thank you, dear Bertie."

Bertie walked his mother to the next carriage and then returned to the others.

"Is she all right?" asked Albert.

"A bit teary," said Bertie.

"Poor Mama!" sighed Alice.

"Your grandmother's death has hit her very hard," said Albert. "Sometimes she has sunk into such a depression that I worry about her."

"I didn't realise she was still suffering so," said Bertie.

"Your mother is not as hard as she appears," said Albert. "That is why we must all do whatever we can to help her and try to make her happy."

The royal party arrived in Kerry and spent the first night in Kenmare House. The following day they travelled to Muckross House on the stunning shores of Muckross Lake for what was the highlight of the tour. The owners of the house were on the steps to greet the royal family and all the servants stood on the forecourt in line as a welcoming party.

"Your Majesty, I cannot tell you how much we are honoured," said Colonel Henry Herbert as he bowed.

"It is our great pleasure to be here," smiled Victoria.

Colonel Herbert was especially delighted to see Bertie who had stayed at the house on his previous trip in 1858.

"Welcome back, your Royal Highness," smiled Colonel Herbert.

"It's good to be back, Colonel," said Bertie happily.

As Bertie and Alice walked into the house, she whispered, "I believe the Herbert family have gone to such expense to host us that they are risking financial ruin!"

"Oh dear, what a calamity!" said Bertie, distressed that the Herbert family had put themselves under such pressure.

"They are paying a dear price to secure their social standing and their place in history," said Alice.

That night, Bertie sat at the window in his room, looking out at the lake under the moonlit sky, smoking a cigarette. The place was so beautiful and tranquil he was lost in his thoughts. Just three more weeks in Ireland and then he would return to his normal life. He decided he would make the most of it while he was there. He would never have this opportunity again. As he thought of Donald and his married mistress and the glamorous Clarissa he had rejected, his envy suddenly turned to excitement. Why should he be different from them? Why should he be denied the life his officer friends were leading?

Bertie strolled along the lakeshore with Alice. He always loved when he had time alone with her. He was only eighteen months older than her and so they had been very close when growing up. She was known for her caring nature and Bertie always felt he had a sympathetic ear with her, somebody who understand his problems and how he thought. She didn't intimidate him like his elder sister Vicky and he never felt he was in competition with her like he was with Vicky. Now Alice was engaged she would soon be going to live in the Grand Duchy of Hesse where she would be married to Prince Louis, heir to the throne there.

"Isn't it so beautiful here, Bertie? I never imagined a place could be so beautiful. When you told me so after your last visit here, you were not exaggerating." She looked across the still lake at the trees and mountains on the other side.

"Yes, it is a place where one feels strangely cut off from the rest of the world," he said, his hands clasped behind his back.

"I wish Hesse was as beautiful as this. If it were, I think I should have no problem going to live there and falling in love with my new home."

"My little sister is to be married! I can scarcely believe it. I will miss you terribly."

"We can write all the time, Bertie, and visit," she said.

"But it won't be the same, will it? How often do we see Vicky now that she has moved to Berlin?"

"That's what growing up means, Bertie – getting married and having families and homes of our own . . . though I do not know where in Hesse is to be my home. They cannot decide where we are to live. There is considerable opposition from the good people of Hesse to spending too much money on a residence for the future heir to the Grand Duchy and his new English wife. Despite the fact that Mama has given a dowry of thirty thousand pounds for me to the Grand Duchy, and with it being a small rather undeveloped country the money is very much needed. I fear that I am to become the poor relation when I marry Louis!"

Bertie looked at his sister. "But I thought that the match had the approval of all concerned, particularly Mama and Papa?"

"It does. Louis has the full royal approval, but it still doesn't alter the fact that the royal house of Hesse is a relatively poor one." She gave a little laugh. "It is typical that Vicky will be the Empress of Prussia and I the wife of an impoverished neighbouring Grand Duke!"

"But you do love him, Vicky? You do love Louis?" Bertie asked.

"Oh, yes. I know our courtship was brief before our engagement, but I adore him. I know we'll have a very happy marriage."

"Then you are fortunate, like Mama and Papa have been in their marriage. Mama has always said she wants her children to marry for love, like she did. But how can this be possible when we are presented with such a small pool to choose from?" said Bertie, his frustration bubbling to the surface. "I mean there are so many people in the world and we could fall in love with any of them and yet we are prevented from doing so and instead are presented with a small group of foreign royals and instructed we must fall in love with one of them!"

"But it makes sense, Bertie. How could somebody who is not royal ever hope to fit into our ways or us into theirs? We are a unique group of people and only one of us can ever hope to really understand what is expected of the other."

"Well, Mama and Papa made sure our upbringing at Osbourne House was not in any way ostentatious. We were given a normal middle-class upbringing, few luxuries. They prided themselves on presenting a middle-class lifestyle to the people. I cannot understand Mama and Papa. They have made sure to give us a normal upbringing and to be dutiful and conscientious and like everyone else and then when it comes to marriage we are suddenly told we are not like everybody else, but royal, and cannot marry anybody who is not one of us. I mean, we are not even permitted to marry into the English aristocracy as they are not considered good enough."

Alice stopped walking, forcing Bertie to do the same. "Something's happening to you, Bertie. You've never spoken like this before."

"Well, I think you are right, something has happened to me. My time in Ireland has allowed me to think for myself. It has allowed me to meet new people, wonderful people whose company I enjoy. Interesting, exciting people who make me feel alive. And who are far more fun to be around than some stuffy foreign royal!"

"Bertie! You shouldn't say such things! Most of those people you are dismissing are our relatives!"

Bertie began to walk on at a quick pace with Alice struggling to keep up with him.

"I say it because it's true! My eyes have been opened and I think I shall never be able to go back to who I was, living my life on Papa's terms. Do you know that I never even spoke to a woman properly until I came to Ireland? As in, had a proper conversation that wasn't stifled and supervised and controlled. I never had a proper drink or had a game of poker or stretched out on a beautiful summer's day drinking a beer while watching a game of cricket!"

"Poker! Beer! You mustn't let Papa ever know you did such things!" pleaded Alice.

"Of course I won't – do you think I am mad? I just wish that you too could have had the chance to experience real life before you are married off to a life of drudgery in some foreign land!"

Bertie stopped walking and turned to her.

"I don't see it as a life of drudgery," Alice said, looking hurt. "It's the life I want. I want to do good things like Papa has done. I want to improve hospitals and care for the ill in my new country."

"Oh, Alice!" he said, putting his arms around her. "And you shall do all those things! Maybe the problem is with me. Maybe I have a restless nature. Maybe I am to be never satisfied and always looking for the next excitement."

"These feelings you have will pass, Bertie. You will become satisfied with your life and your role. You won't be looking for poker games or beer but will be content to dedicate your life to duty and for the good of your people."

He smiled at her. "Perhaps you're right . . . Come, dear Alice, it will soon be dark and we had better return to Muckross House."

"We have made a decision," said Victoria to Bertie as she and Albert sat on a couch in their sitting room in Muckross House.

"And what is that, Mama?" Bertie asked, dreading to hear the answer.

"Once you have finished your training in Kildare in three weeks' time, you are to travel to the court in Prussia to visit your sister Vicky."

"I see," said Bertie.

"And where you will be formally introduced to Princess Alexandra."

Bertie stood in silence as his face went red from anger.

"I shall write to Vicky as soon as we return to England to inform her to make the necessary arrangements," said Victoria.

"And do I have a say in this?" asked Bertie.

"No," said Albert. "Your time here in Ireland has demonstrated to us that there is no point in wasting any more time on matrimonial matters."

"I have not wasted my time here!" said Bertie angrily.

"That is a matter of opinion!" said Albert, becoming angry as well. "The fact is, we gave you what you wanted. You have been allowed your time in the military, and now you must get on with your life as the Prince of Wales."

Bertie stood in silence, barely able to conceal his anger.

"If it were left to you, dear Bertie, at eighty years of age you would still be dithering about who should be your wife!" said Victoria.

"May I go?" Bertie asked.

"Indeed you may!" said Victoria.

Bertie swung around and marched out of the room.

CHAPTER 24

Nellie sat in her bedroom at her dressing table, staring at her image in the mirror. She did not know what to do. Since O'Brien had sacked her from the Palace she had been consumed with a feeling of panic. And anger towards James for what he had done to her. She had made enquiries to other theatres and music halls about positions but, as O'Brien had warned, James had badmouthed her everywhere and she was not wanted. She had made a bad enemy in James and now she desperately was thinking of ways that she could get through this. She opened her jewellery box and started sifting through her items. She could sell these pieces and they would buy her some time, but not much time. She tried to be strong. She had been in far worse positions in her life and she had got through them. But then she always had James before. Now she was on her own.

There was a knock on the flat door and Sadie went to answer it.

"Good afternoon, Sadie, is Nellie at home?" asked James as he walked past her into the sitting room.

"Well, you have a cheek to show your face around here!" spat Sadie.

"Why?" he asked innocently.

"You know why, and you know that I know why!"

"I don't know what you are talking about."

"You know full sure what I'm talking about. Why are you

162

doing this to her? What has she ever done to you?" demanded Sadie.

"Oh, get off your high horse, Sadie. A high horse does not suit somebody as low as you. I don't know what you are being judgemental about – you are as guilty of living off her immoral earnings as I am."

"But she wants to leave that life behind now, and you aren't letting her!" accused Sadie.

"Why should she leave the life she was meant for?" said James.

"Why, you – if I were a man I'd hit you!"

"Well, you aren't a man, and I wouldn't advise that you try to hit me whether you be a man or a woman. Now, stop wasting my time – is she here?"

"She's in her bedroom," said Sadie.

"Well, fetch her! I haven't got all day!"

Sadie gave him a dirty look and walked off down the corridor. She knocked on Nellie's door and entered the room.

"Sorry, Nellie, but he's here – Captain Marton is in the sitting room and wants to see you."

Nellie swung around. "What does he want?"

"He didn't say," said Sadie.

Nellie sat in thought before getting up. "All right, Nellie, I'll see him."

"I'll go with you," said Sadie, following her out the door.

"No, Sadie. Stay in the kitchen. I'll be all right."

"If he tries anything, just shout!"

Nellie nodded and walked down the corridor and into the sitting room where James was standing beside the window.

"Nellie! You look lovely today!" he said, with a smile.

She walked straight across the room to him and slapped him hard across the face.

He put a hand to where she had hit him and rubbed his cheek. "I'll give you that one. But you would be very unwise to try it again."

"What are you doing here?" she demanded.

"Well, I've come to see how you are getting on."

"You know very well how I'm getting on since you got me fired from the Palace and badmouthed me around town," she said.

"Yes, well, I thought I'd have heard from you before now."

"Heard from me! The only reason you'd have heard from me was if I'd arrived down in Kildare with a gun to shoot you!"

"Oh, Nellie, that temper of yours! It's getting out of hand – you really need to control it before it gets you into trouble."

"What do you want, James?"

"I want to know what your plans are, now you have retired from the Palace?"

"None of your business!" she spat.

"But I worry about you – how are you going to afford to live from now on?"

"Ha! Worry about me? The only thing you've ever worried about is your pocket, you miserable bastard! Get out of here, or I'll get that poker from the fireplace and the damage I did to that house in Dalkey will be nothing to what I do to you!"

He started laughing.

Her mouth dropped open at his audacity. She turned and marched to the fireplace, picked up the poker and raised it in the air. "Do you doubt me?"

"Nellie, Nellie, Nellie! This is a fine welcome I get. I come all the way here to help you and I get threatened with a poker!"

"How could you possibly want to help me? When all you've done is try and destroy me?"

"Just put the poker down and hear me out – for five minutes – that's all I ask."

She stared at him in fury and then lowered the poker.

"Well?" she demanded.

"Nellie, I never wanted to cause you any harm or upset –"

"Ha! You've a funny way of showing it!"

"I want to put things right between us," he said.

"Then get your sorry arse down to the Palace and tell O'Brien to hire me back!"

"Well, I can't do that," he said.

She raised the poker again.

"Nellie, you haven't given me five minutes yet," he reminded her.

"Well, get on with it!"

"Put down the poker first – you're making me nervous."

She dropped the poker.

"Thank you," he said. "Look, Nellie, you gave me a terrible shock when you said you wouldn't work for me any more. I mean – imagine how I felt? I had come to rely on the money we earned –"

"*I* earned," she interrupted.

"You earned. I have a lot of debts and living expenses and you've left me in a bit of a pickle."

"That's your pickle, not mine."

"I need you to do something for me," he said.

"My days of doing things for you are over. I know what all this is about, James. You're trying to force me to go back to work for you. And it's not going to work. I don't know what I'm going to do, but I'm not going back to that life again."

"I'm not asking you to return to that life," he said.

"You're not?" she said, relieved but not trusting him for a moment.

"No. But I do want you to meet somebody for me."

She threw her hands into the air. "Then you *are* asking me to return to that life!"

"No, this is different. This man is like no other that you have met before or ever will again. I just want you to meet this man and it is important that you please him. My future relies on it."

165

"I can't believe you."

"If you do this one last thing for me, I will leave you alone. I will visit O'Brien and insist he rehires you at a much higher salary. I will also pay you handsomely for the time you spend with this man."

"*You'll* pay me! What kind of a job is this?"

"As I said, it's like no other. But if you do your job right, you'll never look back and I'll never bother you again. You have my word."

"Not that your word ever counted for much." Nellie paused and considered. "So who is this man that's so important to you?"

He stared at her before he spoke. "The Prince of Wales."

She was stunned into silence.

"I want you to meet the Prince of Wales," he confirmed.

"Are you joking me? I can't meet the Prince of Wales! And I'm sure he has no interest in meeting me!"

"You're quite wrong, Nellie. He has seen you."

"Seen me? How?"

"I brought him to the Palace on the last night of your performance there. He was quite taken with you, I can assure you."

"You are talking bullshit as usual." She gave a harsh laugh.

He came towards her and spoke earnestly. "I've never been more serious, Nellie. He was totally taken with you. Asked so many questions about you. He was shocked when I told him I knew you."

"And he wanted to meet me?" Nellie was incredulous.

"Not exactly – we didn't discuss the prospect. But I have become quite friendly with him and I've learned to read him –"

"Yes, you're good at reading people to your own advantage," said Nellie.

"I know if I engineered a meeting with you he would quickly fall for your charms."

"You are being ridiculous, James. He's the Prince of Wales, he would have no interest in a woman like me."

"You're wrong, Nellie. The Prince is nothing like you would imagine him to be. He's battling with his role in life, unsure of his position and has very little experience of women except royal princesses and countesses. He's never met a woman like you and that is what attracts him to you."

"You've got it all worked out!"

"I just know that if he met you and spent some time with you, he'd really like you."

"This is madness! I wouldn't know what to say to a Prince or how to behave with him."

"But that's the very thing, Nellie. You just be yourself and, of course, demonstrate all the etiquette and manners that I have taught you over the years. I mean, the beauty of you is that you can act like a lady even though you are very far from one."

"Does he know what I am? Does he know what I've done?"

"No, of course not. Telling him you are a prostitute is one step too far for a royal prince. He must never know that about you. He would be shocked and insulted. No – you are Nellie Cliffden, famous actress of the stage. It appears odd, but Bertie is impressed and spellbound by such things. His background has been so stuffy and regimented that he appears to be quite blown away by anything glamorous and by show business."

"Bertie!" She repeated his name in wonder.

"It won't be like the other jobs you've done for me, Nellie. Bertie will not know that you are there for the purpose you are there for. You will charm him, romance him and ultimately seduce him."

"And what is in this for you, James?"

"Isn't it obvious? I have become friends with the Prince of Wales. I've been given this opportunity to become part of his inner circle and I don't want to lose that. Being a friend and confidant of the Prince of Wales will give me opportunities that I could only ever dream of before. If I introduce him to his first love, what better way can I cement our friendship?"

"His first love? I think you are overestimating the role I can play in the Prince's life!" she said.

"I want him to thoroughly enjoy his last weeks in Ireland and I want to be the one responsible for that. I have a future here, an opportunity. If I can ingratiate myself a little more with Bertie, then I expect when he leaves for England I shall be leaving with him."

"Leaving for England?" she asked.

"Yes. I aim for Bertie to recommend me for a transfer to Aldershot and a promotion and perhaps even an official role in his royal staff as an equerry. And you are the key to achieving that, Nellie. I'm done with draughty barracks in Kildare and constant rain during drills. I want to move up in the world and Bertie is my chance."

Nellie walked towards the window and looked out. "So – I am to sing your praises to – Bertie – and encourage him to promote you?"

"Yes."

"And what becomes of me after? When the Prince had returned to his life in England and you've moved on to greater things?"

"Well, then you are left alone to live your life in any way you choose. As I said, you will be reinstated at the Palace Theatre and, if all goes according to plan, I will pay you handsomely."

"And then you will never bother me again?" she asked.

"I promise I will leave you alone. I'll never make contact with you or interfere in your life again. By the end of September, you will just be a footnote in mine – and the Prince's – lives."

Nellie stared out the window for a long while before turning around.

"All right, I'll do it," she said.

"Excellent!" said James, delighted.

"But if you double-cross me, James, I swear –"

"I will not double-cross you, Nellie, I promise."

"So – what is the plan? How and where am I to meet – Bertie?"

"He is in Killarney at the moment with the rest of the royal family. He was not too happy about going. The drill he performed before his parents wasn't too successful and they constantly belittle him and undermine him."

"I see!" said Nellie, shocked and hardly believing she was hearing this information about the royal family.

"Since Bertie has come to Kildare, he has seen another side of life that has been kept from him – he enjoys partying, gambling, drinking and – which is where you come in – women."

"No doubt you have been the Prince's educator in all these vices – that's what you do, isn't it, James? That's what you did to me."

James smirked. "Well, Nellie, if I can corrupt the Prince of Wales, then what chance did you ever have with me?"

"Indeed," said Nellie soberly. "What chance does any of us have?"

"So – I imagine when Bertie returns from Killarney he is going to feel despondent and somewhat depressed at his family's treatment of him and the fact his time in Ireland is nearly over. So, I am going to suggest a party – where you, my dear, will be the guest of honour."

"Me the guest of honour at a party for the Prince of Wales!" Nellie rolled her eyes.

"I will be in contact with you soon with the arrangements." James walked over to her and put his hands on her shoulders. "I am so glad we are to be friends again." He smiled down at her. "I've missed you, Nellie." He bent and placed a kiss on her neck.

She moved away from him. "I just want this over with as soon as possible and you out of my life."

"And that, I promise you, will happen. But, in the meantime, try to enjoy yourself. What an honour for you! You are going to dance with the Prince of Wales!"

More than that, thought Nellie ruefully.

James walked to the door and gave her a smile before leaving the flat.

Nellie stood still, trying to comprehend what had just happened.

Sadie came rushing down the corridor. She had been listening to every word.

"You're not going to do it, are you, Nellie?" she demanded, looking horrified.

"What choice do I have?"

"Don't do it, Nellie! It can only end badly for you. You can't get involved with the Prince of Wales! It's too dangerous. Men as powerful as that are to be avoided by women like you. He will use you and destroy you."

"I've met quite a few important men and none of them have destroyed me yet," said Nellie. "In fact, the man most likely to destroy me has just walked out that door – but I'll make sure he has little chance of doing that!"

"But this is different, Nellie. You'll be out of your depth with a royal. He'll eat you up and spit you out and you don't know what the consequences will be for you."

"Sadie, this is the only way I can get my job at the Palace back and make sure we don't have to leave the flat here and face a future – well, I don't know what future we will have if I don't do what James tells me."

Sadie looked at Nellie, her face creased with worry. "I hope you know what you are doing, Nellie."

"I don't know what I am doing, Sadie, but I have no choice."

CHAPTER 25

Bertie smiled broadly as he entered his quarters at the garrison in Kildare.

"Oh, it's good to be back!" he declared. "I never thought that I would say that about a garrison after a few days in the lap of luxury in Muckross House, looking out at the stunning views of the lakes of Killarney!"

"It's good to have you back, sir," said James. "We certainly missed you around here."

"Did you?" Bertie was surprised.

"Of course, sir – you have become the life and soul of the party!"

Bertie looked chuffed at hearing this. "Well, I've been very lucky to meet such a fine bunch of chaps. Especially you, James. You've been such a support to me – listening to my problems and tales of woe!"

"I am only glad I could be of some help, sir."

Bertie flung himself down on the couch and lit up a cigar. "And now I am told that once I leave here I am to travel to Prussia to meet the Danish Princess. No choice, it's a royal order."

"Oh!" James pulled a face and sat down in the armchair opposite him. "What a rotten business, sir."

"Certainly is a rotten business being a prince. Forced into marrying somebody I do not even know. But, chin up, I'm going to make the best of the rest of the time I have here. You know, if Donald invites me to another soirée at Henrietta Fitzgibbons, I think I would be delighted to go and next time might even enjoy myself! You might have a word with him, would you? Tell him I am game?"

"Of course, sir. In fact, speaking of ladies, I was speaking to one recently who was quite taken with you," said James.

Bertie sat up straight. "Really? Who?"

"The actress, Miss Nellie Cliffden," said James.

"Nellie Cliffden? The woman on the stage at the Palace that night? But I didn't meet her."

"No, but she spotted you from the stage. She was asking me who was that fine man I was with that night."

"Really?" Bertie's eyes were wide with excitement. "Did you tell her who I was?"

"No, I thought discretion was called for, sir."

"Of course, indeed," nodded Bertie.

"But she was extremely interested in you. Wanted to know who you were. I said you were just a visiting officer from England. But it didn't dampen her interest in you. I've known Nellie a long time and I've never heard her being so taken with a man before."

"Gosh – how flattering!"

"She asked if she could meet you."

"*Really?*"

"But I said it was quite out of the question."

"Oh!" Bertie's face dropped in disappointment.

"I mean, the Prince of Wales can't be seen out in town with a young lady, even as celebrated an actress as Nellie Cliffden. It could draw gossip."

"Yes, I hate gossip. But what of Nellie? I mean, I'd hate to disappoint her if she is so bent on meeting me – and, if the truth be known, I think I would be quite interested in meeting her too. She seemed so captivating!"

"Well, I would hate to stand in your way," said James. "Let me think about it. As I said, it's too risky to be seen in public. Maybe if we organised an evening here at your quarters? We

172

could have the other officers here too and maybe a couple of their friends. Nobody could say anything then, could they?"

"No – that's a great idea. Apart from Major Hazeledon – if he found out we had smuggled in women, he might not be too pleased."

"But Hazeldon won't know there are women present. How would he? He won't even know anything out of the ordinary is happening. Some officers enjoying a few drinks in their quarters – what's unusual about that – we do it all the time."

Bertie jumped to his feet. "Yes – good! Jolly good! When is it to happen?"

"Leave it with me, sir, and I shall organise everything. Sooner rather than later, I'd say, as your time here is so limited."

"Yes, James, as soon as possible!"

"You've done *what*?" said Charles as James finished speaking at their table in the mess.

"I have organised a party in Bertie's quarters. And I am inviting a woman along, an actress by the name of Nellie Cliffden."

"Is that wise?" said Charles.

"Absolutely! Look, we all agreed that it was our role to introduce Bertie to some women. We tried it at Henrietta's party, but he just did not feel comfortable in such surroundings. I know it was a private party, but he still felt exposed. Besides, most of the women there were married, and Bertie felt it just wasn't right. Sorry, Donald!"

Donald pulled a face at him.

"And who is this Nellie Cliffden?" demanded Charles.

"She sings at the Palace Theatre. Quite a beauty, plenty of the right manners to impress a prince, and most of all up for the job!" said James.

"A woman of low morals!" said Charles.

"Isn't that what is needed? I mean, it's either married or low morals, let's be honest!" said Donald.

"I don't know," said Charles. "I feel we are playing with fire. Bertie isn't a chess piece to be moved around for our entertainment."

"Bertie is quite happy to be moved around," said James. "Look, it's now or never, and it's Nellie or no one. He has been told that he has to go to Prussia by the end of the month to meet this Danish Princess he doesn't want to marry."

"Poor chap!" said Donald.

"So, are we in agreement to push ahead and introduce Bertie to Nellie?" asked James.

"Agreed!" said Donald.

Charles hesitated before nodding and saying, "Agreed."

CHAPTER 26

James sat in an armchair in an elegant boutique on Sackville Street as Nellie paraded a number of gowns before him.

"Too red!" he dismissed one gown she modelled for him

"Neck too high!" he dismissed another.

"Neck too low!" he rejected a further dress.

"For goodness' sake, James," snapped Nellie, bored with constant fittings. "What are you exactly looking for? If you could give us some idea then we might be able to find it!"

"I'll know it when I see it," said James.

Nellie turned in frustration and re-entered the dressing rooms with the baffled shop assistant.

Finally, she emerged in a gold gown with sequins.

"Oh, yes!" Standing, he walked in circles around her, inspecting the gown. "This is perfect!"

"Thank fuck for that!" snapped Nellie, causing the sales assistants to gasp at her language. She picked up her skirts and, turning back into the dressing rooms, said to the assistants. "Get me out of this dress as fast as you can! I'm tired and starving!"

James looked very pleased as they sat in a carriage, surrounded by shopping boxes.

"Everything is perfectly set for the night," said James. "When he sees you in that dress with those jewels, Bertie will be swept away by you."

"Good for Bertie!" mocked Nellie.

"Aren't you just a little excited about meeting the Prince of Wales?"

"No, I am not! I am sick of the very mention of his name. It's all we have talked about for the last two days – tell Bertie this, tell Bertie that . . . I just want the whole affair to be over as quickly as possible and have him and you, more importantly, out of my life for good!"

"It won't be long now, Nellie, till that happens."

"Good! Lest I remind you that you are actually blackmailing me to partake in this – this plot!"

"Hardly a plot!"

"Seducing the man to advance your career! That sounds like a plot to me," she said, turning and staring out the window.

"I say, I'm terribly nervous for some reason," said Bertie as Tommy rushed around his quarters making final preparations for the evening ahead.

Donald and Charles were sitting, legs crossed, smoking cigars.

"Why ever so, sir?" said Charles.

"Well, it's this girl that James is bringing to the party," said Bertie.

"The actress?"

"Yes. James says she really likes me, but what if she doesn't like me when we meet and talk? She might have no interest in me then."

Charles and Donald exchanged knowing looks.

"I don't think there's much chance of that!" said Donald.

"I hope not. She's the most beautiful woman – wait till you meet her! I hope she won't find me stuffy. She's used to such a different world."

"That's for sure, but I wouldn't worry about it, sir. I am sure you will have many things in common," said Donald as he smirked at Charles.

"You look perfect, Nellie," James said as they made their way through the Kildare countryside.

Nellie ignored him as she looked ahead.

"You won't forget anything I told you? What to say or how to behave?" he said.

"I won't! Tell me who will be at this party tonight, other than the Prince of Wales?"

"Just some fellow officers, Charlie Carrington, Donald Kilroy and Edgar Forrest and a couple of their lady friends."

"Who exactly are these lady friends?"

"They are of no consequence – a lady called Henrietta Fitzgibbons and one named Clarissa – they are friends of Donald's."

Nellie sighed. "More than just friends, I imagine."

The carriage reached the garrison. Nellie bowed her head and looked away from the window as it halted by the soldiers on sentry duty.

"Good evening, gentlemen," said James through the window.

"*Sir!*" said the soldiers, saluting him.

The carriage proceeded. Nellie looked out as it made its way through the cobbled lanes of the camp until it pulled up outside a manor house.

James opened the door, stepped out and offered her his hand. She took it and climbed out of the carriage.

"Ready?" he asked, and she nodded.

They walked inside and up the stairs. Nellie could hear laughing and music playing as they reached a door. She suddenly felt very nervous and fought a desire to turn and run away. She felt herself trembling at the thought of meeting the Prince of Wales.

James opened the door and gestured for her to walk in.

She held her head high as she entered the room. The party was in full swing. There were a couple of musicians in the corner playing a fiddle and accordion. Young officers were laughing and talking loudly to two women who were dressed expensively.

On seeing James and Nellie, they all stopped speaking.

"James! We had almost given up on you!" said Charles as he walked towards him.

"Forgive us, we were a little delayed," said Nellie.

Charles looked at Nellie and smiled. "You must be Nellie Cliffden?" he said.

"Indeed I am, sir," Nellie said and curtsied.

Charles glanced at James and laughed.

"Nellie, this is Captain Charles Carrington," said James.

"Oh!" said Nellie, realising she had mistaken him for the Prince of Wales.

James quickly took her arm and led her to the others.

"May I present to you the famous actress of the stage, Miss Nellie Cliffden. Nellie, this is Captain Edgar Forrest and Captain Donald Kilroy – these ladies are Mrs Henrietta Fitzgibbon and her friend Clarissa."

"Pleased to meet you all," said Nellie.

The men were all smiling at her warmly, the two women viewing her coolly.

Then Nellie spotted a young man hovering behind the others, looking anxious.

"And, Nellie, may I introduce to you His Royal Highness, the Prince of Wales," said James.

Bertie stepped forward and smiled at her.

"Your Royal Highness," said Nellie as she curtsied again.

"Please, call me Bertie."

As she rose from her curtsy, she looked into his eyes and saw that he was as nervous as she was.

"Well, Bertie," she said, "what do I have to do to get a drink around here?"

There was a momentary silence and then they all started to laugh.

Charles immediately put a glass of red wine in her hand.

"Thank you, Charles," she said and he looked pleased that she had remembered his name.

"Miss Cliffden," said Bertie eagerly, "I never saw such a performance as the one you gave that night in the Palace Theatre."

"Then you've led a sheltered life, Bertie! And that was one of my off-nights – you should see me when I'm at my best!"

"How many nights a week do you perform there?" asked Bertie.

"Usually five, but I'm on a holiday at the moment," said Nellie, giving James a dirty look.

"But she will soon be back on the stage there," said James, giving her a meaningful look.

"Have you been on the stage long?" asked Bertie.

"I suppose it's like you being born a prince, sir – I was born to it!"

Bertie laughed. "This is true. We are all prisoners of our destiny."

"Indeed. Though, if you don't mind me saying, sir, some destinies are better to be born to than others!" she said with a wink.

He began to laugh. "That is also very true, Nellie!"

Henrietta was staring at Nellie.

"Whoever is she, Charlie?"

"Some actress friend of James'."

"She's very beautiful – but why is she here tonight?" asked Henrietta.

"His Royal Highness saw her perform on the stage and was interested in her apparently," said Charles.

"I see! And yet he didn't show any interest in the ladies at my soirée," said Henrietta.

"Perhaps she's his type," suggested Charles.

"Hmmm, and I can guess what type that is," said Henrietta.

"We had the most wonderful time in Killarney. Have you ever stayed at Muckross House, Nellie?" asked Bertie.

Nellie glanced at James, wondering if Bertie was being serious.

"Of course I have," said Nellie.

"Oh, you know the Herberts then? When did you stay with them there?"

Nellie looked thoughtful. "Let me think – it was the season before last – just before I stayed with the Russian Tsar and after I stayed with the King of Spain."

Bertie was momentarily confused before he began to laugh. "I see! You've never been to Muckross House, I take it?"

"No, sir, never. And I can't imagine I ever will," said Nellie.

James looked on nervously, wondering if Nellie was overdoing it, but Bertie seemed to be lapping up her personality and wit.

Nellie finished her drink and held the glass out to Bertie. "Be a darling, Bertie, and get me another glass of wine."

James cringed. He felt she had just blown it. He had told her to speak to Bertie like a normal person, but she had just overstepped the mark.

Bertie reached out and took the glass. "Of course, it will be my pleasure. Tommy! Bring over the wine!"

Tommy came rushing over with a bottle and filled the glass. Bertie then handed it back to Nellie.

"Thank you, sir," she said, smiling at him as she took a sip.

Nellie was in Bertie's arms as they danced to the music.

"Watch your step, sir, my feet are small compared to yours!" she warned.

"I'm so sorry. I was always a clumsy dancer."

"Just don't try so hard!" ordered Nellie. "Take it slowly and follow me."

"All right!" he said and began to follow her steps as they swirled around the room. He was gazing into her face as they danced.

James looked on and was very pleased at how the night had progressed. He caught Charles' eye and they nodded to each other. Charles whispered something to Donald and Edgar who nodded as well and whispered to the ladies. Then they all put down their glasses and quietly left.

"I think if I dance any more I will collapse!" said Bertie. "I'm not used to all this dancing, Nellie, unlike you who are on the stage every night."

"Indeed, sir. But you are actually a very good dancer, once you get into your stride." As they stopped moving, she stepped back from him.

Bertie looked around. "Where has everyone gone?"

"I was so caught up in the dancing, I didn't notice them go," said Nellie.

"More wine?" he asked.

"Yes, please."

Bertie looked around and saw that Tommy had fallen asleep.

"Tommy!" he shouted and Tommy jumped up. "Fetch us some more wine and then you can go to bed."

"Yes, sir," said Tommy. He filled two glasses and handed them to Bertie and Nellie.

"In fact, you can all go to bed," said Bertie and signalled to the musicians to stop playing.

They packed away their instruments and left the flat with Tommy.

"All alone!" said Nellie with a shy smile.

"Oh, I didn't mean – of course you may go too, Nellie, if you want?"

"No, I don't want to go home," she said, going to sit down on the couch.

"I -I'm so glad. That is – I don't want you to go. I'd rather you stayed for a while. I've enjoyed your company so much tonight."

She patted the seat beside her and said, "Why don't you come and sit near me."

He walked towards her slowly and sat down, fumbling with his glass.

"I was so happy when James told me that you had seen me in the theatre that night and asked about me," he said.

"Oh – eh – yes! You stood out in the crowd," she said.

"I couldn't keep my eyes off you. I never saw a woman like you before."

"I can scarcely believe that, with all the princesses and duchesses you must have met."

"Have you ever met a princess or a duchess?" he asked, making a face.

"I can't say I have."

"They are a dull lot – prone to talking about horses and races and the weather!"

She laughed. "Yes, there's only so many times you can say the sun is shining or the rain is pouring."

"You are a tonic, Nellie."

"You're – you're not what I expected," she said earnestly.

"What did you expect?"

"Somebody more – kingly – I presume," she said.

Bertie's face fell. "I think that's what everyone thinks. A man born to be king who is not very kingly is not a good fit."

"I don't mean it in a bad way, I mean it in a very good way. You are far more pleasant than I could ever have imagined."

"Pleasant? I don't know if that's a compliment. I'm not meant to be – pleasant – I am supposed to be majestic and autocratic."

"Who says?" Nellie asked.

"What do you mean?"

"Who says you have to be – majestic – and autocratic, whatever that means?"

"Well, it's just what is expected by everyone," he said.

"Well, I think you are just perfect the way you are," she said, smiling.

"Do you?" he asked, surprised.

"To tell you the truth, I really didn't want to come here tonight. But you have made it so worthwhile."

"Really?" He was delighted.

"Yes – really."

She waited for him to kiss her. But when he didn't, she took his glass of wine and placed it on the table in front of them and then leaned forward and kissed him.

"Well – that was . . ." he said as she drew back from him.

"I'm sorry, Bertie – perhaps I am being too forward?"

"No, not at all! I want you to be forward. It's so refreshing to have a woman being forward!" He smiled and then he frowned. "At least the ones that are not married."

Nellie laughed out loud.

"It seems to me that ladies of my class are allowed to do nothing before they are married and too much after they are!" he said.

"Feast or famine!" she chuckled.

"But – you – you are different, Nellie. I admire you so."

"Do you?" she asked cynically.

"Yes, you live life on your terms. You earn your money, rent your own flat, perform on the stage, and yet look beautiful at all times."

"You are very good for my self-esteem, sir," she said and looked at him curiously. She was used to hearing flattery from the men she met. But Bertie was different. He flattered her in ways she had never heard before, but most importantly it seemed as if he was being earnest.

"I envy you, Nellie."

"That's strange, because I envy you!"

"No, seriously, it must be wonderful to lead the life you lead, to be answerable to nobody and do whatever you want whenever you want to," he said, gazing into her eyes.

"I think you are imagining my life is better than it is, sir," she said.

"But I've never met anybody as free as you," he said.

"We are all prisoners of something in this life, Bertie – it's just that our walls are made of different things."

He stared at her. "Wise words, Nellie. When did you become so wise?"

She shrugged. "I'm not sure I'm wise – more streetwise."

He continued gazing at her and then gently leaned in and kissed her, putting his arms around her.

She stood up and reached down for his hand. "I take it the bedroom is through that door?"

He nodded.

"Well, aren't you going to give me the grand tour?" she asked.

He smiled and nodded and led her to the next room.

CHAPTER 27

The light shone through the Georgian window in Bertie's room as the early-morning birds sang loudly and a trumpet sounded somewhere in the distance.

Nellie was awake and had her hand under her head, looking down at Bertie as he slept. As the trumpet continued to play it stirred Bertie from his sleep and his eyelids flickered open.

"Good morning," she smiled down at him.

He smiled back. "Good morning to you."

She continued to gaze at him smilingly.

"What were you thinking – as you looked at me before I awoke?" he asked.

"I was thinking I could murder you while you slept and cause political turmoil throughout the world in a second," she said and she burst out laughing.

He stared, astonished, for a second but then he laughed too.

"Well, I am very glad you are not of a violent or controversial nature, in that case," he said.

She touched his face gently and whispered, "As if I could harm a hair on your head."

"Oh, Nellie!" he whispered and drew her to him and kissed her. "I don't want this to ever end."

Suddenly there was a noise in the sitting room and Bertie sat up quickly.

"That's Tommy, my batman. What time is it?" he said anxiously.

There was a knock on the door and Tommy called "Sir?"

"Oh – hide!" urged Bertie.

"Where?" she asked, looking around.

"Through there, into the bathroom!" he said.

Nellie slipped out of the bed, tip-toed into the bathroom and closed the door.

Bertie swung his legs out of the bed, slipped on a dressing gown and, tying it, went to the door.

He opened the door, keeping one hand on it, stopping Tommy from entering.

"Yes, Tommy?"

"Is Sir ready for his bath?" asked Tommy.

"Oh yes, I mean no – I can run it myself this morning, Tommy."

"Run it yourself, sir?" Tommy was puzzled.

"Yes – and I won't be needing you for the rest of the morning either. You may leave."

"If Sir is sure?"

"Quite sure," confirmed Bertie as he closed over the door.

He then listened at the door and heard Tommy leaving the flat.

"*He's gone!*" he called and returned to the bedroom.

Nellie came out of the bathroom wearing one of his dressing gownss.

"Well, I've had to hide from a few wives in my time, but never a batman before!" Nellie whispered to herself.

"What?"

"Nothing!" she said, coming to him, putting her arms around his neck and kissing him. "I had better go or else risk being discovered," she said.

"I don't want you to go. I want you to stay here all day and night," he said, holding her tightly.

"That's impossible, Bertie," she said. "I am sure you would be quickly missed and they would send the troops to come and find you."

Bertie suddenly looked worried. "Oh, dear, but how to get you out of here? How are you to get home?"

"If I know James, and I do, he will have arranged everything," she said, as she left his arms, went to the window and peered out.

"Really?"

"*Ah ha!* There he is!" said Nellie.

Bertie came rushing to the window and looked out. James was waiting in the laneway across from the building beside a carriage.

"My goodness, what a manager!" marvelled Bertie.

"Indeed, James is a brilliant manager," she said, remembering the pact with James that she must praise him at any opportunity. "James can arrange anything any time. He is utterly trustworthy and reliable."

Bertie smiled at her. "Yes, I find him so. You are very good friends with him, aren't you?"

"Oh, yes, James and I go back a long time. Well, I had better get ready," she said and, turning quickly, gathered her dress from the floor and hurried to the bathroom.

Bertie signalled from the window to James who nodded back and got into the back of the roofed carriage which then moved forward and pulled up in front of Bertie's building.

Nellie emerged from the bathroom and donned her cloak, pulling up the hood. Then she and Bertie hurried outside and to the top of the stairs.

Bertie looked down and saw the coast was clear.

"Oh gosh – if we are caught!" he said, looking terrified.

Nellie giggled. "I feel like we are naughty children!"

They hurried down the stairs.

At the front door, Nellie turned to Bertie.

"Well – it's been – memorable!" she said.

"I – I'd like to see you again."

She threw her hands up in the air and said, "What's the point?"

"Every point, Nellie. There's every point in seeing you again – if you would like to?"

She nodded and smiled. "Very much so. We can make the arrangement through James."

She leaned forward and kissed him and then ran out the door and into the awaiting carriage.

James banged on the roof of the carriage and it took off.

"Hide on the floor, in case anyone sees you," said James.

Nellie got down on the floor and waited there until they were safely out of the garrison.

"You can get up now," said James.

Nellie scrambled up and took the seat opposite him.

"Well?" he asked.

She nodded.

James began to smile. "Well done. Does he want to see you again?"

Nellie nodded. "Yes."

"Excellent!" James banged the roof of the carriage and shouted, "*Pull over!*"

He jumped out of the carriage and held the door open as he spoke to Nellie. "I have to get back to report to duty. The driver will take you back to Dublin."

Nelle nodded. "When will I see him again?"

"Leave that to me – I'll make the arrangements." James slammed the carriage door shut and shouted, "*Drive on!*"

As the carriage continued its journey back to Dublin, Nellie stared out the window. She bit her lower lip and began to smile.

CHAPTER 28

Nellie opened the door of her flat and found Sadie waiting for her inside.

"Nellie!" Sadie said, rushing to her and giving her a hug. "Are you all right? I was that worried about you being down in Kildare the whole night."

"I'm fine, Sadie. Absolutely fine," said Nellie, going over to the mirror over the fireplace and looking at herself.

"Did you meet him?"

"Oh, yes, I met him," said Nellie, turning around and smiling at Sadie.

"And what's he like?"

"Sadie, he's just – he's just not what I expected. I've met many men from many walks of life but I've never met anybody like him." She sat down on the armchair by the fireplace.

"Go on."

"He's so down to earth. You'd never think he was a prince. He just seemed like anybody else . . . but he's so polite and kind and genuine."

Sadie smiled and sat down. "Sounds like you enjoyed meeting him?"

"Well, I have to be honest – yes, I did," said Nellie. "He is so tender – he genuinely liked me."

"Putting on an act, like the rest of them," scoffed Sadie.

"No, he wasn't putting on an act. He wouldn't know how to put on an act if he tried."

"Nellie, remember you were there on a job," cautioned Sadie, "just like the rest of the jobs you've done."

"Well, I know that, Sadie. But it was nice – just once – to be treated the way he treated me."

"Well, that's because he doesn't know the whole truth of why you were there, Nellie. He might have treated you somewhat differently if he knew you were paid to be there and you did it to get that James Marton out of your life once and for all."

Nellie's smile dropped. "I know that, Sadie."

"The Prince has no idea who and what you really are. He thinks you are a famous actress who wants to spend time with him. Don't deceive yourself by thinking anything else." Sadie's voice was harsh.

"I know exactly what I am and why I was there, Sadie, you don't have to remind me."

"Good! Because it's one thing for a woman like you to kid the rest of the world, but if she ever tries to kid herself – then she's in serious bother!"

Nellie stood up abruptly. "I'm going to have a bath."

Sadie watched with concern as Nellie left the room.

Bertie entered the Officers' Mess at lunchtime and saw his friends sitting at their usual table.

"Good afternoon, gentlemen," said Bertie as he sat down.

"Good afternoon, sir!" they replied in unison.

"Smashing evening last night," said Donald.

"Yes, thank you, sir, for the use of your quarters," said Charles.

"That's quite all right. Your lady friends got home safely – Henrietta and Clarissa?"

"Oh yes, Henrietta and Clarissa were dispatched back to their homes in good time," said Donald.

"And how was your lady friend, sir? Did she get home all right?" asked Charles.

"Nellie?" Bertie gave James a quick look. "Oh, yes, she got home safely."

"Did the evening's entertainment go on for long – after we left?" asked Donald.

"Yes, I suppose it did. I kind of lost track of time," said Bertie.

"I imagine you did, sir!" said Charles and they all laughed loudly.

"Now – now! Leave him alone!" said James in good humour.

"We are just anxious to know how Bertie's evening went. After all, we all played a part to bringing it together," said Donald.

Bertie sat forward. "My time with the beautiful Nellie went better than I could ever have imagined!"

"Well done, sir!" said Donald. "She is rather beautiful."

"And witty," added Charles.

"And clever," said Donald.

"An all-round good sport!" said Charles.

"I rather thought she was all those things," said Bertie, smiling and standing up. "And now if you can excuse me. I missed early morning drill, so need to make up my time."

"Of course, sir," said Donald.

Bertie leaned down to James and said, "I need to speak to you, if you could call to my quarters this evening?"

"Of course, sir," nodded James.

The officers waited until Bertie had left the mess and then all turned to each other smiling broadly.

"Well – job done!" said Donald.

"He does seem rather happy, doesn't he?" said Charles.

"Who'd have thought?" said Donald. "An actress! Wherever did you meet her, James?"

"Through mutual friends. She is part of that whole bohemian crowd in Dublin that we hear tell of," said James.

"And how would you know that bohemian crowd?" asked Charles.

"Well, there are quite a few people from the gentry amongst them," said James.

"I see!" said Donald. "She puts on a good act, but I can't

see any daughter of a gentry family ever being allowed to get up on a stage."

"Or to end up in a man's bed before marriage, let alone on the first night that she meets him!" said Charles.

"I don't know – hasn't history shown us that the daughters of the most illustrious families have quickly fallen for the charms of a British monarch?" asked James.

"*Hmm*, and they usually end up literally losing their heads over it," said Donald.

"Or retired to wealth once their affair with the king is ended," said James.

Charles turned to James, his face serious. "What are you up to, Marton?" he asked abruptly.

James laughed. "Nothing, nothing at all! I am just trying to make Bertie's last few weeks in Ireland as memorable as possible for him. Isn't that what we agreed to do?"

"Well, by the look of that smile on his face, I would say you have succeeded in your mission, Marton," said Donald.

CHAPTER 29

There was a knock on the door of Bertie's quarters.

"Come in!" called Bertie.

The door opened and James walked in.

"You wanted to see me, sir?"

"Yes, yes! Come in, James!"

James walked in and closed the door behind him.

Bertie poured them two glasses of whiskey and they both sat down.

"Did – did our friend get home all right?" asked Bertie.

"Yes, I believe so – the driver was instructed to take her back to Leeson Street where she lives," said James.

"Leeson Street," repeated Bertie. "Well, I don't know what to say! She's marvellous – absolutely marvellous."

"I'm glad you were pleased with her, sir."

"Pleased! I thought she was amazing! I kept telling her I never met anybody like her!"

"And she was very taken with you, sir," said James.

"Was she?" Bertie sat forward eagerly. "What did she say?"

"She just said she had a wonderful night and would love to see you again."

"Did she? Did she say that? I asked to see her again, but I wasn't sure if she meant it when she agreed."

"Oh, she mean it, sir! Very much!" said James.

"Well – when can I see her again?"

"Perhaps tomorrow night?"

"Excellent! What about her stage appearances? Can she manage to be free?"

"Oh, I am sure she can," James sat forward. "If I can suggest she visits you here again? I think it is the safest place for you to meet. No prying eyes."

"Yes, yes – good – jolly good! I shall look forward to it. I don't know how to thank you for all this, James. You've been a true friend. Arranging everything and acting as the go-between for us."

"It's been my absolute pleasure to assist any way I can, sir," smiled James as he raised his glass of whiskey and took a drink.

That night Bertie sat writing in his diary. Thoughts of Nellie kept interrupting his writing. She had taken his breath away. He couldn't believe somebody could be so refreshing, so vibrant, so different from everything else in his life so far. He couldn't wait to see her again. He was filling in his diary for the previous day as he had not got a chance to do it the previous night as Nellie had been there. He took up his pen and with a flourish wrote: *NC – First Time.*

Sadie opened the flat door and scowled to see James standing there.

"Good evening, Sadie."

"Oh, it's you again, is it?"

"Is Nellie at home?"

"She is, more's the pity," said Sadie.

He walked in and saw Nellie by the fireplace.

"Hello, Nellie," he said, smiling.

Nellie didn't say anything.

Sadie walked to her and stood beside her with her arms folded.

"Could I ask for some privacy?" said James.

"It's all right, Sadie, you can leave us," said Nellie.

Sadie walked out in a huff.

"And please don't listen in to our conversation!" James called after her.

James walked towards Nellie, taking off his gloves.

"Such a cantankerous crone!" he said. "I don't know how you can bear to have her around the place."

"What do you want, James?"

"I have spoken to the Prince and – he wants to see you again," he said happily.

Nellie tried not to show her equal delight. "Well, I had expected that," she said coolly. "He told me himself."

"This is all going swimmingly well, Nellie. Better than I could have expected. He's quite enamoured with you."

"Is he?" Nellie tried to look disinterested.

"Singing your praises, he was! You've cast a spell on him, to be sure."

"I am merely doing my job in order to be rid of you forever," Nellie said.

"Well, you are doing your job most impressively. Keep this up and who knows where it will lead for me."

"Where are we to meet?" she asked.

"At his quarters again tomorrow night. It will just be you and him this time."

Nellie was delighted to hear this. She was so looking forward to seeing Bertie again and the idea there wouldn't be anybody else there to distract them was wonderful.

"I shall collect you by carriage again and sneak you into the camp," said James.

Nellie nodded.

"Just keep up this act and we will do just fine," said James.

CHAPTER 30

The next night Bertie walked quickly around his quarters, checking everything was to his liking. He had lit candles all around and Tommy had set the table beautifully for two and was just laying out a roast lamb dinner under silver covers.

Bertie took out his watch and saw it was nearly seven. Nellie was due to arrive any minute.

"That's fine, Tommy – you can leave now!" he said.

"But does His Royal Highness not need me to stay to see to the wine and see to your guests?" asked Tommy.

"No – no! We can manage just fine! Now – *shoo!*" he said, gesturing that Tommy should leave quickly.

With a look of confusion on his face, Tommy left the quarters.

Bertie hovered around the table double-checking everything. Then he hurried to one of the front windows and peered out for any sign of a carriage. He felt so nervous and yet excited.

Soon he saw a carriage pull up outside. The driver got down and opened the door.

Nellie stepped out.

"She's here!" he said to himself and then rushed to the mirror over the fireplace to check his appearance.

He waited for the knock on the door.

A few moments later it came.

He hurried to open the door.

Nellie walked in and slid off her cloak. She was dressed in a turquoise and silver crinoline and a silver veil draped over her head covered her face.

She moved forward and stood there facing him. Then she slowly removed her veil and let it drop to the floor.

He stared at her shimmering in the firelight.

"Hello, Bertie," she said softy.

He walked quickly to her, took her in his arms and kissed her.

"I wondered if maybe I had dreamed you up. That you weren't as beautiful as I thought you were – but you're even more so," he said.

"I could get used to you being around!" she said as she gently pushed him away and walked further into the sitting room.

"What's all this?" she asked, confused as she looked at the feast laid out on the table.

"It's for us – for you," he said.

"For me?" she said, turning quickly to look at him.

"Oh dear, did I do the wrong thing? Have you eaten already?"

She placed her hand under his chin. "No, I haven't eaten yet. But I didn't expect all his. I – don't know what to say."

"Oh, you don't have to say anything," Bertie said, pulling out a chair for her.

She sat down at the table.

"I think this is the nicest thing anyone has ever done for me," she said, looking across the table at him as he sat down.

"Do you like it?" he asked.

"I love it!" she said as she surveyed the food.

He picked up a bottle of wine and poured them two glasses.

"I am afraid I got rid of Tommy for the night, so we have to serve ourselves. It will be a laugh!"

She picked up her glass and took a drink. "I'm glad you got rid of Tommy – it gives me more time alone with you."

As the dinner wore on, she listened intently as he spoke of his tour of America and Canada the previous year.

"Tell me," she said. "Are the streets of New York really made of gold?"

"No, they are made of cobble much like anywhere else!"

She giggled. "What a pity!"

"Am I boring you with all these tales of America?"

"No! I've never met anybody who's been to America before. I've always been fascinated with the place. So to hear your stories, I can't tell you what it means to me," she said honestly.

He smiled, delighted with himself. "You know, I think you are the first person who has been really interested in my tour of America. My family feigned interest, but always quickly moved the topic on to something else."

"Well, I imagine your family have seen so much of the world that tales from America aren't going to impress them like they do me," said Nellie.

"If you are so fascinated with America, why don't you go and see the place for yourself?"

She laughed. "I can't just head off to New York like you can, Bertie! The passage alone would cost me a fortune. If I was ever going to New York, it would be for good and never to come back."

"To emigrate?"

"That's what's normal for people who don't live in your world. We don't go on holiday to New York!"

"And would you like to? Would you like to emigrate to New York?"

"I don't know. Maybe one day. Maybe I could be a famous actress on the stage there?" she said with a laugh.

"Why not? And I could come and see you when I am king!"

"Oh, I'd like that!" she said, reaching over, taking his hand and stroking it softly.

Nellie was lying on the couch in Bertie's arms as they gazed into the fire.

"I think my parents will never understand me," he said as he stroked her golden hair.

"And I shall never understand them."

"Do we ever really understand another person?" she asked.

"Perhaps not. I've always been such a disappointment to them, you see. My elder sister, Vicky, has always been so intelligent and bright, so much brighter than me."

"I find that hard to believe," Nellie said.

"Oh, she is! You should have seen us when we were children with our governesses and tutors. She picked everything up in a second whereas things had to be explained over and over again to me."

"Maybe you were just being taught things that didn't interest you," mused Nellie.

"Well, we all have to learn English, maths and geography, Nellie, whether we have an interest in them or not!"

Nellie said nothing as she thought of her own lack of schooling. The truth was she had taught herself to read and write but that was the limit of her education before she met James who taught her what she needed to know. She didn't want Bertie to know that about her though. James had also taught her how to hide her shortcomings over the years.

"Do you know, if my parents had only had girls, then Vicky would have inherited the throne from my mother? There would have been two Queen Victorias, one after the other, each as brilliant as the other. But then they went and had a boy – me!"

Nellie sat up and looked at him. "Bertie, maybe you are not like your sister, but that doesn't mean you don't have talents in different ways."

"Well, I had hoped that I did – and that my time here in the military would prove that. But, alas, I seem to have been a failure as an officer as well."

"Well, I think you are wonderful," she said, leaning forward and kissing him.

"Do you – do you, really?"

"I think you have a special gift with people. You are very likeable, Bertie. People warm to you quickly and like you, and I think that's a much more important quality for a king to have than geography."

"Yes – yes, I never looked at it that way," he mused.

"I've always had a thought. I think if the King and Queen of France had been nicer to people and eaten less cake, then they might not have had their heads chopped off by that guillotine."

"They did come to a sticky end, didn't they? Do you know, you are right, Nellie – I have always felt this about the monarchy. That we should be close to the people, not give them any reason to resent us."

"Share your cake with them!" She reached out to the table in front of them, took a piece of the cake on the plate there and ate it.

"Goodness, is that the time?" he said as the clock tower struck outside, indicating it was one o'clock.

"It's time for bed," she said as she stood up and held her hand out to him. He stood up and, putting his arm around her waist, led her to the bedroom.

199

CHAPTER 31

The trumpet was blowing the next morning.

"I'd better get up before your batman arrives in," said Nellie, pulling herself away from his arms.

"I've told him not to come this morning," said Bertie, pulling her back to him.

"Oh, I see!" she said, kissing him. "Then we are in no rush."

"What are your plans today?"

"Well, I suppose, go back to Dublin," she said.

"But you have nothing pressing on?"

She shook her head. "No, nothing urgent."

"In that case, I feel a cold coming on." He faked a cough. "I think I shall not be able to report for duty today."

"But, will you not get into trouble?" Nellie was surprised but delighted at the thought of spending more time with him.

"Well, what can they say if I am ill? Besides, does it really matter if I report to duty or not? I've already done my drill before my parents, and demonstrated spectacular mediocrity. Now I am just biding my time here until they give me the necessary ranking I will be granted whether I deserve it or not, just by the virtue of being the Prince of Wales."

"It must be nice to be given things whether you deserve them or not," she sighed.

"But it's always been a burden to me, feeling guilty about receiving things that I don't merit. But you know, now, for the first time in my life, I don't really care!"

"And what has brought on this sudden change of heart, Bertie?"

"Well, you have, Nellie – you have," he said.

"To think that anything I have said could influence the Prince of Wales!" she mocked.

"Anything you could say would influence me, Nellie."

Nellie waited at the front door of the manor house while Bertie walked to the fence that divided the garrison land from the surrounding countryside. Reaching it, he looked about and seeing the coast was clear he signalled to her.

Nellie pulled her cloak around her expensive gown, hoping she might look like a peasant woman, at least from a distance. She walked to the fence, trying to appear casual.

"There's a big gap in the fence here," he said.

"I'll never get through that gap, not in this crinoline!" she said.

"Yes, you can!" he said as he stepped through the gap.

"I can but try!" She followed him, pulling in her skirts and squeezing through.

"There! Told you could do it!" he said.

She looked across the beautiful countryside. "And what do we do now that we are on the other side?"

"We walk and talk and enjoy the beautiful day," he said, offering her his arm.

She took his arm and beamed at him as they set off walking.

They seemed to have been walking for hours and had reached a river and were strolling along its banks.

"I feel like naughty schoolchildren escaping from school," said Bertie. "In fact, that is what my sister Alice and I did once, when were growing up at Osbourne House. We escaped from our governess for the day and went playing in the countryside. Our governess nearly killed us when we returned home!" He laughed.

"You mention Alice a lot. You're obviously very close to her," said Nellie.

"Oh, yes! Alice is my treasure. We always confided in each other and would cover for each other if one of us was in trouble. I'll miss her dreadfully now that she is to be married and has to go to Hesse."

"Oh, she's engaged to be married?"

"Yes, her future husband was introduced to her by our sister Vicky, of course," he said.

"But she's happy with the marriage?"

"Oh, yes. She seems very happy with Louis, her fiancé."

As they strolled along, he had an overwhelming desire to discuss his parents' desire for him to meet Princess Alexandra and their intention that he should marry her. Nellie seemed to have such a unique and fresh perspective on everything he told her. But he realised he could hardly discuss this topic with her. It wouldn't be right to discuss another woman with her.

"Such a beautiful country. I will be so sad to leave it and return home," he said.

"You wouldn't have thought it so beautiful if you were here twelve years ago."

"How so?"

She looked at him incredulously. "The Famine of course!"

He looked embarrassed. "Oh, yes, of course, the Famine."

"Anyone who saw the sights then could never forget it. The devastation, the starvation."

"It must have been terrible," he said.

"The things that were going on here were terrifying . . . while you played truant with your sister in Osbourne House," she said, unable to stop the bitterness from coming out.

He looked alarmed. "I didn't mean to cause offense."

"Sure how could you mean to cause offense when you know nothing about such things? But your mother knew, sure enough, and didn't do much to help."

"Well, she may be the Queen, but she has very little real power," he said.

"Ah, she had power enough if she wanted to help. A few words from her could have made all the difference."

"Her hands were tied, Nellie. I am sure if she could have done anything, she would not have allowed all those people to die," he said.

"Well, there are many people who will never forgive her. She cares nothing for us Irish – who are supposed to be her people! Maybe, like her ministers, she looked on the Famine as no more than we deserved!"

He stopped walking, looking concerned. "You mustn't say such things about Her Majesty, Nellie."

"Why not? It's not as if you've said anything good about her yourself!"

"Perhaps I have said too much."

She suddenly remembered herself. She had been so charmed by Bertie that she had nearly forgotten who he was. She had nearly forgotten what her mission with him was. She was there to do James's bidding, no more. And she didn't want to jeopardise that by speaking so out of turn.

She bit her lower lip. "I shouldn't speak about your mother like that. But what I'm saying to you about her is only what others here are saying all the time, Bertie. Or maybe you are not aware of that?"

"I am aware there is a lot of agitation in Ireland, yes," he said.

"Well then, your time here is an opportunity to learn about that unhappiness and I can see that you are going to be a great king, Bertie. You can build the bridges that need to be built. I'm telling you now, if you don't you might lose this part of your kingdom for ever."

His face became clouded with worry "Lose Ireland? That's unthinkable."

"Maybe it's time to start thinking about it, Bertie. Because I hear it in Dublin all the time. Since your mother's visit, even more so. People talking about Ireland breaking away from the Union, leaving the Empire even," said Nellie.

"I – I can hardly believe that could ever come to pass." He was astounded.

"One million dead and more than a million having to emigrate and nobody from your government came to help – how could you possibly think that anyone in Ireland would want to stay united to Britain?"

"Who says these things? Who are these people?" Bertie demanded.

"I know lots of different people, Bertie, from the people in the streets to the bohemian set. I listen to what they say."

"Well, tell me more, Nellie. Tell me more of what they say. I need to know if I can ever be their king."

She took his arm as they continued along the river and she continued to speak.

Laughing, Nellie and Bertie entered his quarters.

"And then I shouted at him – get out of here or it's not just a lost sheep you'll be looking for!" Nellie said, concluding a story she was telling.

They both stopped laughing and stood stock still when they saw James standing in the sitting room waiting for them.

"James!" With all the excitement of spending the day with Bertie, Nellie had forgotten completely about James.

"May I ask, where you have both been?" asked James, looking alarmed.

"We decided to spend the day enjoying the countryside," said Bertie.

"But I had a carriage waiting to take Nellie back to Dublin. When she didn't appear, I thought something dreadful had happened!"

"Sorry, James, we didn't think," said Nellie.

"Well, you should have thought! I've been beside myself with worry. And, sir, I understand you sent a sick note to Major Hazeldon, saying you couldn't attend drill practice today?"

"Yes, what of it?" shrugged Bertie.

"Well, if I might say so, that is a tad irresponsible, sir," said James.

Bertie walked confidently into the centre of the sitting room. "Oh, for goodness sake! Hazeldon doesn't care one jot if I turn up for drill practice or not! He is just biding his time until I leave, now that my parents' visit is over."

"I hardly think that's true, sir!"

"Perfectly true, Marton!" Bertie looked annoyed. "His account to my father of my time here was less than glowing. So – if I could not get a glowing reference after working my bottom off, then I can scarcely see the point of killing myself with work for the rest of my time here. They will allow me to graduate regardless of how many drill practices I do or do not attend."

"Bertie's right," said Nellie.

"Is he indeed?" said James, giving Nellie a warning look.

"Perfectly right, Marton. I will be given my full officer status simply on the merit of being the Prince of Wales."

James tried to decipher what was happening as he looked on. Bertie seemed to be talking with a confidence he hadn't witnessed before. And there seemed to be some secret communication going on between him and Nellie. Secret exchanged looks and smiles.

"Of course, it is not my business to advise you, sir," he continued as calmly as he could. "But due to the fact that I – smuggled, for want of a better word – Nellie in to meet you, then I am alarmed at your lack of caution today – in case it was discovered that Nellie was here and the repercussions it would have for all of us."

"We were very cautious. Nobody saw us – not even Tommy," said Bertie.

"Especially not Tommy!" said Nellie, and they exchanged a private look and giggle again.

"Sir, anyone could have seen you out in the countryside, without your being aware – or here in the garrison as you left and returned, perhaps from a distance and again without your being aware. You must be more careful if you wish this relationship to continue."

Bertie looked alarmed at this and Nellie even more so. She could see James was very angry though he was trying to conceal the fact.

"Yes, you are right, Marton – we shall be more careful in future."

"I am relieved to hear that, sir. I should hate it if scandal overtook you here in my country – and if I was partly responsible." He bowed to Bertie, his face grave. "Nellie, the carriage to take you back to Dublin is down the lane outside now. I suggest we go to it immediately."

"Now, here! We haven't even had dinner yet!" said Bertie.

Nellie took heed of James's warning look and turned to Bertie. "I had better go, Bertie. I need to change my clothes if nothing else!"

"Oh!" Bertie looked disappointed.

"Could you give us a minute, James?" requested Nellie.

James nodded. "I'll wait outside the door for you – it would be better if you are not seen emerging from the building alone."

Nellie watched as James left the room and then turned to Bertie and smiled.

"Why did you agree to go?" he asked, taking her in his arms.

"Because I must! I actually do need to change my clothes!" She smiled up at him.

"But – this isn't a very nice end to a perfect day," he groaned.

"But there can be other days and other nights – if you want?"

"Oh, yes, Nellie. I most definitely do want!" he said, leaning down and kissing her.

She kissed him back and pulled away.

"I'd better go. James is waiting," she said, hurrying to the door.

He grabbed her hand and held on to it.

"When will I see you again?" he asked.

"I don't know! We'll get James to arrange it."

"Tomorrow? Tomorrow night?" he asked.

"Yes, yes, I'll see you tomorrow." She disentangled her hand from his and blew him a kiss as she hurried to the door.

She turned back to take a final look at him before she winked and left.

"What do you think you are playing at?" demanded an angry James as the carriage drove off.

"I'm not playing at anything," she said, looking innocent.

"Taking off like that for the day! I was worried sick when you didn't show and then when I called at his quarters and there was nobody there!"

"There was no need to worry, James, we were perfectly fine."

"I wasn't worried about you, Nellie! I was worried something had happened to the Prince of Wales!"

"Something did happen to him. He enjoyed himself! He had a lovely day with somebody who treated him as a man, not something to be nervous of, or curious about or anything else. I think it's the first time in his life he's been treated as normal!"

James raised his eyes to heaven. "He's not normal, Nellie. Whatever you and he are pretending to be when you are alone together – he is not normal!"

"We're not pretending to be anything. We are just being ourselves."

"Nellie, you are being paid to be with him. He is a client like all the rest you've had."

Her became angry. "I know that! I'm not stupid."

"Well, the two of you look rather stupid together. With your giggles and your furtive glances!"

"I don't know what you are complaining about! I'm only doing what you asked me to do. If I wasn't making the Prince happy then you'd have another thing to say. And I am making him happy. He wants to see me again – tomorrow."

"That's good," said James, becoming more relaxed. "That's very good."

"You plan is working out, James. You should be thanking me and not giving out," she said and looked out the window angrily.

He reached out and touched her knee but she shook him off. He wondered if he had gone too far. He couldn't afford to lose her co-operation.

"I am thankful, Nellie," he said.

"Well, you've a funny way of showing it."

"I can see that you are making him happy, but I am just worried that he is making you happy as well," he said.

"And would that be such a crime?"

"I don't want to see you getting hurt," said James.

"*Ha!* As if you ever cared about *me* getting hurt!"

James looked out the window and saw they were safely out of the garrison.

"*Stop!*" he called out the window and the driver halted the carriage.

James stood up and, opening the door, stepped out.

"I will collect you tomorrow at five," he said before he closed the door and the carriage continued its journey to Dublin.

CHAPTER 32

"Where have you been?" demanded Sadie as Nellie came in through the door of the flat that evening.

"I've been with the Prince, where else?"

"All day?"

"Yes, he cancelled his schedule and spent the day with me!" She began to waltz around the sitting room. "Oh, Sadie! What a day! We went strolling through the countryside, down by a river. It was beautiful. It was the happiest day of my life, I think!"

"Well, you haven't had too many of those to compare it to!"

"It was just magical. I feel like – a princess!"

Sadie leaned forward in her seat, looking horrified. "'Tis far from a princess you are, my dear!"

"I know that – but he has a way of making me feel like one!"

"That's because the only women he's ever probably dealt with have *been* princesses! He probably doesn't know how to deal with you any differently!"

"I don't care how or why – I just care that he does." Nellie stopped twirling and sank to the floor in front of where Sadie was sitting. "He wants to see me again tomorrow night."

"Again! So soon!"

"Yes! He actually wanted me to stay tonight as well but I said I had no change of clothes so I had to come home."

"This is all very – strange, Nellie. I don't like it. You're forgetting yourself and this is going to end in tears if you don't remember yourself quickly!"

"Why are you being so unpleasant to me?" asked Nellie, moving away from her.

"I'm not being unpleasant! I'm being truthful," replied Sadie.

Nellie became angry. "Well, keep your truth! I've had truth all my life and all it's ever given me is unhappiness. This, for the first time, is just a little bit of fantasy for me – do you begrudge me that?"

"I just don't want to see you getting hurt," said Sadie.

"Why is everyone so interested in protecting me all of a sudden? Hurt! I've been hurt so many times that I can't remember a time when I didn't feel hurt. This is the first little bit of happiness I've had, and I'm making him happy too. What's wrong with that?"

"Everything! When it's built on lies! He'll tire of you quick enough, quicker than you'll ever believe, my girl, and where will you be then?"

"I'll be the same as I ever was. But until then I am going to enjoy being with him. Because he makes me feel like no one ever did before."

"You hardly know him!" scoffed Sadie.

"I knew him straight away. With Bertie, there are no secrets, there's nothing hidden."

"That's because he's young and stupid and knows no more," said Sadie.

"I know this won't last forever, Sadie. I know it won't last long at all. I know he'll be leaving Ireland soon and that will be the end of me being with him. But, until then, I want to make memories that I will treasure for the rest of my life. The time I spent with the Prince of Wales. Don't you see this has made me feel important, that I matter, for the first time in my life?"

She turned and walked down the corridor.

"I'm going for a bath."

CHAPTER 33

The next evening Bertie waited anxiously in his sitting room, looking out the window. Again, he had a feast laid out on the table and champagne waiting for Nellie's arrival. He saw the carriage pull up outside and quickly went to wait by the fireplace. A few moments later the door opened and Nellie walked in. She looked at him and then went rushing into his arms and kissed him passionately.

"I've been counting the minutes until I saw you again," he whispered into her ear.

"And I you," she whispered back.

He reached to the mantelpiece and took down a box which he held out to Nellie.

"What's this?" she asked.

"Open it and see," he urged excitedly.

She opened the box and saw a diamond necklace inside.

"Oh, Bertie, why?" she asked, looking up at him.

"Because I wanted you to have something special. I went out to a jeweller's today and, when I saw this, I just had to get it for you."

"I wish you hadn't," she said, closing the box and handing it back to him.

"But why ever not?" he asked, surprised. He had never known a woman who did not enjoy being given diamonds before.

"I just wish you hadn't," she said as tears began to fall down her face.

211

"Nellie!" he said, shocked at her tears. "Have I done something wrong?"

How could she ever explain to him? The life she led and what she had received in return. And for him to give her diamonds made her feel that this time with him was just like the times with the others. Her time and favours in return for financial rewards. It was reducing something that she was treating as special and different to a financial transaction.

"Oh Nellie! Please tell me what I have done wrong?" he begged.

"Nothing!" she said. "I just – don't want anything from you, Bertie."

"But it's just a necklace!" he said.

"You had no right to buy it for me!" Her sad tears gave way and now she became angry and slammed the box back on the mantelpiece and walked away from him.

"I think I'd better go," she said, looking out the window to see if the carriage was still waiting there. Unfortunately, it had already gone.

"Go! But why? I couldn't wait to see you again," he said.

"Well, you've ruined it all now by getting me diamonds. I thought you respected me. I thought we understood each other," she said, still angry.

"I do! We do!" he said. "I didn't mean to offend you. I just thought it would be a nice thing to do for you. I want to please you, Nellie, to make you happy."

"Well, you don't please me! You don't please me at all by buying me diamonds when you hardly even know me!" All Sadie's words of warning came back to her. Her mind was in turmoil. The real reason she was there with him. How she had allowed herself to get carried away. But Bertie knew nothing of that. She had thought he had just wanted to be with her because he liked her. But now he was trying to buy her like all the others. He thought he could buy her and that she expected financial reward. And what hurt her most was that this was the truth. This was who she was.

"Tell your batman, or whatever he is, to go and get James and tell him to return the carriage to collect me straight away so I can get out of here!"

She knew James would be furious. She knew she was would probably never be allowed to return to the stage again, now she had messed this up. But she didn't care. Her pride was surfacing and she couldn't ignore it.

He looked at her anger in amazement. "I would never have thought that buying a necklace could cause so much trouble," he said.

"Well, think next time you decide to buy a gift for a lady," she said.

"But I've never bought a gift for a lady before. I didn't know what was the right thing to do. I know Papa buys gifts for Mama all the time and it pleases her, so –"

"Oh, you and your mama and your papa! Grow up, Bertie, and stop acting like a pampered child all the time!"

Bertie's eyes opened even further in amazement.

"Well, this is a fine way to speak to the Prince of Wales!" he said.

"Ah, get over yourself! You're no different from anybody else once you get past your fancy titles and castles and your empire!"

"I don't know what to say!"

"Good! Then say nothing, I'm tired of hearing the sound of your voice!"

"My! Have you always had such a temper?"

"Only when I'm crossed," she said.

"Well, if you don't mind me saying, I think it is you who are coming across as a pampered child."

"Me!"

"Yes, you! Somebody tries to do something nice for you and you throw it back in his face. What's a chap to do?" Suddenly Bertie was angry. "You are coming across as somebody who has been given a little too much attention from men."

"That's not true!"

"Yes, it is. You think you can treat a man any way you want."

"No, I don't."

"You forget, I've seen you perform on the stage. I've seen how you address the men in the audience. Making jokes at their expense. Well, not I, Nellie, not I! I won't be treated with such disrespect. I was only trying to do a nice thing, and I won't have it thrown back in my face."

He turned and stormed to the fireplace and held the mantelpiece with both his hands as he trembled with anger.

She studied him for a while. She began to feel sorry for him as he stood there trembling with a mixture of upset and anger.

"Well," she said eventually, "I didn't think you had it in you!"

"Had what in me?" he demanded, turning around and facing her angrily.

"A bit of life! That you could stand up for yourself at last!"

"Don't make jokes at my expense, Nellie."

"I'm not! I'm telling you the truth." She walked over to him and smiled at him. "If you show more of that spirt, we'll make a great king out of you yet."

"Are you going?" he asked.

"Do you want me to?"

He shook his head. "No, I'd like you to stay."

"Even after that display I just treated you to?"

"Yes," he said. "You won't frighten me that easily."

"Good!" she said, looking up at the box containing the necklace. "And what about that?"

"Let's just pretend I never got it," he suggested.

"Most sensible thing you've said tonight," she said.

CHAPTER 34

Victoria sat in the drawing room at Buckingham Palace reading a letter from her daughter Vicky.

"What joy!" she declared, putting the letter down on her lap.

"What news from Berlin?" asked Albert, looking up from the newspaper he was reading as he sat on the couch.

"Vicky has answered my request and she has invited Bertie to go to Prussia at the end of this month to meet the Princess Alexandra!"

"So soon?"

"Yes, we can always trust Vicky to be prompt in such matters. Vicky writes that Alexandra will be travelling to Prussia at the end of September and for Bertie to be present at the same time. She is suggesting Speyer as a suitable venue for the two to meet."

"That does sound all very positive."

"Oh that Bertie and Alexandra should meet and fall in love!" sighed Victoria. "And that will be that! No more worries about Bertie! Would that not be bliss?"

"It certainly would remove our concerns for his future. But what if they do not like each other? We must not get our hopes up too high, Victoria. Bertie has a stubborn streak, not unlike you, and it seems to be increasing as he gets older."

"We can only hope that his time in Ireland has eradicated all that insolence he has demonstrated."

"I did not see much sign of it being eradicated while we

were in Killarney," said Albert.

"I am going to remain positive about the whole matter, Albert. I just know that Alexandra is the one for Bertie and we must hope he agrees."

"We certainly hope that he does. Because we have done an exhaustive search of all the royal houses and Alexandra is the only one that is left! If not her, then I fear nobody will be marrying our son and becoming the future Queen of England," said Albert.

Nellie lay in Bertie's arms in the darkness of his bedroom.

"You were almost funny earlier," said Nellie.

"How so?"

"Becoming all masterful in a moment," she said.

He chuckled. "Well, you did provoke me so!"

"I thought you very attractive when you became all masterful."

"Did you?" he laughed.

"You should try it more often."

"Perhaps I shall," he said.

"You should try it with your parents," she said decisively.

"*Hmmm*, I don't know if I should go quite that far!"

"Why not? They'll respect you all the more for it."

"Anytime I have tried to be – masterful – has not resulted in them respecting me," he said. "Though it might be different now."

"Why?"

"Because now I have you," he whispered.

"You have me for now, Bertie. But we both know this isn't going to last very long."

"But why not?"

"Well, you are returning to England in a couple of weeks," she said.

He lay in silence.

"Bertie? Are you all right?"

"Yes – I just can't bear the thought of going back. Of leaving you."

"Oh, my darling!" she said, holding him tighter.

216

CHAPTER 35

"Is this true, Marton, the rumours that I am hearing about Bertie?" asked Charles as the officers sat around their regular table in the mess.

"What rumours?" asked James casually.

"I've heard rumours from some of the men about a woman being seen sneaking in and out of Bertie's quarters," said Charles.

"How should I know?" said James coyly.

"Come on! If there is a woman creeping in and out to see him, then it's obviously that actress that you introduced him to!"

"I wouldn't know about such things," said James dismissively.

"Marton!" warned Donald.

James looked at their accusing eyes and knew he couldn't keep the truth from them any more. He would risk being ostracised from his close officer friends if he kept this matter from them any longer.

"Yes, it's Nellie," he said in a whisper, leaning forward. "She's been coming in and out and seeing him most nights."

"My gosh!" Donald was shocked. "And how's she getting in and out?"

"I arrange a carriage for her," admitted James.

"Marton!" exclaimed Charles.

"Well, I didn't mean it to go this far. I didn't even think he'd want to see her again after the first time!"

"But this was all just supposed to be a bit of fun!" said Donald.

"Well, it is fun. Clearly it is fun for Bertie when he keeps asking her to come," said James.

"There will be war if Hazeldon ever finds out," said Charles.

"Yes, I think you've let this go on a bit too long, Marton," said Donald. "It's risky letting them continue to see each other."

"Well, what can I do? It's not my job to break them up. We all agreed to do this together. We all agreed that we should set Bertie up before he left Ireland. And that's what we've done and it's worked very well."

"A little too well," said Charles.

"Bertie is gloriously happy," said James. "Enjoying his time here in Ireland immensely, isn't that the main thing?"

"Yes, but can you trust the girl, James?" asked Charles. "What if she speaks of her affair with the Prince to anybody?"

"Oh, Nellie won't tell a soul, I promise you that. She is completely trustworthy," said James with a smile.

CHAPTER 36

Bertie sat reading a letter from his mother as Nellie massaged his temples.

"Anything the matter, love?" she asked, seeing his face concerned.

"Oh, no, nothing at all," he said, quickly putting the letter back into the envelope and flinging it on the table beside him.

"What is it?" she insisted.

"It's just from my mother," he sighed loudly. "She has written to tell me I am to go to Prussia when I leave here."

"To see your sister?" asked Nellie.

"*Hmmm*, and others," said Bertie.

"What others?" she pushed.

"A Danish princess called Alexandra."

"And why are you meeting her?" asked Nellie.

"To see if she's a suitable prospect for marriage," he admitted.

Nellie stopped massaging his temples.

"I see! And is she a – suitable prospect for marriage?" asked Nellie.

"Well, I don't know. I haven't met her yet," he said. "I have no interest in meeting her, I can assure you of that."

"Well, why are you meeting her then?" Nellie demanded.

"Because I have no choice. It is what is expected of me," he said.

Nellie walked to the window. "And what does she look like

219

– this Princess Alexandra?"

Bertie followed her and stood behind her. "She is supposed to be quite beautiful. Indeed, I have been shown a photograph of her and she lives up to her reputation."

Nellie felt an anger burn inside of her and a jealousy to match.

"Well, I hope the two of you will be very happy together!" Nellie sniped.

He laughed and then bent down and kissed her neck. "She might be beautiful but she still doesn't hold a candle to you."

"You're all charm," Nellie said and, turning around, looked at him wryly. "I don't know why I'm so upset. I knew this day would come. That you would sail off to marry some princess and I would return to the stage."

"It doesn't have to be like that," he said.

"How can it be any other way? You return to England next week."

"Come with me," he said. "Come with me to England."

She burst out laughing. "Don't be so ridiculous."

He grabbed both her hands and held them tightly.

"I am being very serious, Nellie. I've been thinking about it so much. I can't bear to leave you next week. The thought of never seeing you again, it's unbearable for me."

"It's unbearable for me too. But what choice do we have – you must return to your life and I must return to mine," said Nellie.

"But it doesn't have to be that way. You can come to England too."

"But – but for what purpose?" she said, her mind clouded in confusion.

"For the purpose of us still being together," he said. "I know I am asking you to give a lot up – your flat, your career on the stage."

Nellie's heart was pounding as she moved away from him. "Stop talking like this, Bertie. It isn't fair on me. We are to part next week, and that is the end of it."

"I can't leave you, Nellie, I can't go back to the life I led before I met you. Never sure of who I was or what I was doing. You make sense of me, of my life. Without you, I'm nothing."

"But, where would I live? What would I do? What about Sadie?"

"I can organise a house for you to live in – bring Sadie with you. You can work on the stage or not, it's entirely up to you. I shall provide for you one way or another, if you'll accept,"

"I think you've gone quite mad!" she said.

"I have! I have gone mad! Mad with love!" He laughed loudly as he swept her off her feet and swung her around.

On the carriage ride back to Dublin, Nellie was lost in thought. She didn't know what to think after Bertie's proposal. If it had been any other man, she would have believed him to be joking and not sincere. But Bertie was not like any other man and she knew he would not say such a thing without meaning it completely. Her head was telling her to ignore Bertie's proposal, say goodbye to him next week when he left for England and get back to her normal life as soon as possible. Her heart was pulling her in a very different direction. The thought of never seeing Bertie again was impossible for her to bear. The thought of just returning to her previous life was now a poisonous thought to her. Even if she was reinstated at the Palace Theatre and resumed her life as an actress, she didn't think that would be enough for her any more. She had changed over these past weeks. She had changed in Bertie's company. The way Bertie had treated her made her realise she was worth so much more than she had thought before. In the way she had instilled a confidence in him that he had never had before, he had done the same for her. But what future could they possibly have together? What future could a commoner, and they didn't come more common that she did, have with a king? She didn't understand royalty or know anything about it. Who was this

Danish princess Bertie's parents wanted him to marry? But he had shown no interest in her, so he could not marry her, surely?

Nellie buried her face in her hands as she tried to figure out solutions to their relationship and ways they could make it work.

CHAPTER 37

Nellie sat in her flat, reading a book she had borrowed from the library.

"What are you reading?" asked Sadie as she came out of the kitchen.

"It's a book on Henry the Eighth," said Nellie, not looking up from her reading.

"Isn't he the lad who killed all his wives?"

"Not all of them. He had six wives . . . not all of them royalty." She snapped the book shut and looked up. "In fact, his second wife, Ann Boleyn, the one he left his first wife for and who he left the church for, was a commoner, just like me."

"I see! So?" Sadie's eyes narrowed.

"So, I'm saying nothing is impossible. A king can marry a commoner, even when all the odds are stacked against them like in the case of Henry the Eighth and Ann Boleyn."

Sadie stared at her and then burst out laughing. "You can't be seriously thinking that you could marry Bertie!"

Nellie's face was serious. "And why not? If Ann Boleyn could do it, then why couldn't I?"

"Well, I know nothing about it, but I doubt this Ann Boleyn was a whore like you for a start," said Sadie.

Nellie slammed the book on the table. "How dare you!"

"I dare because it's true! I knew this was going to end in tears! Now you, foolish girl, have gone delusional and thinking that you could marry the Prince of Wales!"

"He's asked me to move to England with him when he returns there next week."

"What?" Sadie's mouth dropped open.

"He's asked me and I'm going."

"But you can't! You just can't! Oh Nellie, I'm pleading with you, stop this now before it goes any further!"

"It's gone too far already, Sadie. I'm in love with him and he's in love with me."

Sadie sank down into a chair and buried her face in her hands.

"I can't live without him, Sadie. I don't know what I'd do without him. I've been given the chance of true happiness and I can't walk away."

Sadie looked up. "And what happened in the end to this Ann Boylen? Was she one of the ones he killed?"

"Well – she – she was beheaded. But that was centuries ago, things have changed now," said Nellie. "Don't worry about a thing, Sadie – you are to come with me, Bertie insisted on it."

"I think I might be better off staying here than watching you destroy your life," said Sadie.

"Don't be silly. Everything will be all right, more than all right, just you wait and see," said Nellie with a smile.

Bertie downed a glass of bourbon and then began to pace quickly up and down in his sitting room. He had sent his batman to fetch James. He wasn't sure how he could or whether he even should break the news to James about his intentions to move Nellie to England. He wasn't thinking straight, he knew. But all he knew was he could not bear a life without Nellie in it. He had become so attached to her, so dependent on her advice and her love. He remembered what his life was like before he had come to Ireland. He could not return to that life of being constantly domineered by his parents and the palace. He had found a new strength here in Ireland, and Nellie was a big part of that. He was following his heart and that was all that mattered. Why should he be forced into a marriage with a Danish princess he did not even know, when he had found true love, so unexpectedly, with an Irish actress?

There was a knock on the door.

"*Come in!*" called Bertie.

James opened the door and walked in.

"You wished to see me, sir?"

"Yes, yes! Come in, James."

Bertie refilled his glass of bourbon and poured another one and handed it to James with a half-hearted smile.

He began to pace again.

"Is anything the matter, Bertie? You seem unsettled?"

"Yes, it's Nellie . . ."

James frowned. What had she done? When everything was going so well, what had she done to upset Bertie?

"Has she – displeased you in some way?" he asked.

"Gosh – no! Not in the least – not at all! Nellie could never displease me even if she tried!" He gave a wry smile. "And sometimes I wonder if she does try to displease me with some of the things she says to me!"

"So what is the matter then?"

"I've invited Nellie to come with me to England when I leave next week," said Bertie.

James nearly dropped his glass. "To England! But for what purpose?"

"For no other purpose than that I want to continue seeing her and do not want to sever my ties with her."

"But – what has Nellie got to say about this?"

"Well, I think she in favour. She hasn't said no – though she hasn't said yes either. She can be very . . ." he smiled happily, "maddening sometimes."

James put down his glass. "Bertie, I advise against this plan. I don't think you have thought it through. Surely – surely – surely you are not suggesting that Nellie be introduced to court life in London?"

"Well, no, I know this isn't a possibility – at least for now –"

"Or ever – Your Royal Highness!" snapped James.

"It is no business of anybody else's what I do and who I meet in my private time. And I wish to continue to meet Nellie – I can't bear to leave her behind, James."

James decided to try sympathy. "Bertie, I know Nellie is a wonderful woman and I can see that her beauty and glamour may have a cast a spell over you. But I think it's wise for you to understand that Nellie would never be accepted in your world, no matter how infatuated you are with her."

"I know that, James!"

"I think there is a huge element of naiveté and lack of experience influencing your judgement here, Bertie. There will be other women, equally as beautiful and glamorous as Nellie –"

"I don't want to meet them! The only other woman I am going to be meeting is that Danish princess with whom I will be stuck for the rest of my life – if I don't do something to escape the fate that is being forced on me by my parents."

"Perhaps, then, you are seeing Nellie as an escape route out of this marriage you are being threatened with? A lifeline to save you from it?"

"I don't know what I'm thinking – but I know I love Nellie."

"Love!"

"And she's coming to England with me."

"But where should she live? What would she live on?" asked James.

"She needn't worry about anything like that, I'll look after her," said Bertie.

"But how will you meet? Do you plan to go out in public with her?"

"We shall manage just fine – with your help," said Bertie.

"*My* help?"

"Yes. I am putting a request in to Hazeldon to have you transferred to Aldershot. You have become a very good friend of mine, James, and I reward my close friends. I need friends like you in my life as I venture forth to carry the great burden of monarchy that has been placed on my shoulders by virtue of birth."

James was stunned. "Your Royal Highness," he said, bowing, "it will be my pleasure to serve you in any way that I can."

"Good, jolly good!" beamed Bertie. "Then we have a lot to organise, James. We must assist Nellie in any way we can to help her with this move. I'm asking her to give up so much, her life here. I am asking a huge sacrifice from her, and I just want her to be happy."

"Yes, that's my dearest wish too," said James.

"So, let us make plans," said Bertie.

CHAPTER 38

As Sadie opened the door of the flat James rushed past her and, seeing Nellie standing by the fireplace, went to her, picked her up and began swinging her around the room.

"Oh, you beauty! You absolute beauty!" he exclaimed.

"James! Put me down! Put me down at once!" demanded Nellie.

He placed her back on the floor. "I've spoken to Bertie and he's told me everything! How you are moving to England to be close to him!"

"I haven't said yes!" said Nellie.

"But you can't say no!"

"There's a lot to think about, James. I can't just up sticks and go."

"Why ever not? There isn't much to hold you back here," said James.

She walked to the window. "I've been in turmoil since Bertie asked me. Sadie says I would be crazy to go. That no good can come from a relationship when we are so far apart socially."

"Did she indeed?" said James. giving Sadie a dirty look.

"I don't know what to do, James," said Nellie.

"Could you leave us, please, Sadie?" said James.

"No, I will not! I'm not leaving you to fill that girl's head with any more of this nonsense. The Prince of Wales! It's all right for him with his castles and his empire – he'll be all right,

228

to be sure. But what about my Nellie – what will happen to her when he's done with her and moved on to his next conquest?"

"Nellie has me to protect her," said James.

"You've done a great job on that so far! Selling her to any man that comes along to line your own pocket and then casting her aside when she wouldn't keep living the sordid life you threw her in!"

"Well, you can't complain! You've done very well out of it all!" countered James.

"I never wanted Nellie to fall into the life she's led!" Sadie said, his voice rising. "I want the best for her – to finally meet a nice man who will love her for who she is and mind her. She's so desperate for love she's believing all this shit the Prince is spewing on her."

"It's nothing to do with you!" James snarled. "You're here to put the kettle on and run her a bath, no more! Keep your opinions to yourself because you do not matter a jot to anyone!"

"*Stop it!*" Nellie screamed.

They both looked at her.

"Now, look – you are upsetting Nellie!" said James.

"*I'm* upsetting her?" spat Sadie.

"Sadie! Will you leave us alone, please," Nellie demanded. "I need to speak to James alone."

Sadie looked furious as she turned and reluctantly left them.

"Interfering old cow!" said James.

"Oh, be quiet, James! What did Bertie tell you?"

"He told me he can't live without you and he was moving you to England. We spent the afternoon discussing the details. He is returning to Cambridge University when he arrives back in England. He is going to rent you a house outside the town where you will reside – and that's all there is to it, really. Quite straightforward."

"So I am to be his kept woman? His mistress?" she asked.

"Well, no, because you can only be a mistress if he were

married," he pointed out.

"Rubbish! What does it matter what name it's called? Besides, he tells me his parents want him to be married as soon as possible to some foreign princess," she said.

"He has no intention of marrying that girl, Nellie. It's you he wants."

"I know, I believe him. I just don't want to be hurt. I care for him deeply. Sadie says our relationship cannot work, ever. Our worlds are too far apart. But I was reading –"

She broke off.

"Reading what?" he asked, then spotted a book on the table and went and picked it up. It was a book on Henry the Eighth. She had left it open at a page about Ann Boleyn.

"You've been catching up on your history, I see," he said.

"Well, all these figures from the past were names I just heard and knew nothing about. And here I am now with the man who is next in line for the throne. It's hard for me to comprehend."

"Nellie, this is your chance to make something of yourself. To become part of a world you could only ever dream of."

"Do you think that Bertie could ever marry me?"

James looked at her, trying to keep his face straight. Was she really so naïve?

"I do not know, Nellie. History has taught us to expect the unexpected. But in any case he's is love with you and the women who have been in kings' lives, women who are kings' favourites are often very well looked after financially and in every other way."

"So, it is as I suspected – I am to be the future king's whore, no more or less. I am to continue the life I have always led, except the man who will be keeping me will be a prince."

"I am not saying that!" he said, irritated. "Oh, Nellie, try to see this for what it is! Royal marriages are based on politics and forming alliances with other countries and not based on love."

"Bertie says his own parents are a love match," said Nellie.

"Well, then they are the exception. That's why the role of a king's lover is so important, because the relationship is based on love and attraction. And that's a powerful position to be in, the real power behind the throne."

She sat down quickly with her hands in her lap. "And why are you so happy about all this? You were warning me before not to get to close to Bertie."

"That was before I realised how deep his feelings are for you. Before I realised he was so serious about you that he is taking you to England . . . and I am to go as well."

"Go?"

"To England," he said.

"You!" she said, startled.

"Bertie is requesting a transfer for me. He's come very much to rely on me and wants me close by in England to be able to advise him, and also to assist you and him in any way I can."

She shook her head knowingly. "This has all worked out perfectly for you, James. More than you ever imagined. You have certainly more than gained favour with the Prince of Wales – promotion and a special role as his friend and advisor."

James walked over to the window and stared out. "Why shouldn't I have it? I've worked hard to get here. I didn't have the advantages and connections the other officers had. I had to fight my way up on merit. And here I am now, part of the Prince's inner circle."

"Thanks to me," she said.

He turned and faced her. "Yes, thanks to you. This is only the beginning, Nellie. If we play our cards right and you trust me, we will go to the very top."

CHAPTER 39

Bertie sat confidently across the desk from Major Hazeldon in his office.

"Ah, the ten weeks that you have been with us have passed so quickly, Your Royal Highness!" said Hazeldon.

"Yes, they have."

"I sincerely hope you enjoyed your time here with us?"

"I certainly did, Major. It has been a wonderful experience, memories that I will cherish for the rest of my life."

"I am so pleased to hear it," said Hazeldon, genuinely pleased that his intention of having Bertie enjoy his time and give good reports on the camp had come to fruition. "Well, you have performed all your tasks with diligence and excellence and have graduated to the officer ranks with credit."

"Oh, come now, Major. I think you are allowed to be as honest with me as you were with my father," said Bertie.

"I don't think I quite understand you, sir?" The smile dropped from Hazeldon's face.

"I have been an average student here with average results, let us be honest. The words *diligence* and *excellence* we can leave out of the equation. There is no reason for you to hold yourself in any way accountable for my mediocrity. I take full responsibility for it myself. Some men are born to be great officers, and others are not. Unfortunately, I was not."

Hazeldon didn't know what to say so just nodded. He

realised there was a change in Bertie from the anxious, eager-to-please young man he had been when he had arrived ten weeks before. He was self-assured, more confident and less willing to compromise himself. Perhaps the disappointment and realisation of knowing he had not made the grade as an officer had made Bertie more circumspect about life.

"You will be returning to your studies in Cambridge, sir?" he asked, to move the conversation on.

"Yes, Cambridge beckons. Just one more thing, Major. I'm requesting a transfer for Captain James Marsdon to Aldershot."

"But this is news to me!" said Hazeldon, taken aback. "Captain Marton has not asked for any transfer and he is assigned to this camp for the foreseeable future."

"Yes, but I've already discussed it with him and he's agreeable." He knew that in such a situation the Bertie of old would be trying to explain and justify his request. But, now, he was determined not to justify himself any more. He was the Prince of Wales, and he knew Hazeldon would not deny or question his request. Which was the way it should be.

CHAPTER 40

Donald leaned against a fountain smoking a cigar in Henrietta's garden as he watched her pruning roses.

"We are going to have to cool our relationship for a while," said Henrietta abruptly as she snipped a rose from its stem.

"Why?" asked Donald, startled.

"I received a letter from Jack and he's returning from South Africa next week," she said.

"Bugger!" said Donald, looking disappointed.

"*Hmm*, I don't know what you are complaining about – I have to live with him!"

"Well, how long will he be back for?"

"Indefinitely, or so he says. But hopefully he'll be posted to one of the colonies soon again."

"Well, what do we do in the meantime?" asked Donald.

"Well, you won't be able to come here any more. Jack accepts my life as it is, but he wouldn't want me to rub his nose in it."

"Yes, I see. Most inconvenient . . . well, what are we to do? Where shall we meet while he's here?"

"I am too circumspect to rendezvous in hotel bedrooms on a regular basis, Donald, that I am sure of," she said.

"You could always come and stay with me in the camp in Kildare. I could sneak you in like we did for the party with the Prince of Wales," suggested Donald.

"And I am far too circumspect to be sneaking into military camps! That was a once-off because the Prince was having a party. Your quarters are far too cramped and that bed too small for me to be going back there again!"

"Well, I don't see the Prince's girlfriend complaining much about being sneaked in," said Donald.

"The Prince's girlfriend?" said Henrietta, stopping her pruning and standing up to look at him.

"Yes, the actress who was at the party that night. Do you remember her?"

"Oh, yes, I remember her all right! Did they end up together?" She looked surprised.

"They most certainly did," Donald confirmed.

"I didn't think he'd have it in him! He rebuffed Clarissa's attentions pretty quickly."

"I don't think he wants to mess around with married women, not in his position," said Donald.

"Really? How noble of him," said Henrietta, her face turning sour. "That woman, Nellie Cliffden – "

"Yes?"

"I've been enquiring about her. She's a singer at the Palace music hall, given to performing the most vulgar acts."

"Well, she seems to please the Prince. She's been visiting him at his quarters ever since that night."

"She also has a disgraceful reputation. She has been seen out with many men. Why would the Prince want anything to do with a woman like that?"

Donald shrugged. "Well, if what I hear is correct, when he returns to England this week, she is to return with him."

"*What?*" Henrietta dropped the pruning shears she was carrying. "But why is he doing that?"

"He is quite smitten with her, by all accounts," said Donald.

"How shocking! I don't know where peoples' morals have gone these days! If the press ever found that out!"

Donald jumped off the fountain wall and threw his

cigarette on the ground as his face became serious.
"Henrietta! This must go no further. It is completely
confidential, do you understand me?"

"Of course," she said as she picked up the shears and
started pruning the roses again.

Henrietta and Clarissa had met for afternoon tea in the
Shelbourne.

"And she's been visiting him in the camp in Kildare ever
since that night!" Henrietta informed her.

"I don't believe it!" said Clarissa.

"Donald would have no reason to lie."

"But can he be sure?"

"He's sure. The Prince was smitten – that was the word
Donald used – with Nellie Cliffden so much that she is
moving to England to be with him."

Clarissa's eyes widened in her astonishment.

"Nobody knows, apparently – it's being kept all very hush-
hush," continued Henrietta.

"So she is to be the Prince's mistress?" said Clarissa.

"It looks that way."

"A common actress from the stage?"

"If she were only that!" said Henrietta. "I have been doing
some subtle enquiring about our friend Nellie Cliffden, and
the rumours that circulate about her are shocking!"

"Well! Go on – pray continue!"

Henrietta glanced around and then leaned forward and
began to speak in whispers to Clarissa.

Nellie rushed into Oliver's studio.

"You're late!" he said. "I was expecting you an hour ago,
Nellie. I have to go somewhere this evening – so come on, sit
over by the window quickly and I'll start sketching."

He sat down and took up his pencil and paper.

"I can't stay, Oliver – I'm leaving for London in a couple
of days and just dropped by to tell you of my plans."

"London!" He stood up quickly and dropped his pencil and paper. "What for?"

"I'm moving there, Oliver. I'm not coming back."

"But this is all very sudden, Nellie! What has brought all this about?"

"No particular reason," she said. "I just need a change and England seems as good a place to go as any."

"Are you in some kind of trouble, Nellie?"

"No!"

"Has this something to do with that incident in Dalkey? Are the police after you?"

"No, nothing like that! Everything's fine, I promise you," she said with a smile.

He searched her face for some kind of upset but could find none. "And what about your job at the Palace?"

"What about it?" she scoffed. "The Palace has shown me no loyalty, so why should I show them any?"

"And do you have a job to go to?"

"No, but I'll find something. Don't worry about me, please. James is coming too."

Oliver raised his eyes to heaven. "I should have known he would have something to do with it! What's he got you involved in now?"

"Nothing, Oliver, everything's fine, I promise you. In fact, I've never been happier."

"Well, this is a fine state of affairs, running out on me like this! How am I going to find a model as good as you to replace you?"

"Oh, you'll manage something, Oliver," she said and kissed his cheek. "I'll write to you."

She turned and rushed out the door.

"*Make sure you do!*" he called after her. "*Mind yourself – and be careful, Nellie!*"

Tommy had carried all of Bertie's clothes and possessions down to the carriage that waited for him outside.

Bertie took a final look around the sitting room in his quarters. He felt sad leaving the place as he thought of all the happy times he'd had there. But most of his happiest times had been with Nellie. And she was coming with him.

Bertie left the quarters and walked down the steps and into the carriage. The carriage made its way through the lanes of the garrison until it reached the square where all the soldiers had gathered. As the carriage drove past them, Bertie waved at the soldiers as they all cheered him.

"This time tomorrow we'll be starting our new life, Sadie," said Nellie as they frantically packed their belongings.

"Where are we staying when we arrive in London?" asked Sadie as she carefully folded Nellie's gowns into a trunk.

"We are staying in Claridge's Hotel until we move into our new house," said Nellie.

"Claridge's! Who would have ever thought!" said Sadie.

"Indeed! Admit it, Sadie! You must be a little excited by our new life," said Nellie.

"I'll admit no such thing!" said Sadie as she continued folding gowns away.

"If you are retiring from the stage, will I pack this – you'll have no need of it any more?" asked Sadie as she held up the wig Nellie used on stage.

"Of course pack it and bring it with us! You never know when I might need it again!"

CHAPTER 41

Sandringham 1871

It was four days since Victoria had arrived at Sandringham, having been informed that Bertie's health was rapidly failing. All the time she hoped against hope that he would begin to recover from the terrible typhoid that had gripped his body. But he continued to decline. She had sat by his bedside with the rest of the family, watching the medical staff do all they could but to no avail. He continued in his delirious state, often making no sense.

Victoria would often reach out and take his hand and try to calm him, hoping his mother's voice would somehow get through to him. But he seemed unaware of her or any of the others' presence. She was now with Alice and her second eldest son Alfred in the study. As she watched the snow falling outside, she was painfully aware of what date it was – December 13th. The next day would be the tenth anniversary of Albert's death. Fate seemed to be playing the cruellest trick on her. She was now facing the same nightmare again a decade later. She had hardly survived her husband's death, she despaired at the thought of now losing her son.

"Mama?" prodded Alfred, stirring her from her deep thoughts.

She stopped looking out at the falling now and returned her attention to her children.

"Yes, Alfred – what were you saying?"

"I was suggesting, Mama, that we must let the Prime

Minister know the current situation. We are getting constant enquiries from his office about Bertie's health and he has a right to know how bad the situation is."

"Yes – yes. Inform the Prime Minister," agreed Victoria.

"And, also, we should issue a bulletin to the press and the public," said Alfred.

"And what should we say in the bulletin?" asked Victoria.

Alfred glanced at Alice before speaking. "That the Prince of Wales is gravely ill and we request prayers."

"According to Prime Minister Gladstone, the press and public don't care one jot about us any more," said Victoria bitterly. "He says that we have become irrelevant – why should we expect them to pray for Bertie, if this be the case?"

"I know for a fact there has been great concern throughout the country since it became known that Bertie has taken ill," said Alice.

"Really?" Victoria said sceptically.

"Of course – he is their future king," said Alice.

"Will he be a future anything, if the doctors are to be believed?" asked Victoria.

"The people have a right to know," urged Alfred. "With your permission I will telegram the Prime Minister and issue the bulletin."

Victoria nodded. "Very well."

Alfred stood up and left the room.

"I never thought I would have to go through this again in my lifetime," said Victoria.

"We must be strong," said Alice, wiping away a tear with her handkerchief.

"I think – I think he will die tomorrow, on the anniversary of his father's death," said Victoria.

"Please – Mama!" begged Alice.

"It is all too – familiar – the memories of your papa's death keep flooding back to me," said Victoria. "Is he still calling the name of – that woman?"

Alice looked at her mother. In all the years since the

scandal, she had never heard her mother refer to Nellie Cliffden by her name.

Alice nodded. "Yes, he is – at regular intervals."

Victoria shook her head in confusion. "But why – why is he calling for *her*?"

"He is delirious, Mama, he does not know what he is saying or who he is calling for," said Alice.

"Do you think – is there a possibility that Bertie has continued to see her over the years? That they are still in contact – involved still in a relationship?" Victoria was straining to understand.

"I do not know about Bertie's private life, Mama," said Alice.

"You may be the only person who does not know of Bertie's private life, Alice. The affairs and rumours have persisted over the years since he married Alexandra. It would not be outside the realms of possibility that the woman is still part of his life."

"Does any of that matter now?" asked Alice.

"I would say it matters to poor dear Alexandra. It must be torture for her to hear her husband calling for another woman as he lies there . . ."

"I believe Alexandra is made of sterner stuff than you think, Mama. If she has risen above the rumours and scandals circulating around Bertie over the years then she will not crumble just because he is calling for Nellie Cliffden now."

"I sometimes wonder did I do right, with his marriage to Alexandra? Was it the right decision? I only ever had his best possible interests at heart – but did I do right?" Victoria looked tortured as she spoke.

"Of course you did, Mama. You had no other choice after what happened. You weren't just trying to save Bertie, but the monarchy itself. The scandal was engulfing us all."

Victoria suddenly begn to cry. "I always did what I thought was best – for Bertie. But our relationship has now nearly become non-existent. I was so intent on stopping him from bringing down the monarchy by his actions that I have been blind to my own faults and lack of action that may now bring it crashing down around our ears."

Alice had risen from her seat and gone to comfort her mother when, in the distance, they could suddenly hear shouting.

"Bertie is having another fit," said Alice.

"We must go to him," said Victoria, standing. "We must go and comfort our dear Bertie."

CHAPTER 42

1861

The carriage pulled up outside Claridge's Hotel in London. James stepped out and offered his hand to Nellie as she climbed down, followed by Sadie. The porters from the hotel rushed forward quickly to take their trunks and suitcases. Nellie stared up at the building in awe. Since they had arrived in London that morning, Nellie had been mesmerised by the city. It was so much bigger than Dublin, so much busier with teeming people going back and forth.

"Good afternoon, sir, good afternoon, madam," said the doorman as he held the door open for them.

"Good afternoon," said James as he walked in.

Nellie nodded to him as she walked by.

Inside the foyer, Nellie stared at the grandeur of the interiors and looked at everything from the ornate ceilings to the marble floors. She suddenly felt overawed and intimidated and frightened. She stopped walking and froze.

James turned back to her. "What's wrong, Nellie?" he asked.

"This! All this, that's what's wrong!"

"There doesn't seem to be anything wrong with it to me – it all looks beautiful," he said.

"I never knew – I never thought it would be like this! I don't belong here, James! This place isn't for the likes of me!"

"Don't be so ridiculous!" He leaned towards her and spoke quietly. "Nellie, you are the companion of the Prince of

243

Wales. You need to start realising who you are and the position you are in. If any of these people knew who you were, they would fall at your feet."

"But that's just it, they don't know who I am and I can't say. I have to be this dirty little secret. This isn't what I expected, James. I've only met Bertie in his quarters in the camp. When we were there it was just the two of us and nothing like this place. But he's used to this, this is his world – how can I ever fit into it? When he sees me again, he'll realise I don't fit in and won't want anything to do with me again. He only liked me because he was out of his natural environment in Kildare."

"It's too late for doubts now, Nellie. Come on, we have to check in," said James as he took her arm and led her to the hotel reception.

"*Tut-tut-tut!*" said Victoria as she read a copy of *The Times*. "Have you read this article about Bertie, Albert?"

"Indeed I have," said Albert.

"'*Who is the Prince of Wales to marry – a matter of national importance!*'" Victoria read the headline out loud before casting the newspaper to her side in disgust.

"Do not let it upset you, my dear," urged Albert.

"Now our son's lack of a wife is not just a matter of concern for our family, but the whole nation!" She grabbed the newspaper and began to read it again. "The paper has made a list of seven prospective brides that *they* consider would make suitable wives for our son!"

"I have read it, Victoria. Unfortunately, even *The Times* has not come up with any new candidates for us to consider. The seven princesses they suggest have already been investigated and discounted by us – with the exception of their fourth suggestion – Princess Alexandra."

"According to *The Times* Princess Alexandra is theirs and the nation's favoured choice," said Victoria.

"Which is fortunate for us, as she is also ours and Vicky's

244

favourite choice," said Albert. "Who would have thought the press would have had such good taste!"

"Who would have believed there would be such a dearth of Protestant royal princesses of eligible age that we are left with a Dane!"

Albert looked fretful. "As I have been saying from the start, Bertie marrying a Dane will not be plain sailing for our family. If Bertie marries Alexandra it will put our dearest Vicky in Prussia in a luckless position as the Prussians and Danes have been so recently at war. There is terrible ill-feeling between the two nations and Bertie marrying Alexandra will look like we are siding with the Danes against our own daughter and her family."

"At yet our dearest Vicky is willing to jeopardise her own political position in her new home in order to find her brother the right wife – not that he appreciates it one little bit!"

There was a knock on the door and, when it opened, Bertie walked in and bowed to them both before approaching them.

"Dear boy! Welcome home!" said Albert, rising to greet him.

"Good afternoon, Papa – good afternoon, Mama!"

"Bertie," acknowledged Victoria as Bertie bent to kiss her cheek.

Albert and Bertie sat down, smiling at each other.

"So, Bertie, your tour of Ireland is complete," said Victoria. "Your military training is finished and you are ready to embrace the next chapter of your life, I take it?"

"Yes, Mama. I feel like a changed man since my time in Ireland."

"We are so glad to hear it!" said Victoria.

"Your mother has been writing to you about your trip to Prussia to visit your sister and be introduced to Princess Alexandra?" said Albert.

"Yes, I received all correspondence," acknowledged Bertie.

"Good!" said Victoria. "You are to set sail on Friday. You will be spending a few days in Prussia and we hope it all goes well – we *sincerely* hope it all goes well."

"Just in time for you to return to your studies in Cambridge," said Albert.

"Yes, Papa," said Bertie.

Victoria and Albert glanced at each other for a few moments as they all remained silent.

"So – if there is nothing else, I have some matters to attend to," said Bertie.

"Yes, that is all. You may leave," said Victoria.

"Thank you, Mama, thank you, Papa," said Bertie as he nodded to them and left them alone.

Victoria looked at Albert. "Is this really our son who was just before us?"

"He seemed most agreeable to everything," said Albert, surprised.

"No temper tantrums, no sulks, no protests about his forthcoming trip to Prussia and meeting Alexandra," said Victoria.

"You see, I told you that his time in Ireland would change him," said Albert happily. "He's matured from being sulky and trying to shirk his duties to being a serious-minded and responsible young man."

"Would that we could believe that this transformation is permanent! What joy it would give us!" said Victoria.

"It is excellent, my dear, that he is now in perfect form for meeting Alexandra and making a good impression."

"Yes, if he comes across as agreeable to her as he did to us today, she will not hesitate to accept his proposal of marriage, I am sure!"

CHAPTER 43

Nellie and James were due to meet Bertie for dinner in the restaurant at Claridge's on her first night in London. She was excited to be out with Bertie for the first time in public. James had said that it would be perfectly fine as he would be there too and so nobody would suspect there was a relationship between her and the Prince. Besides, nobody knew who Nellie was in London and so there could be no talk.

Sadie finished dressing Nellie in her hotel room.

"You are trembling, Nellie," said Sadie.

"I know, Sadie. I'm just so nervous about meeting Bertie again. What if, when he sees me tonight, he realises the whole thing was a mistake and he shouldn't have brought me to England?"

Sadie took her by the hand and led her over to the full-length mirror in the corner of the room.

"How could he ever think it was a mistake, Nellie? If he doesn't fall in love with you all over again when he sees you tonight, then I'll eat my hat!"

Nellie squeezed Sadie's hand. "Thank you, Sadie. Always there to lift me up when I'm feeling down."

"Why are you feeling down? Isn't this what you wanted – to come here and be with the Prince?"

"All your warnings before we left are ringing in my ears now. Being here, in this hotel and seeing his world, makes me realise how out of my depth I am."

"It's too late now to let anything ring in your ears. You're here now and best you just get on with it," said Sadie.

There was a knock on the door.

"That'll be James," said Nellie.

Sadie went and opened the door.

James stepped in, dressed in his officer's uniform.

"Are you ready, Nellie?" he asked.

Nellie nodded and walked across the room to him.

"Your Prince awaits!" said James, offering her his arm.

As Nellie walked through the foyer with James, people were taking second looks at her.

"Good evening, sir, good evening, madam," said the maître d' as they entered the restaurant.

"Good evening," said James before leaning towards him and whispering, "We are joining the Prince of Wales for dinner."

The maître d' nodded discreetly. "If you could come with me, sir."

They followed the man across the restaurant.

"What are they all looking at?" Nellie whispered to James, aware people were giving her second looks. She felt so intimidated and so out of place she was sure she must stand out a mile and she wanted to turn and run away. She was sure they could see she didn't belong there and could see her for what she was.

"They are looking at you in admiration," said James.

Nellie blushed and tried to ignore the stares. Suddenly she saw Bertie sitting at a discreet corner table. He was smiling happily at her. She felt like running to him and holding him in her arms.

Bertie stood when they reached the table.

"Good evening, Your Royal Highness," said James, reaching the table and bowing.

"Your Royal Highness," greeted Nellie and made a curtsy.

"Hello!" said Bertie. "Good to see you! Jolly good!"

The maître d' held out a chair for Nellie and she sat down

as James and Bertie sat as well. The maître d' then poured them red wine and handed them menus before leaving them.

"Oh, it's so good to see you again, Nellie!" said Bertie as he beamed at her across the table.

"I can't tell you how good it is to see you!" said Nellie. "A friendly face amongst all these strangers."

"I can imagine this must be difficult for you – everything so different from what you are used to, being so far from home," said Bertie, his face full of sympathy.

"It's all worth it to see you again," she whispered across to him.

"Is your room satisfactory?" asked Bertie.

"It's beautiful beyond words," said Nellie. "I'm frightened to touch anything in case it breaks!"

Bertie laughed loudly before turning to James. "And you, James? Everything is satisfactory for you here?"

"Very good, Your Royal Highness. I am reporting for duty at Aldershot tomorrow but I have been very busy today making the arrangements for Nellie that we discussed before you left Ireland."

"And has everything gone to plan?"

"Everything is arranged. I have rented a small manor house for Nellie just a few miles outside Cambridge. It is very easily reached from your house at the university. It is in private grounds in the country and so you will be able to come and go without any fear of being seen."

"Excellent, James! The finances I gave you covered the expenses?"

"They covered everything quite adequately," James assured him.

Nellie glanced at James and felt certain that he had made sure that whatever finances Bertie provided had paid him a profit as well. She didn't care about that though. She knew she and Bertie needed James desperately. Without him and his machinations their relationship would not have been able to continue.

As the maître d' came back to take their order, she and Bertie stared at each other across the table, longing to be alone together.

"Where are you staying in London?" asked Nellie as they had dinner.

"In Buckingham Palace, where else?" asked Bertie.

"Indeed – where else?" she said sarcastically and winked at him, making him laugh.

As she looked around the restaurant she saw other diners were looking at their table intermittently. They were trying to be discreet and not cause offense by staring at the Prince of Wales' table but their interest had been piqued when they saw the stranger there.

As she saw a woman lean towards her male companion and whisper something, Nellie said, "Was this wise to come here, Bertie? I thought we were doing everything we could to keep our relationship a secret from your family?"

"I see no reason why we shouldn't have come here," he replied. "I am just joining a fellow officer and his lady companion for dinner. What can be wrong about that if anyone should enquire?"

"Exactly," said James, picking up his glass and taking a sip of wine.

Bertie leaned forward. "I need to speak to you tonight, Nellie. My driver has been instructed to wait and not expect me to leave the hotel early."

"Come to my hotel room after dinner," she said. "We can talk there."

"Is anything the matter?" asked James.

"No, I just need to speak to Nellie," said Bertie.

"She's in Room 202. Third floor. Will you be able to get there without being seen?" asked James.

"I should be able to manage it," he said.

"Don't get caught sneaking around the hotel whatever you do!" warned Nellie.

"I shall try not to, my darling Nellie, but I think I have developed a taste for living dangerously!"

"Clearly, you have, sir!" said Nellie.

As James walked Nellie back to her room she said, "I'd say you are doing very well from Bertie's payments to find me a house."

"I don't know what you mean, Nellie. I am merely trying to be a friend to both of you."

"You are only a friend to yourself, James, let's not fool ourselves." She reached her door and turned to him. "Goodnight, James."

Bertie walked out of the restaurant and when he got to the foyer lit up a cigarette. He could see his carriage waiting through the windows. As he smoked he stepped back into the shadows behind some plants. Observing the hotel was now much quieter, he waited until a party of people from the restaurant walked by laughing and talking loudly, and then strode over to the staircase and ascended them two at a time until he reached the third floor.

He hurried down the corridor, checking the numbers on the hotel doors. As a couple approached him, he lowered his head.

"Good evening," they said as they passed him.

"Evening," replied Bertie, not looking up, and then quickly hurried along until he found Room 202 and knocked quietly.

"Nellie! It's me!" he hissed through the door as he knocked again.

Nellie swung the door open and he rushed in, closing the door behind him. They fell into each other's arms and kissed.

"I've counted the minutes until I saw you again," he said.

"And I you," she said as they fell on the bed, kissing passionately.

Bertie heard Big Ben strike in the distance, saying it was two o'clock in the morning.

"I had better go, or my driver will wonder where I have got to," he said.

"I think I preferred when we were in Kildare and we only had to dodge your batman!" said Nellie. "Now we have the entire staff of the royal family to dodge!"

He got out of the bed and began to get dressed while she put on her dressing gown.

"James says I'll be moving into the new house on Friday," she said.

"Good," he said.

"When will I see you again?"

"Ah!" he said as he stopped buttoning his shirt. "That's the thing I wanted to speak to you about. I must go to Prussia on Friday."

"Prussia! So soon!"

"Yes, unfortunately. I really do not want to go, but duty calls," he said.

"I suppose I must get used to your duties calling." She fell silent as he continued to dress, then dreading the answer, reluctantly asked, "To meet the Danish princess?"

"Yes." He came and sat down beside her on the bed.

Her eyes filled with anger as she stood up abruptly. "Why are you going through with it?"

"I have no choice," he said. "My parents insist."

"Just tell them – no!"

"I can't, Nellie. I must go and meet her," he said.

She stared at him, her anger increasing. "I have left my home and my life to come here to be with you, and you – you are just heading off to Prussia to see another woman!"

"As I said, I have no choice. They have ordered me to go and meet her. I must be seen to at least meet her. If I don't –"

"If you don't – what? I told you before that you must start standing up to your parents and leading your own life, Bertie!"

"I can never lead my own life while I'm the Prince of Wales," he said.

"Perhaps it suits you to meet this Danish woman? Perhaps you are very happy to meet her! I was a fool to ever come here. A fool to ever listen to you! I should have stayed in Ireland! You are using me, that's all. I should have listened to Sadie!"

She walked to the window and stood staring out, wiping away a tear.

"No! Nellie – no!" He walked quickly to her and put his hands on her shoulders.

"Get off me!" She shook his hands angrily from her.

"Nellie! Believe me, this is the easiest way for me to deal with the situation. My parents won't give me a moment's peace until I meet Alexandra. Once I've met her, I can tell them I do not like her, and can't or won't marry her – and that will be the end of that!"

"Until the next time! Until the next princess is paraded in front of you to marry."

"Let them parade as many as they want in front of me. None of them will turn my head like you have," he said.

She stood in silence, staring out the window, as she listened to his breathing behind her. "James says that royal marriages are like political alliances, with no love there. And that I should content myself with being your companion."

"No – Nellie, no! I am in love with you and I don't want to be married to some woman over a political alliance. I want what we have together."

"But what future do we have, Bertie? In all honesty, I can't share you with another – I love you too much," she said, turning around and facing him.

He took her in his arms and kissed her.

CHAPTER 44

Bertie had set sail to Prussia on the Friday and arrived in Berlin early the next morning where he met his sister Vicky and her husband Fritz at their palace.

"Oh, it is so good to see you again, Bertie!" said Vicky as she embraced her brother and kissed him.

He pulled back and smiled at his sister. Her lovely face was unchanged, her eyes displaying the intelligence she was known for.

"And you, Vicky! We have all missed you terribly, particularly Mama," said Bertie before turning to Vicky's husband. "And Fritz, good to see you again, my dear fellow!"

Fritz shook Bertie's hand, his moustached face serious. "Welcome to Prussia." He nodded at his brother-in-law in greeting.

"My gosh – you have grown up so much, Bertie!" exclaimed Vicky. "I hardly recognise you."

"Well, I am an officer now, remember," mocked Bertie.

"Indeed you are and such a handsome one. Come, let us take a walk in the gardens!"

Fritz held back. "I will let you two have some time together and will see you for lunch."

Thank you! she mouthed at him as she led her brother out the French windows into the gardens.

"How are Mama and Papa?" she asked as they walked down the garden paths, arms linked.

"Well Mama is very melancholy after the death of grandmother. She seems to be always sad or in a bad mood," said Bertie.

"It has hit her very hard, I realise from her letters. That is why we must give her something to be happy and positive about, Bertie. Something to look forward to in the future."

"You are referring to my future marriage to a woman I have not even met?" he asked sarcastically.

"Oh, don't be like that, Bertie! None of us have met our husbands and wives until we meet them first!"

"*Hmmm*, a strange thought, Vicky," he said.

"I want you to take this meeting with Alexandra seriously, Bertie! As Prussia and Denmark have been at war and there is huge anti-Danish sentiment here, there would be huge ramifications for Fritz and me if it was known that I was pushing for the future British King to marry our enemy."

"I realise that, Vicky."

"I am not recommending this marriage to you out of any personal benefit to me – on the contrary it will harm my reputation in Prussia if the marriage takes place. But I am willing to ignore that as I am trying to put your happiness first."

"Yes, Vicky," sighed Bertie.

"The fact remains, we would all, Mama and Papa especially, prefer you to marry a Prussian princess but there are none available that are suitable! I have carried out an exhaustive search and Alexandra is the only one fit for purpose!"

"Yes, Vicky."

Vicky stopped walking and turned to him. "She is divine, Bertie! A true beauty! With such a pleasant disposition – kind and patient and charming. You will love her, I am sure."

"She sounds all very well, Vicky," Bertie said, becoming exasperated, "but I have tried to explain to our parents that I am too young to be married."

"Bertie! Will you please just meet Alexandra with an open

mind? Can you at least promise me that, after all the work I have put into you meeting her?" It was now her turn to be exasperated.

"All right! But I promise you nothing more, Vicky," he said.

"Alexandra is presently staying outside Frankfurt on the pretext of visiting her grandmother. She will be visiting the cathedral in Speyer on the 14th – and you will be visiting the cathedral at the same time. Both of you will be there on the pretext of sightseeing and we will – accidently – bump into each other. I will then introduce you. We must maintain this charade in case the Prussians discover that I have orchestrated this meeting between my brother and our enemy."

Bertie sighed to himself as she took his arm again and they continued walking down the path. As he strolled along with her, listening to her speak, he felt heavy-hearted. How complicated the whole business of a royal marriage was! How he wished he was back in London with Nellie.

He was there under false pretences. He was there because it had been easier to come than just continue facing the pressure of refusing to come. But his heart was back in England with Nellie. It was unfair to Vicky to get her hopes up that he would marry Alexandra when he had no intention of doing so. It was unfair to this girl Alexandra, who seemed perfectly pleasant, to lead her on to believe that she could be the next Queen of England, when that was not a possibility either.

CHAPTER 45

It was a warm sunny day as Nellie and Sadie walked along the thronged streets of London.

"So, it's all set up?" asked Sadie.

"Yes, James has arranged everything. We are to live in a small manor house outside Cambridge for easy access for Bertie."

"Sounds nice."

"*Hmmm*," said Nellie as she thought about Bertie in Prussia and wondered had he met Alexandra yet. She was fighting a burning jealousy. What if he should like her? What if she swept him off his feet?

She stopped at a newsstand as she saw a headline on the front page of *The Times* –

Prince of Wales Observes Military Manoeuvres on Visit to Prussia.

She picked up the newspaper and glanced through the article. There was absolutely no mention of his meeting with Alexandra. Bertie had said it was top secret due to some political implications she did not understand. Or care less about, if the truth be known.

What a strange world she had entered into, she thought. She saw a smaller article in the bottom of the front page headed –

Speculation Grows over Who the Prince Should Marry

Since his return from Ireland, there is growing conjecture that

the Prince of Wales will be announcing his engagement soon. Speculation is rife as to who is in line to be the next Queen of England . . .

"Are you buying that, love?" asked the newspaper vendor.

Nellie flung the paper back on the stand. "No!"

As they walked on, Nellie felt increasingly angry. As she looked around at all the people passing her by, oblivious to who she was, it was unbelievable even to her that she was sharing a bed with the Prince of Wales as the world speculated as to who he was to marry.

As they strolled down Regent Street she saw over the doors of the most elegant stores the royal crest and the term *By Royal Appointment* inscribed below it. James had explained to her once what that meant. It was a special crest that was awarded to businesses who provided services to the royal family. As she thought of her relationship with Bertie she began to feel she should be given a crest *By Royal Appointment*. She remembered when he had presented her with the diamond necklace when they had first met and she had angrily rejected it. And now here she was, about to be moved into a house in the middle of nowhere where she knew nobody, to be a kept woman.

"Is anything the matter, Nellie?" asked Sadie.

"There's plenty the matter," said Nellie as she went to the edge of the footpath and hailed a hansom cab.

Nellie asked the cab driver to take her to Shaftsbury Avenue. She had heard her friends talk of it back in Dublin. It was where the theatres and music halls were.

"What are we doing here, Nellie?" asked Sadie, trying to keep up with her as she walked quickly down the street. Nellie stopped outside a large theatre called the Europa. Nellie looked at the line-up of performers advertised on the board outside. There were singers, comedy acts, drag acts and dancers. It reminded her a lot of the Palace back in Dublin. She pushed open the door and walked in. She walked through

the foyer and into the main theatre which was empty except
for a woman cleaning.

"Excuse me, I'd like to see the manager," she said.

"Why do you want to see him?" asked a male voice and
she turned around to see a large fat man in his fifties walking
down the aisle.

She smiled at him. "Hello, I'm Nellie Cliffden."

"So?" asked the man.

"I've been the star billing at the Palace Theatre in Dublin
for the last three years," she said.

"So?" he asked, unimpressed, as he looked her up and
down.

"So – I'd like to apply for a job here as a singer," she said,
hearing Sadie gasp behind her.

"I've no need of another singer, I've got too many as it is,"
he said.

Her smile faltered for a second and then she continued,
"But you don't have a singer as good as me, Mr. –?"

"Reynolds," he answered.

"Mr. Reynolds, I will have your audiences queuing up to
get in here," she said.

"They are already queuing up," he said, turning to walk
away from her.

Nellie watched him walk away and thought quickly.

She suddenly began to sing loudly –

"Where are you going, my lovely?
Wouldn't you like if I went there with you?
I'm not asking to go there forever . . .
I'd be happy with one night or maybe with two!"

Reynolds turned in surprise and watched Nellie as she walked
up the aisle onto the stage, singing all the way. He watched
her on the stage as she sang and went through a routine.

"Well?" she asked eventually from the stage as she finished
singing.

"You can start tomorrow night, be here at eight," he said as he began to walk away. He stopped as he passed Sadie and asked, "Who is this?"

"This is my assistant, Sadie – available for work with your other actresses too!" Nellie said.

Reynolds raised his eyes to heaven and walked on.

Nellie clapped her hands together as she surveyed the theatre from the stage, Sadie went rushing up the steps to her.

"Nellie! What are you doing? You can't be an actress here and live in Cambridge!"

"There's a change of plan, Sadie. We are not going to live in some house in Cambridge. If Bertie wants to continue to see me, he can see me on my terms. I've sacrificed enough to be with him already."

Sadie clasped her hands together in delight and hugged Nellie.

CHAPTER 46

Vicky, Fritz and Bertie walked towards the cathedral in Speyer followed by a small party from the Prussian Royal court.

"Isn't it the most magnificent building!" enthused Vicky.

"Most impressive," agreed Bertie.

There were a number of people mulling around, admiring the scenery. He wondered where Alexandra was. He could not wait to get the meeting over and done with.

"Remember when you meet her to be courteous at all times," Vicky whispered to him. "And impress her with your travels . . . tell her about your trips to America and Ireland."

"Vicky!" he said in exasperation. "I do know how to talk to a woman!"

"Well, I know you are a good speaker, Bertie, but this is different. You need to be able to impress her and court her."

"Oh, do be quiet, Vicky!" snapped Bertie. He fought an overwhelming desire to shock her by telling her about Nellie and his relationship with her.

"There she is!" hissed Vicky.

Bertie saw a small party on the steps in front of the cathedral as Vicky made a beeline for them.

"Alexandra!" exclaimed Vicky in mock surprise. "Fancy meeting you here!"

"Vicky! What unexpected joy!" said Alexandra, leaving the party she was with and hurrying over to Vicky.

They kissed each other's cheeks.

261

Bertie quickly observed Alexandra and decided the praise that was being heaped on her by everyone was justly deserved. She was a very beautiful young woman, with a natural elegance that stood out, tall and slender with a strikingly beautiful face.

Bertie could only admire her as he stood back and observed the young women meeting.

"What brings you to Speyer?" asked Vicky.

"Why, I am visiting my grandmother outside Frankfurt and had heard so much about the beauty of the cathedral here that I insisted on coming to see it. What is the purpose of your visit?"

"My brother, Bertie, the Prince of Wales, is visiting us, and he too insisted on seeing the cathedral's beauty – and so here we are! Come – let me introduce you to him."

Vicky took Alexandra by the hand and excitedly led her over to Bertie.

"Bertie – may I introduce you to my very good friend Alexandra," said Vicky.

Alexandra was staring into his face and began to blush.

Bertie bent down, took Alexandra's hand and kissed it.

"It is with great pleasure that I make your acquaintance," said Bertie and as he raised hs head from kissing her hand he saw that her face was now bright red. The colour only added to her beauty and charm.

"It is equally my pleasure," said Alexandra and she bowed her head to him.

"Well, this is wonderful!" said Vicky, taking both their arms and leading them up the steps. "Absolutely wonderful!"

"Are you staying in Prussia long, sir?" asked Alexandra.

"I leave tomorrow," Bertie said.

"Bertie has been so busy of late, Alexandra," Vicky said quickly and enthusiastically. "He has just returned from Ireland where he completed training as an officer. Then he was in America and Canada before that on an official tour. And then next week he returns to Cambridge to continue his studies."

"My – you have been busy, sir!" said Alexandra, smiling shyly at him.

"Please call me Bertie."

Alexandra smiled at him and said his name softly. "Bertie."

On seeing that his wife was going to dominate the meeting and not allow Bertie and Alexandra time alone to get to know each other, Fritz stepped forward and said, "Would you mind terribly if Vicky and I left you alone for a short while? We must go check on little Wilhelm who we left in the carriage with his nanny."

Vicky took her cue from her husband. "Yes, poor little Wilhelm, he is such a handful for Nanny. He can become so disruptive if he is left to his own devices!"

"Please, do not let us detain you," said Alexandra.

Vicky smiled encouragingly at them both. "I won't be long."

Bertie and Alexandra smiled at each other as they continued to walk along.

"Your parents are keeping well, Bertie?" asked Alexandra.

"Yes, quite well. And yours?"

"They are very good, thank you. It is still such a surprise for them to understand that Papa will be the next King of Denmark. He never expected the role would fall on his shoulders, but we cannot help the destiny we are given, can we?"

He smiled at her with understanding. "Those have always been my sentiments. From what I know, your father will make an excellent king when he ascends to the Danish throne."

"I agree that he will. But since my family became heirs to the throne, my parents have tried to keep life as normal as possible for us. We lead quite a simple life in Copenhagen. Of course the Danish monarchy is not in the same league as the British – we are not a rich nation with a rich empire."

"Perhaps not," he said. "But it's a very small club we are in, is it not, Alexandra? There are so few of us who really understand what it is like to be the children of kings."

She smiled. "That is why I am so fortunate to be a friend of Vicky's. Even though our countries are enemies, we understand each other, because we come from the same place. I hope that, in time, you and I might share that bond too."

He smiled as he opened the door of the cathedral for her to enter and followed her in.

CHAPTER 47

Spurred on by the success of getting the job at the Europa Theatre, Nellie had quickly put the rest of her plan into action. She had taken all her jewellery to a merchant's in Bond Street where she had sold it. She had then visited an agency who had found her a flat in Chelsea that she had rented.

On the day she was due to book out of Claridge's and be taken to the house in Cambridge, she and Sadie were busily packing her clothes in her hotel bedroom waiting for James to arrive.

The knock came on the door and Sadie opened it and let James in.

"Are you not finished packing yet?" asked James, irritated. "The carriage is waiting outside to take us to the train station."

Nellie gestured to Sadie that she should leave them alone and Sadie exited the room.

"Well, come on! We can't miss the train!" said James.

"I'm not going to Cambridge, James," Nellie said evenly.

"What are you talking about?" James became even more irritated.

"I've been giving the situation much thought since Bertie left for Prussia and I've decided not to move into that house."

"Is this some kind of joke? It's all planned, I have everything in place," said James.

"I've got myself a job, as an actress in Shaftsbury Avenue.

265

And I've rented a flat in Chelsea," said Nellie.

James's face went red with anger. "How dare you! How dare you go behind my back!"

"That's not for me, James – living in a house all day in the country, waiting for Bertie to fit me in while he flits around the world."

He rushed to her and grabbed her chin in his hand. "You are *not* going to fuck this up on me, Nellie! This is my chance to make something of myself, and I'll not have you ruin it!"

She tried to shake him off, but his grip got tighter.

"*Let go of me!* Let go of me or I'll scream this hotel down and I'll tell Bertie just what kind of a man you are and that you blackmailed me into sleeping with him!"

James' eyes blazed at her but slowly he released his grip. She pulled away from him and went to the window where she stood rubbing her chin.

"You're not in power here any more, James. So you had better listen to me and start to follow my plans for a change," she said. "I love Bertie, I really do. I wouldn't have done all this if I didn't love him. And I know he is in love with me. But I want to maintain my independence, not just from him but from you too. I'd be completely isolated and at your mercy living in that house. And he may soon come to be bored with me if I was there like a pet waiting for him. I'd be no more than one of those shops on Regent Street whose sole purpose is to provide service to the royal family. Me and Bertie have something special. But I won't compromise myself any more. He has to see me on my terms as I see him on his."

James laughed derisively. "Your terms! Who are you to dictate any terms to the Prince of Wales?"

"If he loves me, he'll accept my terms."

"I can't believe you are being so stupid. Giving up a life of leisure for what?"

"For my own life, however I choose to live it," said Nellie.

"Bertie won't like this, he won't accept it," stated James.

"He has no choice."

"I can get you fired from that job, just like I did at the Palace," James threatened.

"If you do that, I'll tell Bertie everything. I'll tell him about you being my introducer to men for money and the life we led together. How long do you think you'll last in the royal circle then, James?"

He stared at her and then shrugged. "Looks like I have no choice but to accept your terms."

She nodded. "When is Bertie back in London?"

"He returns tonight," said James. "There is a garden party in Buckingham Palace which Bertie has invited me to and we were to leave for Cambridge afterwards to meet you."

"Invited to a garden party in Buckingham Palace? Haven't you done well for yourself, James! Well, I will be performing at the Europa Theatre on Shaftsbury Avenue, so you can tell him if he wants to see me, then he can come and see me there!"

CHAPTER 48

"Garden parties can be such a chore," whispered Victoria to Albert as they made their way through the garden at Buckingham Palace, nodding and smiling at the guests. "One has to spend ages idly chatting to minor officials from far-flung corners of our country about the most mundane matters. I always find the weather the most neutral subject to speak to them about."

"It is all part of our duties, Victoria," said Albert.

"Don't we know! I, for one, cannot wait to return to our holiday at Balmoral once this is over! Oh to be in Scotand now!" sighed Victoria. "Where is Bertie? Why is he not here yet? Was he not supposed to arrive back from Prussia this morning?"

"Perhaps he was delayed," said Princess Alice as she walked behind her parents.

"Inevitably!" sighed Victoria before smiling at a middle-aged man and his wife who were all dressed up for the occasion. "Good afternoon, we are so pleased you could be here today."

"There's Bertie!" squeaked Alice excitedly as she saw him and James arrive.

"Maintain decorum at all times in public, Alice!" cautioned Victoria.

"Yes, Mama," said Alice.

They made their way across the lawn to Bertie who was busy chatting amicably to guests.

"Welcome back," said Victoria. "We trust you had a pleasant visit to Prussia?"

"Most pleasant, Mama. Hello, Papa – hello, Alice." He turned to James. "Do you remember my friend from the garrison in Kildare – Captain James Marton?"

"Indeed we do," said Albert warmly. "Very good to see you again. What brings you to England?"

"I have been transferred to Aldershot, sir."

"Excellent!" said Albert. "I am pleased. I heard only good things about you in Ireland and we appreciate all the assistance you gave to Bertie."

"Thank you, sir," said James, giving a small bow.

Albert then engaged James in conversation. He was delighted that James had been transferred as he had impressed him greatly and he was sure he could only be a positive influence on Bertie.

Victoria and Alice drew Bertie aside.

"Well, did you meet her?" asked Alice excitedly.

"Alexandra? Yes, we met."

"*And?*" implored Victoria.

"And she is a very pleasant and sweet girl."

Victoria and Alice looked delighted.

"Thank goodness for that! I knew Vicky would not let us down!" said Victoria.

"Is she as pretty as they say?" asked Alice.

"Very much so," answered Bertie.

"With an agreeable personality?" asked Victoria.

"Very much so," said Bertie.

"What joy!" exclaimed Victoria. "Well – that is settled then! At last! We may now move the courtship to the next level."

Bertie's face became serious. "Let's not get ahead of ourselves, Mama. I have said nothing about courtship."

Victoria's face dropped. "Well, what are you saying in that case?"

"I am saying I have done what you requested and met

with Alexandra and fulfilled my part of the bargain."

"Bargain! What are you talking about, you stupid boy! We are speaking about a royal marriage not a shopping spree!"

"I don't understand, Bertie," asked Alice. "If Alexandra is so wonderful then why are you hesitating about marrying her?"

"Because I hardly know her! And I'm not in love with her – I don't know her well enough. But most of all, as I have tried to say before, I am much too young to get married."

"I do not know what to say!" snapped Victoria angrily. "Everyone has put so much work into this meeting – why do you think that was done? For our entertainment? Even *The Times* has given Alexandra approval, and here you are like a weathercock not sure which way to turn, depending on a gust of wind to make up your mind!"

Albert quickly cut off his conversation with James on noticing his wife's anger and moved towards her, James following him.

"What is the problem?" he asked.

"*He* is!" she said, gesturing to Bertie. "I can't even speak about it any further. I need to be away from him for fear I shall do something that I regret. How a son could frustrate a mother to such an extent is inconceivable – especially as I am in the depths of mourning over my own dear sweet mama, to whom I never gave a day's trouble all my life! Would that my own children could afford me the same respect!"

"Come along, Victoria, we must mingle among our guests," Albert said, leading her away while giving Bertie a stern look. "We shall talk later, Bertie."

"Oh, Bertie!" said Alice. "Whatever is the matter with you? Can you not see how unhappy you are making Mama?"

Bertie looked upset. "I fear that everyone else's happiness relies on me being in a permanent state of unhappiness!"

"We only want what's best for you, Bertie," said Alice.

"Yes, I know!" snapped Bertie. "Everyone only wants what's best for me!"

"I must go and attend to Mama," sighed Alice as she turned away. "It is good to meet you again, Captain Marton."

"The pleasure is mine," said James.

"Oh dear, this situation is only going from bad to worse," said Bertie as he watched Alice join his parents who were mingling with the guests. He noted his mother's inability to hide her distress. "I thought going to Prussia and meeting Alexandra would make them happy, at least for a while. But it seems to have only made them worse."

"You are in a difficult situation, sir, I can plainly see that," said James.

"They are putting me under unbearable pressure. To make a decision that I cannot make. How can I marry somebody when I am in love with another?"

"In your family's defence, they are not aware that you are in love with another."

"No, and I cannot tell them. The truth is that Nellie was all I thought about while I was in Prussia. I cannot wait to see her tonight. Did the move to the house in Cambridge go well?"

James cleared his throat. "There has been a change of plan, sir. Nellie has not moved to Cambridge. She has chosen to rent a flat in Chelsea and taken a job on the stage at the Europa in Shaftsbury Avenue."

Bertie stared at James in shock. "But why has this happened?" he gasped.

"She feels she would not settle, that she would be bored living in Cambridge. She says she would miss the stage too much and wants to maintain her independence to some extent."

"What a bloody-minded obstinate woman!" said Bertie. "I offer her a life of great ease and she throws it back in my face!"

"You know how spirited she can be, sir."

"Indeed I do!" said Bertie. "But where does this leave us?"

"The same place as before, I understand. She says she is performing in the Europa tonight and if you want to see her, to come there."

"I see!"

"I am not sure if it's wise to go to the Europa, sir, in case you are spotted there."

"Oh, I'm going! I don't give a damn any more. I want to see Nellie! Come – let us mingle among the guests before we make an early exit."

CHAPTER 49

Bertie and James walked into the Europa and bought two tickets. His head bent, Bertie followed James through the foyer and into the theatre where they found a table at the back, sat down and ordered beers. The music hall was packed. It seemed to Bertie to be more relaxed than the Palace back in Dublin, with a long bar which was crowded with people ordering drinks to bring back to their tables and seats. Bertie thought the atmosphere was magnificent as he looked around.

"It's a damned sight better than the garden party today!" said Bertie.

"Certainly different, sir," said James, anxiously looking around making sure nobody had recognised Bertie. He realised the crowd were drunk and enjoying themselves and that all their attention was on the stage. Besides, the last person any of them would expect to see there was the Prince of Wales and so why would they recognise him?

"There she is!" said Bertie as Nellie walked out on the stage to great cheers.

"*Well! What an audience we have tonight!*" declared Nellie from the stage. "*And I see a few of you even brought your wives along!*" She peered at the audience. "*I'll correct myself on that – the ladies we have here are much too pretty to be your wives – so let me say you brought your mistresses along instead!*"

There were roars of approval from the audience.

Bertie looked on mesmerised as Nellie continued her performance.

James had spoken to one of the waiters and sent a message to Nellie backstage that he was there to see her with their 'friend'.

As Bertie and James followed the waiter backstage, Bertie felt utter excitement at the prospect of seeing Nellie again.

"I'll wait outside," said James.

Bertie knocked on Nellie's dressing-room door and entered, closing the door behind him.

Nellie was standing in front of her dressing table.

"Oh Nellie!" he said, rushing to her, and they embraced and kissed.

"I missed you so much," she said between kisses.

She pulled back from him.

"I wasn't sure you would want to see me again."

"Of course I want to see you! All the time!"

She walked away from him and fixed her hair. "How was I to know that? You might have been swept off your feet by Alexandra and that would be the end of us!"

He moved towards her. "Don't be stupid. I told you I was only meeting her because I had to. All I could think of when I was away was you."

"So – what's she like – Alexandra?" Nellie didn't care that her jealousy was clear to see.

"She's fine. Nice girl, pleasant, pleasing on the eye," he said.

"Pleasing on the eye!" she remarked. "Sounds like perfect wife material to me – you should marry her!"

"Nellie!" he said, grabbing her and embracing her again. "Is this what all this is about? You not moving to Cambridge and getting a job here? Because you felt I would marry Alexandra?"

"Well, even the papers are saying you should marry her from what I read. Seems to me your life would be much simpler if you did and forgot about me!"

"That won't happen, Nellie. I don't care what happens – I will never leave you."

"If only I could believe that," she said.

"Won't you come to live in Cambridge as we arranged so we can be together?" he pleaded.

"No, Bertie. That's just not me! Living in a country house and having nothing to do all day – I'd go mad! I need to be on the stage. I need to be independent. I've relied on myself all my life. I can't become something I'm not, not even for the Prince of Wales."

He nodded. "I understand. In fact, I admire you even more for what you're doing."

She was relieved but worried. "How can we meet though, with you returning to Cambridge?"

He laughed. "There's such a thing as a train, Nellie! I can come and see you here all the time and you can at least visit and stay in the house in Cambridge, can you not?"

She smiled and put her arms around his neck. "There's nothing I'd like more."

"And what of tonight, where shall we go tonight?"

"Well, the night is young, Bertie. The show isn't over yet. Why don't I get us one of the boxes and we can watch the rest of the show?"

He thought for a moment. "Yes – indeed, why not?"

She grabbed a shawl and they left the room.

James was waiting outside.

"Are you leaving?" he asked, surprised.

"Not at all," said Bertie. "We are going to watch the rest of the show. Why don't you join us?"

"Is that not a bit risky, sir? In case you are seen in Nellie's company in a place like this?"

"There's nobody we know here, and if there is somebody we know then they shouldn't be here either and have as much to lose by discovery as us!" Bertie put his arm around Nellie's waist and led her down the corridor.

They laughed and joked as if they hadn't a care in the world, and James was alarmed at the whole situation.

Bertie clapped enthusiastically from their box as a group of dancing girls performed on stage.

James sat a little away from them, observing them as opposed to the show on the stage. Bertie was drinking heavily which alarmed James.

"I must go to the lavatory. I shall be back in a short while," said Bertie as he stood and stumbled out of the box.

James quickly leaned forward to Nellie. "What do you think you are playing at?"

"I'm not playing at anything, James. We're just having a little fun – what harm is there in that?" she asked, feigning innocence.

"There will be plenty of harm if it is ever discovered that he was here and with you. The whole point of this is to be discreet and you are losing control of the situation!"

"No, James, *you* are losing control of the situation." She smiled unpleasantly at him. "You hate it, don't you? You hate having no control over me – you hate that you can't dictate to me any more. And you have no control over Bertie either. We have both been living our lives for other people – now we are living them for ourselves for a change."

Nellie opened the door to the building she had moved to and led a drunken Bertie up the stairs.

"My, what a handsome building!" he said as he looked at the carved ceilings and the ornate staircase.

"Not as handsome as Buck House, I imagine," she giggled as they reached her flat.

Sadie had been waiting for her and jumped up from the chair where she had been dozing as she waited for Nellie.

"Nellie! I was expecting you back hours ago –"

Sadie gaped when she saw Bertie, then almost fell to the ground in an over-the-top curtsy.

"Your Majesty!"

"He's not a Majesty yet, Sadie, he's still only a Royal Highness for now," laughed Nellie.

"And who is this?" asked Bertie, looking down at Sadie.

"I'm Sadie, I'm Miss Nellie's maid, Your Royal Highness." Sadie rose to her feet, trembling, hardly believing she had come face to face with the heir to the throne.

"She's more of a friend than a maid," said Nellie. "Although she does run a wonderful bath. And what's this *Miss* Nellie malarky, Sadie?"

"I – I – thought it proper," said Sadie.

"Oh, Bertie doesn't care about proper, Sadie! You can drop your airs and graces around him." Smiling, Nellie leaned forward kissed him.

"I think you both have had too much to drink – if I may be so bold," said Sadie.

"Not half enough!" hiccoughed Bertie.

"Don't worry, my love. I have plenty here!" said Nellie as she grabbed a bottle of wine from the cabinet and led Bertie off down the corridor to her bedroom.

"Goodnight, Sadie!" Bertie called.

They slammed the bedroom door after them, leaving Sadie speechless.

In the early hours of the morning Nellie held Bertie in her arms.

"Now – isn't this much more fun than walking around Speyer with a dull Danish Princess?" she asked.

"It most certainly is," he sighed.

"I do love you, Bertie."

"And I you," he said, reaching up to kiss her. "Oh, the idea of returning to Cambridge and my studies next week fills me with dread – after the most wonderful summer of my life."

She became concerned. "When will I see you again?"

"I don't know if I shall be able to get to London next

weekend, so soon after I return to university. I have a House master there who reports all my activities back to my father." He sat up in the bed. "Why don't you come to Cambridge? And stay at the house there – Primrose House? Could you get away from the theatre for a couple of nights?"

She smiled at him. "Yes, I'm sure I can."

Bertie kissed her. "It will be like being back in Ireland again, just the two of us."

CHAPTER 50

In Dublin, Donald Kilroy was lying in Henrietta's bed, smoking a cigarette, as she brushed her hair at her dressing table, dressed in a silk dressing gown.

It was evening and still light outside.

"I must say it's rather boring at the camp now since Bertie left," said Donald.

"I imagine it is, not having royalty around any more. Not that he was much fun the occasions I met him."

"Oh, Bertie is good fun. He's just shy around women."

"He didn't look that shy when he was in the company of that tart of an actress. To think he could be interested in somebody like her!" scoffed Henrietta.

"And James Marton is gone now and so has Charles Carrington – he's gone back to Cambridge. The whole place is decidedly dull now."

"I can imagine." She stopped brushing her hair and turned to look at him. "Well, your life is bound to become even more dull now as Jack returns tomorrow and so this has to be our last encounter until he is posted overseas again."

"Oh God!" Donald groaned. "What an inconvenience!"

"I don't know why you are complaining about inconvenience – I'm the one who has to live with him while he's here!"

She had turned back to the mirror when they heard the front door open and close and voices in the hallway downstairs.

"Who is that? Were you expecting somebody?" asked Donald.

"No, I wasn't," she said, standing up and going to the door. She opened it and went to the top of the stairs and peeped down.

To her horror she saw her husband Jack there talking to the butler, Vernon.

She gasped and ran back into the bedroom, closing the door behind her.

"*It's Jack!*" she hissed.

"*What?*" he said, jumping out of the bed and hastily beginning to dress. "I thought you said he wasn't due back till tomorrow!"

"He wasn't! I don't know what he's doing here! Oh for pity's sake, Donald, get dressed!"

"Can't you see that's what I'm bloody doing!" he hissed as he struggled to put his uniform back on.

"He'll be up in a minute – what are we to do?"

Donald raced to the door, opened it and began to creep across the landing, but when he saw Jack walking up the steps, he rushed back in and closed the door.

"He's on his way up!" hissed Donald.

"I think I'm going to faint!" gasped Henrietta. "Jump out the window!"

"It's three storeys up! I'll break my neck!"

"Jack will break your neck if he finds you here – it's your choice!"

He ran to the window and opened it. But as he looked down he realised he would never survive the jump.

"I'll have to hide in here!" he said, running to a wardrobe and getting in, closing the door behind him.

Henrietta looked on in terror as she heard footsteps outside. She quickly ran to her dressing table and, sitting down, began to brush her hair.

The door opened and in walked Jack.

"*Jack!*" she said, turning around. "I wasn't expecting you until tomorrow!"

"I managed to get an early sailing, so decided to surprise you."

"And what a surprise!" she said, getting up and going to him and kissing him.

"It's so good to see you, my dear. I missed you terribly," he said.

"And I you, sweetheart. I just wish you had given me more notice!"

He looked down at what she was wearing. "Are you going to bed? It's rather early, isn't it?"

"Yes, I was feeling one of my headaches coming on," she said.

"Oh!" He raised his eyes to heaven. "Are they still plaguing you?"

"I'm afraid so," she answered, making a pained face.

He sniffed the air.

"What's that smell?" he asked.

"Smell?"

"Smoke?"

"Smoke?"

"Yes, *smoke!*" he said, pushing her away and smelling the air. "Cigarette smoke!"

"I can't smell anything!" she said, taking her perfume from the dressing table and spraying it into the air.

"Why is the window open?" he asked.

"I just needed some air – for my headache," she said.

He walked over to the bedside locker, stared down at the brass ashtray and picked up Donald's cigarette that had not quite been extinguished.

"What's this?" he demanded.

"Oh, I didn't want to you to find out, but I've taking up smoking! Most unladylike, I know!"

He looked at her knowingly. "And I dare say that has not been the only thing you have – *taken up* – in my absence! *Where is he?*"

"*Where is who?*" she cried.

He went to the wardrobes and began to open them one by one until he found Donald crouched in the last one.

"Sir – what are you doing in my wardrobe?" he asked in outrage.

Donald crept out of the wardrobe and stood cowering. "It's all a misunderstanding. There's a simple explanation!"

Jack looked at his uniform. "A fellow officer!" And he slapped him across the face.

"Jack! You don't understand!" Henrietta said, rushing between them.

"I understand only too well! I've long suspected your affairs, Henrietta, but now here's living proof, hiding in my wardrobe. I doubt you were her first lover, young man, but I can assure you – both of you – that you will be each other's last!"

"Jack! You can't kill him!" begged Henrietta. "You'd be up for murder and then what would I do when they hang you?"

"Selfish to the last!" said Jack. "My mother warned me about you. She said never trust a woman with auburn hair!"

"I'll dye it, dear Jack. I will become a brunette to appease your mother!"

"The only thing that would appease my mother is to hear you're dead! And I think I may as well be hung for a sheep as a lamb!"

"You can't kill me, Jack! You love me!" she cried and burst into tears.

"Save your tears for the divorce court, when I expose you for the scarlet woman you are!"

As Donald looked on at the husband and wife embroiled in their matrimonial war, he decided it was time to make himself scarce. He tiptoed to the door. When he got there, he took one look back at the two still shouting at each other and then hurried out and raced down the stairs.

In the hallway, Vernon the butler was standing holding Donald's cloak and hat with the door open. As Donald raced past him, he grabbed his belongings.

"Good evening to you, Captain Kilroy – I hope you have a good night," said Vernon.

"Bye!" said Donald as he raced down the steps and sprinted down the street.

Henrietta sat on the bed, trying to stop sobbing, as Jack walked up and down in front of her.

"How long has it been going on?" he demanded.

"Just four months, I swear. It started after you left for South Africa."

"Where did you meet him?" demanded Jack.

"At an exhibition in an art gallery – I never meant it to happen –"

"What is his name and where is he stationed?" demanded Jack.

"I can't tell you!"

"*Tell me!*" yelled Jack.

"I can't!" she sobbed.

"Tell me right now, or by God –" He raised his fist and shook it threateningly.

"He's . . . he's Captain Donald Kilroy."

"And where is he stationed?"

"At the Curragh in Kildare," she whispered.

"And this sordid affair took place here – in my bed?"

She nodded. "Mostly!"

"Mostly! Where else did this shameful sexual liaison take place?"

"In the odd hotel room."

"And where else?"

"Once in his quarters in Kildare."

He halted in his pacing. "You publicly visited him at the camp?" he asked in horror.

"No, no – it wasn't like that – we were there at an evening gathering in Bertie's quarters."

"Bertie – who the fuck is Bertie?"

She stifled her sobs.

"Answer me, dammit, woman!"

"Bertie, the Prince of Wales – he's a friend of Donald's."

Jack stared at her in shock. "*The Prince of Wales*!"

Henrietta nodded. "Yes, Bertie had a party for the officers and some of us ladies were invited to attend."

"Ladies? What kind of *ladies*? Ladies of the night? So you've been carrying on like an alley cat while I've been fighting for Queen and Country in South Africa!"

"But you weren't fighting a war in South Africa, were you?"

"Henrietta!"

"I feel only shame!" she said.

"You don't know the meaning of shame! And did the Prince of Wales know that you were carrying on with Kilroy?"

"I think so, yes."

"And he did not intervene?" Jack was dismayed.

"He was too busy having his own affair," said Henrietta.

"His own affair! With whom?"

"With some actress," sniffled Henrietta. "I had never met her before – she was performing in a music hall. I think her name was Nellie."

"You are lying! You are just trying to distract me from you and Kilroy by bringing the Prince into it!"

"I'm not lying, I promise you. Bertie, the Prince, started an affair with this Nellie and continued with it up until he left Ireland. Donal told me everything – they used to sneak her in at night to the Prince's quarters."

"What a disgusting state of affairs Major Hazeldon is presiding over – married women, actresses – he will be shocked when I report all this to him."

Henrietta jumped to her feet and fell to her knees in front of her husband. "*No!* You can't say any of this to Hazeldon! You just can't – it will be a scandal like none other with the Prince involved."

284

He stared at her and then pushed her away.

"Where are you going, Jack?" she cried as he walked out the door. He didn't answer but kept on walking.

Jack walked through the streets of Dublin until he reached his club. He could hardly believe everything that he had heard and seen. He always knew Henrietta was flirty and suspected her of having affairs, but to find her in his home with her lover! And these stories about the Prince of Wales!

As he calmed down and thought about it, he knew there was nothing he could do. His mother would have a nervous breakdown if he left Henrietta or divorced her. And if he went to Major Hazeldon and reported everything, yes, he would destroy this Donald Kilroy, but he would also besmirch his own name. What's more, there would be a full enquiry and the Prince's involvement would come to light including his involvement with this actress. This would be a full-blown scandal and his own reputation and career would be tarnished for tarnishing the Prince. At best, it would be all hushed up and he would be silenced even if it involved posting him to some back-of-beyond part of the colonies permanently.

Henrietta, as ever, was playing her cards cleverly. She had brought in the Prince's involvement to ensure he did not go to Hazeldon about her own affair.

He walked up the steps into his club and went straight to the bar where he ordered a double whiskey, followed by another in quick succession.

He was greeted by various club members but he barely said hello to them as he continued drinking.

Jack was sitting at a table with some of his friends. He had been drinking for four hours solid and it was now one o'clock in the morning.

"We've had a royal visit since you were last here," said one of his friends. "Her Majesty was here and the Prince of

Wales was stationed in Kildare for the summer."

Jack tightened his grip on his glass of whiskey. "Oh, I've heard all about the Prince's visit to Kildare!"

"I understand all went well for him there," said his friend.

"Oh, all went more than well for him, I can assure you of that!" spat Jack.

"Is anything the matter, Jack?"

"Oh, if you knew what I know about the Prince!"

"What are you talking about?"

Jack leaned forward and spoke in hushed tones. "The Prince of Wales was bedding a music-hall actress called Nellie while he was here!"

"Don't be ridiculous!" laughed one of the men.

"You can believe it, because it's true. I was speaking to somebody who was at his quarters and saw the Prince and this Nellie together. And it didn't stop there! Those oh-so-honourable officers stationed there continued to sneak the actress in to service the Prince every night!"

"Who said this?" asked one of the men, becoming concerned.

"It doesn't matter who, but it's true! Any of you who know soldiers down in that camp, ask them if a woman was seen being sneaked into his quarters. Not a common prostitute now – there are plenty of them swarming around – she would have been brought in by carriage with the officers."

"And where is this actress now?"

"I don't know where she is now, but I certainly know where she has been!" said Jack as he downed his whiskey in one.

The following night at a smart dinner party in a manor house in Dublin, a game of charades was being played. The dinner was being held by Lord Denis Leixlip.

"I do find charades quite boring, don't you?" whispered Denis to one of his guests, Roger Smyth.

"I certainly do! Tedious is the only word I can describe them as," said Roger.

"Shall we escape to the garden for a cigar?"

"Good idea!" said Roger and the two men discreetly rose from their seats, left the parlour and went out into the garden where they lit cigars.

"Thank you, Lord Leixlip, for a beautiful meal," said Roger.

"You are most welcome. You and your wife are charming company as ever," said Denis.

"What do you make of this growing call for independence?" asked Roger.

"Quite worrying. I had hoped the royal visit would have quelled it somewhat, but it only seems to have made it worse."

Roger gave a little laugh.

"Something amusing?" asked Denis.

"Well, I imagine if the Prince of Wales had spent more time on his royal duties while here and less on his love life, it might have been a different matter."

"Whatever do you mean?"

"Have you not heard?"

"Heard what?" asked Denis.

"Oh, I see you haven't." Roger looked behind him to make sure there was no one in earshot. "It wouldn't do for any of the ladies to hear of such matters."

"What matters?" demanded Denis, becoming impatient.

"Well, I am not one for idle gossip, but it was the talk of my club last night . . ." He hesitated.

Denis's patience snapped. "For goodness' sake, man, spit it out! What is the talk of your club?"

"The Prince of Wales' affair with an actress," Roger blurted out.

Denis mouth dropped open. "What nonsense is this?"

"It's not nonsense. One of the members of my club broke the story last night and suddenly everybody was talking about it. He started seeing an actress from the Palace Theatre

– you know, that vulgar music hall, when he was stationed in Kildare! Fellow officers of his sneaked her in under the commander's nose every night."

"You should know better than to repeat such nonsense, Roger – it is dangerous to do so," cautioned Denis.

"I assure you it isn't nonsense. I checked today with some pals of mine at the camp and they said they saw a woman going in and out of the Prince's quarters early in the morning and late at night."

"It can't be true!" snapped Denis.

"As true as I am standing here!" confirmed Roger.

CHAPTER 51

Bertie was waiting for his carriage outside the college in Cambridge, after a tutorial. The streets were filled with students back for the first week of university. As he gazed about him, he thought how things had changed so much since last he was there.

"*Bertie!*" came a call from across the street.

He looked over to see Charles Carrington waving across to him. He waved back and Charles came dashing across the road.

"Charles! My dear fellow – so good to see you again!" Bertie greeted him enthusiastically.

"You too, sir! Quite a different setting from the garrison in Kildare, eh?"

"I think I much preferred the garrison," sighed Bertie as he ruefully held up the stack of books he was carrying.

"*Hmmm*, much more fun than reading philosophy," agreed Charles, indicating his own stack of books.

"Where are your rooms?"

"I'm staying at Madingley Hall – outside the town. I am just about to go back there." He pointed down the street. "See, there's my carriage approaching – why don't you join me for tea and we can catch up on what has been happening?"

"Well, if it's not too much trouble?" said Charles.

The carriage halted beside them and they climbed in.

"I read in the newspapers you were in Prussia for military exercises," said Charles as they set off.

"If only that was the reason I was there! I was there on a secret mission to meet Princess Alexandra – remember, the Dane I spoke to you about?"

"Oh! How did that go?"

"As expected. She's a lovely girl but . . ."

"I understand. Say, did you hear about Donald Kilroy?"

"No?"

"Well, he and Henrietta were discovered in bed together at her house by her husband!"

"Surely not!" Bertie was horrified.

"Surely so! There was war seemingly. Her husband is going mad, literally mad!"

"Will he divorce her?"

"I don't think he wants the scandal, but he might just settle on killing her – and Donald along with her!" laughed Charles.

"Kilroy should be more careful – always a mistake carrying on with married women."

They turned into a gateway and down a driveway through spacious gardens. A huge redbrick country house with Tudor features came into sight.

"Is this your accommodation, sir?" asked Charles, amazed by the large building.

"Yes – my mother has rented the whole place for me. I wanted to stay in rooms in the college or town like all the other undergraduates, but they wanted to keep me away from the other students in case they were a bad influence on me!" He laughed. "Rather like closing the barn door after the horse has bolted after my stay in Kildare, don't you think?"

Charles grinned. "Rather!"

"So I stay here with my governor General Bruce and some minders."

Charles had heard about Bruce before – he had been appointed governor to the Prince when Bertie was seventeen and had accompanied him on various travels abroad since then – his main function being to keep an eye on him, it seemed.

In the hall inside, Bertie threw his books down on a desk.

A middle-aged man with a no-nonsense air came out of one of the rooms.

"Good afternoon, gentlemen," he said.

"Oh, General Bruce, this is a friend of mine, Charles Carrington," introduced Bertie.

"How do you do, sir," said Bruce, shaking his hand.

"General Bruce looks after me, Charles. Makes sure I don't get into any trouble, isn't that right, General Bruce?"

"I try my best, sir," nodded Bruce. "Can I get you young gentlemen anything?"

"Tea, perhaps, in a while," said Bertie. "But we are fine for now – I'm sure you have many things to do, General Bruce, so don't let us delay you."

Bruce nodded and retreated from the room.

Charles went to speak but Bertie put his finger to his lips and walked to the door which General Bruce had left ajar and closed it firmly. He listened at the door for a few moments and then walked back towards Charles.

"General Bruce is worse than a nanny!" said Bertie quietly. "He's always listening at doors and reporting back my every move to Buckingham Palace."

"How awful!"

"Luckily he's half deaf and he's easy to lose in a crowd!" Bertie picked up the decanter from a side table, poured them two glasses of brandy and handed one to Charles. "There are minders in permanent residence as well. But I've got to know their routines so I reckon they will be easy to give the slip to. They used to follow me everywhere at the beginning. But I've insisted they allow me to go to tutorials and classes on my own as well as visiting my friends here in Cambridge."

"What a nightmare!" Charles grimaced at the thought of such restrictions.

"I've got some news for you," said Bertie, sitting down on a chesterfield couch and gesturing to Charles to do the same.

"Oh?" Charles said, sitting down.

Bertie sat forward and kept his voice low. "Nellie is in England – she moved here to be with me. I asked her to come, and she did."

Charles nearly dropped his glass. "*What?*"

"I couldn't live without her, Charles. I just couldn't. So I've brought her with me."

"But – but where is she?" he said, looking around the rooms as if expecting her to spring up from behind the furniture.

"Oh, she's not here! I can't let General Bruce or any of the rest of the palace staff know – I'd be sent to the Tower! No, she's in London. She has a place in Chelsea, and a job working at the Europa Theatre in Shaftsbury Avenue. I didn't want her to work, but she insisted on doing so – she's so independent!" He sat back, admiration glowing in his eyes. "I've rented a small country house just outside Cambridge, where we plan to spend time alone together when we are not in London."

"I – I don't know what to say," said Charles, gobsmacked. "How did you arrange all this?"

"James Marton assisted me with it all. He's our cover. I've put him on the Palace payroll."

"I see!" said Charles.

"I've never been happier, Charlies. Never!" sighed Bertie.

"Well, then I am very pleased for you, sir," said Charles, trying to look happy.

"Why don't you visit us at the house? Nellie would love to see you again. We can invite a few others and make a bit of a party out of it."

"Sounds like an invite too intriguing to refuse, sir," said Charles.

Nellie disembarked from the train when it arrived in

Cambridge and made her way across the platform and through the station house to the street outside. She looked around and spotted a carriage. Bertie leaned out and beckoned her over.

Inside the carriage, they embraced and kissed.

"What a beautiful town!" she said, looking out at the spires as they passed through the streets.

"I'm so glad you are here with me to see it," he said, holding her hand tightly. "How's Sadie?"

"Not impressed that I have left her alone. She wanted to come too and was worried that I was coming on my own. How did you slip your minders?"

"I told them I had to spend the weekend studying with Charles Carrington," said Bertie with a mischievous grin. "Charlie says he will cover for me."

Leaving the town behind, they rode through the countryside for several miles until they turned into the gateway of Primrose House. Nellie put her head out the window to look at the house as they travelled up the curved driveway. It was a small Georgian manor house painted white, with beautiful views across the countryside.

They dismounted in front of the house and the driver began to carry their luggage inside.

Nellie took Bertie's hand and they walked through the door. The hall was quite beautiful, with a winding staircase at its end.

"Do you like it?" he asked.

"I love it!" she said. "It's fit for a queen, or at least a Prince's mistress!"

"Don't call yourself that, Nellie. You are so much more to me than a mistress," he said.

She walked into the large parlour which was on the right.

"James did well finding this place," said Bertie. "I don't know what I would have done without him."

She turned and looked at him seriously. "You shouldn't rely too much on James, Bertie."

"Why ever not? He's been a great friend to both you and me, has he not?"

"James has some excellent qualities . . . but I don't think he's the kind of man . . ." She fell silent.

"He's been a good friend to you, hasn't he? Over the years?"

Nellie went to speak again but stopped herself. How could she reveal what kind of a man James was without revealing her own past sins? Besides, she didn't want to make an enemy of James – he was too dangerous.

"I just think James . . . I just think . . . you have me now, Bertie. You don't need to rely on him so much."

She wanted to say more but refrained from doing so. It would be too risky.

"What I love about this place is that we are completely alone," said Bertie. "There isn't another house nearby and no servants or minders or batmen. Just us!" He suddenly looked worried. "James stocked up the larder but – who will do the cooking for us?"

"Since you can't boil an egg, it will have to be me, Bertie!" she said.

Bertie and Nellie were walking through the fields behind the house.

"I've done so much thinking since I met you, Nellie," he said. "And I've decided that from now on I am going to live my life by my own rules,"

"But can the Prince of Wales ever do that?"

"Yes, I can and I will! I'm sick of living by everyone else's rules. Do you know, when I was a child I was kept at Eton while the rest of my family went on holiday in the country. Because of the harsh regime of education my father insisted on and because I never met my parents' expectations, I was left in school while the others went to enjoy themselves."

"It's strange, I always thought that if you had a family and money then you'd never want for anything. Now I realise you can be as lonely with them as without."

He nodded. "I have never met anybody's expectations – so why should I try any more? I've been forbidden smoking and gambling and eating rich foods and the love of a woman I can love back. Well, I have all those things now, and the world hasn't stopped turning, has it? We are still here – I am still here. And now that I have them, I will never let them go again."

"You're right, Bertie," she said, her arm around his waist. "You are the Prince of Wales, but if you can't be happy, what's the point of it all?"

That night, they heard laughing and shouting coming up the driveway to the house and Bertie went rushing to the window.

"*They're here!*" called Bertie.

Nellie came down the stairs.

"Will I do to meet your friends?" she asked, standing at the bottom of the stairs dressed in a blue gown.

"You'll more than do!" he said, embracing her.

There was a loud knock on the door and Bertie went to answer it.

"It took us a while to find the place, sir! It's well hidden away!" said Charles as he walked in, followed by a group of other undergraduates and a couple of women.

"That's what I love about the place," said Bertie, beckoning Nellie over to him. "Charlie, you remember Nellie?"

"Of course – how could I forget?" said Charles, taking Nellie's hand and kissing it.

"How nice to see you again, Charlie," smiled Nellie. "And who are all these fine men you have brought with you?"

"Oh, let me do the introductions," said Bertie. "Nellie, this is Tom Haddington, Viscount Haddington's nephew – this is Stanley Crosston . . ."

"More vodka?" asked Nellie as she circulated the parlour with a bottle, filling up everyone's glass.

By now they were all merry.

"Nellie – I hear you are an actress?" said Tom.

"I am – amongst other things!" she said, winking at him.

"Will you sing us a song?" asked Tom.

"I will surely!" agreed Nellie. "But I'll need somebody to play the piano for me. Any volunteers?"

"I'll accompany you!" said a young man called Peter as he sat at the piano.

"I didn't ask you to accompany me – all I asked was for you to play the damned piano!" said Nellie, causing everyone to laugh.

Nellie bent down and whispered in his ear and he nodded happily. He ran his fingers across the piano keys and began to belt out 'My Irish Molly'.

Nellie began to sing –

"Molly, my Irish Molly, my sweet achusla dear,
I'm fairly off my trolley, my Irish Molly, when you are
near,
Springtime you know is ring time, come dear and don't
be slow
Change your name, go on be game, begorrah wouldn't
I do the same,
My Irish Molly O!"

Charles was standing beside Bertie who was visibly enraptured by Nellie's performance.

"Isn't she marvellous?" said Bertie.

"Yes, quite marvellous, sir. Eh, could I have a word with you . . . outside . . . it's quite noisy in here."

Bertie looked at him in surprise. "Now?"

"Yes, please."

Bertie put down his drink and walked out into the hall. Charles followed.

"What is the problem, Charles?"

Charles chose his next words carefully. "Sir, have you given any thought to the future?"

"The future?" asked Bertie.

"Well, eh, this relationship with Nellie can't last forever, sir, you do realise that?"

Bertie's smiled faded. "What business is it of anyone other than Nellie and me?"

"I do understand that, sir. But I feel I must advise you as a friend that the relationship with Nellie is better off finishing sooner rather than later – before either of you get in any deeper."

Bertie became annoyed. "I have no intention of finishing my relationship with Nellie, nor has she any intention of finishing with me! It is our business and nobody else's!"

"But you can't possibly be considering this affair to be a permanent fixture in your life, sir?" Charles was astounded.

"She is a permanent fixture in my life, Charlie!"

Charles paused and looked back into the parlour where Nellie was concluding the singing of 'My Irish Molly', dancing around, flirting with all the men.

"Women like Nellie are all very well and good, sir, and they have their place, but it's not right that you have elevated her to such a position in your life."

Bertie spoke angrily. "Why is it not right? Because she's not a princess? Because she didn't grow up with governesses or nannies? Because she's on the stage? Because she's not a Protestant?"

"Well – yes! All of that – and then some more!"

"I no longer want to have this conversation, Charlie. I thought you were my friend."

"I am your friend. That is why I speak so frankly."

As Nellie finished singing, the crowd erupted in cheers and laughter. She made a deep curtsy to them, before looking over to where Bertie stood at the door and smiling.

"You'll have to excuse me, Charles, Nellie is waiting for me," said Bertie and he walked back into the parlour.

Charles watched as Bertie took Nellie in his arms and they began to waltz around the room as the pianist began playing again.

CHAPTER 52

Victoria was in the drawing room, finishing reading a letter from Vicky. Albert was at the window, staring out pensively.

"I don't know whether to be heartbroken or joyous having read this letter from Vicky," said Victoria.

"Why?" asked Albert, turning around.

"Because she writes that Alexandra was impressed greatly by Bertie. She writes –" Victoria took up the letter and read from it, "that Alexandra found Bertie *'handsome, gracious, kind, attentive and would very much like to see him again'.*"

"It would be worse if Alexandra found that Bertie was none of those things, would it not?"

"But what does it matter now how she found him! Bertie has dismissed her as a future wife!"

"He has not dismissed her. He said he was impressed by her, but he said he is too young to contemplate marriage."

"Bertie will be sixty years of age and still declaring himself too young for marriage, if the matter is left to him! No, I do not see any reason to continue holding false hopes that he will choose Alexandra as his wife. If he did not decide by now, having met her, he never will. I must write to Vicky and urge her to continue to search for a more suitable bride."

"But she has searched and searched and there are no others. There are no more suitable princesses!"

"I despair!" said Victoria. "I wonder would any of the Catholic princesses in Europe convert to Protestantism to sit on the throne of England with Bertie?"

"Don't be ridiculous! We cannot ask such a thing, or even hint at it. It would be a political nightmare!"

"I know! I am only thinking out loud because I despair so," said Victoria.

Albert began to cough loudly. As the coughing fit continued, Victoria went to him.

"Are you all right, Albert?"

He gestured to her to move away from him as he continued to cough.

"Albert?" she asked, becoming more concerned.

"I am all right – do not fuss," he ordered between gasps.

The coughing eventually stopped.

"You are quite pale, Albert. Should I fetch a doctor?"

"I asked you not to fuss, so please do not!" snapped Albert.

"Very well!" said Victoria before returning to her seat.

Bertie walked into the Café Royal on Regent Street.

The maître d' greeted him.

"Good evening, Your Royal Highness. We were not expecting you this evening but I will have a table prepared for you at once. How many guests will be joining you?"

Bertie spotted Nellie seated at a discreet corner table.

"That's quite all right. I am meeting somebody here and I see she has already arrived." Bertie walked past the maître d' and through the restaurant until he reached Nellie's table.

"Hello," she said, smiling warmly at him.

"Good evening, Nellie," he said, sitting down opposite her.

As the maître d' poured them wine and took their order, Nellie looked around the restaurant. The other diners had noticed Bertie and were whispering to each other while they stole glances at their table.

"Are you sure this is all right?" she said quietly. "Meeting me alone in public like this?"

"Of course! Why wouldn't it be? Is it a crime to have

dinner these days?" asked Bertie nonchalantly.

"People will wonder who I am." she said. "Maybe we should go?"

"Nonsense, Nellie! I'm sick of hiding our relationship from people. We haven't done anything wrong. We are as entitled to be here as anybody else." He raised his glass to her.

She lifted her glass, clinked it against his and smiled.

Throughout the restaurant the main topic of conversation with the other diners was Bertie and his mystery dinner companion.

"I've never seen her before – socially – have you?" said a woman to her friends.

"No, but I could hazard a guess as to who she is," said a man with a disgusted look on his face.

"Tell us! Who is she?" begged the woman whose curiosity had reached fever point.

The man looked at his dinner companions. "Have none of you heard the rumours?"

They all shook their heads.

"Well, you must be the only people in London who have not heard by now." He leant forward and lowered his voice. "The Prince took up with an actress while stationed in Ireland during the summer. A woman of easy virtue by all accounts. She has moved to England to continue their relationship. My nephew is at Cambridge with the Prince and confirms it's true. This Nellie Cliffden has even hosted parties for the Prince."

"No!" The woman was scandalised. "Pray continue!"

"Seemingly it's a standing joke that this Nellie Cliffden is being referred to as the 'Princess of Wales' by the Prince's friends."

"And this is common knowledge?" asked the woman.

"It's been the talk of the gentlemen's clubs and parlours of the stately homes across the country. Nobody has had the courage to mention it to the royal family – yet!"

"I wish they would stop looking!" said Nellie, becoming irritated.

"Ignore them!" encouraged Bertie.

"It's easy for you to say! You've been used to people staring at you all your life. This is all new to me!"

"Just imagine you're on the stage, Nellie! You are used to people staring at you on the stage."

"Yes, perhaps that might make me feel more comfortable," she said, taking another sip of wine.

"I have some news for you," he said, leaning towards her.

"Oh?"

"You know it's my birthday in a couple of weeks? I'm going to take you to Windsor Castle for the event and show you around."

"Oh, Bertie! Won't your family be there?"

"No. They will be away," he assured her.

"Sounds like a lot of fun!" she squealed in delight.

CHAPTER 53

Returning home to the flat after a late-night performance at the theatre, Nellie called to Sadie as she came through the door.

"I want a hot bath, Sadie – and boil the kettle!"

She stopped when she saw James sitting there waiting for her.

"He pushed his way in, Nellie," said Sadie, appearing from the kitchen. "I told him to wait outside but he wouldn't hear of it."

"That's all right, Sadie. You can leave us alone."

Sadie reluctantly left them.

"I wasn't expecting you. What do you want?" asked Nellie.

"I want to talk to you before this gets any further out of hand," he said.

"Before what gets out of hand?"

"You and Bertie!" said James, standing up quickly. "The two of you have been recklessly stupid in conducting your affair. You've been seen out in public together. He's introduced you to his friends. You are even being his hostess at his parties in Cambridge."

"What of it? As Bertie says, we aren't committing any crime!"

"You stupid woman! You should have listened to me and done as I said. Been his mistress discreetly and not let anyone

302

know. You could have gained a lot financially and secured your future. Now, bringing the affair in the open – it has to end!"

"End?"

"I've bought you a ticket back to Dublin. You are to return at the weekend. I'll explain everything to Bertie – there's no need for you to see him again. I'll tell him you had a family emergency."

She looked at him in horror. "I have no intention of returning to Dublin. I'm staying here. I rather like my new life here and, as for not seeing Bertie again, we are in love."

"You are not in love! He's a stupid young man who has become infatuated with his first love. You are a stupid young woman who thinks he's the answer to all your problems."

"I don't really care what you think, James. This relationship has nothing to do with you any more."

James became angry. "I am telling you to get out now while you still can. If you let this go on any further, you will be in danger."

"In danger from whom?"

"From people you know nothing about. Important people that will want you out of the way if this becomes public."

"I'm not listening to any more of this, James. You are just jealous that Bertie and I have found what we were looking for in each other. Bertie cares for me, he really does. In fact, he's invited me to Windsor Castle!"

James sat down in shock. "When?"

"For his birthday," she said.

"To meet his parents! That's not possible."

"No, they won't be there."

"I see."

"But I expect it will be just a matter of time before he wants me to meet them."

James sprang to his feet, grabbed her arms and shook her. "Wake up, you fool!" he hissed. "He can never introduce you to his parents!"

"*Let me go! Now!*"

He released her.

"He can do anything he wants – he's the Prince of Wales!" she said.

"Nellie, his parents wouldn't even employ you as a maid, let alone be introduced to you as their son's lady!"

"Why not? I've been reading a lot of history since I met Bertie and I wouldn't be the first actress or commoner to capture the heart of a king. From Ann Boleyn to King Charles's mistress Nell Gwynn, an actress like me – I think I'll fit in very well!"

"You're mad! They were different times – that could never happen today!"

"Well, it is happening – right now – in front of the noses of all the high and mighty!" she boasted.

"But you're a whore, Nellie! You've been with half of Dublin for a few shillings! What will Bertie think when he finds out that?" demanded James.

She raised her hand and slapped him across the face. "Get out, James! Get out now!"

"You are giving me no choice but to tell Bertie of your previous profession if you don't return to Dublin," threatened James.

"You won't tell Bertie anything, James. Because, if you tell him the truth, that will be the end of your court career with the royal family, and your military career as well. Bertie will banish you because you lied to him about me and never told him about those men I was with. He'll be angrier with you than he ever would be with me. We are trapped together in the web of lies we have created. If I go down, then you go down with me. So for both our sakes, let's hope the truth never reaches Bertie's ears."

He stared at her in anger before turning and marching out the door.

Nellie bit her lower lip and sat down on the couch.

Sadie came into the room.

"He's making sense, Nellie – what will happen if the truth ever comes out?"

"It won't ever come out. It can't," said Nellie, with a steely look in her eyes.

"Maybe we should do as he says and go back to Dublin. Get away from here and go back to the life we know. I'm sure you'll get your job back at the Palace theatre now. In fact, Captain Marton will probably arrange for you to get your old job back."

"I can't go back, Sadie. I've come too far. I can't leave Bertie, not for anything. Now, run me that bath. I'm exhausted."

Sadie sighed and walked away.

CHAPTER 54

The carriage pulled up outside Nellie's building and she got out and paid the driver.

As she was crossing the pavement to the front door a man stepped out in front of her.

"Nellie?"

He was aged around thirty and was smiling nicely at her as if he knew her.

"Yes?" she asked.

"My name is Pierre Lemont. I am reporter with *Le Figaro* newspaper in Paris," he said in a French accent.

"Yes? What do you want?" she asked.

"I just wondered if you had time for a chat?"

"About what?"

"About your relationship with the Prince of Wales."

Nellie's mouth dropped open in shock. She pushed past him and continued to the front door of the building.

"Come on, Nellie! Don't be like that! I just want to ask you some questions, that's all!"

"How did you find out where I live?" she demanded.

"Oh, we have our contacts. We know quite a lot about you already, Nellie. We've been following you around for a while."

Her heart began to pound quickly as she struggled to get the key in the door.

"How did you meet him, Nellie? How did a girl like you get in the company of the Prince of Wales?"

"Go away!" she demanded.

"Come on, Nellie! I've come all the way from Paris to meet you. I could help you. You could do very well out of this with somebody like me behind you."

Nellie managed to get the door open and rushed inside, slamming it behind her and locking it. She leaned against it regaining her breath as the man outside continued to call her name. She rushed up the stairs to her flat and let herself in.

"*Sadie! Sadie!*" she called frantically.

"Whatever is the matter?" asked Sadie, rushing from the kitchen.

"There's a reporter outside the building from a French newspaper. He knows about me and Bertie! Started asking me loads of questions," Nellie told her in a panic.

"Oh shit!" said Sadie.

Nellie rushed to one of the windows and looked out.

"He's still down there! What'll I do, Sadie? What if they print our affair in the newspaper? What will it do to Bertie?"

"Maybe you should have thought about that before you went gallivanting about the place with him!" said Sadie.

Nellie sat down on the couch, trembling. "I have to warn Bertie. Tell him the newspapers are on to us. And ask him what should I do! Bertie will know what to do. He'll have a plan."

Sadie sat down beside her and stroked her hair. "Oh, Nellie! Bertie strikes me as the kind of man who never has a plan! He just drifts along, going with his heart."

"But he'll know what to do, Sadie. He will, I tell you!"

Sadie nodded and smiled. She didn't want to frighten Nellie any further. But she realised that the two young lovers had been living in their own dream world and the outside world was just about to come crashing down on them. And neither of them were in any way prepared for what was coming their way.

Nellie got off the train at Cambridge and anxiously looked around. Since she had been accosted by the reporter from *Le*

Figaro, she hadn't left the flat. She had stayed hidden inside, not even going to work for fear of meeting that reporter again or another one. She had rushed from the flat in the early hours of that morning and luckily there hadn't been anybody around as she made her way to the train station to get the train to Cambridge as had been arranged.

She raced across the platform and through the station and saw Bertie's carriage waiting in its normal place. She rushed over and climbed into the carriage.

"Oh, my darling!" Bertie said, embracing her and kissing her.

She pushed him away.

"What's the matter?" he asked, surprised.

"Bertie, there was a French reporter from *Le Figaro* newspaper outside my building yesterday. He knew about us! He was asking about our affair."

"I see," said Bertie, his face clouding over. "And what did you tell him?"

"I said nothing. I ran inside and locked the door."

Bertie had visibly paled.

"I've been terrified all week, Bertie! They know! What if they write something about us? Or what if it appears in the British press?"

"I am sure it wouldn't. The foreign press is always hunting for stories about us that the British press wouldn't dare print. But it does put us in an awkward position." His face was creased with worry.

"Awkward – that's a bit of an understatement, Bertie!" she snapped.

"How did they find out? Who told them?" he said, shaking his head.

"Oh, come on, Bertie! We have hardly been discreet – dining in the Café Royal – me meeting all your friends at the garrison in Kildare and then in Cambridge!"

"But none of my friends would speak to the press – they are good fellows. And we only dined out alone once. Hardly enough to set tongues wagging. I figured nobody would know who you were so we would be quite safe."

"Oh, Bertie! Does it matter how it started? The fact is it has started!" she gasped. "What will we do?"

"We'll go on as normal, I think. They have nothing on us, nothing solid," said Bertie, but the worried look did not leave his face.

CHAPTER 55

In Berlin, Vicky walked into her husband's study.

"Fritz! I have just received a letter from Mama and she says Bertie was not overawed by Alexandra!" she said, horrified.

"I see!"

"What is wrong with him?"

"Clearly he must be blind," said Fritz. "I think Alexandra is adorable myself."

"Mama has asked me to continue my search for another bride for him. But there are no others! My goodness, there isn't a principality, duchy or kingdom I haven't meticulously searched already!"

"Perhaps, my dear, there is no more you can do. If the boy doesn't want to get married to Alexandra or anybody else for that matter, then what can we do?"

"Well, I am not going to give up, Fritz. I see it as my mission to help my brothers and sisters to find their ideal partner, as I have already done for dear Alice."

"Well, one success is maybe all you will achieve. I think it may be time to leave your siblings to find their own way in life and perhaps concentrate on our own family. Little Wilhelm needs all the attention you can give him – he can be so troublesome when not supervised."

"My parents are relying on me and I will not let them down with Bertie."

Fritz sighed and sat back in his chair. "I did not want to tell you this, my dear. But there are unsavoury stories circulating about Bertie."

"Unsavoury? Bertie?" said Vicky, sitting down in the chair across the desk from him. "Pray tell me what you are talking about?"

Fritz picked up a newspaper and handed it to her.

It was French and there was a front-page article about Bertie. Vicky began to read.

"But what is this?" Shocked, she looked up at Fritz. "They can't write this! It's slander!"

"I'm not sure if it is, Vicky. Gossip has been circulating the gentlemen's clubs and elsewhere for some time – that Bertie has got himself involved with that actress – romantically – as that newspaper reports. The rumours started in Dublin – he met her while there – and spread to London and then to the Continent. I was told of the rumours some time ago but refused to believe them."

"And who is this – actress?" she asked, ashen-faced, looking down at the newspaper again. "Nellie Cliffden?"

"She has quite a dubious reputation. I even heard her being described as a prostitute."

"Oh my God!"

"It is no wonder that Bertie is not interested in pursuing Alexandra – if his heart is with another. This woman, Nellie Cliffden, is now in London at Bertie's behest – they are seeing each other regularly, I understand."

"But what are we to do, Fritz?" she demanded.

"Would you like me to write to your papa and inform him?"

"No! It would kill him and Mama too!" she cried.

"But I fear it is only a matter of time before they discover what is happening themselves. It has not only been reported in the French newspapers, but the Spanish and Italian as well. Respect for you only is preventing it being mentioned in the German newspapers but it's common knowledge in

Berlin. And I've heard in London it is the – gossip of all gossip. "Are you certain you do not wish me to write to your father and inform him of all this?"

"No! I don't want him or Mama stressed unnecessarily. I simply do not believe the rumours or the gossip! No brother of mine would be involved with a woman like that! Bertie simply would not do it. I would urge him to sue those newspapers for slander, but I fear to do so would only bring more attention to the tawdry gossip. I suggest we do nothing and wait for it to blow over."

"Let us hope in that case that it will blow over soon. Because if this goes any further it will destroy Bertie. No woman of breeding will ever consider marrying him if his reputation is tarnished with a woman like that. And I fear that if I will not inform your father of this affair, then somebody else surely will soon."

CHAPTER 56

Nellie was mesmerised as the carriage was waved past the soldiers on duty at the entrance to Windsor Castle and began to drive up to the imposing building.

"Oh, Bertie, I've never seen anything so beautiful!" she said as she peered out the carriage window.

"Do you like it, my love?" he asked, delighted to see her so impressed.

"How could anybody not?" she asked.

The carriage drew up to a side doorway and they stepped out of it. A footman was waiting there.

"Good afternoon, Your Royal Highness." He bowed. "Madam."

"Good afternoon, Anthony. Are any of my royal family in residence or expected tonight?" Bertie enquired.

"No, sir," said the footman. "Your parents arrive tomorrow."

"Good. Jolly good." Bertie offered Nellie his arm. "And Anthony –"

"Yes, sir?"

"I am on my own, if anyone should enquire."

"Yes, sir," said Anthony.

As Bertie led Nellie through the building to his rooms, she was speechless as she viewed the luxurious rooms.

When they got to his flat, she walked around the giant sitting room, marvelling at the ornate ceilings and furniture.

"To think – me here in Windsor Castle!" she muttered to

herself in awe.

"What was that?" he asked.

"I just feel as if I am in a fairy tale. I keep thinking I will wake up and none of this will have happened," she said.

He laughed. "Come and I'll show you around the rest of the castle."

Nellie was fascinated as he showed her the castle, pointing out its different aspects which were steeped in history.

When they got to the throne room, Nellie walked slowly through it, staring at everything, until she reached the throne.

"Is that where she sits – Her Majesty?" asked Nellie as she walked around the throne, almost frightened of it.

"Indeed it is, Nellie, and where all the monarchs sat before her and where I shall sit one day," he said.

"I'm sorry!" she said as she sat down on the throne. "But I can't resist!"

"Oh, Nellie!" He laughed, seeing her on his mother's throne. "Would Her Majesty care for me to get her anything in particular?"

Nellie adopted a posh accent. "Yes, we would like a foot rub!"

She slipped off her shoe and held out her foot to him.

"It is my honour to be of service," he said, laughing as he knelt down and massaged her foot.

Suddenly footsteps sounded behind him. He jumped up while Nellie quickly got off the throne and slipped her shoe back on.

"Oh, pardon me, Your Royal Highness, I didn't realise anybody was here," said a footman, staring at Nellie in shock.

"That's quite all right, we were about to leave anyway," said Bertie.

He offered Nellie his arm and they walked past him and out of the room.

That evening Nellie dressed in one of her evening gowns in Bertie's bedroom. As she fixed her hair in the mirror there was a knock on the door and Bertie entered. He walked over to her and kissed her neck.

"The servants have just left," he said, taking her by the hand and leading her out through his sitting room and into the dining room where the table had been set and a pheasant meal lay prepared.

"I told them not to disturb me for the rest of the night," he said, leading her to a chair.

She sat down and he took a seat opposite her.

"They don't suspect that I am staying the night?" she asked.

"I do not know and I do not care, Nellie," he said as he poured the wine.

Silence fell as they began to eat and Nellie felt her light-heartedness evaporate.

Bertie too looked preoccupied.

"James visited me during the week," she said at last.

"What did he want?"

"He wanted me to return to Dublin," sighed Nellie.

"What? I don't believe it!"

"I assure you he did."

"But why? He had no right to ask you such a thing!"

"I think he was thinking about the repercussions of our relationship for you – and perhaps even for me and probably himself if it becomes public. He says our relationship, now that it is becoming known, can't continue."

"I am tired of everyone telling me what I can and can't do!" said Bertie angrily.

"But he's right, Bertie . . . and I don't want to be hurt."

"What do you mean? Have I ever hurt you? Have I ever done anything to upset you?"

"No, of course not. But when you are forced to finish with me, what will I do then? What will happen to me?"

"If you married me, then there would be nothing that anybody could do," said Bertie, staring at her across the candlelight.

"Don't tease me, Bertie," she implored.

"I am not teasing you – I've never been more serious in my life," he said.

"Don't, Bertie!" she said, rising from the table and going to a window.

"Nellie?" he said, getting up and following her. "Have I offended you?"

"How could you ever marry me?" she demanded. "I would never be accepted by your family, or the country or by anyone!"

"You wouldn't be marrying my family, or the country or just anyone, you would be marrying me."

"But that's just the point, Bertie – whoever marries the Prince of Wales isn't just marrying the man, she's marrying an institution."

"There's the religion thing, I grant you that," he said. "You might have to convert to Protestantism – I need to check the legalities of it. But there is no other reason why we can't be married."

"Bertie, I have no family, I have no money. I'd never be accepted and then there's my past," she said.

"What about it?"

"A famine orphan becoming the Princess of Wales! There would be an outcry!"

"It does not matter to me, Nellie. The world is changing. I saw it when I was in America. People are being judged not by where they are from but by who they are and what they have achieved. Look at Abraham Lincoln – he was born in a one-room log cabin and is now the President of the United States. We can be part of that new world order."

"You make it sound so simple, Bertie, but this isn't America. This is Europe."

"Well, Europe needs to change. And I am in a unique position to help make that change. And by marrying you I can change society overnight."

She looked into his earnest eyes and kissed him.

316

"Is that a yes?" he asked.

She nodded.

That night as she lay in bed while Bertie slept soundly, a million thoughts raced through her head. A few months ago she would never have dreamed of being here in Windsor Castle with the Prince of Wales. But it had happened. Couldn't those same changes that had brought her here sweep her onward to be his wife? As Bertie said, if the President of the United States had made the journey from a one-roomed log cabin to the White House, why could she not make the journey from the cottage she was born in to Buckingham Palace?

She had always had the belief in the back of her mind that their relationship would have to end one day. But now with his proposal they could be together forever. And she could make him happy, she knew she could. She knew how happy he was in her company. Why should he suffer a cold loveless marriage to some foreign royal when he could be with her? As she thought back on her life, she remembered the journey that had brought her there. And now, if she were Bertie's wife, nobody could ever look down on her or mistreat her again.

She sat up and looked at Bertie's sleeping form and fear gripped her. What if he ever found out about that side of her past? No man, however humble, would marry her if they knew about the men she had been with.

But that was another part of her life that was over now. And there was no reason he should ever find out.

CHAPTER 57

Victoria always loved being at Windsor Castle. Even though Buckingham Palace was their official residence, she always felt more at home at Windsor.

In the afternoon she was alone with Alice in the drawing room. Alice, who was working on a tapestry, was seated in an armchair by the fireplace. Albert was in the audience room with government ministers who had asked to meet him urgently over a diplomatic row that was developing with the Americans.

"Your tapestry has much improved over these past months, Alice," Victoria commented.

"Thank you, Mama," said Alice.

"I wonder how long your father will be in his meeting," said Victoria.

"What is he discussing with the ministers, Mama?"

"There has been some incident involving the Northern States of America. They boarded one of our ships illegally and seized two Confederates who were travelling on it," said Victoria. "I do not know what Mr. Lincoln was thinking."

"Is it serious, Mama?" asked Alice, not looking too concerned.

"It could be very serious. It could result in Britain being dragged into the American civil war. Your papa is trying to find a diplomatic solution." Victoria sighed. "Your papa works so hard and rarely is given the credit he deserves. He certainly takes some of the strain of the monarchy from my shoulders by handling these issues for me."

"He is a wonderful man," agreed Alice.

"Do you think he looks rather unwell recently, Alice? He seems so pale and is not in good spirits at all. He complains he is tired all the time – it can be quite difficult to listen to – especially as I am still stuck in my grief over my dear mother."

"Yes, I've noticed he looks unwell and his mood is irritable, to say the least."

"*Hmmm* . . . he works too hard," mused Victoria.

"It is unfortunate Bertie is not here to have dinner with us this evening – it could take Papa's mind off work?"

"Why on earth would Bertie be here for dinner? He is at Cambridge immersed in his studies – we hope!"

Alice looked up from her tapestry. "No, Mama. He was here last night, I overheard a couple of the maids discussing it."

"You or they are mistaken, Alice. Bertie was not scheduled to be at Windsor. He is in Cambridge, as I said."

"They seemed quite certain he was here. They said he was showing a woman around the castle," said Alice.

"Whatever are you talking about, child? What woman?"

"That's all I heard them say," shrugged Alice.

Victoria stared at Alice, trying to make sense of the story.

The door of the room opened and an exhausted-looking Albert walked in.

"Albert?" said Victoria. "Do you know anything about Bertie being in Windsor and showing a woman around the castle last night?"

"No, I do not," said Albert irritably. "And I am in no mood to hear nonsense about Bertie. I am trying my best to divert us from going to war with the Northern States of America!"

Victoria looked at Alice and said, "Leave us, dear child."

"Yes, Mama," said Alice. She stood, gathering up her

tapestry and threads, and nodded to her father as she left the room.

"Is the situation bad, Albert?" asked Victoria, concerned.

"Yes, it could be very bad," he said, sitting at a desk by the window. "As you know, when Mr. Lincoln's troops entered our ship illegally to arrest the two Confederate diplomats they broke international law and now the situation is in danger of spiralling out of control. Our government is seeing the incident as an act of war and are privately threatening to enter the American civil war on the side of the Confederates."

"My goodness!" Victoria was horrified. "So we would be fighting on the side of slavery?"

"I am trying to temper our government's response and explain to them that we cannot become involved in the civil war. The people do not want it and the country cannot afford it, especially so soon after the Crimean war," said Albert.

"Yes, my darling, you must insist they see sense!"

Albert massaged his temples as he began to sift through his post.

"Ah, a letter from Baron Stockmar," he said, managing to smile as he unfolded the letter.

Victoria was glad Albert had received a letter from his oldest and dearest friend. Based in Prussia, Baron Stockmar had been a very trusted friend and ally over the years. He was one of the few people they could rely on totally. He always helped them and his advice was completely dependable. He had even helped Albert devise Bertie' education curriculum when he was growing up.

Albert read in silence as Victoria digested the information about a possible war with the Northern States of America.

Eventually Victoria spoke. "Albert, we simply cannot leave this diplomatic incident in the hands of the Prime Minister. Viscount Palmerstown will lead us into yet another catastrophe like the Crimean war, if left to his own devices.

You will have to intercede forcibly and stop this from going any further!"

She looked at Albert who did not appear to be listening to her but instead was holding the letter from Baron Stockmar so tightly in his hands that his knuckles were white. His face was white as a ghost.

"Albert? Albert – are you listening to me?" she demanded.

Albert stood up from his desk and crossed over the room to his wife, still gripping the letter.

"Whatever is the matter, Albert?" Victoria asked.

He handed her the letter, sat down on the couch opposite her and placed his face in his hands.

"Albert? What is it?" she asked, alarmed. She quickly began to read through the letter.

Albert's voice was low and forlorn. "Baron Stockmar says that Bertie is in a relationship with an Irish actress of easy virtue. That they met in Ireland and that it is the talk of the courts, gentlemen's clubs and parlours of Europe. He says everyone knows . . . but us."

Victoria's mouth was open wide as she read the letter.

"Nellie Cliffden!" She read out the name in horror.

"To think a son of mine would ever stoop to such depths . . . that he would sink to such depravity . . . that he would associate himself with such a person and defile his body and soul." Albert's voice was so low Victoria could hardly hear him.

"But this must be the woman that Alice heard the servants talk of – saying that he was showing her around Windsor Castle!" exclaimed Victoria. "Oh, stupid boy! Idiot of idiots! He has ruined his life!"

"He brought her here? Is it something I have done? Have I not been a good father?" Albert was on the verge of tears.

"He could not have had a better father! It is Bertie himself who has got himself into this mess! As only Bertie could! I have been right about him all his life! Reckless, stupid, selfish, idiotic!"

"I tried to show him the right way to lead his life, I tried to lead him by example. Perhaps I was too hard on him, as he has gone in the opposite direction to everything I have tried to teach him."

"Oh Albert!" said Victoria as she rose from her seat, went to him and cradled his head against her breast. "There is nothing for you to reproach yourself with. You have done nothing wrong! Bertie is just Bertie, and it is our misfortune to have been given such a wayward son. And the empire's misfortune to have such a future monarch."

"If Bertie can even become the monarch now. His reputation is lost. Who will marry him now when he has been publicly shamed with such a woman? He has undone twenty years of our work in a matter of weeks. He has reduced the monarchy to a laughing stock around Europe. He, or we, can never be taken seriously again, or hold our heads up."

"What shall we do, Albert? What can we do?" pleaded Victoria as she was tried to understand the gravity of the situation.

"I do not know. But I fear all is lost with him," said Albert.

CHAPTER 58

Bertie left his tutorial at his college and got into the carriage to drive him back to Madingley Hall. He felt so overjoyed with life. His studies were going well. What he had struggled with all his life was now suddenly coming easy to him. He knew the reason this was so had a lot to do with Nellie. She had cleared his mind and given him confidence. Confidence in himself to ask the questions in his classes that he needed to ask to learn. He was so grateful to her for so many things. He had been lost until he found her and now he had a purpose in life.

At Madingley, General Bruce was sitting in the parlour.

"Good afternoon, General Bruce," said Bertie cheerfully.

"Good afternoon, sir," said Bruce, not in the least cheerful.

Since the Prince's return from Ireland, it had been nearly impossible to pin him down. He was constantly off with his friends, slipping away from his minders. Escaping out windows at night and returning before light. The Prince had become wild and Bruce did not know what to do with him or how to control him.

"There is post for you on the cabinet, sir," said Bruce.

"Good, jolly good!" Bertie gathered up the post and stretched out on the chesterfield in front of the roaring fire. "Thank you, General Bruce!" he said, tacitly dismissing him.

Bruce reluctantly left him alone.

Bertie riffled through his letters. He saw there were some from Ireland – the friends he had made at the garrison were keeping in constant contact with him. He saw there was one from Vicky in Prussia. Then he frowned when he saw there was one from Windsor Castle in his father's handwriting.

He sat up, opened the letter and unfolding it began to read.

Dear Bertie,

I am writing with a heavy heart, on a subject that has caused me the greatest pain I have yet experienced in this life. It is with much distress that I have learned of your liaison with that low common woman. I knew you were thoughtless and weak – but I could not think of you as depraved!

Bertie eyes shot up from the letter as he paled at his father's words. Terrified, he looked down and read on. His father went on to imagine the worst possible scenarios, from Nellie blackmailing him to her falling pregnant with his child.

There, in the witness box, she will be able to give before a greedy multitude disgusting details of your profligacy for the sake of convincing the jury, yourself cross-examined by a railing indecent attorney and hooted and yelled at by a lawless mob. Oh horrible prospect, that this person has in her power, any day to realise, and to break your poor parents' hearts.

Bertie could hardly bear to read the harsh words from his father and glanced to the end of the letter to read –

You must, you dare not be lost – the consequences for this country and the world would be too dreadful. There is no middle course, you must belong to the good or the bad in this life.

Bertie crumpled the letter up and held it in his hands as he stared into the fire. It was as if reality had suddenly hit him. After months of living in a blissful bubble with Nellie, he was being confronted with the reality of his father and mother knowing about their relationship.

324

General Bruce walked into the room.

Bertie ignored him as he continued to stare into the fire.

"Sir – I am to inform you that Prince Albert is coming to see you on the 25th," said Bruce.

Bertie looked quickly at him. "My father is coming here? To see me?"

"That is what I have been told, sir," said Bruce before leaving the room.

Bertie had hardly been able to eat or sleep over the next days as he waited for the arrival of his father. He had read and reread the letter his father had sent him. The words did not become kinder with each read. His father had never minced his words with him, but the letter had been of a tone he had never encountered from him before. Absolute horror and disgust, but what was even harder to bear was his father's sheer and utter disappointment.

As the November nights were drawing in fast, the weather was cold and miserable. Bertie sat at his bedroom window looking out at the rain and grey skies, anxiously awaiting the arrival of his father and all that that would bring. Those glorious days in the sunshine in Ireland, when his relationship with Nellie had started, now seemed like a distant memory as he faced the consequences of his actions.

There was a knock on the door and General Bruce entered his bedroom.

"Sir, your father has arrived to see you."

Bertie nodded and, feeling he was going to meet his executioner, he walked slowly from his room and down the stairs to the parlour where Albert stood facing the fire with his back to him.

"Papa," Bertie said quietly and Albert turned slowly to look at him.

Bertie got a shock on seeing his father as he looked so pale and unwell. He became shrouded in guilt, realising he had been the cause of such anguish for his father. He had expected to see a look of disgust on his face, but instead he could see only sadness. Bertie felt he would prefer to have seen a look of disgust.

"I think we shall go for a walk," said Albert as he headed to the door.

As Bertie looked out at the rain that was teeming down, he wanted to say something but was too frightened to object.

"Yes, Papa," he said as he grabbed a cloak and followed his father out into the rain.

They seemed to walk for ages through the cold rain, firstly though the gardens of the house and then out of the grounds and towards Cambridge. Neither said a word.

Albert had a coughing fit occasionally.

As Albert launched into yet another coughing fit, Bertie mustered the courage to ask, "Are you all right, Papa? Would you like us to return to the house?"

Albert shook his head as he marched on, his eyes peering through the cold rain.

Eventually he spoke. "I am doing all I can to keep the country from going to war with America. The government want to send a stern response, an ultimatum, to Abraham Lincoln that unless the two Confederate diplomats taken from our ship are released, we will declare war on them. I am trying to make our government see sense and to send a much more diplomatic response that will not embroil us in that ghastly war."

As Bertie listened to his father speak he was in awe of him. Even now, when he was faced with the personal ruin of his son and family, he was putting the country first. And Bertie had no doubt but that his father's diplomatic skills would win out and safely manoeuvre the country away from any dangerous course that could embroil it in the American war.

"I am sure they will listen to you, Papa," said Bertie.

"Do you? I am not so sure. Does anybody ever listen to me any more?"

"Of course they do! Everybody respects you greatly, Papa."

"Except you, perchance?"

"That is not true. I respect you greatly too, Papa."

"Then why would you put your mother and I through this scandal? Why, Bertie - *why*?"

"I – I didn't mean to put anybody through anything. I just met somebody and fell in love . . ."

"How could you love a low common woman like that?" demanded Albert.

"If you met her, Papa, you would see how – you would see what's she's like."

"I have no intention of ever meeting her. I will never meet her, Bertie. And I do not wish you to meet her again either. I insist on it. Tell me, who introduced you to her?"

"I would rather not say, Papa."

"I have already heard all the sordid details of how she was sneaked into your quarters in Ireland by your fellow officers. I want their names – give them to me."

As Bertie walked on in the freezing cold rain he remembered the great times he'd had with Donald and Charles and James at the camp. How they had supported him and looked after him, covered for him.

"I will not give those names, Papa," he said with determination.

"Believe it or not, that is the only thing I respect you for in this whole tawdry affair. A sense of loyalty cannot be bought."

"Thank you, Papa."

"Where is this wretched woman now?" Albert asked.

"She has a flat in London, in Chelsea."

"Is she pregnant?" Albert demanded.

"No, Papa!" Bertie was horrified. It was a possibility he had not given much consideration to – he could not afford to think about such consequences.

"That is the rumour that is circulating. That she is

pregnant with your child." Albert gulped as he said the next line. "My grandchild."

"Papa, no – I swear she is not pregnant!" insisted Bertie.

"If she is it will bring down the monarchy. That such a wretched creature should be the mother of the Prince of Wales's first child! Even if it would have no legitimate claim to the throne. How could your legal heir be taken seriously with your firstborn being paraded around London by that Irish . . . harlot?"

"I wish – I wish you wouldn't speak of Nellie like that, Papa. She has not done anything wrong – she merely fell in love with me."

"That, my boy, is doing plenty wrong! She had no right to fall in love with you – or be in your bed – or be anywhere near you! Has she tried to blackmail you?"

"No! Of course not!"

"Have you given her much money?"

"Nothing, Papa! Not a thing! I tried to buy her presents and she refused to accept anything from me."

"As I expected . . . a very clever shrew . . . she is playing a long game with you to entrap you."

"Nellie isn't playing any game with me, Papa. It is I who insisted on meeting her, I who invited her to the garrison in Kildare, I who insisted she move to England. She gave up everything for me."

"She had nothing to give up. Unlike you who had the whole world to lose and lose it you have very nearly done. What self-respecting princess will marry you now, with this scandal circulating around you? God knows the choice of brides for you was limited enough as it was. How could we expect Princess Alexandra to marry you now? Do you think her family would allow her to marry you, after you have been with that woman?"

"I do not know, Papa. All I know is that I am love with Nellie. I cannot imagine living without her."

"And can you imagine living without the throne? Because

you cannot have one without losing the other. It is not acceptable for you to have any future with this woman. If you try to, abdication is the only alternative. And if you abdicate and forsake your destiny so you can be with this actress, then we are all ruined. I know the monarchy will not survive the scandal. All our futures are in your hands."

"You are putting me in an impossible position, Papa."

"You have put yourself in an impossible position, Bertie," said Albert as they continued walking through the relentless rain.

When they finally got back to Madingley Hall it was getting dark.

Albert stood in front of the roaring fire to dry off as Bertie stood apart.

Albert turned to face him.

"I have done much soul-searching since I have learned of this affair. I fear that I may have been too strict with you over the years. That I was trying so hard to shape you the way I wanted you to be shaped that I didn't give you space to develop your own self-control."

"Please, do not blame yourself for anything I have done, Papa. I take full responsibility for my own actions."

"Perhaps it seemed I did not love you as much as the others. But I knew the huge responsibility that had been mounted on your shoulders and I was trying to prepare you for that role. I pushed you too hard, I realise that now. I didn't accept you for who you are. But anything I have done I have only done because I loved you so much."

Bertie's eyes began to well with tears as he cleared his throat. "I know that, Papa."

"I would like us to start again. I want us to be close and to have a mutual respect. Is it too late for that?"

"No, of course not, Papa. I want that more than anything in the world."

"Then I want you to promise me that you will never see this woman again."

Bertie stared at his father in silence.

"Bertie – promise me that you will not see this Nellie Cliffden again," Albert demanded.

"I – I – what will become of her?"

"That is none of your concern. Promise me, Bertie. If you ever loved me and your mother then promise you will not see her again."

Bertie stared at his father before uttering, "I promise."

Albert heaved a sigh of relief.

"Where is General Bruce?" he said. "Get him to bring the carriage to the front of the lodge. I need to return to Windsor. Your mother is waiting for me and I have to help the government draft a statement to Abraham Lincoln."

Bertie went to the bell-pull and tugged it.

Albert walked to Bertie and smiled as he put a hand on his shoulder.

"I am very pleased we spoke today, Bertie. Very pleased with what we have discussed and the outcome."

"So am I, Papa," said Bertie who managed to smile back.

General Bruce entered the room.

"I am returning to Windsor now," said Albert. "Please have my carriage brought to the front."

"Very good, sir."

"I will write to you soon," Albert said to his son before following General Bruce out of the room.

"General Bruce," Albert said once he was alone with him in the hallway.

"Yes, sir?" said Bruce in some trepidation.

"There has been a major breach of security with my son since he returned from Ireland. I know he is not the easiest of fellows to keep track of and has a wilful mind, but I intend to have a full investigation of how he has been capable of continually slipping you and his minders."

"I can only apologise, sir," said Bruce. "Allow me to say that we have exercised every reasonable precaution. But it has proved to be an impossible task to control his – eh, movements."

"'*Reasonable*' is not enough. From now on, I want my son not to be left alone for one minute, apart from when he sleeps. And even then a minder is to be stationed outside his window at all times. He is to be accompanied to and from classes. Quite simply, he is to be under house arrest or the consequences will be dire."

"Very well, sir," said Bruce with a bow, relieved that he had not been summarily dismissed from his post.

Victoria waited anxiously in the drawing room at Windsor Castle for Albert to return. Government ministers were waiting for him in the study to finalise the draft to the Americans. She paced up and down, her nerves racked.

At last the door opened and Albert walked in.

"Albert!" She rushed to him and embraced him.

Albert began to cough harshly as he gently pushed her away.

"What – what is the outcome?" she asked, fearing the answer.

"Bertie has admitted everything but he has apologised and promised not to see her again. Whether I believe him or not is another matter. But I have cautioned General Bruce and instructed him that minders should surround Bertie day and night. He seems genuinely contrite . . . he says he fell in love with her." Albert collapsed into an armchair, exhausted.

"Love!" cried Victoria. "What does he know of love? How this creature has bewitched him!"

"Are the ministers still waiting for me?"

"Yes, they are in the study. We have tried to keep them at bay with tea and scones but their impatience is at boiling point," said Victoria.

"I must go to them," said Albert, standing up and launching into a fit of coughing again.

"You are as pale as a sheet, Albert!"

"I went walking with Bertie in the rain and fear I may have caught a chill," said Albert.

"Let us tell the ministers to come back tomorrow – you must go to bed and rest," urged Victoria.

"This matter cannot wait any longer. State affairs wait for no man," said Albert as he continued to the door, fighting to stave off another coughing fit.

Albert sat at his desk in his study, surrounded by government ministers and civil servants as he redrafted the response they were sending to Abraham Lincoln.

"This reads as very lame in my opinion and shows us to be weak. I doubt the Prime Minister will agree to it," commented a minister.

"This is the only response we can give the Northern States of America without risking war with them," Albert said firmly. "If the Prime Minister does not accept this final draft then he not only risks causing the ruin of Great Britain but of himself also as the British people will not fight a war to ensure the continuation of slavery." Albert then began to cough loudly.

"Are you all right, sir?" asked the minister, alarmed at how ill he looked.

"I am fine, but I must retire to my bed now as I have had a long day," said Albert.

"Yes, of course," said the minister, gesturing to the others to leave.

"Was there something else, minister?" asked Albert when they were left alone.

"Yes, sir. I must discuss with you the terrible news the government has received in relation to the Prince of Wales and a most unsuitable young lady. The Prime Minister has spoken to all the British Press to ensure they do not print anything for now, but he is most concerned with the situation."

"You may tell the Prime Minister that I have spoken to

my son and the relationship is now over," said Albert.

"But, sir, how can you be sure? The Prime Minister is extremely concerned that the Prince's affair will lead to a constitutional crisis."

"The Prime Minister's main concern should be presently to keep our nation out of war with the Americans. Leave my son to me and there will be no further problems with the matter."

Albert rose from his desk. As he walked to the door he had a coughing fit and grabbed a chair to give him support.

"Are you all right, sir?" asked the minister, rushing to his aid.

"Yes," Albert said between coughs as he shivered and manged to keep going to the door.

CHAPTER 59

Bertie sat staring into the fire in his bedroom as he relived the day. He had never seen his father so upset, so distraught. He had never wanted to cause his parents this amount of pain. He was in turmoil. All he wanted to do was to be with Nellie and now it had been pointed out to him in the harshest manner that his relationship with her could never be. He had been living in a fool's paradise. But what was he to do? He couldn't bear being without her but he couldn't plunge his family and the nation into any more crisis.

He thought of his promise to his father not to see Nellie again. But he could hardly just abandon her. And he didn't want to abandon her. He wanted to be with her. He needed to see her and discuss the situation with her.

He got up and went to the window. It was dark outside. He grabbed his cloak and put it on. He opened the window as he had done countless times before to slip past his minders. He climbed out of the window and began to climb down the trellises there until he reached the ground.

He took a quick look around and then began to walk quickly across the gardens to the road. He would just make the late train for London if he hurried.

"Are you going somewhere, sir?" asked a voice as a man suddenly appeared from the darkness.

Suddenly there were three other men by his side – two of them Bertie recognised as his regular minders.

"Yes – eh – I'm a little restless so I wanted to take a stroll," he said.

The man who had spoken shook his head solemnly. He was very big and Bertie thought he looked quite threatening.

"That won't be possible, sir. May I suggest you return to your room immediately. You can use the more conventional route of the front door instead of the trellises on the wall."

Bertie was shocked at the man's unpleasant tone and he saw the other men were all looking at him in a serious, almost menacing manner.

"It's not safe for His Royal Highness to be out alone," said one of the other men.

"Oh, eh, yes, of course," said Bertie.

He turned and was escorted to the front door in silence. There, one of the men knocked loudly and General Bruce opened the door.

"We found him in the garden heading towards the road – he'd got out of his window," said one of the men.

"I see," said Bruce. "Do come in from the cold, sir."

Bertie stepped in and Bruce closed the door and locked it.

"I'll walk you back to your room, sir," said Bruce.

"For goodness sake, General Bruce, I think I can find my own way there!" snapped Bertie.

"Just to be on the safe side," said Bruce.

Bruce escorted him through the building and back to his room where he walked swiftly to the window and closed it.

"I shouldn't try and get out that way again, sir. It will do you no good as there are extra minders in place."

"This is ridiculous!" snapped Bertie. "Am I to be a prisoner?"

"Just following instructions, sir."

"Whose instructions?"

"Your father's, sir," said General Bruce as he left the room and closed the door behind him.

To Bertie's horror he heard the key turn in the lock. In disbelief he went quickly to the door and found that indeed he was locked in.

"*General Bruce! You've locked the bloody door! Unlock it at once!*" Bertie shouted. "*General Bruce!*"

There was no reply.

Bertie turned and in despair sank into a chair with his face in his hands.

"Albert!" called Victoria the next morning in their bedroom. "It is getting late. You will miss breakfast if you don't rise soon."

When Albert didn't reply she turned and walked over to the bed. "Albert?"

She looked down at him and saw he was deathly pale, his face covered in sweat.

"Albert!" she cried, sitting down beside him and putting her hand to his forehead.

"I feel wretched," mumbled Albert.

"You are burning with fever!" she said, jumping up.

She ran to the bell-pull and tugged it and then rushed to the door. She ran down the corridor, shouting at a footman, "Quick – fetch a doctor at once!"

Victoria and Alice stood by a window in the bedroom as a doctor examined Albert with the help of two nurses. Alice held her mother's hands as they both trembled with fear.

The doctor eventually came over to them, his face grave and his voice low.

"Is there somewhere we may speak privately?"

"What is the matter with him, doctor? Tell us now!" demanded Victoria.

The doctor kept his voice low. "Prince Albert is very unwell. He has pneumonia . . . and, I suspect, typhoid."

"Oh my God!" cried Victoria. "My poor darling Albert!"

"But he will be all right?" asked Alice. "He will recover?"

"It is hard for me to say at this stage," said the doctor. "We need to give him the best care we can so that he has every chance of making a full recovery."

"Every chance?" asked Victoria, horrified. "My husband is only forty-two years of age, doctor!"

"I will do everything in my power, ma'm. In the meantime, I think it's advisable to send for family members and inform them of the situation."

The doctor returned to the bedside to tend to Albert.

"Send for family members!" gasped Victoria as she collapsed on the window seat. "Why is he suggesting that? What is he not telling us?"

Alice had tears streaming down her face as she sat beside her mother and held her hands tightly.

"Mama, from my nursing experience I can see that Papa is very sick. I think we must send for the others at once – Vicky and Bertie –"

"*Bertie!*" spat Victoria angrily. "Do not send for him or inform him that Albert is ill. This is all his fault! Your poor father spent hours walking in the freezing rain yesterday with Bertie to try and make him see sense over that wretched woman he has got himself involved with. And this is the result – your poor papa is down with pneumonia. If anything happens to my dear Albert I will hold Bertie fully responsible – I will *never* forgive him – *never*!" She tried to stifle the sobs that overtook her as Alice hugged her tightly.

CHAPTER 60

Nellie was coming from a rehearsal at the theatre when she passed a newsstand and halted abruptly as she saw the front page of a newspaper.

"*Read all about it! Prince of Wales in love scandal!*" shouted the newspaper boy.

She went to the newsstand and picked up the newspaper with trembling hands and began to read.

'A story has been circulating in the foreign press for some time regarding the Prince of Wales and his relationship with a young actress he met during his military training in Ireland during the summer. Buckingham Palace has not commented on the story which has been circulating and gathering pace over the last month . . ."

Nellie quickly fished some change from her purse, bought the paper and hurried out of the station.

Sitting in a hansom cab she read the rest of the article. To her relief, her name was not mentioned, but it gave plenty of other details about her. That she was actress who had worked in 'vulgar' music halls in Dublin.

The carriage stopped outside her building and she got out. To her horror she saw there were six men at the door of the building, no doubt waiting for her.

"Nellie – will you comment on your relationship with the Prince of Wales?" called one of the men as she approached them.

"Nellie – is it true? Are you a friend of the Prince's?" demanded another.

She hurried past them, head down, and let herself into the building.

"Oh, Sadie – have you seen this?" she called as she entered the flat.

Sadie hurried to her, alarmed.

Nellie thrust the newspaper at Sadie. "It tells all – except my name!"

Sadie looked at the headline in horror. "Those reporters have been outside the building all day! Nellie, what are you going to do?"

"What can I do? I told Bertie about the reporters and he said he would sort something out." Nellie collapsed into an armchair in despair.

"But what's he going to do?" demanded Sadie. "He can't just leave you to cope with all this on your own."

"He won't, Sadie. When he took me to Windsor Castle we discussed marriage. He wants to marry me, Sadie!"

Sadie stepped back from her. "They won't let him, Nellie. He's making a fool of you."

"I know when a man is making a fool of me, Sadie. He meant every word."

There was a knock on the door.

"Are you expecting somebody?" asked Sadie.

"No. It might be one of the reporters," said Nellie. "Someone may have left them in."

"Well, if it is I'll get rid of them quick sharp!" said Sadie as she marched over to the door.

She swung the door open and, to her alarm, saw a man dressed in tweeds with a police officer standing behind him.

"Yes?" asked Sadie, closing the door over again as she looked nervously at the policeman.

"I would like to see Miss Cliffden, I believe she's at home," said the man.

"She's not here, sir, can I take a message?" said Sadie.

"We have just seen her enter the building. I am here on government business so I would prefer to do this the nice way –" he paused as he glanced back at the policeman, "rather than the unpleasant way."

Sadie glanced over her shoulder at Nellie who nodded at her to let him in.

The policeman folded his arms and remained outside as the man came in.

Nellie stood up. "Who are you and what is all this about?"

"My name is Thomas Gardenton, I work for the Home Office. I've come representing the minister, Miss Cliffden."

Nellie's mouth dropped open as she looked at the middle-aged man with the stern-looking face and spectacles resting on a pointed nose.

"What business could a minister possibly have with the likes of me?" asked Nellie, pretending innocence.

"I see you have seen today's newspaper," he said as he pointed to the paper on the table. "Let's not play games, Miss Cliffden."

"I don't know what they are talking about in the newspaper," she said.

He sighed loudly. "Miss Cliffden, I've come to meet you today in a friendly capacity. If you don't co-operate with me, the police officer who is waiting outside the door will return tomorrow and the next visit won't be so friendly."

Nellie started to shiver.

"We've researched your past, Miss Cliffden. My, you were busy back in Dublin, were you not? Going to all those parties, some organised by Captain Marton," he said as he patted down his silver hair.

Nellie thought quickly. She could not imagine that any of the men she had been with would speak publicly about her – they had too much to lose themselves. However, the government had gone to great lengths to investigate her and she was sure they could arrest and detain her for questioning whether they had any evidence or not.

"What do you want, Mr. Gardenton?" she asked.

"More important is the question: what do *you* want?" he demanded.

"I want nothing but to be left in peace and to get on with my life!"

"You don't want money then from your relationship with the Prince, or fame?" he asked cynically.

"No! I just want to be with Bertie, and that's all he wants too," said Nellie.

"But you must know that is quite out of the question – even an idiot would know that. The trouble is you have become quite an inconvenience, Miss Cliffden. And we don't know quite what to do with you."

"There's nothing to be done with me!" said Nellie.

"You've become a loose cannon. And there is nothing the royal family or the government, for that matter, hate more than a loose cannon."

"I'm not a loose anything!" she protested. "I've spoken to nobody. I didn't ask those reporters who sit on my doorstep to write anything in newspapers!"

"That may be true but it's of no consequence any more. We are giving you twenty-four hours to disappear."

"Disappear? What are you talking about?" she asked, confused.

"You must leave here, leave London. Disappear back into the life of obscurity you had before you met the Prince."

"And if I refuse?" asked Nellie.

"Then the police will be back tomorrow and they will arrest you."

"On what charges?" demanded Nellie, aghast.

"Oh, I am sure we could find a number of reasons to have you arrested. Soliciting for instance. You won't like prison, Miss Cliffden."

Nellie looked at Sadie who seemed to be shaking with fear.

Nellie held her head up as she walked towards Gardenton.

"You won't be arresting me, Mr. Gardenton, and I will not be 'disappearing' either. You wouldn't risk having me arrested – with all those reporters waiting outside to witness it? You would blow this scandal through the roof. And if you put me in a courtroom, goodness knows what I might say – all the secrets I know might come out in public. So, you can take your threats and leave. I'll not quiver for the likes of you or anybody else."

His face became grim. "I don't think you realise who you are dealing with."

"And I don't think *you* realise who you are dealing with! How dare you come in here and start ordering me about? I am the Prince of Wales' close friend. He will be outraged when he hears that you have threatened me like this. It's you who needs to be fearful, Mr. Gardenton, not I."

"I think you are overestimating your lover's power. Well, I think there's no more for me to say here."

"I'm sure there isn't. Convey my regards to the Home Office and your minister," said Nellie.

Thomas Gardenton turned and left the flat.

Sadie rushed over to the door and bolted it after him.

"Come on, Nellie, we have to pack quickly and get away from here," she said in a panic. "We don't have much time to lose. You heard him – twenty-four hours."

"Hold your horses, Sadie. We're not packing or leaving or fleeing like thieves in the night."

"But did you not hear what he said – that they will be back to arrest you!"

"And did you not hear what I said? He's bluffing. Trying to frighten me into running away. I'll not be frightened into running anywhere – I've come too far," said Nellie with determination.

"But, Nellie! We'll be doomed if we stay!"

"We won't be doomed. Bertie will look after us. I'll not lose him, Sadie, not for anything."

"Oh, you stupid, stupid girl!" Sadie sat down on the

couch and began to cry. "You think you've become invincible since you started sleeping with the Prince of Wales but you've never been in a weaker position in your life!"

Nellie went to her and put an arm around her. "Hush, Sadie, stop those tears. Can't you see the power we have? Those reporters are outside waiting to hear from me. One word from me and I'll make the front of all the newspapers tomorrow."

"For all the wrong reasons!" cried Sadie.

"I'm exhausted. I'm going to go to bed," Nellie said as she kissed Sadie's forehead.

Sadie watched her walk out of the room and down the corridor with a heavy heart.

The next morning Nellie got out of bed and put on her dressing gown. She looked out the window and saw the reporters still down on the pavement. Across the road she could see two policemen walking up and down.

"They are still down there, Sadie," Nellie called as she came out of her room and walked towards the sitting room. "They must never get bored! Standing out in the cold all night! They must be mad."

The flat was unusually silent. Normally Sadie was pottering around, lighting fires or cooking breakfast.

"*Sadie!*" Nellie called loudly but there was no reply.

She spotted a letter on the table, walked over to it and picked it up.

My darling Nellie,

Can you ever forgive me for running out on you in the middle of the night like this? I've always been a coward, in every way. I can't face the police coming and arresting you. And if they arrest you then they will arrest me also. I was in prison once before and I made a promise to myself that, no matter what, I'll never go back there again. No matter what – even if that's means running out on you, my lovely Nellie with the golden hair. I hope you and your prince find happiness together. Sometimes fairy tales come true. But I've never seen one come true yet in this world.

Love from your (unfaithful) servant,
Sadie.

"Oh Sadie!" cried Nellie as she crumpled the letter in her hand and fell down on the couch, sobbing loudly.

CHAPTER 61

Bertie came out of a tutorial and was immediately met by two minders there to escort him back to Mandingley Hall. He spotted Charles Carrington down the hallway.

"*Charlie!*" Bertie called.

Charlie came bounding up to him. "Hello, sir! Where have you been hiding these past days?"

Bertie glanced back at his minders. "I've just been revising. Walk with me a while, would you?"

"Sir, you are to go straight back to Mandingley," said one of the minders.

Charles glanced at the minder and made a face at Bertie. "That's all right, I'm heading in your direction."

"Thank you," Bertie said and they continued to walk a few yards ahead of the minders.

"Are you all right, sir?" asked Charles quietly, concerned.

"No! I am under house arrest since news broke of my relationship with Nellie," whispered Bertie.

"Yes, rotten show, sir. The newspapers show no respect any more," lamented Charles.

"I am not even allowed to send a letter without it being scrutinised by General Bruce. I haven't been able to contact Nellie and I am sure this must be awful for her. I need to see Marton as soon as possible. Can you get word to him to visit me at Mandingley Hall without delay?"

"Of course, sir! I shall do it today," promised Charles.

"He is the only one who can help me. He is the only one who can meet with Nellie and explain to her what is going on," explained Bertie. "And to try and devise a plan to sort out this dreadful mess that we find ourselves in!"

"I understand. Anything I can do to help," said Charles.

"Thank you, Charles."

They left the building where a carriage was waiting and one of the minders held the door open for Bertie.

"Hopefully I shall see you soon," said Bertie, getting into the carriage, looking very grim.

"Yes, hopefully! So long!" called Charles as the carriage took off down the street.

At Windsor Castle, Albert lay in the bed in the Blue Room while Alice wiped his brow.

Victoria was sitting by a window with her fifteen-year-old daughter Helena and her youngest son Leopold, who was only eight.

The doctor was at the other side of the bed, examining Albert as he mumbled in a delirious fashion.

The doctor nodded at Alice and she left the bedside to walk over to Victoria with him.

"If I can have a private word, ma'am?" asked the Doctor.

"What cannot be said here? I do not wish to leave my husband's side for a moment until he is better," said Victoria.

The doctor indicated young Leopold. "I think it's wise we speak alone."

"Please, Mama, the doctor wants to speak to you alone," pleaded Alice.

"Oh, very well!" said Victoria, rising from her chair and walking from the room, followed by the doctor and Alice.

Outside, they crossed the corridor into a sitting room.

"What is it, doctor?" asked Victoria.

"I regret to tell you that Prince Albert is dying, Your Majesty," the doctor said as kindly as he could.

"*Ohhh!*" cried Victoria and she swayed on her feet.

The doctor and Alice caught her and helped her to a seat.

"This cannot be true," mumbled Victoria. "It simply cannot be! He is a young man – a young man."

"He has only days left," said the doctor. "As I explained he has contracted typhoid and pneumonia on top of that – he cannot withstand it."

Tears were streaming down Alice's face. "When you say days, doctor – how many days?"

"Perhaps two, perchance three," said the doctor.

Victoria muffled a scream with her handkerchief.

"I shall get back to attending to him," said the doctor as he bowed and retreated from the room.

"Oh Alice! What shall I do? How can I live without him?" cried Victoria between her sobs.

"We must be strong, Mama, for the younger children," said Alice.

"But how can I be strong, when the person who was always my strength is slipping away from me?" sobbed Victoria.

"I must send for Bertie at once," said Alice.

"*No!*" cried Victoria, managing to control her sobbing. "I do not want him here, he does not deserve to be here."

"But, Mama, we must inform Bertie! We simply have to let him know what is happening to Papa. It would be unforgiveable not to!"

"What is unforgiveable is Bertie and his actions! He will be responsible for killing my dear Albert. I never want to set eyes on him again!"

"Papa would want him here," said Alice.

"Your papa had the same thoughts on Bertie as I have – he is a disappointment to the end. He thought nothing of us when he carried on with that woman, so now I think nothing of him," said Victoria with steely determination.

Alice nodded, not wishing to upset her mother any further.

"I must return to my husband's side," said Victoria.

Alice watched her leave the room and then stood in

thought for a while. Then she went to a writing bureau where she wrote a note and slid it into an envelope which she sealed. She then tugged the bell-pull and a few moments later a footman entered.

Alice handed him the envelope. "You are to take this at once to the Prince of Wales in Cambridge. Do not let anything delay you. It is imperative the Prince receives this by the end of today."

"Yes, Your Highness." The footman bowed and quickly exited.

It was the first time Alice had ever disobeyed her mother. But she did not care. She knew her mother was not thinking straight in her anguish. It was left to Alice to take control.

General Bruce walked into the sitting room where Bertie was smoking. Bruce looked disapprovingly at the cigarette.

"Oh, get over it, General Bruce!" snapped Bertie, his patience at breaking point from the constant supervision.

"Captain Marton is here to see you, sir."

"Oh, very good! Show him in at once!"

General Bruce left and returned a minute later with James.

"Hello, James!" said Bertie happily.

"Good evening, sir. I got a message –" James stopped speaking when Bertie gave a minute shake of his head in warning.

General Bruce was standing at the door.

"Thank you, General Bruce, you may leave us," said Bertie.

Bruce's face was obstinate as he refused to budge.

"For God's sake, General Bruce! Haven't you got some tapestry or something to do?" Bertie lost his temper. "Please leave us alone. My friend has come to visit me and I wish to speak to him without an audience! We will not be leaving the building – we will remain in this room, rest assured!"

At this Bruce nodded and reluctantly left.

"Bloody hell!" cried Bertie. "I am living in a prison, I tell you! I am not allowed a moment's peace and they even lock me in at night. I know how the Princes in the Tower felt!"

"I take it this is all down to your relationship with Nellie?" asked James.

"Of course. My family now know and all hell has broken loose! Now I am under lock and key for fear I slip away and meet her."

"It's in the national newspapers now, sir. It has all got out of hand."

"Have you seen or spoken to Nellie?" asked Bertie.

"No. I did try to warn her last time I saw her of the risks you were both taking, but she seemed blind to what was coming."

"The poor girl, left on her own to deal with all this! And she must be worried sick that I haven't contacted her. I need you to do me a favour, James."

"Anything, sir."

"I need you to go to Nellie and explain to her what has happened – that I have been forbidden to meet her, against my will. My father has made me promise not to meet her again."

"Well, in that case your relationship with Nellie is over," said James in hope.

"Once my father calms down he will see the overreaction everyone is guilty of here," said Bertie.

"I am not so sure of that, sir."

"Well, in truth, neither am I. But the reality is I love Nellie and I am worried sick about her. She's too exposed in London, especially with the press sniffing around, and so I want you to get her and take her to the house I rented for her outside the town here – Primrose House – until all this dies down. She'll be safe there."

"Primrose House! Is it wise she should come to Cambridge?" asked James.

"Where else can she go? Nobody knows about Primrose House except for us, so nobody will dream of looking for her there."

"Forgive me, sir – but, because of the political storm this is causing, sir, I advise you as a friend to sever your ties with Nellie at once and have no more to do with her."

"But I can't, James! I simply can't. I need you to help me, James. I will be for ever in your debt – will you bring her to Primrose House and make sure she gets there safely?"

James felt trapped. He had no choice but to obey Bertie's wishes. "Of course, sir."

General Bruce came into the room. "Will Captain Marton be having tea?"

"No, General Bruce, Captain Marton is leaving," said Bertie.

"Oh, I see!" said Bruce, looking relieved.

"Come see me again very soon, James," said Bertie, giving him a coded nod.

"Of course, sir," said James as he bowed and left.

"That will be all, General Bruce," said Bertie.

"A letter has arrived for you by hand from Windsor Castle, sir."

"Well – give it to me then!" snapped Bertie.

Bruce crossed the room and handed Bertie the envelope before bowing and exiting.

Bertie looked at the envelope and recognised the handwriting.

A letter from Alice, he said to himself happily as he tore the envelope open. He settled down to enjoy his sister's correspondence but was surprised to find that it contained only a brief message.

"*General Bruce! General Bruce!*" he shouted, jumping to his feet, his heart pounding.

General Bruce came rushing in. "What is the matter, sir?"

"Bring a carriage immediately to the front! I must go to Windsor Castle!"

Bruce looked at Bertie sceptically. "For what purpose, sir?"

"*My father is ill – is that good enough reason to go?*" shouted Bertie.

Bruce swiftly left the room to arrange a carriage.

Bertie sank down on the armchair. In Alice's last letter she had already told him their father was unwell. The fact he was now called to Windsor filled him with dread.

CHAPTER 62

As James got the train back to London he was deep in thought. His whole plan had spectacularly backfired on him. Yes, he had the Prince of Wales's friendship and favour which was what he had dreamed of. But he was caught doing the dirty work and the whole situation had become so explosive that he felt it was only a matter of time before the blame would be laid at his door. And if that happened he would be finished. He would be tainted forever. He did concede that Bertie was right at least in his suggestion that Nellie needed to get out of London. She was a sitting duck there, especially with the press hovering around.

Once the train arrived in London, he got the a hansom cab straight to Nellie's building. He was horrified to see the number of reporters that were outside.

"Wait here," he told the driver as he got out of the cab.

Head down, he hurried past the reporters and into the building.

Nellie sat by the fire in her flat, staring into space. She kept hoping the door would open and Sadie would be back. But in her heart she knew that would not happen. Sadie was gone for good. She could not take the kind of pressure Nellie had brought on them. With a dubious past herself, Sadie could not deal with the attention that the scandal had brought their way. Nellie felt abandoned. Her emotions were swirling from being angry for Sadie for leaving, to feeling guilty for putting her in an impossible position.

There was a knock on the door and Nellie jumped up from her seat in terror. She knew it wasn't Sadie as she would just let herself in with her key. Nellie thought of Thomas Gardenton and what he had threatened. That if she didn't disappear the police would come back and arrest her.

There was another loud knock on the door and a man's voice called: *"Nellie – open up – it's me!"*

"James!" she cried as she rushed to the door and unlocked it. "Oh, James!" she said, falling into his arms and hugging him.

He quickly pushed her inside and locked the door behind him.

"I've been so frightened. I'm all alone. I haven't heard anything from Bertie and Sadie has left." Nellie's voice was full of anxiety.

"Oh, now you are pleased to see me, are you?" said James cynically.

"Oh, James, what's happening?"

"I've met Bertie. He can't meet you for now – he is being watched all the time. He understands the position you are in here and wants you to go to Primrose House and stay there until this all dies down."

"Primrose House? But for how long?"

"I don't know, Nellie!" he snapped. "You should have gone when I told you to – back to Dublin and away from this mess. It's too late now!"

"I told you I couldn't go. I couldn't leave Bertie."

"It's like watching somebody walk into fire and no matter how you shout at them they keep on going!"

"Have you ever been in love, James?"

"No! And I never want to be either!" he said as he went to the window and looked out at the street below. "I have a cab waiting outside. Hurry up and let us get away from here. I'll come back another time and get the rest of your things –

just take what you need now."

Nellie ran to her bedroom where she hastily packed a case.

"*Nellie!*" James called. "*Hurry!*"

"I'm ready," she said, emerging from the bedroom.

James nodded, took the case, and they left the flat.

"Keep your head down and say nothing to anyone," he ordered as they went down the stairs.

When they got to the front door the reporters began to fire questions at them. James pushed his way through them with Nellie following close behind him. They ran to the carriage and climbed in, the reporters rushing after them.

"*Go!*" James shouted at the driver and the carriage took off down the street.

Once Bertie arrived at Windsor Castle, he hurried to the Blue Room. When he reached the door, he stopped and prepared himself for what was on the other side.

He opened the door gently and walked in.

He saw his father on the bed, white as the sheets, looking very ill. Alice was beside him as was a doctor, backed up by several other medical professionals. There were ladies-in-waiting in the room also along with equerries and Bertie recognised two government ministers present as well. He saw his mother sitting beside the bed, young Arthur beside her. His sister Helena was desperately trying to stifle her sobbing.

"*Bertie!*" cried Arthur who came rushing to him and threw his arms around him. Bertie held his brother tightly.

Alice left her father's side and came quickly to Bertie and kissed his cheek, then gently pushed Arthur back towards his mother.

"What is going on, Alice?" asked Bertie fearfully.

"It is the worst news, Bertie. The doctor says – he says there is not much time."

Bertie felt his legs go weak under him. "But why did you not tell me before he was so bad? Why leave it to now?" he demanded.

Alice glanced at Victoria but said nothing as realisation dawned on Bertie that his mother had forbidden that he should be told.

"I cannot believe it," said Bertie as he beckoned young Arthur back to him.

It was shocking for them all, but Bertie couldn't imagine what an eleven-year-old like Arthur was feeling, faced with his father's death.

Bertie took Arthur by the hand and walked further into the room. Helena came to him and embraced him, stifling her sobs in her handkerchief. Bertie gently pushed Helena away and went to Victoria.

"Mama," he whispered as he bent to kiss her cheek.

She looked distraught but she was not looking for any comfort from Bertie – instead she turned away from him once he had kissed her.

Victoria gave Alice a scathing look, realising she had been responsible for sending for Bertie.

Bertie tiptoed to the bed and stared down at his father.

"Papa," whispered Bertie as he sat down on the side of the bed and held Albert's hand. "I am so very sorry."

Bertie sat outside the Blue Room in Windsor Castle with his head in his hands. Alice came out of the room and gently closed the door after her.

"Bertie," she said, coming to him and hugging him.

"It's all my fault, Alice. He's going to die, and it's all my fault," said Bertie.

"You must not say that, Bertie. The doctor says Papa contracted typhoid and also has pneumonia."

"You don't understand. He came to see me and walked for hours in the rain. He came to see me over . . ." He couldn't bear to tell her.

"I know, Bertie. I know of everything that has occurred."

He was shocked as she seemed unconcerned about his affair.

"Then how can you not blame me?" he asked.

"He has typhoid, Bertie," she reiterated.

"Mama blames me, I can see it in her eyes. She sits there, her eyes full of accusations. She hasn't spoken to me since I arrived."

"Mama is in shock. She will see things differently in time."

"No, she won't. She'll never change her mind or stop blaming me. You know how she is."

The door of the Blue Room opened and a nurse came out.

"The doctor says you should come at once," she said urgently.

Bertie and Alice looked at each other in dread as they held hands and went back into the room.

Soon after, a bloodcurdling scream from Victoria could be heard throughout Windsor Castle.

As the carriage brought Nellie and James to the train station through the London streets, the bell at St. Paul's Cathedral began to sound loudly and solemnly.

James looked out, listening, trying to understand what was going on as he saw people begin to gather in the streets.

"What is it, James?" asked Nellie, looking out at the crowds.

"St. Paul's only tolls for a national emergency – war or the death of a monarch," he said.

"War? Who are we at war with?"

"Let's hope that stupid incident with the Americans has not led us into war with them," said James before calling out to the driver, "*Pull over!*"

The driver pulled the carriage to a stop and James stuck his head out the window and shouted to the crowd, "*What is it? What is going on?*" He saw women who were crying.

"*It's Prince Albert – he's dead!*" shouted one of the men back.

James's mouth dropped open as he sat back into the carriage.

356

"Prince Albert dead? But how can that be – he's only young," said Nellie.

James sat gobsmacked by the news. As he tried to recover from the shock, he realised that the time bomb that he was sitting beside in the carriage had just magnified several times.

"My poor Bertie!" said Nellie. "I must go to him. I must go to him at once – he will need me."

James sat there, looking at Nellie in astonishment.

"James, did you not hear me? I need to go to Bertie!"

"Be quiet, Nellie – just be quiet, for God's sake!" James whispered at her before shouting at the driver, "*Continue to the train station as quick as you can!*"

Bertie stood at a window in the Blue Room, staring out. The family were weeping behind him around the bed.

"How will we cope? My life too is over, I may as well have died with him," sobbed Victoria.

Alice came to Bertie and hugged him.

"We must be strong, Bertie, for Mama," she whispered.

"How can I be strong, Alice? How can we survive this?"

"We have to, Bertie. You are the Prince of Wales – everything will fall on your shoulders now. You will need to take over the leadership, not just for Mama and the family, but for the whole country and the empire. Your time has come."

"But I am not able to take over that responsibility," he said.

"You have no choice, Bertie. You must put aside all thoughts of your personal happiness now and put your duty first. You have made mistakes, there is no denying that. But you can now rectify those mistakes and show real leadership. It is what Papa would have expected from you. Do you understand?"

"Yes, I understand."

She hugged him tightly.

Nellie and James remained silent for the journey to

Cambridge. As in London, there were people crying on the train. James realised what a calamity it was for the nation that Albert had gone. Everyone knew the Queen relied totally on him and left the affairs of the state to him. Bertie's role would be changed overnight, James knew. And, as the train pulled into Cambridge, it was glaringly obvious to him that Nellie was totally unaware of the political implications of Albert's death. For now, more than ever, the continuation of the royal family was on Bertie's shoulders. And James suspected that Bertie already knew that Nellie now had to go.

They got a cab from the train station in Cambridge and travelled out to Primrose House.

As they entered the house, Nellie was reminded of the last time she was there and how she and Bertie had enjoyed their time there so much.

"What do we do, James?" she asked as she lit a fire in the fireplace. "What can we do for Bertie?"

"I think the best think you can do is as he last asked and stay here until things quieten down – now more than ever," he said.

CHAPTER 63

The next day Victoria sat in the drawing room, her face tearstained, looking heartbroken.

"I will not be attending the funeral," she said.

"Nobody expects you to, Mama – it is not the custom for a widow to attend her husband's funeral," said Alice. "Nor any women for that matter."

"Regardless of custom, I could not face it anyway. I fear I would collapse in public. And such grief in public would not be fitting," said Victoria. "You, Bertie, shall be the chief mourner."

"Yes, Mama," nodded Bertie.

"You and Arthur will walk behind the coffin as it is brought to the church, as your brother Alfred is abroad."

"Arthur is distraught, Mama. I am not sure if it is wise that he be put through such a public ordeal when he is still so young," said Bertie.

"Arthur is a prince first and last – youth does not protect princes from their responsibilities or their – foibles," she said, looking at him pointedly.

"The whole nation is in mourning. Everyone is wearing black – even farm labourers are wearing black armbands," said Alice.

"That is as it should be. Your dearest Papa served this country with all his heart and changed it so much for the better –" Victoria suddenly burst into tears. She rose from her seat and left the room.

"*Mama!*" Bertie called as he started to go after her.

Alice held him back. "I shall go to her," she said and she followed her mother.

Outside in the hallway she found her mother sitting on a chaise longue in floods of tears.

"Oh, Mama," said Alice as she sat beside her.

"I cannot bear being in his company!" wailed Victoria. "I cannot bear even seeing him. He killed his father and destroyed our lives!"

"Mama – don't!" begged Alice.

"When I think of your poor papa and that sordid business Bertie was involved in – it is too much for me to bear!" She began to wail loudly.

Alice looked at her mother, distressed that there seemed no comforting her or even speaking to her.

The streets in Windsor were thronged with people as Albert's funeral cortege made its way through the town to the church. As Victoria dictated, Bertie and Arthur walked behind the coffin.

Arthur was crying continuously, unable to stop, and Bertie fought the almost overwhelming need to reach out and comfort him. He knew his mother was right – they had to perform in public. As he walked solemnly on, Bertie had never felt so conscious in his life of so many hundreds of eyes looking at him. He walked with as much dignity as he could. He had never felt so exposed, so lost and yet having to maintain a public façade. This was his life now, he understood. As he felt the hundreds of eyes upon him, he wondered how many of them had heard about Nellie. How many of them knew of the scandal? He felt acute embarrassment that his private affair had been so exposed and that these people, his future subjects, thought of him as sordid and irresponsible.

As well as a walk of mourning, for Bertie it felt like a walk of shame.

Nellie sat in the parlour at Primrose House with the

newspapers in front of her. There was a village a couple of miles away and she had walked down to get them and some groceries. Even in the village there was an eerie feeling as all the doors had black ribbons tied to them and nobody was smiling and or even talking. All were dressed in black.

As she read through the newspapers it was as if there was no other news in the world but Albert's death. She peered at a photo of Bertie on the front of one of the newspapers. She had heard nothing from him, not a word.

James had deposited her at Primrose House, told her to remain there, keep quiet and not draw any attention to herself. He said he would be in contact with her soon.

She stood up and went to the window, looking out over the countryside. She could only imagine the anguish Bertie must be feeling. She longed to be with him and comfort him. She knew she was the only one who could comfort him. That she was the only one he could speak freely with and tell his innermost thoughts to – thoughts that he was not allowed to share with anybody else. How she wished to be at his side!

It won't be long, she told herself. He will come to me soon.

CHAPTER 64

In the week following Albert's funeral, Bertie threw himself into caring for his mother at Windsor Castle. He waited on her hand and foot, tending to her, bringing her anything he felt she needed. He was met with a cool response from her at all times. Often, she could barely look at him. Often, she did not even bother getting out of bed.

"I fear she is suffering from some kind of breakdown," Alice said to Bertie in the drawing room. "The doctor says her grief is so acute it is worrying."

"What can I do to help her get through this?" Bertie asked.

"You are doing everything you can, Bertie."

A footman came in and bowed.

"Yes?" said Bertie.

"Her Majesty is asking for Princess Alice."

"Not for me?" asked Bertie.

"No, sir."

Alice gave Bertie a sympathetic look as she left.

Bertie sighed heavily and took up that morning's *Times*. The newspaper was still filled with the death of Albert. Bertie went to the editorial and was surprised to see it was solely about him:

This newspaper now strongly advises the Prince of Wales to leave his former life of frivolity behind. He must step into the great void left by his father and perform his royal duties

362

to the best of his abilities. Her Majesty must allow the Prince to accept those responsibilities and allow him to handle state affairs in the way his father did . . .

The editorial went on to say that the nation was adrift after Albert's death and the royal family would be lost if Bertie did not perform his duties. Obviously aware of Victoria's lack of trust in her son, the newspaper was also telling her that she had no choice but to allow Bertie responsibility if the monarchy was to survive.

Bertie stood and looked into the fire. He had changed so much in the short space of time since his father's death. He wanted to be the best he could be. *The Times* was right – the time to leave frivolity behind had come. He had hardly thought about Nellie since he had come to Windsor. So immersed in his own grief and with so much to do, he had not had the time to even think of her. But when he did think of her he was overcome with feelings of shame – guilt that he had allowed himself to become so involved with her when deep down he knew the pain and anguish the relationship would cause. He had never expected that pain and anguish to result in his father's death but, now that it had, he was filled with revulsion for himself and his own actions.

Nellie sat on her own at Primrose House on Christmas Day, looking out at the snow that had fallen. It was now nearly two weeks since Albert's death and she had heard nothing. James hadn't visited or written. She kept going to the window and staring down the long laneway, expecting to see Bertie's carriage approaching. But still nothing. She was feeling isolated and lonely and didn't know what to do. She also missed Sadie dreadfully.

Christmas had come and gone at Windsor with no celebration. As Christmas had been Albert's favourite time of the year and he had reinvented it and how it was celebrated in Britain, it made it even harder for the family to endure.

The more Bertie tried to assist his mother the more she pushed him away, which compounded his guilt and made him feel depressed. He would do anything to please her and make her life even slightly more bearable in her grief, but she would not allow him.

As soon as Christmas was over, Victoria, Alice and the children departed for Osbourne House leaving Bertie alone at Windsor.

"Mama, can Bertie not come with us? It is so soon after Papa's death," begged Alice.

"The reason I am leaving Windsor is to be away from him! What is the point of going to Osbourne House if he is to come with us!"

In early January Victoria sat at her desk in Osbourne House, writing a letter to Vicky. Her anger with Bertie seemed to be increasing by the day. As the New Year began, such was her anger at her son that she felt it was interfering with her mourning her husband. She poured out her anger in her letter to Vicky as she wrote *Oh! That boy – I never can or shall look at him again without a shudder.*

Alice came in and Victoria paused in her writing.

"Mama, the Prime Minister is here to see you."

"Show him in, my dear. And you may sit in on our meeting," said Victoria.

Alice felt exasperated. Her mother was relying on her for official business when everyone knew that role should be Bertie's. And yet Alice knew there was no point in pointing this out again to Victoria as she would either start sobbing in grief or explode in anger.

"Very well, Mama."

Alice went to open the door and Lord Palmerston, the Prime Minister, walked in and bowed to Victoria.

"Good afternoon, Your Majesty," said Lord Palmerston.

"Good afternoon."

"How are you coping with your great loss?"

"I am coping as best I can. I am consumed with work. Now that Prince Albert is no longer here, everything falls on my shoulders. I arise at four in the morning to get through the mountain of paperwork that is thrust upon me."

"Is the Prince of Wales not here? I had expected him to sit in on our meeting," said Palmerston.

"There is no need for him to be here. We have Alice to assist us."

"With the greatest respect, ma'am, I am most disappointed that the Prince is not present."

"We do not have all day, Lord Palmerston," said Victoria coldly. "So I suggest we get on with the business at hand."

"But the business at hand is the Prince of Wales, ma'am – for him to now take active duty in state affairs. This is the express wish of your government, the press and the people."

"We care little for express wishes, Lord Palmerston. The Prince of Wales will not be able to take an active role in state affairs as he is due to go on a very long overseas voyage," said Victoria.

"Voyage, ma'am?" asked Palmerston, surprised.

"To the Middle East – for four months," said Victoria.

"The Middle East! But for what purpose?"

"For the purpose of finishing his education. Bertie will not be returning to Cambridge. His education, such as it was, is now complete there. It was Prince Albert's intention that Bertie be sent on a tour of the Middle East and I see no reason to alter that plan."

"But, ma'am, there is every reason. The Prince of Wales is needed here at home, now that Prince Albert is deceased."

"Who needs him here at home?" Victoria demanded.

"The government and you, ma'am!" said Palmerston.

"I have no need for him, and I suggest he has little to offer to your government either, Lord Palmerston," said Victoria.

"But, ma'am! There will be an outcry!" said Palmerston.

"I care little for outcries or public wishes. I care only that the monarchy is conducted in a right and fitting fashion. And

I will ensure it will. I think that dreadful business in Ireland demonstrates how immature the Prince is and how unfit for royal duty he is."

"I am aware of that dreadful – business – ma'am. But young people make mistakes – surely this should not blight the rest of his life?"

"It killed my husband, Lord Palmerston, and has reduced the good name of this royal family to a laughing stock not only in this country but around Europe. And those are the shoulders you expect me to lay state affairs on? I think not!"

"And when is the Prince to set sail for the Middle East?" asked Palmerston.

"As soon as possible, early February by the latest. It is the best place for him. He will be well chaperoned and have no opportunity to meet that – wretched woman – again. Nor to get into any further trouble until he is married off."

"As you wish, ma'am," said Palmerston, realising there was no point in trying to argue with her.

"In the meantime, I am writing to my daughter Vicky to tell her to press on with the formal wedding negotiations with Princess Alexandra of Denmark without further delay. As this is a diplomatic negotiation with Demark as well as a marriage contract, we would appreciate your government's full co-operation."

"Of course, ma'am. And I am very pleased the Prince of Wales has decided on Princess Alexandra, a most suitable candidate from what I hear."

"Indeed. And it is very important that it is presented to the public and the press as a union of love. The young couple are very taken with each other. We do not want to convey that the marriage is in any way arranged, as that would be distasteful."

"Without question," said Palmerston.

"Now, if you will excuse me, I need to finish my correspondence before dinner. You will be joining us for dinner, Lord Palmerston?"

"I look forward to it, ma'am," Palmerston said before bowing to Victoria and Alice and leaving.

Alice turned to her mother. "Mama! Lord Palmerston is right that you should not be sending Bertie overseas at this sensitive time," she gasped.

"I want him as far away from me as possible – the Middle East will do! I cannot abide even looking at him. Being in the same country as him is too much for me!"

"And what of this marriage to Alexandra?" cried Alice. "Bertie has not agreed to any such thing!"

"He will, Alice. He will not dare object – not now. Not after everything he has done."

The following week, Bertie greeted the Prime Minister at the drawing room in Windsor.

"Thank you for seeing me, Lord Palmerston."

"I felt I needed to, sir, as you were not present at my recent meeting with Her Majesty. Since your father's death there are some very important items I felt I needed to discuss with you but, alas, your mother said otherwise."

"She will not change," said Bertie, feeling a mix of anger and sadness.

"It appears not. You are to be excluded from state affairs by her decree."

"Damn it!" Bertie lost his temper. "Even the King of Belgium, my uncle, has implored her to see sense and not exclude me. He has tried to act as a peacemaker, telling her I only want to assist her, to make her load lighter. But she will have none of it. She is as ever turning to my sister Vicky for all support and advice while poor Alice acts as her secretary. I am a nonentity."

"The public, sir, are talking as are the press because you are not by your mother's side. It reflects as badly on her as on you."

"You have seen for yourself I can do nothing about the situation. She blames me for my father's death. She blames me for everything."

"It is a delicate subject to raise, sir, but your relationship with the – eh, young lady – is definitely now ended?"

Bertie went to speak and then closed his mouth tightly.

"Sir?" pushed Palmerston. "I cannot remind you enough of the delicate situation the royal family finds itself in since your father's death, and one whiff of scandal could lead to – dare I say the word that is being used so much today – republicanism."

Bertie shut his eyes for a second and then he spoke quickly, "The affair is over, you have my word."

Palmerston looked visibly relieved. "I'm glad to hear it. Where is the young lady now, may I ask, sir?"

"How should I know?" asked Bertie defensively.

"In my experience these types of women do not go away easily. An actress of the stage, I believe she is? I do hope she will not prove troublesome in the future."

"Nellie will not become troublesome," said Bertie.

"Good. Sir, you are aware you are being sent away to the Middle East on tour?"

"Yes, banished from court and from my mother's sight," said Bertie cynically.

"And plans for your marriage to Princess Alexandra are to proceed – your sister Princess Vicky will conduct the negotiations."

"Marriage!" cried Bertie in horror.

Palmerston was taken aback at his reaction. "Yes, sir, did you not agree? Your mother believes it is the only thing that will rescue your reputation and make you fit for royal duty."

Bertie sighed loudly. "How fortunate you are, Lord Palmerston, that you were not born a royal prince!"

"Indeed, sir, I agree with you on that point without question," nodded Palmerston.

CHAPTER 65

Nellie was in her bedroom at Primrose House, sewing. She had packed in such haste when leaving her London flat that one of her dresses had got torn. She now had it displayed on a mannequin that was in the house, carefully sewing the tears.

When she heard a carriage coming up the driveway her heart began beating quickly. She had been alone there for over a month. Apart from when she walked the two miles down to the village for groceries she had seen nobody. Sometimes she felt she was going mad in her isolation. She peered anxiously from behind the curtain and saw it was James stepping out of the carriage.

She ran to the door and unbolted it.

"James! Where have you been all this time? How could you just leave me here? Where is Bertie?" she said, looking out at the carriage, hoping in desperation to see him waiting there.

"He is at Windsor Castle in mourning," said James, stepping inside.

The driver carried in some suitcases and left them in the hallway, before going back to the carriage for more.

"What are these?" asked Nellie.

"The rest of your things from the flat in Chelsea. I collected them for you – you won't be going back there," said James.

After the driver left, Nellie shut the door and confronted James.

"I am going mad with worry, James. Why hasn't Bertie come to see me, why hasn't he contacted me?" she demanded.

"See sense, Nellie! He has just lost his father and one can only imagine the protocol and affairs of state he must be dealing with," said James.

"Yes, of course. I am being selfish. I just thought he would want to see me. That he would need my comfort and love," said Nellie.

"These are strange times we live in, Nellie. The whole country has been turned upside down by Prince Albert's death. It is like a rudderless ship."

"So what am I to do? Just wait here for ever more until he can come and see me?"

"I have received an invitation to go see him at Windsor Castle. I understand Charles Carrington has been asked to go as well," said James.

Nellie's face lit up with joy. "But that's wonderful news! He obviously needs to speak to you about me and that's why he has asked to see you."

"I imagine you are a topic he needs to discuss, yes," agreed James.

"Tell him I send all my love, James. Tell him I am here and waiting for him and I'll wait forever if I have to," she said.

James nodded. He had no doubt that Nellie was the reason why he and Charles were being summoned to Windsor Castle. But he didn't know what to expect. He remembered Bertie being the light-headed fool who thought he could have Nellie, have the throne and have all the benefits that came with being the future king. But James suspected that Albert's death would have brought Bertie down to earth with a bang.

"Can I go with you to Windsor to see Bertie?" Nellie asked.

"Are you mad? Of course not! You might not be the focus of the newspapers' attention any more as they are distracted by Prince Albert's death. But if you are seen anywhere, they will be onto the story like hounds after a fox again – which is the last thing Bertie needs right now."

"Yes, of course. It's just that I know, because Bertie told me so, that his father was the reason why we couldn't be seen together – because his father was such a controlling and disapproving man. But now, with Prince Albert gone, there's nothing to stop Bertie from being with whoever he wants to be with, is there? He can be his own man at last." She smiled at James. "I'll make us some tea."

"Poor demented fool," James whispered under his breath as he watched her walk out.

CHAPTER 66

Two days later James arrived at Windsor Castle at the same time as Charles.

"Sad circumstances have brought us together this time," said Charles as they shook hands.

"Yes," agreed James.

"Have you seen her?" asked Charles.

"Yes. I visited her a few days ago. She's still at Primrose House."

"And what's the plan, Marton? She can't stay there forever!"

"I suspect that is what we are here today to discuss with Bertie," said James.

They followed a footman through a vast array of halls until the footman stopped at a door and knocked before opening it.

Charles and James walked in and saw Bertie standing by the fireplace.

"My dear fellows!" said Bertie as he approached them warmly and shook both their hands.

James immediately saw that Bertie looked different. Gone was the happy-go-lucky exuberance he displayed before. Here was a man who had aged quickly and looked as if he had the world on his shoulders.

"It's very good to see you, sir. I cannot enough express my heartfelt condolences," said Charles.

"As do I – my heartfelt condolences," echoed James.

"Thank you," said Bertie. "I won't lie to you that it's been a ghastly time. How things change! Was it just a few short months ago that we were drinking beer and watching cricket without a care in the world on the plains of Kildare?"

"It seems a long time ago," said James.

Bertie walked to the fireplace and took a cigar from a box on the mantelpiece. He offered them one but they both declined. He lit the cigar then invited them to sit which they did. He remained standing at the fireplace.

"I won't delay you long," he said. "I am rather busy as I have to soon set sail on the royal yacht for the Middle East for a protracted time."

"Oh – and when will you return, sir?" asked Charles, surprised.

"Not until early summer . . . also the arrangements for my expected forthcoming marriage to Princess Alexandra are to begin in earnest very shortly."

Charles and James exchanged looks.

"Oh – I see! The Dane?" said Charles.

"The Dane," Bertie confirmed.

"I thought you were most reluctant to marry her?" said James.

"Things change, times change, everything changes. What is unacceptable one year is yearned for the next, do you not think?" said Bertie.

"If you say so, sir," said James.

"Marriage to Alexandra is what my family needs, my mother needs, the country needs – and if I am to be honest to myself for the first time in my life – what I need too."

Charles and James both made an effort to conceal their surprise.

"We hope you will be very happy with her, sir," said Charles.

"Which leaves the little matter of our friend," said Bertie.

"Nellie?" said James as if he were unsure who Bertie was referring to.

"Indeed. I have been foolish, beyond foolish. I have let my heart rule my head. I am immersed in shame and guilt for the upset I have caused my family. In my last conversation with my father I promised him that I would not see Nellie again. I cannot now betray that promise – you can see that, can't you?"

"I can see that, sir, but it sounds to me as if you are trying to convince yourself rather than us," said Charles.

Bertie clasped his hands together as tears welled in his eyes. "Dear Lord, I have no need to convince myself! As I look back on my relationship with Nellie, I can hardly believe that I could deceive myself that there would not be consequences. Now I must live with those consequences for the rest of my life."

"Forgive me, sir, but is this not a conversation you should be having with the young lady rather than us?" asked Charles.

"I would if I could but I can't! I promised my father I would not see her again – so how can I break that promise?" He paused. "Where is Nellie now?"

"She is still at Primrose House where you told me to take her last time we met, sir. I visited her a couple of days ago," said James.

"And she is well?"

"As well as can be expected."

"It is good that she is still there. It wouldn't do for her to be back in London in case the press got wind of it and started to stir up trouble again. That we have to avoid at all costs."

"So – you would like me to tell her the relationship is over?" said James.

"Oh, would you, James? I would be eternally grateful. My god, a fellow couldn't have better friends than you chaps!"

"I can tell her that, sir. But she will be heartbroken. I believe she cares for you very deeply."

For a moment James and Charles saw the façade Bertie

was presenting crack and he looked as if he was about to break down in tears from the strain of the emotion he was going through.

"Tell her – I wish her well," said Bertie.

His friends again exchanged looks.

"And where is she to go now, sir?" asked Charles.

"Wherever she wants. She, unlike me, is not bound by duty," said Bertie.

"But is this not a rather delicate situation we are all in? Can we expect Nellie to just slip back into normal life after she has been the lady friend of the Prince of Wales for several months?" asked Charles.

"I can't see why not," said Bertie.

"But if she returns to the stage everyone will know who she is and it will draw unwanted attention," said Charles.

"I am sure she can go back to Dublin," said Bertie. "Nobody will know who she is there."

"That just isn't true, sir," said James. "Her notoriety is even greater in Dublin than it is in London, given that she is from there."

Bertie looked flustered and uncomfortable – these were questions he would rather not face and didn't have any answers to.

There was a knock on the door and a footman walked in.

"Her Majesty has arrived, sir, and is waiting to see you," said the footman.

"Thank you," said Bertie and he quickly shook Charles and James' hands. "It was so good seeing you again and I will write to you from the Middle East and look forward to meeting you again when I get back."

"Indeed, sir," said Charles as James smiled and nodded.

After he left, the two men looked at each other in bewilderment.

"That's perfect, sir! You toddle off to the Middle East and leave us to clean up your mess!" said James.

"I suppose it is a mess that we got him into in the first

place," said Charles. "Well, actually, you got him into!"

"Why do I feel as if everyone is abandoning this sinking ship?" said James.

"It's not sinking – it's sunk!" said Charles. "Will she go without trouble?"

"I don't know. Nellie can be obstinate and difficult. She's sacrificed a lot for him – even her beloved maid ran out on her when the going got tough."

"But where does he expect her to go? How is she to live – if she cannot go back on stage anywhere in Britain?"

"I do not know."

"Well, in any case she has no choice. He wants no more to do with her. I just hope she goes quietly," said Charles.

"So do I," whispered James.

"It is good to see you, Mama," said Bertie as he met her in the audience room after leaving Charles and James.

Victoria nodded to him coldly. As she viewed him she noticed he looked extremely nervous and uncomfortable. It was the first time they had been alone since Albert's death.

"You are all prepared for your trip?" asked Victoria.

"Yes. I travel to the royal yacht tomorrow and set sail the day after that," said Bertie. "Though I would prefer to stay here and be of whatever assistance I could be to you."

"Let us not discuss all that. I've already discussed it with too many people."

"Yes, Mama."

"And it has been decided that we are to start the marriage negotiations with the Danish royal family for the hand of Alexandra. I would hope you have no objections? It is what your father would have wanted."

"I have no objections at all, Mama," said Bertie. "I believe Alexandra and I can be very happy together and make you and the family proud."

Victoria managed to smile as she was flooded with relief on hearing at last a firm commitment from Bertie.

"Your father would be very happy to hear you speak so. I cannot imagine the negotiations will be that difficult. The Danish royal family, though well connected, are not rich and a marriage into the British royal family will be a gigantic leap up the hierarchy for them. In short, we hold the upper hand."

"Yes, Mama. Do I need to do anything during the negotiations, to play my part?" he asked.

"No, leave everything to Vicky and me. What you can do is to keep your head down, stay out of trouble and do nothing further to risk this marriage from taking place. Is that clear?"

"Yes, very clear," he said as he went red with embarrassment.

"Very well. You may kiss me before you leave."

He walked towards her and nervously placed a kiss on her cheek.

"We shall see you in four months," said Victoria, her eyes turning away from him.

He bowed and left the room.

CHAPTER 67

James was deep in thought when he left Windsor Castle. The least of his concerns was Nellie's predicament and how devastated she would be on hearing the news that Bertie had finished with her. Or what she would do with her life now. He was more concerned with himself. He had hoped that being summoned to meet Bertie so soon after his father's death would be a mark of the friendship that had developed between them and that Bertie would continue to rely on him now that so much more responsibility would be placed on his shoulders with his father's passing. But from the meeting, James realised that was not to be the case. He could tell from the way Bertie had interacted with him that the friendship would now fade away quite quickly. They were from different worlds and James was not the same background as somebody like Charles Carrington who would always be part of Bertie's circle. James's friendship with the Prince had been forged through his relationship with Nellie. Now that the Prince was finished with Nellie, he no longer needed a friendship with James as he now donned the mantle he was born for. James's membership of the royal court was to be as brief as Nellie's. James only had one more duty to perform for Bertie and that was to get rid of Nellie. Once that was done, he would slip back into a life of obscurity.

He was bubbling with resentment and anger. He had loved being part of the Prince's inner circle. And he had come to

378

expect and rely on the generous allowance he had been continually given for 'Nellie's expenses', little of which had found its way to Nellie of course and which she knew little about.

James had a sleepless night at his quarters in Aldershot and next morning set off to meet Nellie at Primrose House. By the time he got a carriage out to the house he knew what he must do.

Nellie was waiting anxiously for him and swung the door open when she saw he had arrived.

"Well – how is Bertie?" she demanded as he walked past her into the parlour and poured himself a glass of brandy.

"He's not good, Nellie, as can be expected. Beside himself with grief and all the weight of responsibility that has been thrust upon him," he said in a melancholy voice.

"My poor Bertie . . . did he talk of me?" she asked. "Did you send him my love and tell him I am thinking of him all the time and want to help him in any way I can?"

"Yes . . . yes, I told him all that . . . and he told me to tell you that he loves you back in equal measure."

"Oh!" Nellie suddenly felt weak and grabbed on to a chair. She was overcome with relief. She sat down and started to wipe away tears. "I thought – when I hadn't heard from him for so long – I thought he didn't want to see me any more."

"That couldn't be further from the truth! He says he longs for you day and night. He longs for the time he can be with you again."

Nellie dabbed at her eyes. "All this time in this house going mad with loneliness . . . it's all been worthwhile to hear those words. When is he coming to see me?"

James walked towards her slowly. "There is a problem with that – as he is being sent overseas."

"*Overseas! Where?*"

"The Middle East."

"*The Middle East! What for?*"

"He doesn't want to go – he loathes having to go."

"Why is he going so?"

"His family are sending him away."

"Not because of me?" Nellie was aghast.

"No – no, of course not. He has to go on some diplomatic mission. He has no choice."

"And will I not see him before he goes?"

"No, he sets sail tomorrow," said James.

"Tomorrow! And how long is he to be gone?"

"Not that long, not that long at all. A couple of weeks, that's all."

"But surely it would nearly take that long to sail there and back!" said Nellie.

"He said to tell you he will be back as soon as possible. That the only thing that makes his life bearable is the thought of seeing you again."

"But I don't know if I can take this much more, James! The isolation and loneliness here in this house. I don't think I can take being without Bertie another day let alone however long he is going to be in the Middle East."

James came quickly to her, went down on bended knees and grasped her hands.

"Nellie, you must! You must for Bertie! He's relying on you to be strong and wait for him, he told me so himself. You should have seen him, Nellie, looking so depressed and unhappy – like a broken man!"

"My poor Bertie," said Nellie.

"As bad as what you are going through here, imagine what he is going through. Bereft of his father and the whole country looking for him to carry them through these terrible times."

"I just want to help carry him through it all, that's all I want to do, James," said Nellie.

"Well, you can. By staying here and waiting for him – just knowing that you are here waiting is what is carrying him through all of this. Can't you keep doing this for him?"

Nellie nodded. "Of course I can. I'd do anything for him."

Charles opened the door of his rooms at Cambridge and saw James standing there.

"James! Come in! An unexpected surprise."

"Yes, I was in the vicinity so decided to pay you a visit."

Charles pulled. "In the vicinity? I take it you called out to Primrose House to see our friend?"

James nodded and sighed.

"How did she take the news?" asked Charles.

"Not very well."

"I can imagine. No girl wants to be jilted. But it makes it even harder when the chap's friend is sent to deliver the unfortunate news. What is she going to do now? Go back to Ireland?"

"No. She has no intention of going anywhere."

Charles looked puzzled. "What is she going to do then – stay in Primrose House indefinitely? Did Bertie leave enough rent money to enable that? Or paid in advance?"

"No, he certainly didn't. We have got ourselves a very unfortunate predicament, Charles."

"In what way?" Charles was alarmed.

"Nellie's not going to go away easy."

"Oh dear God!" Charles sank down on an armchair. "She's taking it that bad, is she?"

James nodded. "She's furious. Inflamed. Out for blood."

"But surely Nellie knew this day would come? Perhaps hastened by Prince Albert's death. But, in all reality, she's been deluded if she thought Bertie would not tire of her in time and move on."

"It's not as simple as that. It appears Bertie made Nellie a number of false promises. The word *marriage* was even used," said James.

"For God's sake! What was he thinking of?" Charles was shocked.

"He probably got carried away in the first flush of love," said James.

"There's being carried away and then there's – being a total idiot! He should have never led her on like that," Charles said angrily.

"I agree. But that is what he did and now she is threatening all sorts."

"Threatening? Threatening what exactly?"

"To go public. Not just with her relationship with Bertie . . . but with other sensitive information she has learned about the royal family from Bertie. Not just embarrassing information, but information that could seriously derail the monarchy."

"What kind of information?" demanded Charles.

"She wasn't specific. But she was privy to a lot of family secrets that Bertie, in his naivety, disclosed to her."

"And she would do this now? When they have just buried Prince Albert? She would sink to such a depth?" Charles' shock was increasing by the moment.

"A woman scorned, Charles – hell hath no fury."

"It's disgusting behaviour, and she always appeared such a nice woman – common, but nice," said Charles.

"Oh, Nellie can fight dirty. I think it would be very unwise for us to ignore her – we do so at our peril."

"But Bertie has set sail for the Middle East. He's not even here to deal with her."

"Which leaves us dealing with the mess," said James.

"So what does she want? Revenge – to damage the monarchy as revenge?"

"Not exactly. She feels she has invested a good part of her life in Bertie and sacrificed a lot for the relationship. She feels she cannot go back to living a normal life. She cannot continue in her career. And so she wants compensation."

"Ah – I see! She's out for money, which I suspected was what she was after all along. Common little tart!" Charles was disgusted. "And to blackmail the royal family now when they are at their lowest ebb. What a bitch!"

"I don't think she sees it as blackmail."

"Well, she can dress it up any way she wants, but it's blackmail at the end of the day," Charles sighed. "Well, I suppose we will all have to club together and give her what she wants. We can't go to Bertie or anyone else in the royal family about this, not when they are grieving so. What is she looking for? I shall have to order cheaper brandy for next few months I imagine."

"I'm afraid cutting your brandy bill won't cover the money that Nellie is demanding, Charles."

"Well, how much is she demanding?"

"Forty thousand pounds," said James.

"*How much?*" shouted Charles as he jumped to his feet in absolute shock.

"Forty thousand pounds – in cash," said James.

"But she cannot be serious! We can't scrape that kind of money together – not in a month of Sundays. That's a king's ransom!"

"Or a prince's ransom," said James. "She is quite determined. If she does not receive the money she will destroy Bertie, and probably the whole royal family along with him."

"But what will we do?" demanded Charles as he began to pace up and down furiously. "We can never find money like that."

"No. That's why I think the royal family will have to be informed. Either they or the government will have to come up with the money for Nellie to ensure her silence. Otherwise she will go to the press. She has also said she will return to the stage and make her relationship with Bertie the centrepiece of her act. Can you imagine the masses queuing up to see the Prince's mistress sing and joke about their relationship? It would be the hit of the year."

"I cannot believe this is happening!" wailed Charles. "And Bertie gloriously sailing to the Middle East in ignorant bliss!"

"I think there is no choice but to pay her off, Charles.

With the marriage negotiations now proceeding, this scandal would derail them in an instant."

"But who do we talk to?" asked Charles.

"You have the contacts in the Royal family, Charles. You will know who to speak to about this. Clearly whoever you talk to will want to keep it from Her Majesty's ears, if they can," said James.

CHAPTER 68

Victoria was at her writing desk in her sitting room while Alice was on the nearby couch sorting out her correspondence. Alice glanced at her mother and was consumed with worry. Victoria's grief over Albert's death was still extreme. She had ordered the Blue Room where Albert had died to remain untouched and she intended to keep the room as a shrine. The only thing that distracted her from her state of mourning was the endless marriage negotiations she was conducting with the Danish royal family. Alice thought of how little negotiation had been conducted for her own forthcoming nuptials compared to Bertie's. But then, Alice reasoned, she was just a younger daughter marrying a comparatively poor German Prince. Bertie was the heir to an empire. Victoria was putting excessive energy into the negotiation and marriage treaty, but Alice was glad that there was at least one thing to distract her from her mourning. Victoria's longstanding desire to see her son married to the right woman took precedence even over mourning her beloved Albert.

Victoria put down her pen as she finished writing a letter to Vicky.

"I have written to Vicky to assure her that the rumours that have been circulated around the Prussian court that Alexandra had a teenage fling with an army officer are completely false – malicious rumours being put forward by the Prussians to derail the marriage treaty."

"How cruel of people to make up such wicked lies about poor Alexandra," said Alice.

"The Prussians will say anything to stop Bertie marrying their enemy, a Dane," said Victoria. "I have made exhaustive investigations and Alexandra has been chaperoned all her life. She is without a smear on her character. Thank goodness for that, for where would it leave us if Alexandra was suddenly out of the running?"

"Indeed – where would it leave Bertie?"

"Would that the sordid details circulating about our own family were equally false!" said Victoria with a shudder.

Alice nodded sadly, hoping her mother would not dwell on the Nellie Cliffden affair again.

"We have agreed that Alexandra will receive an income of £10,000 annually once she has married Bertie, for her sole use. And if she is widowed, she will receive an annual pension of £30,000," said Victoria. "I need to get government approval for the figures. I am due to meet a government official on Wednesday to discuss same."

"There is something very unromantic about it all. I am quite glad that I am a younger daughter of not much consequence to anyone politically and my darling fiancée has a small estate."

"You will know yourself one day the importance of your children making good matches, Alice. I hope your children, though not coming from the upper echelons of royalty, will remember their lineage and marry well."

"Yes, Mama."

"We have the upper hand at all times in this marriage treaty. The Danes know how lucky they will be for Alexandra to become Queen of England and we can almost dictate the terms in their entirety." Victoria almost looked gleeful.

Alice stood and brought her mother's letters to her desk.

"I have sorted your letters in order of importance, Mama.

You have received a letter from Copenhagen from the royal court and I put that top of the pile."

Victoria lifted the letter and looked at the handwriting.

"It is from Alexandra's mother, Princess Louise. No doubt discussing more details of the marriage treaty. Such a meticulous woman – she is probably requesting an extra tier on the wedding cake, or some such other mundane detail."

Victoria opened the letter and Alice saw she began to pale as she read on.

"Is everything all right, Mama?"

"We are lost!" declared Victoria.

"What is it, Mama? Has something happened to Alexandra?"

Victoria dropped the letter on her desk. "She has found out about Bertie's fall!"

"No!"

"Princess Louise's cousin, the Duke of Cambridge, felt it his duty to write to her and tell her about Bertie and his relationship with *that woman*. She knows everything! And the Duke told her that Bertie and I were on the worst possible terms!"

"No!"

"Princess Louise says Alexandra has been put in an impossible position."

"Are they calling off the wedding negotiations?" gasped Alice.

"I do not know! But I do know we are in danger of losing Alexandra. The Russian Czar has said that he is determined his own son will marry Alexandra or her sister Dagmar! Oh Alice – what are we to do?" cried Victoria.

CHAPTER 69

James sat in a quiet corner of a tea room off Piccadilly Circus. Charles walked in and surveyed the room until he spotted James and made his way over to him.

Charles did not look his usual jovial self as he sat down opposite James – he looked tired and worried.

"Have you been speaking to Nellie since we last met?" asked Charles.

"No. I am due to meet her tomorrow," said James.

"I had been hoping that she might have changed her mind – had second thoughts about this whole blackmail malarkey," said Charles.

"I can assure you, Charles, that she will not be changing her mind. In fact, I would hazard a guess that if there is any delay in agreeing to her terms, the sum she demands will go up significantly."

"Go up! How could she possibly ask for more?" said Charles, shocked.

"We shouldn't mess with her, Charles. Who knows what she is capable of?"

A waitress came with a pot of tea and poured two cups. They waited until she had left before they continued speaking.

"I received a letter from Bertie," said Charles.

James was surprised. "I see."

"From Constantinople." Charles took the letter from his

pocket and handed it across the table to James.

"How is he?"

"Oh, he sounds in great form! Enjoying the mysteries of the east as he sails on the royal yacht. While he leaves us here to clear up his mess."

"Does he mention Nellie?"

"Oh yes – he mentions her all right," said Charles, reaching across and pointing to a line in the letter.

James read the line out loud. "*I trust that you have cut the acquaintance of our friend N.*"

He looked up. "Would that it were that easy! To simply 'cut the acquaintance' and she would be gone!"

Charles reached over and took back the letter. "We know that – but he doesn't."

"Are you going to write to him and tell him that she is demanding money?"

"No! How can I? He has just lost his father, fallen out with his mother and is about to be engaged to a woman he doesn't know. It will finish him off if I tell him his lover is blackmailing him to boot!"

"But you can't tell him she has simply sailed off into the sunset either!" said James.

"I will write to him to say she is still in contact with us," said Charles, "but will say nothing of the blackmail. He has firmly closed the door on Nellie and is ordering us to get rid of her. We risk personal social ruin if we don't manage to do so."

"It will cost forty thousand pounds to get rid of her, Charles," said James. "Have you made any move in the matter of procuring it?"

Charles looked around before leaning closer. "I have spoken to my contacts in the royal household and informed them of the situation. They have told me the royal family is like a rudderless ship since Albert died. Her Majesty is in deep mourning and it is out of the question for her to be broached on the subject. She has already banished Bertie to the Middle East over it. However, realising the seriousness of the situation, my contacts have advised me to bring the matter to the government – to a Thomas Gardenton, who is the advisor to the minister who handles royal matters. My contacts have already informed him of the matter and he wishes to meet us to discuss it further."

James digested this information. "I know that name. He is the man who visited Nellie at her flat in Chelsea and told her to disappear before the scandal went any further."

Charles shrugged. "Then he clearly is the right person to deal with the matter as he is already familiar with it. He will know what to do."

"Do you think the government then will negotiate the payment for Nellie from the royal family?" James asked, trying to piece together what was happening.

"I cannot say, James. We are meeting Thomas Gardenton in his office in Westminster tomorrow. I am sure he will tell us then what is likely to happen."

Victoria sat at her writing desk late into the night drafting and redrafting her reply to Alexandra's mother. Alice sat by her, her face a mask of concern.

"We must try to portray Bertie as the innocent party in his – fall," said Victoria. "That he was an innocent abroad led astray by an unscrupulous woman!"

"Will it work?"

"We can only hope," said Victoria as she finished the letter and handed it to Alice for approval.

Alice read through the letter, reading parts aloud. ". . . *wicked wretches that led our poor innocent boy into a scrape . . . We have forgiven him this one sad mistake . . . and we look to his wife as being his salvation.*"

"Well?" asked Victoria.

"Yes, Mama, it reads well – however untruthful it may be."

"Truths have little place in a marriage treaty, Alice!"

390

"Clearly – you also write that you and Papa had forgiven Bertie and you have never quarrelled with him."

"Well, your papa had forgiven him," said Victoria.

"But have you forgiven him, Mama?"

"It's of no consequence to anybody if I have forgiven him or not. The important thing is we must let the Danes *think* there is no issue between me and my son. For they will not allow Alexandra marry into a family where there is a bitter feud."

"Then you haven't forgiven him," said Alice sadly.

"Alice, I am too busy trying to save him to entertain thoughts of forgiving him! Oh, how I wish your papa was here. He would know exactly how to handle this situation. But I am left alone – the burden falls on my shoulders alone." Victoria suddenly burst into tears.

"Mama!" said Alice, rushing to her to comfort her.

"I don't know what we shall do if Alexandra abandons us now," sobbed Victoria. "The game has changed considerably and now the Danes hold all the cards. We are at the mercy of any terms they dictate to us – and it is all the fault of *that woman*!"

James managed to hide the nerves that were tearing him up inside as he met Charles the following day at Westminster. He was playing for very high stakes, he knew. If the truth ever emerged that he was behind the blackmail plot he would be ruined forever. And yet if all went according to his plan he would be rich beyond his dreams.

Thomas Gardenton stood as they were shown into his office.

"Captain Marton – Captain Carrington," greeted Thomas as he shook both their hands and they all sat down.

They sat in silence for a short while before Thomas spoke. "This is a very unfortunate business."

"Indeed it is, sir," said Charles. "None of us want this – we are as alarmed by it as you are."

"Nellie Cliffden has been a big concern for this government since we became aware of her involvement with the Prince," said Thomas. "I visited her myself in an attempt to persuade her to – eh, go away. I see my endeavour utterly failed."

"Spectacularly failed, if I may say so," said Charles.

"I felt from the start that Miss. Cliffden was only interested in financial gain, however much she denied that to me when I challenged her. I have unfortunately been proven correct," sighed Thomas.

"I feel confident that once the payment is made to Nellie, we will never hear from her again and she will no longer be a threat to the royal family or the government," said James.

"And how much of a threat is she?" said Thomas.

"She's a considerable threat," said James. "If she speaks publicly about the affair she will all but ruin not only the Prince of Wales but the rest of the royal family as well. His Royal Highness was not very discreet in divulging to Nellie intimate details of the royal family and their relations, often very bad, with each other."

Thomas frowned. "We could try to silence the British Press from printing any of it."

"It will not stop the foreign press," said James, "and it will become so widespread on the continent and in America that it will only be a matter of time until the British press are forced to report what Nellie says. She is also reputed to be working on a new musical for the stage, detailing her relationship with the Prince, that the public can go and see for a cover-price of one penny."

"Dear Lord!" exclaimed Thomas, becoming angry. "Does Miss Cliffden realise the trouble she is in? That she could be arrested for blackmail?"

"Indeed, she says if such a thing happens she will welcome the opportunity to reveal all about her relationship with the Prince when she stands trial to a packed public gallery – and the press will be forced to report the details of the affair," said James.

"She's very clever, this woman. How looks can be deceiving! But forty thousand pounds! Is she mad? How does she think she will ever be paid that?" said Thomas.

James didn't falter as he continued. "She has hinted she has private letters from the Prince, very damaging private letters if she were to make them public."

"Oh – I see," sighed Thomas heavily.

"There is also the possible problem of a baby."

"*Baby*!" shrieked Thomas.

Charles paled. "She is not pregnant – is she?"

"I cannot say for sure," said James. "I didn't mention it to you, Charles, as the very suggestion is so frightful. But she has hinted at the matter – and I have a fear that she may be holding it as her trump card. Of course, a pregnancy would have unforeseen and uncharted consequences for the royal family and the country as a whole."

"Where is Miss Cliffden now?" asked Thomas.

"She's –" began Charles.

"Charles! She has expressly forbidden that her location be divulged to anybody," said James.

"I would like to meet her in person to discuss the situation," said Thomas.

"Out of the question. She refuses to meet anybody . . . and the fact of the matter, Mr. Gardenton, is that she does hold all the cards," said James.

"Has anybody been in contact with the Prince and informed him of what is going on?" asked Thomas.

"No," said Charles. "As I am sure you know, he is in the Middle East and is unaware of what is happening. I did receive a letter saying he wishes all ties with Nellie to be cut."

"Which will never happen if she is pregnant with his child and refuses to go away," said Thomas with another sigh. "I am meeting with Queen Victoria tomorrow where I will address the situation. I am not looking forward to it. I cannot imagine the effect all of this will have on her. What a vicious woman the Prince got himself involved with!"

Thomas was shown into the audience room in Windsor Castle.

He approached Victoria who was sitting on a couch and bowed low to her.

"Your Majesty," he said.

"Mr. Gardenton," she said with a nod.

As ever, Thomas like all government personnel, was expected to remain standing during his audience with the Queen.

"I have devised a number of building projects to honour the memory of my late great husband," began Victoria. "Statues for public places, busts for public buildings. We feel the country cannot honour his memory enough."

"I have seen some of the projects being suggested, ma'am."

"I take it there will be no objection to the budget for the programme," stated Victoria.

"I have heard of no objection."

"That is good. Prince Albert dedicated his life to this country and it is the least that can be done in return. Did he not save us from war with the Americans while he was at death's door?"

"We were honoured to have Prince Albert as our Prince Consort," said Thomas.

"I also forwarded you the sums being agreed to for the allowance to be bestowed on Princess Alexandra if and when she becomes Princess of Wales. Were the figures acceptable?"

"Again, there has been no objection raised so far. Although official approval has not yet been given, I cannot see any objection being raised," said Thomas.

"Good. For the marriage negotiations do not need any unnecessary complications, now since they have entered into such a delicate stage."

"A delicate stage, ma'am?"

"My son's indiscretion with that actress has been brought to the Danish court's attention." Victoria gave a shudder. "They are far from amused and the whole marriage is very much at risk of not going ahead."

"I see!" Thomas frowned on hearing this news.

"We are trying to appease the Danes as much as we can. But now the Russian Czar has intervened and let it be known he would like his son and heir to marry either Alexandra or her sister. Alexandra is suddenly in high demand whereas my son is very much tarnished. We are fortunate that my son is abroad, away from scandal and the risk of getting into trouble. For we feel the slightest upset would now derail the marriage treaty for good and my son and this monarchy would be lost forever."

"I see!"

"Our future relies on this marriage. That scandal killed my dear husband and I fear if the marriage to Alexandra does not go ahead it will not be long until I join him."

Thomas stared at the Queen in horror. He quickly realised that the Nellie Cliffden affair was now risking international diplomatic relations. Also, he realised that there was no way he could broach the subject of Nellie's blackmail with the Queen. She simply could not take the news or deal with the aftermath.

As Victoria continued to witter on about busts of Prince Albert, Thomas was wracking his mind trying to think of a solution to the problem of Nellie Cliffden.

Bertie was enjoying his Middle East trip immensely. From Cairo to Jerusalem, he had now arrived in Constantinople. Although he was being chaperoned and supervised at all times, it felt very good to be away from England. As he tried to come to terms with his father's death and the disgrace he himself had brought on his family, he began to look to the future. The marriage negotiations with Alexandra, he was informed, were at last coming together and he looked forward to the future he might have with her. Occasionally he allowed himself to think of Nellie. But thoughts of her were too painful. All memories of his love for her and their wonderful times together were now overshadowed by the fact his family blamed the relationship for the death of his father and the overwhelming guilt he felt because of that. He was angry with himself for being so irresponsible. He should not have allowed himself to get involved so far with Nellie, as now it was crystal clear to him the relationship was doomed from the start.

As he sat at the open window of his hotel, overlooking the city of Constantinople, he began to look through his post. He opened the first letter and to his delight saw it was from Charles Carrington. He read through the letter, chuckling at the stories Charles had written about Cambridge. Suddenly, Bertie frowned as Charles came to the topic of Nellie. Answering Bertie's query in his last letter, asking had all acquaintance been cut with her, Charles responded that acquaintance had not been severed. He wrote that Nellie was proving to be a tad troublesome.

"*Damn it!*" shouted Bertie, rising to his feet. Why were Charles and James still in contact with her? Why had they not, as he had instructed, cut acquaintance with her? And how was she being troublesome? What could she be doing to cause trouble? Charles went to his writing desk and began to pen a letter to Charles. He began the letter by reporting on the different sights he had seen on his travels since he had written last. Then he came to the point of the letter and wrote:

I am sorry to see by your letter that you still keep up an acquaintance with NC, as I had hoped by this time that THAT was over.

Bertie signed the letter. He would have it posted the next day to Charles. He had now given a clear instruction to Charles that none of his circle should have any more contact with Nellie and that he expected them to obey his order. He

396

did not need Nellie in his life or any disruption that might cause. It was his friends' duty to get rid of her, Bertie thought, as they were responsible for bringing her into his life in the first place, and the ensuing havoc.

James and Charles had been summoned to the office of Thomas Gardenton. As James was shown in he maintained a cool exterior, but inside he was a bundle of nerves.

"I have met with the Queen," said Thomas.

"I am sure it was very distressing for her to hear the . . ." Charles searched for the right word.

"Blackmail plot. Gentlemen, in the end I did not inform Her Majesty of Miss Cliffden's demands."

Charles and James stared at him, taken aback.

"What – but why not?" demanded James.

"I decided it would be too much for her to bear, to hear of such a sordid plot against her son," said Thomas.

"So – what happens now?" asked Charles. "What do we do about Nellie?"

"The government has agreed to give in to Miss Cliffden's demands. Under these circumstances we have no choice. We cannot risk destabilising the monarchy further in these already very unstable times. We are making the payment without consulting Queen Victoria."

James was overcome by a feeling of relief.

"You are doing the right thing," said Charles. "I have received another letter from the Prince, from Constantinople, demanding we get rid of Nellie."

"Perhaps that is easy for him to say when the money is coming from the public purse and not his," said Thomas.

"When is the payment to be made?" asked James.

"Next week. I shall have the money ready on Tuesday," said Thomas.

"I will inform Miss Cliffden of what has been decided and return next Tuesday to collect the money and deliver it to her," said James.

"Very good, gentlemen," said Thomas.

Charles and James stood up, and shook his hand and left.

James managed to contain himself until he got back to his quarters at Aldershot. Then he punched the air in delight, poured himself a beer and took a large gulp.

It had worked. His plan had worked. In a few days he would be richer than he ever thought he could be. His whole plan of introducing Nellie to the Prince had paid off spectacularly for him.

As he lay out on the couch, he thought about Nellie – Nellie who had been patiently waiting at Primrose House all these weeks for Bertie to return to her loving arms. She would be devastated when he broke the news to her, but that really wasn't his concern. He wondered what would happen to her in the future. She would be all right, he reasoned. Women like her always were.

Nellie walked down the quiet country road from Primrose House to the village and bought some groceries. She saw copy of *The Times* for sale in the shop and bought that as well. She was relieved to see that there was no awful headline about Bertie screaming at her.

When she got back to Primrose House, she prepared herself lunch as she thought about Bertie and what he might now be doing in the Middle East.

She was nearly going insane with boredom. James had said that Bertie should be back by now, but she hadn't got any word yet.

After lunch she sat in the parlour and looked through the newspaper. She spotted an article about Bertie and began to read it, desperate for information about him.

The article said that Bertie had arrived in Constantinople as part of his four-month grand tour of the Middle East.

"Four months!" Nellie exclaimed out loud as she looked up from the paper.

She read on to see that Bertie was not due to arrive back in England until June.

"*June!*" she shouted out loud.

But James had said Bertie would be back any day. He never said that Bertie was going for such a long time. She could not be expected to stay at Primrose House on her own until June! And Bertie would not want to be without her until then – not if he intended for them to be together, as James had said.

She read on: "*Rumours that an engagement between the Prince of Wales and Princess Alexandra of Denmark are continuing to circulate, but Buckingham Palace have not commented.*"

Nellie dropped the newspaper on the floor as she stared out the window. It suddenly all made sense to her. Bertie was going to be married to Alexandra. He had been sent out of the country to be away from the scandal of his affair and to be away from her. James was lying when he told her Bertie intended them to be together and was still in love with her. Bertie had finished with her.

She broke down as the reality hit her. She sobbed for what seemed like hours. What would she do now? Where would she go? How could she get over the love of Bertie? And one thought kept going through her mind amongst all the others: why was she being kept here at Primrose House?

CHAPTER 70

James was on tenterhooks in the days before he was to return to Westminster to collect the money from Thomas Gardenton.

On the morning he was to go to Gardenton's office, he got up early, bathed and dressed.

"This time tomorrow you will be a rich man," he said as he looked in the mirror.

His batman entered his quarters.

"Padron me, sir, but you are requested to go to Major Crofton's office," said the batman.

"What does he want?" asked James, irritated.

Major Crofton was his superior at Aldershot. He had taken a liking to James and would spend hours talking about cricket to him in his office. He really didn't have time for one of Crofton's long dreary conversations that day. He could not be late for his meeting with Gardenton.

"He said it was urgent," said the batman.

"Oh, all right!" snapped James.

He made his way through the camp until he reached the headquarters and announced his arrival to Crofton's secretary. To his dismay he was then left waiting nearly an hour outside in the corridor.

At last Crofton opened his office door.

"Come in, Marton," he beckoned.

"Good morning, sir," said James.

He noticed that Crofton didn't look his usual jovial self – in fact, looked rather sour. Then, to his surprise, he saw Major Hazeldon seated behind Crofton's desk, to the left of Crofton's chair.

"Good morning, Major Hazeldon," he said, trying to keep the surprise out of his voice.

Hazeldon merely nodded.

Crofton sat behind his desk beside Hazeldon. Unusually, he did not invite James to sit.

"Major Hazeldon has come from Ireland to relay some very disturbing news to me," said Crofton.

"Yes, sir?" said James as his heart started to pound.

Hazeldon leaned forward. "Marton, I understand that you are the culprit behind all this unseemly business between the Prince of Wales and the Irish actress."

"I, sir?" James feigned innocence.

"Yes, *you*, sir!" snapped Hazeldon. "Do not try to deny it. I have made exhaustive enquiries since the whole situation was reported to me by Prince Albert before his untimely death. You introduced the Prince to this woman. You smuggled her into the camp night after night – for what depraved acts I shudder to think. You organised the woman to follow the Prince back to England so they could continue their sordid affair. You have been a known associate of this woman for a number of years. You have introduced her not just to the Prince but to a number of men in Dublin leading to this woman's fall and ultimately the Prince's fall as well. In short, sir – you are a disgrace to your family, regiment and country!"

"I – I – who says these things?" demanded James.

"A number of sources. But my main source of information is the husband of the mistress of another of my officers, a Mrs. Henrietta Fitzgibbons whose husband reported his own wife's adultery with one of my officers, Captain Donald Kilroy. Kilroy is being named in the ensuing Fitzgibbons' divorce. The lady, for want of a better term, also told me of

401

the background and sordid details of the Prince's affair. I have verified the accusation with many sources, including the Prince's former batman, Tommy Spillane."

"Am I allowed to defend myself?" asked James.

"You may if you can!" said Crofton.

"I only acted in the interest of making the Prince's stay in Ireland enjoyable," said James.

"And you succeeded in nearly destroying his reputation. Next line of defence?" said Hazeldon.

"I was not the only officer involved in this," said James.

"But you were the one who orchestrated it. Next defence?" said Hazeldon.

"But we all played our part!" said James.

"It would be typical to try to bring down your fellow officers with you. Donald Kilroy is being disciplined over his own involvement with this married woman but I see no reason to punish any others for their involvement with the Nellie Cliffden scandal but you!"

"That is because they are from prestigious families and I am not!"

"No – that is because, despite their faults, they have never lived off immoral earnings. Next defence?"

James gave a laugh. "It was only high jinks!"

"You may call it what you what," said Crofton. "You have brought the reputation of your regiment into disrepute. I am relieving you of your duties as of today. You are no longer an officer, a soldier or a member of this regiment. You are dismissed!"

James stared at them in disbelief.

"But –" he began.

"You are dismissed! Good day, sir!" said Crofton loudly.

James thought for a moment, then saluted them, turned and walked out of the office.

CHAPTER 71

Nellie was in her bedroom at Primrose House sorting out her clothes. She guessed she would have to leave Primrose House now, though she had no idea where she could go. She could wait for James to contact her, or try to contact him, but she knew he would only lead her back into the life she had before. And she would never return to that life again. She thought about going to the Europa Theatre and asking for her job back. But she realised she could not do that, when everyone knew who she was now. She felt so alone. Like she always had before. Now she didn't have Sadie any more, or Bertie. She felt like she did years ago after she left the workhouse, alone with nowhere to go.

She had very little money left. Not even enough to get her back to Dublin. A least if she got back to Dublin, she could go to Oliver and he would try to help her.

As she continued to pack, she glanced out the window and saw a figure walking up the driveway from the road. It was a man on his own – a gentleman – and she could see a carriage parked down at the road. It wasn't James, she could see that.

She began to panic as the man reached the house and there was a knock on the front door. She steadied herself, went downstairs and opened the door.

She got a shock to see who was standing there. It was Thomas Gardenton, the government official who had visited her at her flat in Chelsea.

"Good afternoon, Miss Cliffden. May I come in?"

"Do I have a choice?" she asked.

"Not really," said Thomas as he walked in and looked around the hallway.

She closed the door and showed him into the parlour.

He sat down on an armchair, putting the case he was carrying on the floor beside him.

"So, this is where you have been hiding," said Thomas.

"How did you find me?"

"We got it out of Charles Carrington."

Nellie nodded and sat down opposite him.

"How can I help you, Mr. Gardenton?"

"Let's not play games, Miss Cliffden. I've come quite a way to meet you and you have caused everybody considerable trouble."

"I never meant to cause anybody trouble. I fell in love, that's all," she said.

"You charge a high price for your – love," he said, raising an eyebrow. "You agent has driven a hard bargain for you."

"My agent?" she asked, confused.

"He should know by now that it has cost him a high price personally," said Thomas.

"What are you talking about?" asked Nellie.

"Captain Marton. He has been dismissed from the army this morning due to his involvement in this whole vulgar episode."

"James – dismissed from the army?" Nellie was shocked.

"I am sure his share of the winnings will compensate him," said Thomas as he lifted up the case by his side. Opening it, he took out a canvas bag and handed it to Nellie.

Hesitantly, Nellie reached out for the bag and took it. She opened it and saw it was filled with neatly tied stacks of money.

She took out one of the wads of money and looked at it in amazement.

"It's all there – forty thousand pounds – you may count it if you wish," said Thomas. "But I'd rather you didn't – I need to catch the next train back to London."

Nellie was speechless.

"I have come personally to meet you rather than hand the money over to Marton. I want to tell you to your face: this is it. Do not ever try to get more money from the royal family or the government. You have promised to disappear and never to be heard of again – we expect you to meet your side of the bargain. This is the last we want to ever hear from you. Do I make myself clear?"

Nellie nodded quickly.

"I also came to see if – as Marton hinted – you are pregnant. Are you?" asked Thomas.

"Pregnant!" gasped Nellie. "No!"

"You've played a clever game, Miss Cliffden, holding out for the big win. But every gambler should know when to leave the table, and the time has come for you to do that now. Do you understand me?"

She nodded.

"If we should ever see or hear from you again, then we will throw the book at you. There is a very lengthy prison term for blackmail, I warn you of that."

Clicking his case closed, Thomas stood up.

"I will leave you now to get on with the rest of your life. Take my stern advice and don't let that be in England – or Ireland," he said.

Nellie nodded blindly as she followed him to the front door.

"Good day, Miss Cliffden," nodded Thomas as he opened the door and walked out.

She watched him walk down the driveway to his carriage. Then she looked at the bag of money she was holding, in shock.

James was consumed with anger after he had left Crofton's office. To be dismissed from the army in disgrace without even a pension! He was being picked on because his background wasn't as good as the others, that he was sure of. They wouldn't dare do this to Charles Carrington. As he hurried to Westminster to meet Thomas Gardenton, all he could think of was getting his hands on the forty thousand pounds. He would show them. He would show them all. Because he had something none of the rest had – a cunning mind. He had masterminded a plot to become rich and now he was going to collect his winnings.

He arrived at Gardenton's office and was asked to wait.

As an hour and another hour ticked by, he was ready to explode with impatience.

"Where is Mr. Gardenton?" demanded James. "I haven't all day to wait for him!"

At that moment Thomas came down the corridor. "I would have thought you would have a lot of free time on your hands, now that you have taken early retirement from the army."

James was dismayed to realise that Thomas knew he had been kicked out of the regiment. He realised the government had played their part in his dismissal.

"Come in," said Thomas, opening his office door.

James followed him in.

"So you know about my dismissal?" said James without preamble.

Thomas turned to face him. "Oh, yes – in fact it was we who strongly suggested it to your regiment after we did a full background search on you, Marton. We can't have men masquerading as officers when they clearly are not gentlemen."

James fought the urge to explode in anger and reminded himself why he was there.

"I have come as arranged for Nellie's money," he said. "She is waiting for it."

"No, she isn't as I have already given it to her," said Thomas.

"What did you say?"

"I said I have given it to her."

"When? How?" James couldn't believe his ears.

"I travelled to Primrose House this morning and handed the money to Nellie myself. We thought it wiser to hand the money over to her directly, so she could never claim she didn't receive it. We also feared, given your character, that you might abscond with her ill-gotten gains."

"But – but – how did you find out where she was?" James stammered.

"Charles Carrington told us when we informed him of your sordid past role in Nellie's life and also that you were being dismissed from the army," said Thomas.

"*You stupid fucking bastard!*" shouted James, erupting in anger and sweeping everything from Thomas's desk onto the floor. "*Do you realise what you've done? Do you fucking realise what you've damned well done?*"

Thomas looked at him, alarmed. "Please calm down, Marton!"

"*I could kill you with my bare hands for what you've done!*" shouted James.

"I will call the police if you do not leave at once!" said Thomas.

"*Oh – fuck off!*" shouted James as he turned and stormed out of the office.

James was disorientated as he made his way through the streets of Westminster. He was reeling from the shock of being dismissed from the army and now discovering that Gardenton had given Nellie the money. His meticulous plans had backfired. He had to get to Nellie as soon as possible. He had to get that money from her. His future relied on it. He could only imagine how angry Nellie would be with him. But Nellie was smart and she knew how to survive. He could make her see that he did it for them both and that he was just trying to secure their futures. He had always held sway over Nellie and now he needed to exercise it more than ever. He would have to share some of the money with her of course. But he could think of how to deal with her after he had the money.

A terrible thought ran through his head that she might have run away with the money. He couldn't even entertain that thought, it was so atrocious. He hailed a hansom cab and instructed the driver to take him to the train station as fast as possible.

CHAPTER 72

Darkness was descending as the train made its way to Cambridge. James was rehearsing what he would say to Nellie and how he could win her around. But what if he couldn't? What if she would not fall for his story and would not forgive him? What if she refused to give him the money? James stared out the train window, becoming more and more angry and agitated by the thought. If she gave him any trouble, he could quite happily place his hands around her delicate neck and choke her. As he thought about his disgrace and army dismissal he realised it was all Nellie's fault. Had he not implored her to leave Bertie before the story broke and became public? Had he not told her the consequences would be dire if she did not return to Dublin? And the consequences were indeed dire – he had been disgraced. None of his friends and colleagues would see him again. He would be ostracised from society. All hopes that one day he would marry a lady of breeding and financial independence which would assure his place amongst his set were now scuppered. No lady would ever look at him now, a disgraced and discharged officer.

His anger was reaching boiling point as the train arrived into the station at Cambridge. Nellie was poison. She had not only caused the fall of Bertie but now him too! She should pay for what she did. Why should she reap any rewards from the money that he had worked so hard to extract from the government and royal family? Who would miss her if she was gone? If she disappeared? All she did was cause trouble for everyone. He would be doing the world a favour by getting rid of her.

As the carriage he hired pulled up outside the gateway of Primrose House, to his relief he saw lights on in the windows. He paid the driver and didn't ask him to wait. He did not want any witnesses to his showdown with Nellie or what the outcome might be.

He walked up the driveway. There were lights on downstairs and also upstairs. His heart was pounding as he neared the house. What if the lights were on but she had left? But she wouldn't do that, he reasoned. She would surely have turned off the lights before leaving if she was going to flee. Unless she was in such haste to leave that she didn't bother?

Suddenly he saw a figure in her bedroom upstairs. To his relief he saw it was Nellie. He dashed quickly to the front door and, finding it unlocked, rushed in. He darted across the hallway and up the stairs. He steadied himself as he walked down the corridor and breathed deeply. He needed to approach her calmly. He needed to win her over first and get her to hand over all the money before he dealt with her.

He reached her door and gently pushed it open. He saw Nellie standing at the window, looking out. Her back was to him, her golden hair glimmering in the low light.

"Nellie?" he said softly.

She didn't turn to him.

"Nellie," he said gently. "I know how this might seem to you. I've been speaking to Gardenton and he told me he visited you today – and gave you the money. It must come as a terrible shock to you that Bertie will not be returning to you. I didn't want to tell you because it would hurt you so."

She said nothing and continued to stare out the window.

"What I did, I did for us, Nellie – for you. You had to get something out of it. After being with Bertie for so long – you deserved that money. I know I should have told you what I had planned to do, but I didn't want to worry you. Of course, I was going to tell you as soon as the money was paid over."

She said nothing.

"Nellie! Look at me. Please. I know you must be angry. Angry with Bertie for finishing with you – angry with me for not informing you of what I was doing. But it's worked – has it not? We are rich, Nellie. Richer than we ever thought we would be!"

She continued to ignore him.

Suddenly his anger spilled over. *"Nellie! Say something – damn you!"* He strode towards her. *"Don't you dare ignore me, you bitch!"*

He reached out and grabbed her by the hair. To his shock her hair came away in his hand. He was holding a wig.

It wasn't Nellie standing at the window. It was a mannequin dressed in one of her gowns.

He shouted in rage as he kicked the mannequin to the floor.

James sat on Nellie's bed with the wig in his hand. He had searched the whole house and there was no sign of her or the money. She had run away, taking the forty thousand pounds with her. He sat there, his world fallen apart, as he thought of what he could do. Where had she gone to? He decided she would not have gone to London as she was too well known there and the risk of being found was too great. Besides, he knew that Gardenton would have given her a stern warning to leave the country. She wouldn't have returned to Dublin as she would realise that James could too easily track her down there. The obvious place for her to flee to was the Continent. She would have travelled to Calais to make the quick crossing to France. But maybe that was too obvious, and she might have gone to somewhere like Amsterdam. He racked his mind thinking of what Nellie was likely to do.

He suddenly looked up. He remembered her saying once that her father and brothers were in New York but she didn't know where they were there. Forty thousand pounds would help her track them down, thought James, track down the family she had always longed for. She had said to him another time that she always wanted to go to America and felt it would suit her. He jumped up and threw the wig on the bed. He felt sure it must be where she was heading. He needed to find her before she got on that ship. For once she had stepped off it into the New World, she would be lost to him forever.

CHAPTER 73

Nellie had left Primrose House soon after Thomas Gardenton had left. Recovering from the shock of what had happened, she knew there was no time to lose. As soon as James discovered that Gardenton had come to her directly to give her the money, he would come looking for her.

To discover that James had been deceiving her, holding out hope that she still had a future with Bertie, when all the time he was blackmailing the government on the pretext that it was her doing was frightening to Nellie. It made her understand that James would sink to any level to get what he wanted. And he wanted that forty thousand pounds.

She had rapidly packed what she needed and then had a thought as she looked at the mannequin in the corner of her bedroom. She dressed it in one of her gowns, placed her wig atop it and stood it by the window looking out. She imagined James arriving at the house in a panic, thinking she might have absconded and then overcome with relief on seeing the mannequin in the window. She imagined how he would explode in frustration and anger when he realised he had been duped. The thought made her smile. A small act of revenge for all the tricks James had played on her in the past. To let him know what it felt like to be made a fool of.

Liverpool was teeming with people waiting to get ships to America. Irish, Scandinavians, Germans, Italians, Russians –

all descended on Europe's busiest port to buy a passage to a new life in America. The city streets were also thronged with ticket agents. Nellie passed by these, many of whom looked dubious, and headed straight to the Britannia Adelphi Hotel where she booked a suite for the night. She had heard of the hotel many times in the past – it was where the wealthy passengers stayed before embarking on their journeys to America. With forty thousand pounds in her bag, she would not be dealing with one of the street agents selling tickets for the ships.

She booked into the hotel under the name 'Sadie Primrose'. She knew she could no longer use her real name, not even in America. Her name had become notorious. She quickly composed the name, combining that of her much-loved and missed maid and the house that she had been imprisoned in but which had also shielded her from a hostile world for months. She then asked for the hotel to send up their ticket agent to her suite.

"When would you like to depart, Miss Primrose?" asked the ticket agent.

"As soon as possible – tomorrow morning? I need to get to New York as quickly as possible over an urgent family matter."

"The ticket to travel first class is twenty pounds," he said. "That will get you on a ship in the morning. If you travel second class the wait could be up to six days."

"I shall be travelling first class," she informed him as she handed over the money.

"Very good," he said and wrote her a ticket.

She felt relieved. She pitied the majority of people travelling who often had to wait up to ten days to get passage on a ship. And their time in Liverpool while they waited was often horrendous, as they were ripped off by everyone from ticket agents to the keepers of the rundown hotels they were forced to stay in.

"The ship will take eight days to reach New York. I hope that will get you there in time to attend to your family business," said the agent.

"Yes, that should be perfect," said Nellie with a smile.

"A complimentary carriage will collect you in the morning and take you to the docks," said the agent as he left.

"Thank you," said Nellie.

She closed the door after him and sighed with relief.

It had been that easy. There was no paperwork to sign, no visa needed, no prove of identity. All a person had to do was show up in Liverpool with enough passage fare to get on a ship and they could set sail for a new life in America.

As she looked around the luxurious sitting room of the suite, she could scarcely believe she was there. She felt she didn't belong in such beautiful surroundings.

"Of course you belong here, Nellie," she then said out loud to herself and with a wry smile added, "Weren't you nearly the Princess of Wales!"

James arrived in Liverpool by train the next morning. The journey to get there had been appalling. It had taken him two hours to get a lift from a local cab from Primrose House back into Cambridge. Then he had to wait another two hours before a train was leaving for London. There he managed to get on the night train to Liverpool. Nellie, he realised, had got a head-start on him. He was convinced that she was in Liverpool.

As he raced from the train station into the thronged streets of the city he realised that it was not going to be easy to find her.

He was immediately approached by ticket agent.

"Looking for a ticket to New York, sir?"

James realised it was an opportunity to get some information.

"How quickly can I set sail?" asked James.

"Well, sir, that depends on how much you want to pay. Steerage is five pounds but you won't get on a ship for maybe ten days." The agent looked at James in his well-tailored suit. "I'd say that wouldn't be a comfortable enough voyage for a man like you, anyway. Second class is five pounds, and you can get passage in five days. If you are willing to pay first class I can get you on a steamship which sets sail at eleven in the morning."

Digesting the information, James walked away from the agent and down the busy street.

"*Which is it to be, sir? Second class?*" shouted the man after him.

James realised that Nellie would have bought a first-class ticket the previous night when she arrived. Which meant she would be setting sail that morning. As he looked at his watch and saw it was nine o'clock he realised he did not have much time to catch her.

At the docks, Nellie walked past the long queues for steerage and second class towards the top of the docking platform. The whole port was teeming with people. She showed her ticket to the shipping staff and they courteously waved her in behind the ropes that were cordoning off the embarking area. She looked out at the ship in the water and felt excited that she would soon be on it and setting sail to her new life.

Small rowing-boats were used to ferry the passengers out to the ship. She joined the small queue of very well-dressed people who were standing at the steps down to the rowing-boats. She viewed her fellow first-class passengers and saw they were a mix of families, couples and businessmen. Most had servants travelling with them. She was the only woman travelling in first class on her own.

She waited her turn to reach the ticketing desk and then handed her ticket to the man there.

The man looked at her ticket and stamped it. "Thank you, Miss Primrose, and I hope you have a very pleasant journey with us to New York."

"Thank you, I am sure I will," smiled Nellie, taking her ticket back from him.

"If you could follow the other passengers down the steps to the boat, you will brought out to the ship."

"Thank you," said Nellie.

"Is that your only luggage, madam?" One of the shipping staff indicated the suitcase and bag she was carrying.

"Yes."

The man clicked his fingers, summoning a porter who took the suitcase from her. The bag she held on to.

"*Nellie!*" came a roar behind her.

She froze as she recognised James' voice.

"*Nellie! It's me – James!*"

She ignored the shouts and followed the porter towards the steps.

James saw that Nellie was carrying a large bag and knew the forty thousand pounds was in it.

"Excuse me, I need to go in there for a minute to talk to somebody," James said to shipping staff as he made to walk past the ropes.

"Can I see your ticket please, sir?" asked one of the staff, blocking his path.

"I don't have a ticket – I am not getting on the ship – I just need to see that woman," said James, pointing at Nellie.

"Sorry, sir, no access without a ticket," said the man.

"It's an emergency!" pleaded James. "Please let me in!"

"You cannot enter unless you have bought a ticket like everyone else," said the man.

"You don't understand – it is urgent I speak to that woman before she gets on that boat! Will you please tell her that I need to speak to her?" James pointed again at Nellie. "That woman there with the blonde hair! She is a friend of mine. Her name is Nellie."

The man looked at Nellie who was standing at the top of the steps down to the boat, seemingly unconcerned by the ruction James was causing.

"One minute, please," said the man to James.

He hurried to Nellie who was just about to walk down the steps.

"Excuse me, madam," he said to Nellie.

She froze.

"Yes?" she asked.

"There is a man there who wishes to speak to you urgently. He says it's an emergency."

Nellie understood that if she acted nervously she would be lost. It was time to rely on her acting skills.

She adopted a haughty English accent. "Which man wishes to speak to me?"

"Him there," said the man, pointing to James. "He says he knows you."

"*Nellie!*" called James, frantically waving at her. "*Please! We need to talk!*"

"The man is mistaken – I have no idea who he is. And my name is certainly not Nellie!" she said, showing him her ticket.

The man looked at her ticket. "I apologise, madam. He just seemed so insistent."

"My good man, he looks to me as if he is an escapee from a lunatic asylum. See that he doesn't come anywhere near me."

"Certainly, madam. I apologise for disturbing you."

The man walked back to the ropes.

Nellie took a final look at James who was getting even more agitated and then continued down the steps to the rowing-boat.

"Sorry, mate, the lady doesn't know you and doesn't want to know you either. Best you clear off," said the man to James.

"*Doesn't know me! I bloody rescued her from the gutter!*" shouted James.

"Please, sir, you are disturbing the passengers," said the man.

"*Nellie! Nellie!*" James shouted.

"Her name isn't Nellie!" said the man. "You're getting her mixed up with somebody else."

"There is no mistaking that one!" James took out his

wallet. "I want to buy a ticket for that ship."

"We don't sell tickets here. You will have to go back into the city and find an agent who sells them."

"But that will take ages, the ship will have sailed!" said James.

"In any case you won't be able to buy a ticket – the ship is sold out," said the man, becoming impatient. "Now please step out of the way."

Nellie sat into the rowing-boat with the other passengers, her heart beating quickly. As the boat was pushed away from the dock and the oarsmen began to row, her panic began to calm.

James had stepped back from the ropes and stood watching. He became frantic. He couldn't let her go. He ran towards the ropes and jumped over them.

"*Hey – get back here! You can't go in there!*" shouted one of the staff.

James raced to the steps and ran down them to the water. He saw the boat Nellie was on hadn't moved too far out from the dock. He dived into the water and began to swim after the boat.

"*Oh my goodness! That man!*" cried a woman in the boat, pointing.

Nellie turned her head and her eyes widened as she saw James trying to swim after the boat.

"*What is he doing?*" shouted another passenger.

Nellie watched James swim while the shipping staff on the dock shouted at him to return. She became frightened as the oarsmen had stopped rowing to look at him. He would soon reach them.

Abruptly, he stopped swimming. He looked to be struggling in the water, his arms flailing about.

"He's run into trouble – there's a strong current there and it's got him," said one of the oarsmen.

"James," Nellie whispered before crying out to the oarsmen, "*Go back and rescue him!*"

"*Do not!*" commanded the woman beside her. "We don't want a lunatic on board a small rowing-boat like this!"

"*Help! Help!*" James' cries now carried through the air.

"*We can't just let him drown!*" shouted Nellie as she stood up.

"Sit down, woman! You'll drown us all if you topple this boat!" said a passenger as he grabbed her and pushed her back down on her seat.

"For God's sake, will somebody do something!" Nellie pleaded, seeing James weakening as he struggled against the current.

"They are going to fish him out now, if they get to him on time," said an oarsman, pointing to a rowing-boat that was heading out from the dock towards James.

"For goodness' sake! We paid for first class to avoid any disturbance and we are faced with this!" said the woman beside Nellie.

"*Will you shut up!*" Nellie shouted, forgetting her assumed accent and making the woman cower away from her.

Nellie watched terrified as James stopped struggling in the water. She held her breath as the boat from the dock reached him. The oarsmen grabbed him from the water and dragged him on board.

"Is he all right? Is he alive?" asked Nellie as she strained to see.

The boat headed back to the docks. She watched as the men dragged him from the boat and laid him out on the pier.

"He'll survive," said one of the oarsmen. "Look!"

James' form began to move on the pier and Nellie felt herself flood with relief.

"Can we now please get on with the task at hand! I can't take much more of this small boat!" said the woman beside her.

"Right you are!" said the oarsman and they started rowing vigorously again out to the ship.

Nellie continued to stare at the pier as a gang of people gathered around James and lifted him to his feet.

On the ship, Nellie was shown to her room. It was a beautiful stateroom. As she looked around at the gold taps in the bathroom and the Persian rugs on the floor, she wondered if she would ever get used to such luxury. As she placed the forty thousand pounds in the safe in her room, she realised she might have a very good time trying.

She felt the ship move as it began to set sail. She left her room and walked through the corridors and up on the deck where so many of the passengers had gathered to watch as they departed the shore. There was cheering and a sense of excitement from everyone. And Nellie felt excited too. A chance to start a new life with a new name in a new country. She was doing what everyone wanted her to do – disappearing – and they would never hear from her again.

She walked to the other side of the ship and, as she looked out at the sea they were about to voyage across, she thought about James. He had risked everything for money and had nearly died. She thought about Bertie – her darling, loving, sweet Bertie – and wondered if he would ever enjoy the life he was being forced to lead. Would he be happy? Would he ever think of her and the happy times they had together, or would she simply be forgotten?

As she walked the deck, she promised herself she would focus on her new life now. She wouldn't be looking back over her shoulder. The world that had so briefly and dramatically been fixated on Nellie Cliffden would not be hearing from her again.

CHAPTER 74

1863

As Queen Victoria was still in mourning for her beloved
Albert, it was decreed that the ladies attending the wedding
of the Prince of Wales to Princess Alexandra of Demark
would were restricted in the colours they wore. Nor would
Victoria take part in the carriage procession to St. George's
Chapel in Windsor where the wedding was taking place. She
made her way privately there and, dressed in widow's weeds
and a mourning cap, she sat on a small balcony overlooking
the altar, isolated in her mourning.

Bertie stood at the altar beside his best man, Vicky's
husband Fritz, under the watchful eye of his mother on the
balcony above. The guest list had been kept to a minimum
but the Prime Minister Lord Palmerston was present, as were
other notables such as the writers Charles Dickens and
William Thackeray and the poet Tennyson.

The marriage service was conducted by the Archbishop of
Canterbury. Bertie saw his mother begin to cry and step back
from view on the balcony when the famous soprano Jenny
Lind chanted the Chorale of the music that had been
composed by Prince Albert during his lifetime.

Finally, the marriage ceremony completed, Bertie and
Alexandra turned to Victoria in the balcony. He bowed and
Alexandra curtsied before they turned to the congregation.
Alexandra then took Bertie's arm and they set off down the aisle
to begin their married life as the Prince and Princess of Wales.

EPILOGUE

Sandringham 1871

Victoria had fallen asleep in her armchair in her bedroom at Sandringham. The night before Bertie had reached the worst crisis of his illness so far. His screams echoed throughout Sandringham. Victoria had sat by his bedside grasping his hand, trying to soothe him, trying to say anything that could calm him, to no avail. She saw the doctors become more frantic until finally Bertie fell into a deep sleep. As she watched him unmoving and silent in the bed, Victoria found his quiet state more terrifying than when he was ranting incoherently. She could see the doctors whispering to each other and knew they were of the opinion that the end was near for Bertie.

On Alice's insistence, Victoria had gone to her bedroom to try and get some rest. But it was pointless for her to go to bed, for she feared she would be called back to Bertie any minute for his final hour. As she sat in her armchair, looking out at the snow-covered grounds of Sandringham, she whispered: "Spare my dear beloved child."

She thought back to him as a child and his life through the years. She thought of her own relationship with him. She thought of how their relationship could have been repaired, if she had only allowed it. Bertie had tried his best to help and assist her and make amends after the whole Nellie Cliffden affair but Victoria had pushed him away. She had been lost in her grief and anger. Bertie had even obliged her by marrying Alexandra without any argument. But all she had done over the years was to remind him of what he had done and try to punish him for his behaviour. And even exclude him from the royal role he was born to.

As the years passed by, Bertie had simply stopped trying to appease Victoria. He stopped trying to gain her favour or her forgiveness. He knew it was a fruitless exercise and so he had simply distanced himself from her and got on with his life as he saw fit. And now he was dying and she would never have the opportunity to put it right between them. As the tears fell down her face, she fell into a deep sleep.

Victoria stirred from her sleep and saw it was bright outside. She stood up from her armchair and went to look out the window at the snow. She listened intently but there was only silence throughout Sandringham. Victoria put her face in her hands. She had hoped that the ranting and shouting from Bertie would have started again. It would show he was still alive. But the eerie silence was deafening.

She turned and walked from her bedroom and down the corridor outside. There was nobody about, no servants, and she was overcome by a sense of terror. Was Bertie dead and they were all in silent mourning, too anguished to come and break the news to her? Tears started to fall down her face as she reached Bertie's bedroom. She paused at the door, dreading what was on the other side. She put her hand to her forehead and tried to prepare herself. She had to be strong for the others.

Suddenly she could hear voices on the other side of the door and then somebody was laughing. Laughing? Or was it crying? It must be crying, she thought. But the person laughed again. There was no mistake: somebody was laughing.

Confused, she put her hand on the doorknob and opened the door. She marched into the room. She saw Alice and Alfred and Alexandra standing in front of the bed, blocking her view of it. The doctors were gathered around too. And then the laughter again – and Victoria could see that it was Alexandra who was laughing. Was the woman in shock?

"Your Majesty," said one of the doctors on seeing her and bowed.

Alfred, Alice and Alexandra turned to her and they were all smiling happily.

Victoria walked further in the room. And then she saw Bertie. But he was no longer lying out on the bed as he had been for so long. He was sitting up in bed. And he was smiling.

He was smiling at her.

"Bertie," she muttered as she stumbled towards him in shock.

"Isn't it the most marvellous thing, Mama?" exclaimed Alice. "Bertie woke up this morning and he is recovering! He feels much better!"

"Like his old self!" exclaimed Alfred.

"The fever has broken, Your Majesty," said the doctor, grinning in delight.

Hardly allowing herself to believe it, Victoria stared at Bertie who was smiling at her all the time.

"Bertie – is it true? Are you better?" Victoria whispered.

"I woke up this morning, Mama, and I feel fine. Weak and tired, but fine." he confirmed.

"Oh Bertie!" cried Victoria as she flung her arms around him and pulled him to her, kissing him again and again.

Bertie looked shocked as Victoria held him tightly.

He looked at Alexandra who was now crying along with Alice and Alfred. Alexandra nodded to him and gestured to him to embrace Victoria.

"I thought I'd lost you, I thought I'd lost you for good!" said Victoria.

"Mama," whispered Bertie as he put his arms around her and they hugged each other tightly.

"I don't know what is wrong with me," said Alexandra.

"I don't know whether to laugh or cry."

"Try doing both!" said Victoria as she pulled back from Bertie and ran her fingers through his hair, looking at him proudly. "Can I get you anything, my son, do you need anything?"

"Yes, I have a terrible thirst. I think I should like a Bass Ale!"

"Wonderful, Bertie, you can have whatever you want!" said Victoria as she embraced him again.

In the days that followed, Bertie continued to recover. The doctors at first feared another relapse but to everyone's relief that did not happen. Victoria stayed at his side, nursing him with Alice.

One evening Victoria and he were alone in the bedroom. She was sitting on the side of his bed, gazing at him.

"If I had lost you," Victoria said, "I don't think I could have borne it."

"I am sorry for all the concern I caused you," he said, frowning. "The last thing you needed was to be worried so about my health."

"For goodness' sake, Bertie! There is nothing for you to apologise for. You have spent your life apologising – and all you have been apologising for was simply for being you. Because I made you feel inferior – feel that you were not good enough, that you always could do better."

"But that was because I always could do better!"

"Your best is good enough, Bertie. It is time, for once, that I ask you for your forgiveness."

"You!" he was incredulous.

"Yes – I. For all the times I didn't give you the unconditional love you deserved. For all the times I pushed you away. For all the times I could have been kinder."

"You have nothing to be sorry about," he said, looking away.

She grabbed his chin and turned his head towards her.

"I was so lost in my own grief when your father died, that I couldn't see anybody else's. Particularly yours. I blamed you because I felt I had to blame somebody. And I was so used to blaming you for everything that it came naturally to me. I acted appallingly."

"But – it was I who acted appallingly," he said, forcing the tears that were threatening away. "What I did that summer before Papa died – I let you all down so badly. And I shall never forgive myself."

"There is nothing to forgive, Bertie. I was wrong in blaming you. And now I want a new start, if you will let me?"

"It is all I want," nodded Bertie.

She reached forward and kissed his cheek.

As Gladstone was shown into the audience room, he was struck by seeing a broad smile on Victoria's face as he approached her and bowed. He couldn't remember the last time he had seen her smile. In fact, he wasn't sure if he had ever seen her smile and hadn't been sure she was capable of doing so.

"Your Majesty, may I offer you my congratulations on the recovery of the Prince of Wales," he said.

"You most certainly can, Prime Minister. We are overjoyed at my son's return to good health. We have much to be grateful for." Her smile widened even further.

"The whole nation rejoices with you," said Gladstone.

"It has been very touching to see the outpouring of goodwill that the people – and the press – have shown during my son's illness. It has helped carry us through the dark days."

"Indeed, the Prince's brush with death has changed the royal family's fortune with the people. The joy at his recovery is quite outstanding. Perhaps they did not realise what they had until they nearly lost it?"

"Indeed, that can be said for us all." She looked at him wryly. "No more talk of republicanism in that case?"

"No – the Prince's illness has brought the royal family closer to the people than ever."

"I should like to discuss with you the matter of giving my son more responsibilities now that he is returning to good health. I think it is about time that he performs the duties he was born to – don't you, Prime Minister?"

"Indeed, I fully endorse the Prince now being given an official role, ma'am."

"And I was thinking that we might hold a thanksgiving service in St. Paul's Cathedral? It would be a way of returning all the goodwill to the people that they have shown us. A royal procession through the streets of London to the cathedral where we can see the people and they can see us."

"Us?" said Gladstone confused. "But surely you would not take part in the procession as well?"

"Of course I would. I intend to be by my son's side when we travel to the cathedral. Where else would I possibly be?"

Gladstone regarded Victoria in shock. She was going to do what he had begged and pleaded with her to do for years. She intended to be seen out in public. Not only that, but at her son's side after all these years of bitterness and feuding.

Gladstone bowed deeply to her. "I think it will be a great day, Your Majesty."

"Good, Prime Minister. I thought you might be in agreement with me," Victoria said, allowing herself to smirk at him.

The streets of London were packed with people the morning of the thanksgiving service for Bertie. Banners and flags were erected all along the route from Buckingham Palace to St. Paul's Cathedral. The carriage procession was ready to set off.

"They say there will be thirteen thousand people squeezed into St. Paul's Cathedral for the service. Can you imagine such a number?" said Alexandra who was already seated in the carriage.

"And how many more thousands will be lining the streets?" said Bertie. "But I suppose it is only to be expected. It is the first time in ten years that they will see their Queen."

"This day isn't about me, Bertie," said Victoria as a valet stepped forward to assist her up the steps into the carriage. "It is about you."

Bertie smiled at Victoria as he ushered the valet away and assisted her up the steps himself.

He sat down beside his mother in the open-top carriage opposite Alexandra.

"I do hope we did not rush this thanksgiving day," said Victoria. "You still look pale and quite frail. We could have waited until you were stronger."

"Mama, I am perfectly fine. It is three months since the fever broke and all I have been doing is recuperating at Sandringham. I think I should have gone mad if I could not get back to London by now."

Trumpets sounded as the procession took off. As it left Buckingham Palace there was a huge cheer from the crowds. Victoria and Bertie waved and smiled as their carriage continued through the streets to the cathedral.

"One forgets the joy it is to see the people," said Victoria as she waved happily.

"It is they who are overjoyed to see you after such a long absence," said Alexandra.

"I cannot describe how touched I am to experience such warmth," said Bertie, becoming emotional from all the cheering. "I never thought I would have such love."

As the carriage went through Temple Bar, Victoria reached over, took Bertie's hand and lifted it high above them – and then she kissed it which caused a great roar of approval from the crowds.

Victoria looked at him and smiled. "You always had our love, Bertie. But we never knew how to show it.

Author's Note:

Victoria reigned for a further thirty years until her death in 1901. Although she continued to make public appearances during the rest of her reign, she never came out of mourning for her husband Albert.

On his mother's death, Bertie ascended to the throne as King Edward VII. As Prince of Wales and later as king, Bertie was admired and loved for his ability to connect with ordinary people, and for his diplomatic skills abroad he became known as the 'Uncle of Europe'.

Although his marriage to Alexandra was a happy one, he continued to have mistresses and had a weakness for actresses, having a long-time affair with the famous Lillie Langtry. He disguised his rendezvous with his mistresses in his diary by entering them as royal appointments, writing only the initials of the women, a habit he started during his relationship with NC – Nellie Cliffden.

Killarney did become a world-famous tourist destination after the royal visit. However, their hosts the Herbert family never recovered financially from the cost of the royal visit to Muckross House. The house was put up for sale and is now a national park open to the public.

Bertie's favourite sister Alice was celebrated for the work she did in improving nursing in her adopted country of Hesse. She died at the age of 35 from diphtheria on the anniversary of her father Albert's death. Her daughter

Alexandra married Czar Nicholas of Russia and was assassinated along with him and the rest of his family by the Bolsheviks during the Russian Revolution.

Rumours circulated for years over what became of Nellie Cliffden, but all that is certain is that she disappeared from the world stage she occupied briefly during her relationship with Bertie as quickly as she had appeared on it. A true actress, she knew when to make her exit.

THE END

Also by Poolbeg

The LEGACY of ARMSTRONG HOUSE

A. O'CONNOR

2017 – At Armstrong House, Kate and Nico Collins are looking forward to a bright future with their young son Cian. When archaeologist Daniel Byrne arrives in the area to investigate life there during the Great Famine, he soon crosses paths with Kate. Through Daniel's work, Kate is horrified to discover that a vicious sexual assault occurred in their home in the 1860s when the occupants were Nico's ancestors Lord Edward and his wife Lady Anna. Kate sets out to use all her investigative skills to discover the circumstances of the crime, the identity of the victim and the guilty party.

1860s – After Lawrence, the long-awaited heir to the Armstrong Estate, is born Lord Edward and Lady Anna take great joy in watching him grow up. But somebody else is watching – Edward's cousin Sinclair who has always felt cheated of the Armstrong legacy by the unexpected birth of Lawrence. As Anna's past comes back to haunt her, life at the house is a tangled web of deceit, blackmail and betrayal that shatters in the summer of 1865.

2017 – As Kate's detective work edges closer to discovering the truth behind the assault, she and Daniel uncover a mystery that goes much deeper. Kate realises that if the truth is ever revealed it will not only destroy the legacy of the Armstrong family but also her marriage to Nico.

ISBN 978-178199-821-2

Also by Poolbeg

On SACKVILLE STREET

A. O'CONNOR

1869 – When Milandra arrives to live on Sackville Street as a young widow, she becomes the talk of Dublin. Firstly, she scandalises society by refusing to wear the mandatory widow's weeds. She then sets her sights on marrying young solicitor Nicholas Fontenoy, despite the fact he is already engaged to Bishop Staffordshire's daughter, Constance.

But is there something darker behind Milandra's professed love for Nicholas? As she attempts to lure Nicholas away from Constance, a chain of events is set off that leads to bribery, blackmail and murder.

1916 – Now in her seventies, Milandra is one of the wealthiest and most respected women in Dublin. Back in her mansion on Sackville Street, after spending Easter with family, she is astonished to be confronted by a gunman. She fears he has come to rob her, but quickly realises she has been caught up in something much bigger.

Then, as Dublin explodes with the Easter Rising, Milandra's granddaughter Amelia desperately tries to reach her grandmother who is trapped in her house at the very centre of the conflict. Meanwhile, events unfolding on Sackville Street will unravel decades-old mysteries, secrets that were to be carried to the grave.

ISBN 978-178199-868-7